Also by Loralee Dubeau

There's a Whole in the Sky

THE HONEY PIT

FINDING THE
GRANDMOTHER'S WAY

LORALEE DUBEAU

BALBOA.
PRESS

A DIVISION OF HAY HOUSE

Balboa Press books may be ordered through booksellers or by contacting:

Balboa Press
A Division of Hay House
1663 Liberty Drive
Bloomington, IN 47403
www.balboapress.com
1 (877) 407-4847

Because of the dynamic nature of the Internet, any web addresses or links contained in this book may have changed since publication and may no longer be valid. The views expressed in this work are solely those of the author and do not necessarily reflect the views of the publisher, and the publisher hereby disclaims any responsibility for them.

The author of this book does not dispense medical advice or prescribe the use of any technique as a form of treatment for physical, emotional, or medical problems without the advice of a physician, either directly or indirectly. The intent of the author is only to offer information of a general nature to help you in your quest for emotional and spiritual well-being. In the event you use any of the information in this book for yourself, which is your constitutional right, the author and the publisher assume no responsibility for your actions.

Any people depicted in stock imagery provided by Thinkstock are models, and such images are being used for illustrative purposes only. Certain stock imagery © Thinkstock.

Print information available on the last page.

ISBN: 978-1-5043-2794-7 (sc)
ISBN: 978-1-5043-2796-1 (hc)
ISBN: 978-1-5043-2795-4 (e)

Library of Congress Control Number: 2015902404

Balboa Press rev. date: 4/23/2015

DEDICATION

To the many women in my life both past and present, that challenged, guided, inspired and loved me. Thank you for your teachings.

PREFACE

In the spring of 2010, I was a year away from completing the rewrites for my first novel, *"There's a Whole in the Sky."* During a time of prayerful reflection, my life's teachings and experiences intertwined and began the creative journey of my second novel, *The Honey Pit, Finding the Grandmother's Way.* Although the story was on my mind, I needed to put this second novel on hold until the publication of my first novel in 2012.

By the end of the summer of 2013, while teaching classes, workshops and consulting with clients, *"The Honey Pit, Finding the Grandmother's Way"* could no longer be held back. The words and images were consuming my daily thoughts and dreams, becoming a frustrating obsession, until at last I decided to put client consults on hold for a while and put pen to paper. I let the inspirational story and teachings unravel itself and the writing process was effortless as I dreamed the story into creation each day.

For the next thirteen months my focus was entirely on writing and letting the novel birth its existence into reality.

Though a writer draws from personal experience, I have found that a fictional story must be allowed to find its own creative voice and direction. One cannot control or silence a message during the birthing journey.

I am grateful for a creative imagination, personal life experiences and the many teachings I have received from grandmothers from all walks of life and beyond.

This novel will take you on a journey of self-discovery, as you become immersed and intrigued with the lead character. I hope the joy and excitement I experienced from writing *"The Honey Pit, Finding the Grandmother's Way"* touches your heart and inner spirit.

Blessings to you,
Loralee Dubeau

CHAPTER ONE

As I sit on this hill, far across the country in an unfamiliar and harsh setting, I am beginning to wonder why in the hell I chose to do this. The temperature is a blazing 115 degrees and scorching my skin. I am praying to ask for guidance as to why I was led to Texas on this initiation quest.

Nine months ago it all made perfect sense. Several of the women from our lodge community were offered this opportunity to participate in a women's ceremony and four of us had agreed to start the process. Due to the demanding nature of the preparations, the other three women decided they could not complete the requirements. So now I find myself, the only New Englander crazy enough to commit to the ceremony.

Within a few hours, I was left with forty or so women from all parts of the United States. They had come together as a women's society to support those who came every year since the ceremony had been brought back into practice.

I sit here, separated from the one other woman from Texas who, like me has also completed the nine months of preparations. I wondered if she was questioning herself on the other side of the hill the way I was, *what in the hell have I gotten myself into?*

When I had arrived on the land in the small town of Wizard Well, Texas, I was met by locusts. The swarms had arrived like a dust cloud and were flying and jumping everywhere. The noise was a never ending sound of mastication of the tall grass that made my skin crawl. I felt I was in a western horror flick soon to be eaten alive by a plague. Many of them jumped into my mouth and entangled in my hair when I tried to greet and get acquainted with my soon-to-be sisters. I had traveled to many places in the southwest and had seen dangerous snakes, scorpions and spiders, but the locusts were unbelievable!

So now I sit, with the sun beating down on me and burning my skin. I am fasting and my throat is parched. Perspiration from my body is making my cotton dress stick to my form like a second skin, while the sound of locusts swarming and chewing is making a crazed unbearable noise. I don't know if I want to scream or cry.

I had been through several Native American vision quest ceremonies years before when I began the serious spiritual road of my distant ancestors. While some of the conditions had been tough, these were the most severe. Only this was not a Native American vision quest. It was a Native American woman's initiation ceremony, which I would eventually learn comes with its own experiences.

After countless pleads with the sun, begging for a cool breeze of some clouds, my prayers were finally heard. The sky began to darken and the clouds blew into formation. The clouds became black in the sky and the wind grew more vocal. The temperature dropped, as the coolness of the wild wind bent the tall grass as it bowed to a higher power. I watched the sky and saw a small funnel start to form.

"Oh no," I cried. "Please Spirit, not a tornado! Please let this pass. Please protect this land, the critters and the people. Oh Thunder Beings of great power from the west, please pity us all."

I rose and stood in reverence to what I was witnessing, the birth of a tornado and the balance of nature. I raised my arms above my head holding burning sprigs of cedar in a shell as an offering.

The growth of the funnel cloud seemed to be stalling as it came closer. As it moved quickly overhead, the sky changed to a pinkish-gray, brightened for a moment and then unleashed a torrential downpour of golf ball size hail. The ice balls were pelting me as I covered my head with my arms. I cooled off very quickly as the storm and funnel disappeared and the hail passed. I began to shiver.

I offered a long prayer of gratitude for my life and the mercy that nature had shown me. Hail had certainly been much more forgiving than a tornado.

My attitude adjusted. I was no longer distracted by my uncomfortable situation or questioning my being here in this moment. I had been on a spiritual road all my life and had seen this moment once again, as a sign of how quickly one's life and perception can be transformed. I continued to pray for a vision for my life and the initiation into the women's society. I prayed for hours and began my deepened altered state of awareness.

CHAPTER TWO

At forty years old, one expects one's life to be settled and stable. Mine had unraveled in the last couple of years and would continue to change for the next several years until I was altered in every way possible. I had learned in the past when you lived with expectations of how life should be, you are usually waiting, not following. I, Laurel Cannon, was now following.

Following what, you might ask? Following my spirit's calling, visions and dreams. Not always the dreams that you choose but rather the ones you receive to guide you.

In my dreams as a small child I was always praying in ceremonies with Native American Indian people. I had never seen nor witnessed these ceremonies in my waking life until I was eighteen-years-old, when I started to travel and meet Native American Indian elders. It wasn't until then that I participated in ceremonies that would shape my life and give profound understanding, connection and meaning.

At present, I am divorced from a man who swept me off my feet. I realized that I was not happy being in a relationship that was toxic to my entire being. I was fearful of his every move, due to his rage and outburst. I was no longer a confident, happy person. The fear and stress caused a negative change in me that I could no longer bear. The marriage lasted three months before I left.

I wanted to get back to my happy adventurous self. Only, I would never be the same. Everything in me had changed. I had experienced a fear, sadness, disappointment and embarrassment that truly affected me. I would have to dig deep to find the true me. Deeper than I ever thought was possible. What I would find was nothing I could have imagined.

CHAPTER THREE

Born in the mid 1950's in Webster, Massachusetts, my childhood was happy. Like many other children, I was doted on by my mother, Tracy and loved unconditionally by my father, Roger. I was an only child until I was seven. I had my own bedroom in our little two bedroom apartment.

My mother was very homey. She was a talented seamstress and handmade all of my dresses. She could create and sew just about anything. She was also a great cook. She made sauces and baked goods all from scratch. She was a talented homemaker and very good at making our small apartment a loving home.

My parents attentively listened to my singing. Music was always available on the record player or radio. My biggest crush as a child was the Beatles. I was caught up in the frenzy. My parents bought the first Beatles album for me along with the next seven over the years. I must have sung and performed in my bedroom thousands of times in preparation for the show I would present to my parents. I am sure they grew tired of the record, my tiny voice and impromptu dancing.

Although both of my parents were attentive I adored my daddy and he was the one I waited for each dinnertime. When we sat down to eat, I would capture his attention with all of the day's events from start to finish. The adventures I had in our little backyard with the bugs, frogs, rocks and dandelions amused him.

My father was my hero. To my innocent eyes he was good at everything. He could fix anything inside and outside our apartment and often helped our neighbors. Everyone seemed to like him and he got along with everyone. He was smart and mechanically inclined. He was very athletic and usually excelled in any sport or game he played, even a board or card game. I was like most little girls, in awe of her daddy. The sun rose and set around him. I listened to every word and instruction he gave to me.

As I came of school age, I was excited to go to school. I loved pretending to teach my stuffed animals and dolls, as if I was in a large classroom with my small chalkboard that Santa brought me for Christmas. My bedroom became my safe place to dream and play, while the backyard became my place of exploration and adventure.

On most sunny days, my mother would take me outside to play for an hour. She would sit in a beach chair watching me run around and explore jungles, beaches, mountains and even other planets. I could navigate with my imagination in great detail.

I also could be very still and observe a bee as it landed and removed the pollen from a flower's center, or as the ants carried tiny crumbs of food on their backs into the mazes underground. Nature was my teacher and I observed without interference. I learned slowly how life worked.

During warm months I wore dresses. Not fancy ones like I did on Sundays but, still, it was a dress. It was a time that little girls were expected to have their hair brushed, curled, in ponytails or in pretty barrettes so that their hair could stay proper and clean. However as an explorer; my face, hands and clothes would become dirty and muddy from my beach pail's creations.

Sometimes the dress got in the way, much to my mother's displeasure. Having to bathe daily was probably more of a nuisance to her than it was to me, since I loved the sanctuary of sitting in warm, relaxing water.

Once I started school and engaged with other children, I realized that I was very sensitive. Although at the time I did not know what the word empathy meant, it was exactly what I experienced. I could see and sense things about the other children. It was as if I was inside of their minds, feeling what they felt and thinking what they thought. I felt their anger and sadness, but more often than not, their happiness. My mind would be empty of thought and then sadness or anger would engulf me. The words I heard in my mind were not my own, but of another person. As I became one with another's thoughts I could see events happening for them further in the future. It was hard to distinguish my thoughts and presence from another's.

I had noticed this sensitivity several times before with my parents and grandparents, but within a room of over thirty children it was intense. Sometimes I was not sure if it was my own emotions or another's taking over. There seemed to be no boundary of where my body began, where it extended and ended. The waves of what I could feel would leave me exhausted and depleted. As a child I had a lot of energy but as the school year continued, I began to tire and needed a short nap after I returned home from school instead of playing outside.

As I continued first grade, I began to have problems with my kidneys and urination. I had a lot of physical pain. After many tests, they found that I was born with a twisted double ureter to each kidney that became infected. Although it did not require surgery, it did require some weeks of medication that turned the water in the toilet a pretty shade of blue every time I urinated.

During the time of the infection, I would become feverish and go into a deep sleep. As rest and liquids were prescribed, I succumbed to the deep slumber leaving the world of my bedroom far behind.

I would journey to places far away with people of indigenous cultures. They looked like Native American Indians from different tribes and eras in time. I understood that they were ghosts who had crossed the plane from their earth bodies, but had agreed to become helpers or teachers to those who could access other dimensions of existence. I was easily able to see them when they came to work with me. Not all of the apparitions were human looking; some emitted a shroud of light.

The shrouds of light were my favorite because it was from them that I learned about the energy of the universe. I learned about the matrix that lives inside everything in the universe. It is all one large ball of light energy and each living thing can impact the matrix because it is all connected like a giant spider's web. It extends out into the universe and connects the planets, stars, the Milky Way and all galaxies. It was profound to learn as a young six-year-old how small you are in the vast universe, spinning on a blue and white ball of land that balances in the energy of blackness and yet so connected and affected by every tiny atom in creation. I learned through their teachings that the colored bands of energy within me were given only a certain amount of life force to use wisely in my body. Every emotion or thought I created or experienced could either bring me more energy or take it away. Anger, fear and sadness lowered the life force and dimmed the light I would see. Joy, happiness, gratitude and relaxation would energize the life force.

Even though I did not understand the word 'life force', I understood what I could see and feel. I could see the color bands and lines inside a body and if they were dimmed or blocked. The band and lines looked like spider webs that ran vertically and horizontally and the spiral bands that ran in a column up and down the spine could become clogged and weak.

The explanation that I understood from these beings was that my body was being overloaded by picking up other people's energy and I was allowing it to cling and deplete me. The kidneys were the place in the body that filtered emotions and the energy was getting stuck there because I was not releasing outside influences. I needed to learn how to reenergize myself.

It took seven weeks for my body to fight the physical infection and with the teachings of these other worldly guides; I healed and came to understand one thing: I was expected to help others on the earth by teaching them about the energy matrix and help those heal who were ready to join consciously with the living matrix.

This would not be an easy task. Each day during my sickness a different guide would greet me in dream time and help me heal the energy field inside and outside of the body. They would treat me with songs, stones, rattles, drums and colored lights. Through each experience and understanding, I became stronger and learned how to protect my empathic nature of receiving and to transform the dense energy, thoughts and emotions around me. Even though I did not learn it all in those seven weeks, I learned to visualize and run an energy line from the cosmos through me to the earth below, then up the back of my spine, over the top of my head, then down the front of the body and underneath my feet to the earth as a simple alignment. I learned that visualizing colors in different places in my body helped with energizing and balance.

Some days, I would visualize different colors to the bands and other times I would expand the energy like a bubble around me. Many times I would continue to run the energy around me vertically and then horizontally to clean and energize myself.

I respected the energy that was given to my body and the life force that gave me breath each day and allowed my body to perform voluntary and involuntary functions.

During my illness, the school was kind enough to send a small amount of class work home so that I would pass into the next grade and not fall behind.

When I returned to school seven weeks later, I could still see energy and feel others thoughts, but I was not bombarded and overwhelmed. I had learned to desensitize by clearing and refocusing my attention on something else.

One of my helpers took me on a journey to an island with palm trees and a beach near a great volcano and explained to me the laws of nature.

"Every living thing has a spirit or life force. So every living thing is made up of energy. All things in life are in continuous movement. So we can influence the movement and affect it and other life's movement can influence and affect us. So in the end, we are all connected and in relationship. We need to continuously adjust to the movement going on around us, by using our mind and actions to focus loving thoughts on nature's creatures, animals and people. If we choose to give our energy in a loving way then the flow of energy that returns from other living things in nature will energize us. That is the dance of the living matrix."

To prove his point he pointed to a hibiscus flower.

"If you look closely you will see a tiny bee removing some of the pollen. See the tiny bit on its body that it has collected."

As I peered closer I did in fact see it. He sternly shook the flower and the bee was thrown out of it to the ground and the pollen dust was lost from its body on the ground.

"Now we have influenced the pollination of other flowers and we have been destructive to nature, to the bee and to the flowers, all by one careless act. Now let me show you something else. Let us sit here quietly and focus on calling more flying insects to the flower by focusing our mind and visualizing the flower opening up and attracting new insects to feast on its nectar."

I stilled myself and quieted my breath in a slow rhythm, as I pictured the flower opening and receiving the flying insects, each touching down gently receiving the sustenance. He whispered to me to open my eyes and there before me, were the dancing insects fluttering around the flower while others landed inside the flower to partake of its nectar. I gasped in excitement.

"Now the balance has been returned. You must be careful with your energy and focus, along with your actions for the results affect much more than you realize."

Flowers became very important to me from that day on. Their energy was precious and their beauty and scent brought me pleasure. It is no wonder why years later, when I was in my twenties, I was led to train and work with the healing properties of the essence of flowers.

As a teenager my hormones and body began their physical changes. I became even more sensitive, especially in large crowds. It took me longer to clear my energy field and the density that I felt.

My increasingly heightened intuitive sense allowed the dimension beyond the earth to open up without warning. One minute I was listening to the teacher in Geometry class and the next a ghostly spirit appeared in front me and placed pictures in my mind to produce a telepathic conversation. The spirit somehow was attracted to me and instinctively knew I could see and understand its need.

Not all of the deceased spirits communicated with ease. Some of them struggled to explain what help they needed. Some needed help crossing and moving to the spirit world and others needed to give messages to loved ones.

The help that was needed was not always readily apparent. At first I tried to ignore them and pretend I did not see them. The first couple of times it worked. Then as they came with more frequency, I asked them to go away, but they were reluctant and stubborn. They disappeared briefly and returned with more persistence.

Many times I had several of them following me around because I couldn't figure out what they needed. The sooner I helped them, the faster they moved on.

The deceased spirits do not talk. Most will communicate telepathically; some through pictures, others through spelling words in my mind. My degree of comprehension developed throughout my teenage years and into my twenties.

Many of the deceased do not fully understand that they are dead, so they float to old places where they once had lived, to the people closest to them or to the nearest light they see. My vibration must have emitted enough light for them to find me - and find me they did.

For those spirits that wanted to give messages, sometimes they would come to me a few days before I would meet their loved ones. Many times they would appear in the middle of class or while I was doing homework. Sometimes they appeared in ghostly full body or sometimes just their face would float in front of me. As I got older, I could decipher the message faster. If it was still to be a few days before seeing their loved one, I would tell them to leave and return when the time came.

Most of them needed to communicate unfinished business, like telling someone that they were okay, and that they loved them. Others had more specific messages. One young woman came back for me to tell her mother to stop wearing her jeans, and that she needed to let her go so she could move on. When the deceased spirits came through, my life was interrupted and not my own. It became very difficult.

After high school I began to travel. I was interested in learning about my distant Native American Indian lineage. As I traveled throughout the United States, Canada, South America, Mexico, Central America, Europe, the West Indies and many islands in the Caribbean, I began to meet and learn about many indigenous cultures. All have similar beliefs of origins from the stars and a brotherhood of connectedness to all living things for which I could fully relate.

I observed and listen to their stories, ways of life and, in many cases, participated in their rituals. In time I shared some of my own personal experiences. All were very accepting and non-judgmental. It was the first step for me to accept my gifts and not fear that I would be laughed at or ostracized.

My fear lessened as I grew into my twenties, but I still needed to have a way to take care of the deceased spirits and not have them show up at any time and disrupt my life.

Thus was the beginning of intuitive readings. I would read the clients energy field and if there was a deceased spirit that would show up for the client, the message would be delivered. It gave an opening for the deceased to enter when I would be available. This seemed to work much better, and though a few spirits continued to show up at random, most appeared in the readings.

I continued to travel and learned different forms of energy healing modalities: crystals, stones, chakra balancing, Reiki, Huna, acupressure, friction, color and light therapy, flower essences and aromatherapy.

They were all wonderful tools, but if you did not have the gift of seeing and feeling energy to begin with, you really were just following a procedure and it would not be as beneficial to others as it could be. I had seen this many times over the years. Many people work with tools, but few can interpret and understand what is going on within the client to access what is needed or will be helpful.

I moved from my parent's home in my twenties to be on my own and I began a career in the booming fiber optic industry. Slowly through word of mouth, I continued my intuitive readings and energy sessions part-time on the weekends. I was not completely open about sharing my gifts, but shared that I was available part-time for consults to those whom seemed to be accepting to the idea.

I continued my travels and received teachings from a Lakota elder named Black Deer for several years. He gifted me my first Sacred Pipe, a sacred being or child he explained.

"Laurel, the Sacred Pipe is made of a stem that comes from the standing ones that reach up to the sky. It is a masculine power. The bowl is made from the red clay from the earth. It is a feminine power. When they are connected together in ceremony for prayer, it becomes a living being, one of great power that bridges us on earth to the spirit world and cosmos where our prayers can be heard. Although it has much power it is still like a child, one that has to be cared for, protected and nurtured by praying with it. It is not a possession to parade around but a being wrapped in a bundle to be honored."

He also put me on four vision quest ceremonies. He taught me how to pray from the heart, true emotion and not the head, meaningless words.

Black Deer was considered a ceremonialist and holy man, what one might call a medicine man. From what I learned, Native American Indian cultures don't like the term shaman; it is not indigenous to America. The people call them doctors, healers, holy people, and men and women who work with the medicine ways.

Over the years, I have been led to male and female elders and teachings from Seneca, Blackfoot, Cherokee, Cree, Hopi, Navaho and Sioux tribes. I was grateful for the lessons and ceremonies that continue to shape and evolve my life.

CHAPTER FOUR

My life was balanced. I was working in the optic field enjoying my work and using my spiritual gifts with a small amount of clients. I took weekends off to travel to see elders up and down the east coast and weekly excursions two or three times a year to the west coast.

I didn't need a man. I was fairly self-sufficient. My father and mother taught me well. As I look back on it now, I was trying to be like my father: a smart, strong, mechanically inclined, responsible and independent person. I dated men on and off but not for very long stretches. I guess I was not ready to divulge all of my talents and secrets. I did share some personal spiritual experiences with one or two men after dating for a couple of months, but through their snickering, disbelief and the look of fear in their eyes, I decided to withhold any further information and broke the relationships off.

I was not interested in raising children. I had enough wonderful babysitting experiences with my younger brother, Tom. I began babysitting for him when I was ten. As a toddler Tom was a handful. I played with him when my mother was busy with household work. There was a seven year age difference, so I felt more like a mother than a sibling.

I knew even at a young age that I wanted to help people and be of service to the world. So at eighteen I began my traveling and training. I wasn't quite sure at the time what I was training for, but it was a call I could not resist. Praying to the source of power and mystery greater than me was my true comfort. I had a direct line of communication, devotion and understanding that allowed me to have an inner sense of joy and peace. I understood who I was in those moments for I had touched the connection to all life in the universe and had become one with it.

Years went by quickly and I was in my late thirties. While at a friend's birthday party I was introduced to a man named Blake. He had been divorced and had a teenage son who lived several states away. So in a way he seemed to be quite available, alone by himself in a nice house with several acres of land. We seemed to get along quite well and we were interested in similar things. It wasn't long before he asked for my number and we began to date.

He very quickly swept me off my feet and after three months he proposed with a beautiful ring. I was overwhelmed as he professed his love for me. It took me a few moments to answer. My first response was not an answer, but a question for him.

"We don't have to marry right away; we can have a long engagement right?"

To which he answered, "Of course, anything you want."

So I agreed and accepted his proposal. Looking back on it now, I felt cornered. I didn't want to hurt his feelings, especially since he loved me *so much,* or so I thought.

We all want to feel loved as humans. At that time like everyone else, I must have really wanted to feel loved in a relationship. I realized now that I was afraid to be and share all of who I was. Though I shared my travels, beliefs and even performed energy sessions on Blake when he hurt his back, the secret of dead spirits and readings was something I had not completely shared with him. I did however share that I was being called to serve people in some way and although he agreed, I don't think he really understood.

After the proposal, Blake began to pester me to move in with him and set the wedding date. He wanted us to be together, not living apart. I should have realized then that he was in a hurry for some reason. I wasn't. I had a good job in a still booming business, had clients on the weekend and supported myself very nicely, living in my own apartment.

As he pushed and manipulated, I agreed in fear of losing a good man. After a month, I was now living in his house. Due to limited living space, I had to sell most of my possessions except for a loveseat, bedroom set and clothing.

As soon as I moved in he wanted to plan the wedding and get married. He had a vacation in August and wanted our wedding to coincide with the week. So we quickly planned to get everything arranged. It would be a small wedding with only our immediate family invited.

A week before the wedding, Blake came home from work and we had our first major argument.

"Honey, let's get a dog. I think it would be good to have a dog to guard the house," he suggested.

"No. I don't want a dog. Sunshine, (my cat) is still getting adjusted to living here. I don't want another pet to make him feel stressed," I rejected.

"I want a dog. This is my house. I can have what I want," he screamed.

"Calm down, Blake. I thought this house is my home too?" I said calmly.

Enraged, Blake went to the curio cabinet where I had placed four expensive native clay pots I had bought in my travels out west.

"How much do you value your clay pots? You brought them into this house because *you* want them. *I* want a dog," he manipulated.

"No. I don't want a dog," I argued.

Smash. The clay pot was in pieces as he threw it forcibly to the floor. He grabbed another pot from the shelf.

"Say yes, or I will break another one," he said with venom.

"No," I replied again.

Smash, another clay pot broken to pieces. Once again he grabbed the third one.

"I said, say yes," he held the clay pot in mid-air.

"Blake, I really don't want a dog now, please stop. You're behaving like a child," I cried.

Smash, another one broken to pieces.

When he had seen that I was not going to change my mind, he drew his fist and put it through the wall near the telephone.

"Blake!" I screamed.

I was in shock of such violence. Secretly in that moment, my feelings changed from love to fear. The shock of his fist hitting the wall calmed him down.

"I'm sorry, honey. I am under a lot of pressure at work. I might be losing my job," he said regrettably.

Instead of listening to my head and getting the hell out of there I cleaned his cuts, got ice out of the freezer and wrapped his hand with it.

I questioned that day now. I was confused, but it was a good sign that this might not work. The one time when I should have sat down and prayed to ask for guidance, I didn't. On some level as I look back on it now, I must have unconsciously wanted to stay in denial and chose to have the lesson.

One month after the wedding, I received several credit card bills in Blake's name. In the six months prior to the wedding, I had seen and helped pay for the bills. We combined our checks into one account and everything went out on time - or so I thought. After we were married, I received $10,000 worth of credit card bills in his name that were several months past due.

When I asked Blake about them he said he was behind and didn't want to worry me, so he hid them. When I pressed further he took a fit and started throwing things around. I decided to let it go. I took money out of my personal savings account and caught up on the past due payments and interest. I worked extra hours each week to catch up on his bills. In the meantime, he did lose his job on the police force. He went back to his previous construction work career.

Two months later, I came home from work early. Since Blake was working construction now, we were working opposite shifts and I thought he would be glad to see me. Only Blake was not home. He crawled in drunk at midnight and nearly hit my car in the driveway. I didn't understand. We never kept liquor in the house because I did not drink and didn't want it around. Blake would occasionally have a drink at a birthday party, but this was unusual.

He barely made it in the house.

"Blake, you're drunk. Where have you been? You could have killed yourself or someone else," I said with concern.

"What the hell are you doing home? You're supposed to be working and bringing home money. You think you're better than me now that you make more money than me, bitch?" he sneered.

He was looking for a fight and I was not going to engage him further. I got him to bed and the next morning I tried to talk calmly to him.

"Blake, I'm worried about what happened last night? Why did you get drunk?" I calmly asked.

"I went out with friends to a country dance club to blow off some steam," he replied.

"Why would you go to a club without me? That's a good way to get in trouble with other women," I said sternly.

"Look, I will drink and do whatever the hell I want. I'm the man and you're the wife. *You* obey, get it?" he glared.

Who was this man I married?

Now that the cat was out of the bag, he drank as much as he wanted whenever he wanted. I tried to get him to go to counseling with or without me.

I even went to his mother and asked her for help and all she could say was, "Oh is he up to that again? He's just like his father."

She thought he had given up drinking because he was so happy being with me. This was the first I heard of it. It is no wonder he flew into rage. He needed his alcohol and he was not getting it. He had to hide it from me.

The final straw came a week later when he returned home drunk and wanted to build a barn. Not just a simple barn, but a ten thousand dollar barn. Thinking of the credit cards that still needed paying off, I said, "I am not going to pay for a barn we don't need or can't afford" and that sent him over the deep end.

He handcuffed me pulling my arms behind me like a prisoner and told me, "I could kill you right now and bury your body where no one would find you."

I shivered with fear. I asked him why he married me and how could he do this if he loved me.

He screamed, "I didn't want to be alone the rest of my life and I needed someone to help me pay my bills. Since you never were married, I thought you would obey me!"

Then and only then, did I get down on my knees after he went to bed and asked for guidance. And to that guidance I listened, "Get out before he kills you."

Whether it came from inside of me or from an outsider it didn't matter. I followed it. From then on, I have followed my intuition and the spiritual guidance I have received through prayer and ceremony.

I was embarrassed, ashamed and felt guilty at allowing myself to be manipulated by this man. I was hurt. I was angry at myself. I moved out after three months. I wanted to disappear from the pain of this mistake and marriage.

Full of embarrassment, I moved back in with my parents. I hated to face my father. I felt so stupid being betrayed by Blake and being financially broke since I used my savings to pay his bills. The embarrassment I felt for letting my father see my fragility through short bouts of tears was hard to bear. After all, I was the child he raised to be strong, smart and independent. At thirty-nine-years-old I was back at home and having to save money to gain my independence once again. Thankfully my job was still going well but by the time I turned forty I would be divorced.

Why did I attract such a man in my life? What did I lack or wrongly believe to cause this misstep? Why did I not stop the whole drama by saying no when he asked me to marry him? That would take me a few years to understand and to heal.

CHAPTER FIVE

While going through the divorce, I met a wonderful massage therapist, Lisa Parker. I wanted a massage and found her name in the telephone book. I made the appointment for the next day.

"Laurel? Hello I am Lisa. Nice to meet you," she said.

"Hello," I replied as I entered her place of business.

"Are you from town?" she asked.

"Originally, yes. I moved back to town. I am going through a divorce," I replied.

"I understand. I have been married before as well. But after taking the time to heal myself, I found another wonderful man that makes the other marriage a distant memory," she affirmed.

Lisa was full of wisdom and shared my views, especially spiritually. Over time we built a mutual trust that led to a close friendship.

I lived with my parents for four months until I found a place that would allow my furry companion, Sunshine and me to live.

I continued my work in fiber optics. In fact, I was promoted to a shift supervisor and received a hefty salary increase. I could not wait to tell my father my good news on my next visit.

"Dad, I have been promoted to shift supervisor. I lead twenty-five people now. Mostly men," I boasted.

"Laurel, that's great. Did you get a raise?" he asked.

"Yes. A twenty percent increase," I replied.

"That's my girl," he responded.

"That's great, Laurel. I hope you are not taking on too much. That is a lot of people to supervise," my mother added.

"I can handle it, Mom. I am not a weak woman you know. I have worked long and hard for this company during these last fifteen years to learn the industry," I argued.

With my marriage ending, I was able to put my efforts into my work and it paid off. At least something good came out of this mess, though my time for readings, energy sessions and flower essence consults was now being limited due to the increased hours and responsibilities as a supervisor.

I continued massage sessions with Lisa to nurture both my body and mind. She introduced me to the spiritual community that she prayed with on a regular basis. The leader was a Native American man in his forties and a completed sundancer several times over who was taught by native elders to run purification and Sacred Pipe ceremonies.

For years I had traveled to many places for ceremony and now I would be getting the chance to pray closer to home, in my own state. I was thrilled to say the least. Since being with Blake, I had not been in a purification ceremony in over a year.

Lisa introduced me to the leader Bill Marsh who was impeccable in ceremony and in his life. He was tall, dark and very handsome. He had long, dark hair and piercing dark eyes. He could make any woman's heart flutter. His girlfriend Darcy Regan was a sweet, petite woman with long brown hair and a child-like giggle. Her voice carried you through the ceremonies and into another realm. She was a powerful singer in ceremony.

I was accepted into the lodge community of about twenty-five people. I never shared any of my previous ceremony experiences or that I was given permission to lead ceremony. I didn't need to appear as if I knew anything. I just stayed open to learning and observing, as I had been taught by other native elders. I supported and did what was asked and needed for community.

I was in ceremony every other weekend with them and it was wonderful and very healing. My career was unfolding nicely. A year later I was offered a new position as a Training Coordinator, which consisted of breaking down job positions, step by step and teaching experienced people the best way to train new hires efficiently. It also got me another salary increase of ten percent. Since as a supervisor I had done a great job training my employees myself, the company thought I was a good fit for the position.

I shared the good news with my parents the following weekend. I was met with much praise from my father.

"Laurel, that's great. You're a smart girl and it's good to see that your knowledge and leadership is valued. You should be able to take care of yourself financially," he beamed.

My mother was just as happy, but again worried, suggesting that I be sure to save money for the rainy day down the road.

The new position required me to use my teaching skills, which was a calling I had since childhood. I taught meditation classes at a nearby holistic store once in a while, and still conducted intuitive readings on weekends when time permitted. I felt this training coordinator position was exactly what I should be doing and I expected I could make a nice living and a career.

Remember, when you expect and stop following the flow of life, things will fall apart and fall apart it did.

In less than six months, I found the training department dismantled. I had fought in this predominately male industry to be seen as an equal. Learning every position in the company that was necessary to become a lead person, a supervisor, and a training coordinator and now the job was being eliminated. What I failed to see was a sign that the company was slowly losing sales and the industry was changing. So I aggressively applied for another supervisor's position on a twelve to fourteen hour shift four days a week. I knew all of the positions and machines, so I felt it was a good fit. Again, I would be supervising an entire shift of men, but this time they were older than I and had less experience in the industry.

Since I had been working with men for many years, I actually grew to prefer it. They were easier to work with and came with less drama. But I soon learned that I would have to earn their respect because, after all, I was a woman. Most of them did not really want a woman telling them what to do, but when they had problems with the processes or mechanical trouble-shooting, I effectively guided them and they eventually realized my experiences were valuable.

I tried hard to prove my knowledge, earn respect and set an example through the years, so that other women might have a chance to get into the industry. Slowly the company started to hire women about twenty percent of the time. I felt it was a small accomplishment.

As life was going along, with ceremony on the weekends and working fifty-five hours on the four days a week schedule, I was burning out fast. I enjoyed ceremony and our community, but my career was not as happy and fulfilling as it had been. I had no time to teach meditation or take clients for readings the last two months.

Darcy had announced to the women in the community that there was a women's vision quest into a Native American women's society approaching. It was a return of the traditional Women's Ceremony. This society had been established several years ago and led by a native elder in Texas.

Darcy explained that she had been through it and it was a wonderful experience. She noted that there was a lot of preparation required. Each of us had to prepare by fasting food and learning how to bead, make boot moccasins, wrap prayer feathers as giveaways, and create a breastplate, a fringed shawl, a beaded pouch, and a dress. We had to essentially demonstrate the old women ways of creating and outfitting ourselves. It sounded like a lot of work. *Where would I find the time?*

As in all cases, I decided to pray on it. The one thing that always held true for me was to pray and wait to be guided. So I prayed and in four days I received guidance. On the fourth day as I was praying, a group of thirteen elderly spirit grandmothers came to sit with me. I was not a stranger to the spirit world. It was open to me the day I was born and still remains open, though I had never had contact with a circle of so many. I had met with one at a time or two, but never this many and never all women.

They sang a song as they circled me. They appeared to be from many different lineages of women. When they finished singing, one of them spoke.

"You will learn the ways of the grandmothers, but first you must connect to the woman in you."

With that they disappeared. I could not ask for their meaning or for further understanding. I knew it was a message to commit to the ceremony being offered. The next day I spoke with Darcy and agreed along with three of the other women in community, to learn what was needed for the ceremony.

CHAPTER SIX

We met bi-weekly at first to learn to bead on a loom and create the design symbol for the ceremony. Ornate colored beads were picked up gently on a thin, long-neck needle as I followed the graph and design on the labeled paper drawing. Each bead in the design was color coded. Many times the beads fell off the needle and many times I made a mistake and had to remove rows and rows of beads.

I would have to make four of these designs to attach to moccasins and a pouch. It was a test of patience and humility. I was knowledgeable in many things but this was new and allowed me a way of creating with my hands that I had never experienced.

It was getting difficult for the four of us to meet with Darcy and gather to bead. Everyone's schedule was unmanageable. So we decided to go it alone and check in with Darcy with each next step.

I eventually enjoyed beading. When I prayed as I beaded, I started to hear songs in my mind and sang them out loud in a native language that I had not known before. Each time I became more and more enmeshed in the connection to the spirit grandmother's circle as they talked to my mind when I beaded, imparting their wisdom and understandings. I was beginning to weave my heart and spirit with theirs on a deep level. Hours would go by with no sleep. I became part of an ancient time in my mind, around a fire with women sharing, singing and praying as I beaded.

The next step was the dress. I had cut the pattern and needed to sew it together. My mother was an incredible seamstress, so I asked for her help and guidance. She helped me understand the pattern and what was needed to accomplish the task. I had sewn a little before in high school, but I really disliked it. My mother on the other hand, was a wiz at it and enjoyed it very much.

I think back then, I rebelled at being expected to sew because I was girl. I always rebelled against stereotypical women's work. I knew I wanted to reach beyond that boundary.

Now, I appreciated my mother's expertise, knowledge and creative ability. Over the years, she had made curtains, shirts, dresses, skirts and my annual Christmas pajamas. I was beginning to see how resourceful and creative my mother really was.

I completed the ribbon dress, but not without a few mistakes and having to use a seam ripper to take out the stitches and re-stitch. What I learned was to take my time, go slow and pay attention to detail. Again the grandmothers' songs were filling my head and calmed my spirit.

The next step was creating a pair of moccasins. Darcy provided me with a how-to video tape and I purchased my deer skin for the pouch and moccasins. My father helped me use a hole-puncher to make the small holes for stitching the sinew and lacing. He helped me measure the pattern for my calf because the video only had directions for the feet, not the high calf moccasins. I was glad to have his technical help with the tools and his praise when the task was completed.

I must say it required strength. Pulling the sinew through the leather was hard work. I had been blessed with many blisters before they were finished, but through it all, the songs from the spirit grandmothers were always there.

They would visit me during my dreams and I would sit by the fire with them. They told me stories and gave me teachings. When I awoke the teachings were buried in my heart, mind and spirit.

My next step was the shawl. The fringe would take precise measurement and agility of looping the fringe in equal lengths. Although the lengths were all cut properly, holding them together, looping them through the hole I made with the awl and tying them evenly was taxing. Much of the fringe was done over and over until they were even in length. When I surrendered as I had with each task, it was if the spirit grandmothers took over my hands and guided me.

The next task was beading the woman's breast plate. It told the story of her life, what she had experienced and the children she bore. Every bone bead symbolized the events in her life.

Darcy gave me the instructions and the pattern to follow. I bought my red and white colored glass beads and my buffalo hollow bones. I chose *red* for a woman's life giving blood and *white* for the purity of rebirth, after all wasn't the ceremony a new beginning?

As I made the breast plate, I was thinking of a new beginning and a new life, so I did not want to place anything connected to the divorce. The longer I beaded, I realized I needed to honor it for it was a part of my life. So I placed one black bead for the grief I experienced, and hoped years later I would remove and replace it with a white bead.

All through this process I was fasting and praying regularly. I was feeling more emotional, softer and compassionate. I was connecting to people and the environment on a deeper level than I had ever experienced before. It was if my heart was being opened up to receive and transform.

I would find the last task of wrapping the sacred feathers to be the most profound experience of my preparations. Each feather had to be carefully wrapped with special colored thread and in a particular manner, twisting and wrapping with the correct tension and number of wraps.

Throughout the process, my prayers were placed into the work and feathers. As I worked carefully and reverently, a new song came into my mind. It started to get louder and louder. It came through me as if it was being passed down from an ancient time. The circle of grandmothers appeared and again sang with me. Our voices became one in union.

My body became light and goose bumps covered my skin. It was as if I was observing myself from above my body while I wrapped the feathers and sang. It was an ecstasy of transcendence, not feeling the movement of my hands or the muscles used in my voice. It was a power flowing through me, but not of me. The grandmothers would later reveal to me it was a blessing song, one that I would use many times in the future. It would become a part of my medicine (knowledge) as I worked to complete the regalia.

Four weeks before the ceremony, Darcy gave me the privilege of taking care of one of the society's medicines. It was the complete skin of a magnificent brown bear. The fur was chocolate brown and soft to the touch. It was amazing to hold. She asked me to keep it for the month, pack it and bring it to the ceremony in Texas.

It had been a beautiful female bear. I smudged it with sage and cedar smoke and laid it on my bed. While praying, all thirteen grandmothers visited and told me to sleep with this medicine. I was given this skin to work with for a full moon for a reason and that I had dream medicine and the brown bear would teach me.

So it began. I slept with the skin covering me as I fell asleep. This was the first time in four years that Sunshine would not sleep in bed with me.

The first night I dreamed...

I was a small cub following my mother by the river. She led me to some red berries and carefully nudged me to the bush. I watched her nibble on the berries and I followed her lead. They tasted ripe and juicy. A small sweet burst of liquid. Then she led me further into the woods and we fed on a different plant. Each day she led me to the same berries and plants. One day I wandered away from her and I was about to feed on some brown and green berries. Before I had the chance, she growled and swatted me hard with her massive paw, letting me know it was not edible. It was a teaching of recognizing what was safe and what was not.

I dreamed each night of being a cub growing larger and stronger as my mother bear guided each of my steps and taught me how to live and survive. The night before I traveled to Texas, my dream changed.

I was somewhat older and mama was taking me to a different place. It was not the same woods or the same river. It was a further journey to unfamiliar territory. The landscape was dry and the temperature was hotter. I yearned for a drink of cool water from a clear flowing river. It seemed we had walked forever to get here. Mama stood on her hind legs and reached up into a small tree to a suspended branch and inspected a large odd-shaped object covered with swarming insects. She listened closely with her ear and gently sat back down. It was early morning, so we rested for a few hours.

As the day grew hotter we watched more of the small buzzing winged insects fly out of the object. They swarmed, buzzing and flying about. Many had left. I was not sure how many were still in there. As the day passed, mamma once again stood and shook the branch. More of these buzzing creatures flew out and mama swatted them away without harming any of them. I realized if she had done this earlier there would have been too many to swat away. Her timing was perfect. When she knocked the object off the branch and on to the ground, a few remaining insects flew out. As I peered closer, a couple of the insects bit my nose. The quick sting was uncomfortable at first, but then mama scraped some of the wet earth from around the tree's base and rubbed it on the bite. Relief came quickly.

I watched as mama placed her paw inside the odd-shaped object. Her paw pulled out a golden brown, sticky substance that dripped slowly down her paw. She licked her paw with such precision as to not get it into her fur. She motioned for me to do the same. I placed my paw inside and pulled out a small amount. It was messy but I managed to remove my paw and began to taste the incredible nectar. It was the reason we had traveled so far on this journey. It was the sweetest substance I had ever tasted in my young life - one that only my mother could teach me to find. We had our savory feast and felt satisfied, full and content. I was happy that mama and I enjoyed the moment. She looked at me with her loving brown eyes and spoke.

*"**The honey is always in the center like a pit in a fruit. It is kept hidden to be protected. It will sustain, nurture and feed you and allow you to grow. Sometimes it seems hard to reach but it can always be found.**"*

I felt she was passing on great wisdom. I knew I had to remember these words. And then abruptly, I awoke.

I wrote down the dream, just as I had every other night in the past month, but with this dream I underlined the words that the mother bear had spoken. I would not really come to understand the words until much later.

CHAPTER SEVEN

The day came for me to head to Wizard Wells, Texas with Darcy. To our surprise the flight was canceled due to electrical problems found prior to the flight. So we delayed our arrival to Texas for a day.

I found the flight delay a blessing. I felt in the big scheme of things that the Great Spirit was protecting us for safe travel. A medicine man once told me years ago, that if I saw a red-tail hawk following me as I traveled, it was a sign of protection. As luck would have it, a red-tail flew above us for several miles on our way to the airport.

We got to the land the next day after a three hour drive from the Dallas airport and were greeted by several women of different ages. All were excited and working tirelessly preparing food for the ceremony. It was clear that all the women that I met that week were loving, sacred individuals. They were ready to assist and support me through the process. They had built a family of compassion and nurturing and I felt fully accepted.

Two elder grannies in particular caught my eye. They were blood sisters of Cherokee descent. Janice looked a lot like my maternal grandmother who had been deceased for years. Molly looked like my maternal great grandmother who had been a healer, and whom had passed when I was twelve. The two elder sisters were spry and witty. Their laugh permeated my being and put me at ease from the anxiety of the unknown that was yet to come.

They were in their mid to late sixties, only a couple of years apart. One had brown hair and the other a whitish-blonde tint. Both were petite in stature but each of their presences held energy of great wisdom and understanding. They had an amazing fire in their spirits that gave them almost super human endurance and tireless energy as they busied themselves cooking and cleaning in the kitchen and seeing to everyone's needs.

There were about forty women to support us and there were only two women going through the ceremony. Many of the women, including the three from my community who started the commitment months ago, had dropped out of ceremony for individual reasons. As always, I knew everything was just as it was meant to be. The two of us ladies were exactly in the right place at the right time. In twenty-four hours, we would be thrust into the purification lodge in preparation for seclusion on the high hill.

The other woman going on this quest was Sara Mills. She was from northern Texas and was independent and strong-willed. She possessed a tall thin body, very feminine in nature with frosted, long blonde hair and beautiful green eyes. She too was a spitfire with lots of energy to spare. She was kind and intelligent. When I arrived to the land, we had a long chat about our personal lives, struggles and our calling to this ceremony.

The ceremony needed to have an elected grandmother who would hold the energy connected to the women on the hill and pray for them. Since I did not know anyone from the group, Sara suggested the elder Janice. She excitedly agreed to support us.

The evening before the ceremony, Granny Molly and Granny Janice sat us in a circle and told stories about their older sister Karen, who had passed a couple of years before. They talked about her being a great healer and ceremonialist who taught many students. They said that she had lived on this land for years before she passed and her presence was still felt here. They talked of their Cherokee lineage from their father and their escapades as teenagers. They were entertaining and filled with many life experiences and stories. We were cackling so loud that a few of the women in their tents asked us to "keep it down."

"Laughter is medicine," said Granny Molly. "It takes the fear and sadness away. You will have a good night's sleep tonight. This initiation is about transformation. It is the change from who you once were to who you are meant to be."

I wasn't really sure what she meant, but I found myself already in the midst of change in the last year. With the divorce, a change in residence, change in job position and changes in my body's menstrual cycle possibly due to stress, what else could possibly change?

~

So here I find myself on a hill in the depths of this vision quest initiation, battered by the hail, rain, relentless heat and it was mid-morning. A rooster was crowing from a nearby farm. The swarm of locust were still crunching the tall dried grass and covering my blanket where I sat. I was careful not to step on any of them when I stood to pray to each of the directions.

A vision right now would be a most welcomed distraction from the uncomfortable circumstances. But no, I would have to sing and pray for many more long hours.

My mind wandered to Sara, the other quester. *Could she be having an uncomfortable time like me as well? Was she also questioning her sanity as to why she chose to be here?*

Whatever happened during this ceremony, I believed it would affect each of our lives differently in the years to come.

As the day went on and the sun set in the west, I sang the song to welcome the evening star. Slowly more stars appeared and the moon rose to its fullness of light. The moon has always been a powerful force for me. Its reflection soothes me in times of stress. As I gazed upon her I felt a rocking within, like a child that has been comforted by its mother.

My skin was sunburned and I developed a slight chill. I wrapped a brightly colored, striped, lightweight blanket around myself. The locust continued to swarm and chew the tall grass around my blanket at a less ferocious pace.

Usually on a quest, one tries to stay awake because the night can be a very active time for the spirits to bring a vision, but I found my eyes to be very sleepy.

So I rocked back and forth singing quietly to myself. I was too tired to stand and move around when the vision began.

Through the darkness and only the moon's light, the sky brought a brilliant light from the west. As it drew nearer the light split into several smaller lights that formed a ring shape. As I counted each light that had emerged from the one, I realized it was now a circle of thirteen. The lights drew closer until they were right above my head. It looked like the underneath of a spaceship ready to land. The ring dropped lower to the ground. Each ball of light emitted a beam that surrounded my blanket. As the beams faded, a circle of women sat around me. They were not solid, but rather ghost-like apparitions. Each was ornately dressed in their indigenous regalia. Their familiar faces appeared to be smiling, very old and from different cultures. The group was the same women that had appeared to help me in my preparations each month. A woman spoke through telepathy, her mouth never moved. I could hear her clearly.

"We have arrived to welcome you to our circle. We are the Grandmothers. We have called you here and we have worked with you to help you prepare for this night. We will work with you through the coming years, for we have something to teach. I am White Swan," she spoke.

"You will be helping many people to heal in the future. It is what you came to Earth to do. You will teach and help the children. Then you will teach the women and then help the men. All have lost their connection to the grandmother, the great mother within. But first you will heal it within you," she commanded.

My mind raced with many questions. I was shown a small Sacred Pipe and a young boy and girl holding it together. As they came closer they presented it to me in a sacred way, motioning it back and forth until the fourth time when it was laid to rest in my hands. It was small, barely nine inches altogether.

"This will be your child, a sacred being. You did not have physical children born through you in this lifetime. This will be another child to take care of and protect. Each of them will have great power and be a conduit for healing."

Many scenes were placed through my mind. I saw myself leading many ceremonies. I saw myself being older with long graying hair and many people around me. The visions were fast and fleeting. I was overwhelmed. This was not something my ego would choose to do.

Black Deer had often told me, "You know when the spirits have spoken to you, because it is usually something you don't want to know or would ever want to do."

It's what he would call a vision or a calling and it was rare, since most people are not open enough or will commit to a fast and go through ceremony.

As the circle of grandmothers got ready to leave I felt a euphoric sense of bliss along with a deep sadness at the same time. I did not want our time to end. They said they would give me a song to call upon them when I needed help and that I would hear the song again when they came to teach.

The song of their voices started soft and slow. As the rounds increased their voices became loud and fast as if they were drawing a circle of energy around me. I sang quietly along with them. The song had been ingrained into my own womb. I felt a twitch and then movement in my womb, like a butterfly fluttering, and then it subsided.

The women once again became balls of lights and ascended to the sky into a circle before morphing into one light and disappearing.

The next thing I remembered was a tickle on my cheek. I opened my eyes and a small brown spider had crawled upon me to awaken me. I was dizzy and still in a dream-like state. The locust had left my blanket and the rooster was quiet. Stillness had risen with the new day and I pondered the night's events.

Time was slow paced, like a dream. I don't remember being brought down from the hill and placed into the purification lodge that I now found myself in. I sat dazed and ungrounded as if life was passing by in slow motion. I was weak, depleted and laid on the earth face down seeking the cooler air. I made my prayers of gratitude and finally it was over.

I don't remember eating food to break my fast that was prepared by Granny Molly.

"How are you feeling? You need to go and take a nice shower and relax before the next part. Someone will help you get dressed into the ceremonial clothes that you made over the last nine months. You'll be given a new name for initiation into the society. It's all so exciting," she fussed.

After my shower Granny Molly brought an herbal preparation containing comfrey oil to help ease my chigger bites. As an aroma therapist, she also massaged my feet with several oils to help revive my energy. I could barely feel her fingers as she massaged my feet. It was nice to meet a woman, who like myself, could read and sense energy fields. It was a great relief to have her healing expertise. I knew that I had instantly formed a loving, life-long bond with both of the grannies.

I did not feel like myself. I was still in a fog. I slowly dressed into my newly made regalia. I would now be given my new name and acceptance into the society.

As my shawl was being draped over my shoulders, my new name was announced. I could not hear it because as they spoke my ears went deaf. A buzzing sound erupted in my ear drum and I felt dizzy. I was taught many years ago, one's whole sacred name was never used in public, for it contained personal power and wisdom and one would need to grow into the name in the coming years. I could not hear my new name, so I made a mental note to ask Granny Molly and Granny Janice after the feasting and giveaway. As was customary one would shorten and use only a part of the name in ceremony.

Still in slow motion, I completed my giveaway of wrapped feathers and a gift to each person at the ceremony. Though I still could not feel grounded in my body, I was now accepted into the sisterhood. The ceremony taught me about nurturing and compassion. My new sisters had surely exemplified that to me. I had traveled to a place that was not even found on a map and it was there that I met a group of unknown women who cared for me, fed me, helped dress me and offered compassion, love and support. An unfamiliar feeling in today's fast-paced society.

In society many women gossiped, back stabbed, and were unsupportive of each other because of fear and a lack of love within themselves. It was through this ceremony that I caught a glimpse of the healing that I would need to bring to myself first, then perhaps to other women in the future.

Women indeed are important. They give life and are great nurturers. They are emotionally strong, are the partners in co-creating and are sacred beings. Yet we are not treated as such nor do we treat ourselves or other women with this sacredness. It would take me the next years to truly embrace my own sacredness.

CHAPTER EIGHT

I returned home to New England and I tried to readjust to work and life. I had planned a trip to the Yucatan in Mexico months before and I was unsure if I still wanted to go. I was still worn out from Texas. I eventually decided to take the trip and it was there a series of events began to unfold.

The tour group to Mexico consisted of a lively, spiritual, small group of women. I knew some of them prior to the trip, including my friend, Lisa Parker. We were to meet with a healer, Pablo Sanchez in his village and each of us would be able to work with him personally.

The trip was humid and hot and we found ourselves touring a few historic sights off the beaten path, like the village of Catemaco and the place of Trez Zappotas. These were places Pablo had ongoing sightings of UFO's and star people.

So the group climbed to the top of the twelve-story-high mound of one of the Trez Zappotas. I had to climb using my hands and propel myself up the gigantic hill. It was beautiful and breathtaking at the top once I arrived, but it certainly was a tough hike. It was in the middle of a pasture of land that a kind peasant farmer gave permission to Pablo and our group to enter his property.

Once we were on top, the wind began to pick up and the sun burned directly on us in the midday hour. Pablo led the group with prayers and energy opening exercises to connect to the earth and the sky.

The Native American woman leading the tour into Mexico, Star Hawk, conducted a Sacred Pipe ceremony for the group. Once the ceremony was complete, an eagle flew above us and circled. Pablo pointed above and everyone looked up to see a golden eagle gliding and circling as if a blessing was being bestowed upon us all. Star Hawk began to speak to the group in a serious tone and explained the eagle was a sacred sign.

"Through dream and prayer, I am called to gift a sacred bundle given to me by a woman I met on a Montana reservation to one of the women in this group. I was told it belongs with her since she will not have children in this life. It will be her responsibility to care for it. I was gifted this bundle to find the person to whom it needs to be with. It is a Child's Sacred Pipe bundle. It is very small and fragile...,"

Her voice trailed off. I found myself in slow motion, remembering my vision on the hill in Texas, the two children placing a small Sacred Pipe in my hands telling me it was to pray for all children; those coming into the world, those in the world and those leaving the world early.

As Star Hawk knelt in front of me she placed the bundle in my hands.

"Sister, I believe this bundle is for you. Please honor and respect it. If you have questions I can speak with you later."

I held the bundle and I cried. I knew my life would never be the same. It would be changed forever. Would I be ready to accept the change? I could never imagine the magnitude of the impact it would have on my life.

The rest of the trip was physically hard and demanding. There was civil unrest in the country. There were checkpoints along the road with armed military men who checked our passports and threatened our security.

Our daily food source during the day had been bottled water, tortilla chips, packaged guacamole and salsa. The food in the road side stands was cooked with impure water and a few of the women came down with severe cases of Montezuma's revenge.

The long road trip would end in the evening with a clean hotel where we were able to eat a safe meal and refresh with a clean shower. The trip reminded me to be grateful every day for all I had. When we rode through poverty stricken villages, tiny shacks with only a strung hammock inside and no running water; it was hard not feel guilty for all I had at home in my rented two bedroom condo. Though poor, the children were smiling and running happily through the streets. Gratitude is what this trip would teach me. It would be the beginning of my life's journey to help those in need.

I welcomed the return home from Mexico as I needed much rest. I had experienced so much in the last few weeks and, unbeknownst to me, there would be more to come.

I was looking forward to being in the purification lodge with Darcy and Bill and the community. I felt at home and at peace in ceremony. The lodge was hot and intense. Bill was amazing to watch as he performed the ceremony with compassion and reverence and Darcy's voice was like an angel that helped me soar above the heat and stay in the prayer.

When the ceremony was complete, we changed into dry clothes and started with the feast. As we ate and socialized, Darcy and Bill announced that they would be moving further west in the state more than another hour away and invited all of us to continue ceremony with them. I was happy for them, but realized I was already traveling two hours one way every other weekend. I was not sure if I could continue, especially during the winter months. My heart was in angst. I knew I would have to pray to seek an answer of whether to continue with them.

Back at work, I noticed that the sales were dropping immensely and there were whispers of lay-offs. I didn't get rattled, I continued on with a business as usual attitude.

I received a call from the daughter of my former elder Native American teacher, Black Deer. He was coming to Massachusetts for a lecture. She asked if I could support his trip to Massachusetts. I agreed and called to register for the lecture immediately. He had been my teacher early on and put me out on four vision quests years ago. I had traveled out west for seven years to work with him and to be in ceremony. I looked forward to seeing him again. He gifted my first Sacred Pipe years ago and the teachings of its use and care.

The night of the lecture, I greeted Black Deer and spoke with him a few moments. I had not seen him in several years, but I sent letters and gifts to help him out on the reservation. He had aged, now nearly eighty.

He looked at me and smiled, "Big changes coming for you. Your life's gonna be turned around soon. You will feel lost, but it's just preparing you for your real work," he winked.

"Come purify with me tonight after the lecture. We've got a place up in the woods. The people who own this place let me build a temporary lodge for the weekend for my group. It'll be like old times. We'll sing and talk to the spirits," he laughed.

I laughed too... on the outside, but the inside knew better. His laugh always taught me that something big was coming and I knew it would be something I wasn't ready for or probably wanted. He would tell me never to get too comfortable in life because change was always around the corner and you needed to be ready to surrender and accept it, for it was the nature of things.

After the lecture, I followed his group to the woods. I helped fix the sacred foods as I had learned years before. I brought the proper towels and things for the lodge. Since I purified regularly I always had them in my vehicle with me ready to go, as well as camping equipment.

As the seven of us entered the darkened lodge with reverence, Grandpa Black Deer began to sing in his native tongue. He welcomed each of the stones and honored them and called for the flap of the door to be closed. It felt good to be in his lodge again, as his prayers and songs were strong.

When the water was poured over the hot stones, they sizzled and hissed as the steam rose upwards to heat and cleanse us. There is something that happens in the darkened lodge. You become very present, very aware of your body and your being. You are aware of your aliveness and your connection to the earth below and all the creatures, as well as to the elements of fire, water, air, and earth. Everything is one, there is no separation. It's as if you are in a great womb and you are cleaning and preparing yourself to be reborn into a new you each time.

Ceremony is about growth and change because prayer changes things. It changes you and everything around you. It gives you an internal peace, knowing that the prayer is heard and has value.

The heat became more intense after the door flap was closed for the third time. I was sweating and cleansing profusely. Grandpa was speaking to the spirit world and the ancestors. He prayed for each one of us and our healing. Finally, the door flap opened and the cool air streamed in.

Relief was brief as the flap was closed for the fourth time. Grandpa sang, prayed and then stopped to speak in English. He rarely spoke in English during ceremony.

"The woman called Laurel has changes coming. She will walk the path of medicine. She will pray and help the children, then the women and then the men. She is a ceremony person. She will care for seven children in her life. It will not be easy. She will need tough skin. She knows the stars and will learn the power of the moon. The grandmothers will teach her in dream time. She can choose to follow or not, but it is her calling from the Great Spirit. She will have to detach from family, friends and even community to do spirit's work. She will sacrifice her life for Spirit's will. If she follows Great Spirit, the Great Spirit will help her, aho."

I listened carefully but had no words to speak. I took it all in. I welled up with tears. I did not understand it all, but I knew another chapter was unfolding. *Was there was a reason for my divorce and everything else that had come my way in my life?* Some were choices and some were of divine purpose. How did Grandpa know? *He* didn't. Spirit had told him. Spirit spoke through him in ceremony. I just breathed the steam, sighed heavily and surrendered.

After the ceremony, I quickly changed into clean dry clothes and we sat down to eat the feast of meat, corn, berries and water. I sat by Grandpa and offered him a sacredly wrapped pack of tobacco and asked if I could have a teaching on the Sacred Pipe again.

"Grandpa, I know I have watched you many times in the Sacred Pipe ceremony and you have given me teachings for my first Sacred Pipe in the past but I am asking again for the teachings. I was gifted a second Pipe, a Child's Sacred Pipe bundle and I want to make sure I have the teachings to honor it."

He proceeded to talk about the Sacred Pipe as he had in the past, giving the same instructions from the ceremony to its care and use. We sat there for a few hours and I just listened. Then he looked at me and spoke.

"You will also receive teachings from a woman on the Child's Sacred Pipe bundle. There will be a song and some women teachings. It will balance the bundle. Laurel, you will start teaching and working with children soon. Each sacred bundle is a sacred being, like a child. Take care of them, protect them, and listen to them for they will teach you. Each will come at a different time in your life, when you are ready."

"Grandpa, will you bless my bundle for me like you did with the first one you gifted to me years ago?" I asked.

"No. Not this one. A woman will bless it for you. Don't worry. She will find you when the time is right and not too long after, another sacred bundle will come. Remember all your bundles will be different, for each have a different purpose and power. They will teach you if you humble yourself to them. Get ready," he chuckled.

The twinkle he had in his eye as he laughed made me unsure of everything. All that I had learned or had thought I had learned didn't help. This would be a new beginning. I was starting over like a child. *Was I too old for this?*

CHAPTER NINE

I returned to work on Monday. My place of work had become a place of gossip and fear the last two weeks. Lack of production work orders made the employees restless. The company had slightly reduced the staff the previous week with the people who had taken a lot of time off and had disciplinary problems. Employees were disgruntled and fearful of losing their security.

I had seen no new hires over the last months. My manager had told me secretly that the company was considering massive lay-offs in all departments this week. The company of over five hundred people would be downsizing over a hundred employees this week. I had over twenty-five men that reported to me and I was asked to cut the staff in half. I took into consideration what each man knew, his years of experience, and if he could be trained to move to another position.

This was a stressful task. Not only did I have to cut staff but I also needed to cut overhead costs as well. As the week wore on, my heart grew heavier. The men asked if there would be another lay-off and I could not in good conscious deny it.

"Yes, but I cannot tell you who will be let go, but I will help anyone that needs help with a resume or a personal reference," I replied.

Some of the men took me up on my offer and I helped them after hours with their resumes. By the end of the week twelve people in my department were let go.

I knew the upcoming weeks were going to be stressful, so I prayed daily and in lodge every other weekend to stay balanced on all levels. I knew that Darcy and Bill would be moving soon and I would not be able to continue the journey being so far away. As I told them my decision my heart was sad. I felt the changes in the air coming.

In two months, the company was downsized to less than one hundred people. There was barely any work for anyone to do. By September 1st the rest of the employees were given their walking papers and by that afternoon I, as well as the rest of the employees in management, were given severance packages. The company closed its doors for good. The company had put all its production and research into one product that was booming, now the market had change and left the company with no other options but to close.

I had never seen a company close its doors nor had I ever been unemployed. I never experienced the grief over identifying one's job with who you are and the loss of self-esteem when you are trying to find another job. I needed to figure out how to survive and pay my bills.

I remembered Black Deer's words when I prayed, *"Big changes coming for you. Your life's gonna be turned around soon. You will feel lost but it's just preparing you for your real work."*

The next morning I greeted the first ray of sun with a prayer. I loved this time. It was the sacredness and the mystery of another day. The birds were chirping and singing a gratitude for life. I lifted the tobacco to the east direction and asked for the Great Spirit's guidance. Yes, I was feeling lost. No job and my ceremony community had moved away. All was taken from me.

I remembered Black Deer's teaching, *"Something is taken away when change is needed but it will always be replaced with something new. You just have to keep your eyes and ears open and pay attention or else you might miss it."*

Well, I was certainly paying attention now. I was listening. But how long would it take? I had some savings that could keep me going and I could take clients for readings more often since I had the time. Also I could offer to teach meditation classes at night again. So I guess I'm not so lost.

I dreaded the visit to my parents over the weekend to inform them of my job loss.

"Oh that's terrible. You can move back home if you want to make it easier for you," my mother coaxed.

I winced at the thought of it. I was going to take care of myself, come hell or high water. I was not going to move home again, once was embarrassing enough.

"Laurel, you've got to get your resume back out there before the others that were laid off. Keep searching. You have enough experience. You'll find something," my father encouraged.

I was happy he had belief in my abilities, but I was so unsure in my career direction. Sometimes you need to take what you can get. My embarrassment of being unemployed for the first time in my life and worrying about disappointing my father gave me the motivation to find something soon. I needed to get my career back on track.

I had always admired the path my brother Tom took in his career. He had found his niche early in life. At eighteen he joined the Air Force. He was a mechanic for jets and he was making a career of it stationed in Nevada. He traveled to many places to fix mechanical problems on jets. He had made quite a career over the years. My parents were very proud, though he had not been lucky in love. He had two long term relationships that didn't work out. We didn't see each other often. Usually it was every couple of years at Christmas when he came home to Massachusetts.

Discouraged about my unemployment, I met with my oldest friend Margie Donovan. She was an intelligent and honest woman. She had beautiful mid-length dark hair, dark eyes and a wonderful smile. She was a friend to everyone she met. She worked hard to stay in contact with many of her friends from high school, especially me.

We had known each other since we were fourteen. She had gone to college and became a middle school teacher. We had laughed and cried over boys and relationships, gone to dances and movies, and even double dated together for the senior prom.

In fact, she was a true friend and shoulder to lean on when I was going through my divorce. She had comforted me through tears, grief and the shame of my divorce. I would never forget her kindness and love that helped me through those times. I told Margie of my job loss when we met for dinner over the weekend.

"What are you going to do?" asked Margie. "I mean, what do you want to do?"

"I don't want to work in production companies again. I want to enjoy work that makes me happy," I replied.

"What work would make you happy?" Margie questioned further.

"I love spiritual things, ceremony, praying, using my gift of insights. Being an intuitive person is a part of who I am. Guess those aren't credits you can put on a job application. Could you imagine a potential employer glancing at the following resume?

- Works well with people... all people living or dead.
- Is highly intuitive... will figure out answers by asking for guidance from Spirit.
- Great at training and teaching people because of seeing energy fields.

Not your everyday employee," I joked.

Margie laughed.

"As a child, I wanted to teach. I can remember at three-years-old lining up my stuffed animals and dolls on my bed like a classroom and using a wooden spoon from the kitchen and pointing on the wall like I was teaching a class. I wasn't a mother to my dolls. I lined them up on the bed like students and taught them different things. When I turned five, my parents got me a small blackboard, so I could write and teach my dolls. Obviously I was not in school yet because I was young, but I could draw circles and talk," I added.

"What were you teaching?" asked Margie.

"I talked about everything that I could see and understand at that time. Frogs, ants, everything that I could observe became a topic. I was an only child for years before my brother was born. So I had no playmates until school."

I sat there quietly remembering my childhood past when my brother was a toddler. *Why was I walking down memory lane? What was this stirring in me?*

"Oh well, enough about that," I said.

We finished our dinner with hope of meeting again in a few weeks.

Six weeks later, Margie called me.

"Laurel, this is Margie. I was thinking about Thanksgiving. Our school usually reads a book about the pilgrims and the Indians as a part of our curriculum. Do you think you can come into my fourth grade class and maybe do a little talk about your experiences with Native

Americans Indians for about an hour, as a favor to me? I have about twenty-five students. I would like to do something special this year. I will get permission from the principal if the answer is yes."

I thought about it and got excited. A charge ignited in my belly and I felt a flutter in my heart.

"Yes, I would love to. I will think about it tonight and send you an outline for the presentation by email tomorrow," I answered.

I hung up the phone and dashed around the house to get a pen and paper and then sat down to pray. The Child's Sacred Pipe bundle was not blessed as of yet and I could not smoke it, so I held the bundle in my hands after smudging myself. I raised the pinch of tobacco over the sage smoke that was burning in the shell and prayed.

"Great Spirit, Grandfathers of the West, North, East and South, Grandfather of the Sky and Grandmother Earth, I give gratitude for my life and this opportunity to teach this class of children. I ask you to show me what to teach the children and I ask you to bring the woman that will help bless this bundle when the time is right, so I can pray for the little ones coming in, the one's living here and those that are returning to you, aho."

I placed the tobacco in the shell, sat in silence and watched it burn in the hot embers of the sage. The smoke danced around in a circle. *Dance* my mind spoke. Again and again the embers would go out and then relight in another place playing in the shell. *Play* my mind spoke again.

As I watched the embers a song came to my mind. It was a social song of gratitude that I learned while listening to the elders tell stories and sing to the children at one of the camps at a vision quest ceremony. The elder had taught everyone in the circle that day, both young and old to sing it. *Song and stories* my mind spoke to me one final time. Then the embers extinguished. I had received what I needed. Dance, play, song and stories, this would be my presentation.

I sent the outline to Margie. The principal of the school, Mrs. Bartel, gave her approval. In November, I would have the pleasure of teaching twenty-five students in the local elementary fourth grade. Unbeknownst to me, that day would represent the beginning of another level of my own education.

CHAPTER TEN

One week before I presented the children's program, I received a phone call from Star Hawk.

"Laurel, have you had the Child's Sacred Pipe blessed yet?" she asked.

"No. My former teacher Black Deer has given me teachings again on its care and ceremony, but he said that a woman would need to bless it for it to be opened properly," I replied.

"Good, then the vision I have been given is correct. I have seen myself blessing and connecting it to you. Please pray on this to see if it feels right for you. Let me know if you have any other questions. Please don't hesitate to ask," she said.

"Black Deer said there would be a special song that the woman would teach for the bundle," I added.

"Yes. He is right. There is a special lullaby that I will teach you for this bundle. I have been shown this already," she replied.

I prayed for four days and received my confirmation through a dream.

A child was playing outside in a field and she was waving to the sky. As I looked up a giant golden eagle was swooping down towards the child. I ran towards the child calling to her and trying to get her attention. I realized I must get to her before she is swooped up by the eagle for it is not her time to leave this earth. I must protect her. I raced to her and covered her with my body on the ground. The immense eagle landed, gave a shrilling call and waited. I raised my head. The bird landed on the ground and crouched down as if it were nesting. It started to whistle a tune. I listened carefully over and over until the tune became a part of me. I began humming along with the eagle. I found myself rocking back and forth holding the little girl and she became calm and sleepy. The eagle stretched its wings in formation for flight. It looked directly into my eyes and I heard its thoughts clearly in my mind.

"It is time to birth the child. You must remember the song. A hawk from the stars will help you."

With that it raised its wings and took flight high into the sky.

I awoke in bed humming the song over and over, *a hawk from the stars, Star Hawk.*

I understood. I could not wait to call her. I had received my confirmation.

Star Hawk would conduct the ceremony two days later, to bless the bundle. We agreed on a discrete place and time for the ceremony. I invited my friend Lisa Parker and another woman, Anna Becker from the trip to Mexico, so that the four of us who had witnessed the gifting of the bundle would be part of the ceremony. Four is a sacred number in Native American Indian teachings, reminding one of the connections to the seasons, the four directions and body, mind, heart and spirit.

When the day arrived the weather was dark and cloudy with a cold chill in the air. As we sat in the circle a mist of rain began. Star Hawk handle both the bowl and stem with reverence and careful attention as she blessed both pieces with the sacred smoke. She blessed and connected both pieces of the Sacred Pipe to my heart. She asked me to sing four songs. I sang the prayer songs that I had been taught long ago by Black Deer.

One song was for health and healing, one was for the Sacred Pipe, another was a gratitude song and the last one was a children's song. As I sang for health and healing the wind picked up and the rain drops became larger. I began the second song and the rain turned to large snowflakes that melted when they touched the ground. On the final song the snow stopped, the clouds parted and the sun came out to shine its full blessings. It was a powerful ceremony. Tears fell from my eyes as I sang honoring the weather's role in the ceremony.

Finally I filled the Child's Sacred Pipe with a sacred mix of tobacco and smoked it in prayer. The taste was sweet and the trail of smoke from my breath rose to the sky in beauty. When the ceremony was complete and the bundle was closed, Star Hawk sang the last song. As she sang, I began to recognize the song. It was the same tune the eagle had gifted me in the dream. I hummed along with her.

When she finished she said, "This is the song I was going teach you, but I see you know it already."

"I only know the tune. An eagle in a dream gifted the tune but not the words," I replied.

"Before I leave today we will have private time and I will pass the song on to you and give you any further teachings you might need."

I did a giveaway to Star Hawk as well to my two friends. A giveaway is done after a ceremony. It completes the ceremony. It honors the person conducting ceremony for their time and energy and a way to give back for what one has been blessed with in ceremony.

I gifted each of my two friends a package of tobacco and a lovely silk scarf. For Star Hawk, I gifted the four sacred plants (tobacco, sage, sweet grass and cedar) along with a small Pendleton blanket and a gift card that could be used for her travel and personal expenses.

There is no charge for any type of ceremony. However, it is always honorable to give a generous exchange or giveaway for all the blessings you have received. It is the natural order of things that allows one not to become greedy and ungrateful. The reciprocity cycle of receiving and giving go hand in hand. It is a way to share abundance. It amazes me that in today's society so many do not practice this way, for the level of fear, violence and poverty could be transformed.

I spent private time to learn the lullaby song from the Star Hawk. I also shared my experiences with Black Deer and his Sacred Pipe teachings with her. The ceremony forged a bond of friendship between us that will last forever. I was grateful for the way the vision I received in Texas was slowly falling into place.

CHAPTER ELEVEN

I kept in touch with Granny Molly and Granny Janice every month. We chatted by phone. On my last call to Granny Janice her tone of voice was very serious. She asked if I would come to Texas and support her in the Sundance ceremony. She said her granddaughter was diagnosed with cancer and that Spirit was calling her to pray for her healing by committing to the Sundance.

I knew that supporting her dance would be for five years. A dancer commits to dance for four years and the last year is a gratitude year. But many dancers who complete their commitment to the Sundance end up recommitting to the dance until their bodies no longer can dance.

I prayed on the matter and then agreed to support Granny Janice. Before it was official I still needed the approval of the camp's native elder and leader Wind Woman. Granny Janice asked Wind Woman if I could support her. Wind Woman stated that I would have to meet her in Texas in the spring to support the committed dancers in her camp on their vision quests that she conducted before the Sundance. It was then she would see my level of work ethic, support and commitment to her camp. As customary, when we met, I would gift her tobacco and offer my five-year commitment to support the Sundance.

So, I would need to save money to travel to Texas twice next year, in the spring for the vision quest and then back in the summer for the Sundance. I am currently unemployed. *What the heck did I just commit to? How was I going to be able to do this?* The unemployment check barely covered my rent. I decided to take appointments for readings and flower essence consults full-time to supplement my income. I had learned that if I was truly meant to do this, I would find a way or the Great Spirit would find a way for me. *Trust Laurel, let go and trust.*

Three days before Thanksgiving, I was excited to meet with Margie's fourth graders. I taught the social songs and told the old stories to entertain the children. I also spoke about honoring the earth, the land, the plants, trees and all the animals. I spoke of respect to all of life and our connection to each other and to use only what you need and to save the rest for future generations. There were lots of questions about dream catchers and stereotypical beliefs that I helped clarify.

I have learned from elders that many teachings in society are incorrect about native peoples. While I am not an authority, I felt compelled to share what my native teachers had taught me in their words not mine. It seemed to move the children emotionally.

As the class came to an end, I noticed the principal Mrs. Bartel, in the hallway observing my presentation. She later commented on my ability to keep the children's attention because they could be quite unruly at times.

I just smiled and said, "I prayed about it beforehand. I asked for help to give the children what they needed and that I would teach them to be better human beings."

Mrs. Bartel gave me an awkward stare and then it was as if a light went off in her. She smiled and nodded her head in approval.

The day went well. It gave me great joy when I thought of the time I had spent with the children. I went home and opened the Child's Sacred Pipe Bundle and conducted a ceremony of gratitude, blessing each and every child I encountered.

A week later, Margie called me and asked if I would be willing to go back to her school to present to three more classes. The principal was so impressed that she had agreed to ask the Parent Teachers Association to fund the event. Mrs. Bartel felt that I should be offered payment for my time. I was thrilled. The payment would be enough to pay my airfare to Texas in the spring.

After presenting to the three classes at the local school, I started to receive phone calls from other elementary schools in other towns throughout the state of Massachusetts and Connecticut. I began to give presentations twice a week until Christmas. By the holidays I had saved enough to buy both airline tickets to Texas and enough for gifting and supporting the food for the ceremonies. Everything that I had earned was used to support both ceremonies. Spirit had given me the opportunity and the means to travel.

Though I was still looking for a full-time job, nothing seemed to be available. I had applications everywhere. I had interviewed for half-a-dozen positions and I was kindly told I was over qualified. So far all possibilities were dead ends, but I continued to trust and pray.

My day to day would begin with a prayer ceremony at sunrise and ended in prayerful devotion at sunset. I had no idea that this was the beginning of what my life would become and the person that I was meant to be. In time, it would become my calling to be of spiritual service to people.

CHAPTER TWELVE

The winter was quiet. The months of January and February were frigid and snowfall was heavy.

My life had become a time of reflection. I lost my identity as a wife, supervisor and training coordinator. Then my next test appeared. My landlord was putting my condo on sale in April.

Are you kidding me? I had to find a new place to live and I didn't have a full-time job. Who was going to rent to someone who didn't have a job? My unemployment benefits would run out in September. I could possibly get a six month extension but that was it. I was trying. I was not sitting around all day. I searched the internet and newspapers. For several hours each day I called and brought in applications. What more could I do? An increase in clients helped supplement but it was not weekly guaranteed full-time money. *Don't panic,* I told myself. *Just pray.*

Prayer seemed to become my new job, filling and consuming my life in every spare moment. I prayed for the people who might be traveling in the snow, who were in pain, suffering and dying. And I remembered the children who were lost, hurt, sick, abused and hungry. There were so many people and so little time.

Life was prayer. Prayer was a life. As a child I loved to pray. It was the most sacred and fulfilling connection to the mysterious energy of creation. It was so much a part of what gave me great joy and peace. From the moment I was taught to pray at two or three-years-old by my mother, there was an overwhelming, goose bump feeling that still holds true for me to this day. I got excited when I prayed to the energy of God or what I now call the Great Mystery of Spirit.

I could hear a voice, but not my own. I had known that my prayer was both heard and answered all in one. I could see and hear the spirits of loved ones and many others who had died and gone before me. I knew I was never alone, even if I physically or emotionally might have felt a moment of abandonment. I knew it was not the truth. I knew there was a higher energy of oneness and connection that I could feel when I prayed. It was real, true and a great comfort.

As the weeks passed, I continued to scan the papers and internet for work. I applied wherever there were openings. April was around the corner and I would be off to Texas to support the Sundance vision quest and meet with Wind Woman. Afterwards I knew I would need to find a new place to live.

I kept in touch with the grannies, Molly and Janice every week now as the ceremony got closer.

Eventually I returned to Texas in April and both grannies were as excited to see me as I was to see them. They prepared me for the protocols for meeting Wind Woman and answered any questions I had. I had been through quests and other ceremonies over the years, but every tribe and elder had their own tradition. One should never think they know everything. There is always something to learn.

In the past, Black Deer told me, "Listen with your ears and open your eyes to learn something. Not by opening your mouth. A wise person listens and speaks only when they have something to say that could benefit others. Otherwise it is just diarrhea of the mouth and it serves no purpose."

His words used to make me laugh, but I realized that they were true. If you talk all the time from your ego, you really can't learn from others who may have something to share and teach you. No one will listen to someone who does not listen to others. If everyone is talking and no one is listening then we miss the opportunity to learn, connect and evolve.

Since I have followed the Great Spirit, I have learned a few things and will continue to learn. Someday, I may have something of importance to say when I'm older. But until then, I will humble myself to listen, observe and set good examples by my actions. For if I am not learning, I am not living and one can never know enough.

As the grannies and I traveled together to Wind Woman's land, the weather was a scorcher. It was already 110 degrees. The beads of sweat were pouring out of me as we drove along the highway.

"Not used to this heat, eh?" Granny Janice commented.

"No, guess not," I replied.

"Here, put this bandana around your forehead. It'll keep the sweat out of your eyes. There's no vanity at ceremony. Everyone will be dirty, sweaty, sunburned and worn out by the end of the quest. Supporting is hard work. Your legs and back will get tired and your hands will get pruned from washing loads of dishes. At night, as exhausted as you will be, you won't be able to sleep for the energy is high," Granny Janice warned.

"It takes much work to support. When you get to Sundance the work and energy will be more intense. Consider this sundancer vision quest support your kindergarten. Everyone's stuff comes up to heal in ceremony. You will feel other peoples' emotions as well as your own. That can be the best part. Any emotional and mental stories you carry will come up for you to reflect upon and heal. Bless your heart girl; you don't know what you are in for," Granny Molly chuckled.

My mind was whirling. I understood what she was talking about. In community we learn to work together and our personality can create conflict to work through and release our heavy baggage from personal history and stories we feed ourselves. It also helps those who need to learn to use their voice. Yes, I have seen and learned some of those hard lessons. This quest was preparation for the largest ceremony called Sundance, with over five hundred or possibly more people. What would come up for me to learn? I knew that I needed to keep my mouth shut, perform the task I was asked and observe what I could.

We drove for two hours to get to the land. The tall sagebrush and blue bonnets were in bloom and made the journey worth the while.

When we arrived at the land it was barren and dry. The trees were small like bushes, not nearly as tall or as green as in Massachusetts. Everything looked as if the sun had beaten the hell out of it. A large gate closed the entrance from the dirt road. A man came holding a shell filled with sage and smudged around the car. He recognized the grannies, reminded us of the protocols and let us in. We drove slowly down the dirt road, but the dust and small pebbles kicked up and made a trail of smoke behind us. We parked the vehicle in the designated parking and had to walk a half mile further up the road to the ranch house. I was introduced to a few people. Reminded once again of the protocols, I was given my tasks for the next four days.

This quest support was harder than any other former quest I had supported. The temperature was nearing 116 degrees by noon. The Sundance energy was present even though it was a quest ceremony and that made for more intensity. I got little sleep. Many of the supporters got physically sick, several got bit by the fire ants, two people got stung by scorpions and one other woman suffered a heart attack. I was tasked with keeping the fire going, cooking, dish duty and other odd jobs that were needed since the amount of supporters had dwindled. I was grateful that I was able to handle all the tasks that were asked of me. I tried to understand why the supporters were failing.

Granny Molly explained the energy and her understandings.

"Laurel, I know you see energy as well as feel it. I feel energy but I don't see it as clearly as you do. The sequestered dancers' prayers are bigger energy. A vision quest is a prayer for guidance and direction. The Sundance prayer is for a healing for someone they love and for the renewal of the entire human race and all of life. It is a big prayer and a heavy energy to be transformed. So this is not a regular vision quest. This ceremony has the energy of both quest and the dance. The dancers are questing in preparation for the dance, to understand what sacrifice is needed to offer for their prayer to be heard. Many of the supporters cannot handle the intensity of the energy so many of them have had problems. I'll be interested in how well you do, but so far you are doing well. Pay attention, it will be fun," she said.

From our previous discussions, I could not think of this ceremony as fun. Hard work and serious commitment, yes, but certainly not fun. I was here in Texas and committed to support the vision quest for the dancers, especially Granny Janice and I wanted to just stay in my prayer and service.

By the end of the quest, I was exhausted. I barely had a moment to rest during the four days. Somehow the energy and my prayers held me together. The group of fifty people gathered for the feast and the quester's giveaway. I was ready for a hot shower and a nice hotel bed, or any real bed for that matter. In another eight hours my comfort awaited me.

Granny Janice took my hand and led me to make my introduction to Wind Woman.

"This is my friend, Laurel. This is this woman that I would like to support me at the dance. May she have permission to support in your camp?" she asked.

Wind Woman approached me and smiled. I offered her a sacred wrapped package of tobacco.

"You have worked hard, dear one. I didn't think a New Englander would make it in this heat. You surely have been tested. You must have some good strong medicine in you to still be standing even when many of the other supporters have gone down with sickness, bites and other circumstances. I'll see you in camp at Sundance in June," and with that she handed me a small red button.

"This button was gifted to me years ago when I was dancing in my first Sundance. The medicine man could see I was having a real hard time. I didn't think I was going to finish the ceremony. I was crying and suffering in pain. He came to me and pinned this on my dress. It somehow lifted me to a place beyond my pain. I want you to have it. I think it will be of importance to you, maybe not today but someday. See you at Sundance," she said as she walked away.

I didn't look at the button while she was speaking. I just thanked her for the tiny object that was as big as a nickel. For most people, it would have seemed so insignificant for all the work I had done. When I turned it over and looked at it, it brought tears to my eyes. The small red button with white lettering read one small inscription of three little words, "You Are Loved."

Powerful and uplifting; it brought me closer to the energy of the Sundance. My permission to support and be part of her camp was granted. Her comment, "See you at Sundance" was my golden ticket.

CHAPTER THIRTEEN

The return to Massachusetts was uneventful. Exhausted as I was, I had several clients lined up for flower essence consults starting tomorrow. I went to bed early to catch up on some much needed sleep.

The morning sessions went well. The first afternoon appointment cancelled and another woman named Geri, unexpectedly called to set up an appointment. Since I had the time as fate would have it, I had her Skype in. As soon as the session started, a woman's spirit appeared over her left shoulder and wanted to make contact.

The spirit began to rush her thoughts as if she was anxious and out of breath. She held her chest and tapped on it. She exhaled heavily over and over and appeared to be short of breath. She sent my mind a picture of Geri as a little girl. I understood that she was her mother and that she had died of lung cancer. Many pictures were coming through. She had died when Geri was nine-years-old. Geri was getting married and she was missing her presence at her upcoming wedding.

"Geri, before we begin the flower essence consult, I need to take care of a spirit that has come through to speak to you."

The woman was stunned.

"What are you talking about?" she questioned in disbelief.

"Please just listen. Your mother's spirit has appeared to me. She is communicating with pictures to me. She is showing me she died of lung cancer when you were nine-years-old. She knows you are sad and wishes that she was here to attend your wedding. She is happy you have chosen a good man. She wants you to know her spirit will be with you on your wedding day. She wants you to happy. She also wants you to know that *you are loved.*"

Chills ran up my spine. I remembered the pin I was gifted. The words were a reminder and of importance to me. I relayed the message to Geri.

Geri was overwhelmed and wept. The message gave her comfort. Her mother's message was received and her spirit disappeared.

Once Geri composed herself, she thanked me and we proceeded to complete her consult. It never amazes me how everything works in sync. My appointment cancellation proved to be exactly what was destined for Geri. I was grateful to be paying attention to allow the flow of the divine to come through.

The next several weeks flew by and I found myself back on a plane to Texas and the Sundance. The grannies once again picked me up at the airport and quickly we were on our journey further south. Only this time the heat was hotter and the drive took four-and-a-half moving hours instead of two.

We made a few stops to keep ourselves hydrated and fed, grounded and alert. The energy of Sundance can be uplifting and leave the mind spacy, especially for the people who are going to be dancing in the Mystery Circle, as Granny Janice was proving by not wanting to eat or drink.

We finally arrived at the land late in the afternoon. A gate keeper was burning sage and quietly smudged the car to clear the dense energy.

He asked which camp we were there to support and we all replied, "Grandmother Wind Woman."

He gave us directions to the camp and we set off slowly down the four-mile dirt road. The sun beat down on the car and there was no breeze coming through the rolled down windows. The sweat was pouring out of me. There wasn't a dry spot on me.

"Still not used to the heat?" asked Granny Janice.

"No, I guess not. It seems hotter than last month," I said as I wiped my forehead.

"Here," she said as again she threw a bandana to me.

"Put this on your head. Better remember to bring one next time," she winked.

I was introduced to a few people and we unpacked and set up the tent, that I would later find out, I would *not* be sleeping in. The Sundance energy is like a strong buzzing, the vibration is so high that although you are physically tired you cannot sleep. At least that is how I experienced it.

My assignment from Dan Germaine, the camp director, was to help in the kitchen. The head person of the kitchen was called the "kitchen mom" and I was to take direction from her. Her name was Sally Walton.

She was a stocky woman with a tough demeanor and in her fifties, I guessed. Her face was dry, wrinkled and worn proving her many years of support in the Texas sun. She explained to me that the kitchen was the heart of the camp and each camp held the energy of support for the dancers. We needed to keep the energy clean and clear.

"Keep the sage burning, prayers for the dancers going and your energy loving and uplifting. If someone enters the camp, greet them with love and compassion. Offer them a cold drink of water or sweet tea or offer to fix them food if they're hungry. Just do your best and let me know when you need a break," she instructed.

She gave me a slap on the back and inhaled my cleanliness.

"You smell good. Don't worry. By tomorrow you will smell and look like the rest of us," she smirked.

I began my task in the kitchen. During the next four days the dancers purified and ceremonially chopped down the large cottonwood tree and replanted it in the center of the dance circle.

Thankfully, we had a small tin roof over the kitchen that gave us some relief from the sun while we cooked. The dishwashing station however was not as sheltered. It was opened directly to the sun from a tornado the week before.

I was able to keep my emotions in check as I washed dishes. The water washed away any emotions that would come up. I felt tired and worn and very raw emotionally. A couple of times the tension Sally was feeling boiled over and she yelled at the women in the kitchen. Only later did I realize she was feeling all the emotions of the camp in the kitchen and was trying to do her best to shift it.

Angry, frustrated, sad, tired and depleted - she felt it all. She was in charge and she got hit with the energy first. Sometimes she did not release it in the best way, like yelling at people in the camp and breaking down crying. Only at the end of the week, would I learn not to take it personally.

Between the suffering heat and the gas burners in the kitchen, I could not complain, for I remembered the dancers out in the Mystery Circle suffering in the sun, tired, thirsty and hungry. It was then I drank a glass of water and prayed for their strength to complete their dance and prayer. Every time I felt pain or fatigue in my body, I was reminded to feed and take care of myself to revive the energy of the dancers and the camp's connection to them.

I learned from the grannies, the Sundance is a prayer for the generations to come, a completion and renewal of another year. Each dancer has their own calling to the dance, in many cases to ask for a loved one's healing. It was not a macho or ego thing and the preparation of one's self was a serious commitment. I was so honored and touched to support those that were giving so much for their loved ones.

Late afternoon, Granny Molly came to the kitchen.

"Laurel, I need to go to the arbor to check on Janice. I am feeling she is struggling and she needs our prayers and support. I need you to come with me," she directed.

I looked towards Sally.

"Sally, can I leave kitchen duty to accompany Granny Molly to the arbor?" I asked.

"Well…," she paused.

"Sally, she has been here more than her shift and as an elder I need her to come with me," she demanded.

"Ok, Laurel. I will see you tomorrow morning," she agreed.

Granny Molly knew when to pull out the elder card. As is customary in the native community, elders are respected and given what they ask for and need. Sally dare not cross hairs with Granny Molly's request.

As we walked the long rugged terrain to the arbor, I could hear the drum and the male singers. I could smell the fresh burning cedar in the air. The arbor was the length of a college football field. It was covered with boughs of cedar that provided a little shade for the supporters. The inner circle or "Mystery Circle," is where the dancers danced barefoot on the dry grass. They were in lines around the large cottonwood tree.

The tree was beautiful. Its top branches were moving with the slight breeze. Colorful tobacco filled robes of black, red, yellow, white, blue, purple and green were wrapped around the branches and waving to the people below.

I stood there in awe of its beauty as it brought tears to my eyes.

When I looked closer, I could see energy lines like spokes on a wheel, turning slowly through the dancers to the tree in a clockwise formation. This funnel of energy was rising up the tree to the sky, making a connection to the sky and following the sun's travel. I felt the energy in my body as the sun's energy traveled back down the tree to the earth. It was as if all the prayers were heard and answered, infusing the earth and the dancers with a sacred power. Men laid down on the buffalo robes while their flesh was cut and bones pierced their skin, on their chest, arms or backs. I began to feel the pain in my body as I looked on. I prayed for their strength while I wiped the tears trickling down my cheeks.

"What do you see, girl?" Granny Molly asked. "I know you see something. Don't take on their pain. It is their prayer. Be strong. Sing and dance with your feet to build the energy of support for them. They do this for the people, all people. Don't turn your eyes away, witness it. Feel the love they have for all of us and send that love back to them with strong prayers."

I composed myself and prayed with love and compassion asking the Great Spirit to see their sacrifice for the good of all. I started to dance in the shade of the arbor covered by cedar boughs, moving my feet to the beat of the drum. I felt the surge of energy from the earth and sent it out from my heart into the circle to whoever needed it. A sound came out of my mouth from deep within me. It was a strong, loud, tremolo. Other women began to do the same. It was such a unified sound that the hairs on the back of my neck stood up. I had never expressed such a sound with an incredible wave of energy released.

"That's it girl. What do you see now?" Granny Molly asked again.

I looked around the circle and found Granny Janice. I looked into her energy field. She was doing okay for the first day. As I looked at others, I had seen that some bodies were moving in and out of this physical dimension. Going from physical to ghostly form, then as they began to disappear the Medicine Chief would come and fan smoke around them and they would come back to the physical form.

On one man, I could see several thin wispy energy cords that were connected to several women in the dance. I realized quickly that he had or was still, sleeping with these women. I closed down the barrier of my visionary eyes and looked away. I relayed all that I had seen to Granny Molly and she was in amazement.

"Girl, you got the gift. What you have seen is correct. Please keep an eye on Janice each time we come to the arbor to make sure she is okay."

"Sure Granny," I agreed.

CHAPTER FOURTEEN

By the seventh day, which was the actual third day of Sundance ceremony, I was exhausted. There was one more day of the dance before the large feast and celebration. Again it was late afternoon, when Granny Molly and I went to check on Granny Janice and support the other dancers. When we got to the arbor we watched as Granny Janice approached the tree and the Chief pierced each arm inserting the buffalo bone. He secured a sacred feather on each side.

"Oh no," Granny Molly cried. "What is she doing? She didn't tell me she was going to pierce. She is too old for that. She doesn't have to suffer like that. She gave life to three children. She has given enough of her blood," she wept.

"Let's pray for her and send her strength," I said.

Once the piercing was completed, I noticed she was a little wobbly on her feet, but she stayed at the tree and prayed. In that moment, I understood. Her prayer for the dance was for the complete healing and curing of her granddaughter who had just found out that she had breast cancer. That was the reason she was committing herself to dance for four years with the fifth year being a gratitude and giveaway year. Her love for her granddaughter was so great and her trust in the unseen power of the Great Mystery of Spirit was so strong she was willing to sacrifice even at her age of sixty-eight. She would be seventy-three by the time her commitment was over.

What an amazing and loving woman she was. Her call to the dance could not have been an easy decision. She was just a tiny, frail woman, but her heart and conviction did not waiver.

Her will was strong and as she had told me during her Sundance vision quest, "Laurel, if I prepare myself in the right way, I know Spirit will take care of me. Sacrifice is needed for Spirit's help, but suffering is optional."

Her level of trust was impeccable. We watched her pray going back and forth to the tree four times. We were escorted inside the Mystery Circle to stand behind her for support. The Chief and his helper were going to pull the piercings and break the skin and flesh on each arm to remove the bones and tied feathers. I entered the Mystery Circle and I could feel a surge of energy through my feet and run up my spine, a high and intense shock wave. I felt compelled to run towards the tree and touch it and weep, but I stopped myself. Instead, I followed the leader and fell behind Granny Janice at an arm's length distance.

I prayed using a hawk wing and fanned her from behind without touching her. I had faith that she could endure what was to come and that her prayer would be answered.

Both men pulled the bones quickly at the same time and they both broke loose from her skin as blood ran down her thin, bony arms. Granny Janice stumbled for a moment, but never fell. Every one cheered and screamed in loud tremolos. She was escorted back to the tree and her wounds were cared for before she began dancing once again.

Granny Molly and I were escorted out of the circle and back into the arbor.

"Granny, when I was in the Mystery Circle I could feel an electric charge running horizontally on the ground from the tree. It was as if the tree was pulling me magnetically to it. I had to fight the urge to run up to it and touch it. I could see the energy from the tree passing like a cord through each dancer giving them life and support. As I followed the energy up the tree I could see the sun in the sky pouring its rays down into the tree, the people and the earth giving them life. The dancers prayers passed through the horizontal lines up the tree and to the sky and the sun gave its energy back to the dancers. I felt it and it was amazing. The Great Spirit, mysterious source of the sun and sky passes its healing energy down to the earth and to the dancers that commit, sacrifice and pray and answers their prayer," I revealed.

"There's a lot going on in there. The sacred energy in the arbor, the power of the earth, sun, sky and stars, the tree and the dancers' prayers combines all the living energy of the Great Spirit that flows through everything. The energy moves up and down as you've seen, but when you entered the circle you felt and saw the power move through you and that is a gift," she nodded.

When we returned to camp my energy started to wane. Sally wanted me back in the kitchen to help in the preparation of the evening meal. As tired as I was, I pushed forth to relieve the others that had been working tirelessly while I was at the arbor.

I chopped the vegetables for the salad. First the cucumbers and then as I began to slice the tomato Sally rushed to me and angrily raised her voice.

"What are you doing? Don't you know how to cut vegetables?"

"How would you like me to cut them?" I asked sheepishly.

The other ladies in the kitchen lowered their heads and said nothing, not wanting to have the wrath come down upon them as well.

"The *right* way," she sneered.

I had been taught to respect people, especially someone who is older than me. I always tried to be fair and complimentary, but in this moment I felt I was being attacked and wanted either to cry or lash out. Lashing out was not my way. So I excused myself and said I needed to use the port-a-potty.

Granny Molly saw me and called out to me.

"Laurel, come here. What happened?" she asked.

When I approached her, I could not hold the tears back any longer. They flooded out of me like a torrential rain storm.

"Sally screamed at me. She complained that I was cutting the vegetables wrong. I felt attacked and when I asked how she wanted me to cut them she said the "right way." How am I supposed to know the right way if she won't tell me? I am so tired. I can barely hold myself up. It has been seven days and we have one more day. I am trying to serve and do my best for the people, but I don't know if I can hold up any longer."

"It sounds to me that something has come up for you to heal. Sally triggered something in you, something very vulnerable and deep. Come with me to my tent."

"But Sally…"

"Don't mind Sally. You need to take care of yourself," she said sternly.

She sat me down on a camp chair and raised my feet. She applied essential oils to each foot while she talked. The scents were calming and reviving.

"I have been working with aromatherapy for years. They work wonders on the senses and moving emotional and mental energies. Kind of like when you work with the flower essences. That's your expertise. This is one of mine. I will apply basil and then peppermint," she smiled.

"Now what emotion did Sally bring up for you, Laurel? Why did it make you cry?" she asked while she continued to rub my feet.

"Well," I paused. "It made me feel worthless, wrong, angry, like an outsider; fearful and abused," I answered.

"What are you angry and afraid of?" she asked tenderly.

"I don't know. I guess I am embarrassed. That maybe I don't fit in here?"

"Let's go deeper, where is "here"? Is it in Texas? What part of your life are you embarrassed about? Sounds like it's something much deeper," she surmised.

"I guess "here" is not really Texas. It's how I feel everywhere. Seeing and feeling energy, seeing dead spirits and hearing their requests. I don't come in contact with many people that I can talk to about it. I think that I fear that there is no one out there who will want to be with me and to love me as I truly am."

I paused for a moment and was dumbstruck.

"I can't believe I just said that. I guess after my divorce I felt really bad about myself which I know is just a reflection of how I *really* felt about myself back then. Blake was only mirroring to me what I already believed."

"Yes, you are right, but I think there is something deeper to it and I believe this is the beginning of getting to the bottom of it. Healing doesn't happen in one day. It's like an onion; it needs to be peeled away.

The layers of the tougher skin need to be released to get to the real core stuff. How are you feeling now?" she asked.

"Much better, I feel more relaxed and less emotional. The anger and fear have disappeared for now. I feel more stable. I think that I need to shift the energy from the divorce, right? I mean, I should bless Sally for bringing that up for me right?" I questioned.

"Good idea. You might also want to remember that you need to love yourself and take care of your needs. You have been giving so much in service that you were not taking care of yourself, like taking breaks and eating and drinking regularly. Young women are not taught to do that, to take care of the self and feel worthy of Spirit's love. We're taught to honor and serve others, but not ourselves, as if we don't matter. We become angry and unbalanced because we have cut ourselves off from the sacredness inside ourselves. We bury our feelings deep inside. We lose our voice by pleasing others and not caring for ourselves. We are trained to be martyrs. We feel alone, unloved and unappreciated. It's not enough for other people to love and appreciate us, we need to love ourselves and take care of our needs in balance with service to others. It can't be done any other way," she explained.

"Laurel, I think you're dehydrated and you need to drink more fluids. You're not used to this heat. I also think you have a deeper wound than your divorce and someday you'll uncover it and gain understanding."

She was right. I had not eaten or hydrated enough. I definitely did not take many breaks, other than to the port-a-potty. After seven days, I was brought to my knees for balance. I understood the pieces of worthiness and needed to release the divorce emotions and energy. I was now in a place of gratitude to Sally for showing me that I still have emotional baggage from the divorce. I returned to the kitchen and felt Sally's glare and disapproval. So I spoke to her lovingly.

"Thank you, Sally. You work hard for this camp and keep the energy moving and shifting. I was getting tired and emotional and needed to take care of myself, so I took a break to move the emotional stuff that came up for me. I didn't want to bring it back to the kitchen. What can I do for you, so that *you* can take a break to take care of yourself?"

I placed my arm around the back of her shoulders while the other women in the kitchen held their breath. Sally's eyes softened and misted.

"Thank you, Laurel. No one understands how hard this is on me. Could you just make sure that the dishes are done, food is put away and everything is wiped down with hot water and soap?" she asked.

"Will do," I replied.

As I made eye contact with the other women in the kitchen, they all smiled and I could feel a shift of energy in the kitchen. It was lighter, less stressful and in a few minutes was filled with laughter.

Granny Molly winked at me as she sat down at a picnic table.

"Energy sure feels good in here... yup, sure feels good," she smiled.

CHAPTER FIFTEEN

The last day in the kitchen went smoothly. By mid-afternoon we were packing up the kitchen and getting ready for the dance to end and the feasting celebration to begin.

It was so humbling to see the dancers leaving the Mystery Circle in a single file, shaking the hands with the circle of people who had supported them. They were in such gratitude for the people's support. For me, I saw it the other way around. It was I who was grateful for their prayers and sacrifice. They had endured so much for their prayer.

Granny Molly and I were privileged to cut up and offer watermelon to the dancers before we started the feast. Granny Janice and the other dancers savored its juicy sweetness.

"Nothing is better than watermelon to break the four day fast," noted Carl who had just completed his four years of Sundance.

"Thank you, Laurel for supporting me. I knew you were praying for me. I could feel it. When I saw you in the arbor, I felt a burst of energy lifting me up. It was like my feet were floating above the ground and not touching," said Granny Janice.

"You're welcome, Gran. Was it physically hard, when you pierced? I'm sorry, is it okay to ask that question?" I asked.

"It is personal, but it's okay to ask me. I wouldn't go around asking other dancers. For me the dance at times was physically hard on my knees and feet. At times I stayed dancing by sheer will and other times, I felt Spirit take hold of me and keep me standing. I felt no pain in the piercing. Spirit had shown me a vision on my vision quest as to how I was to pierce. I didn't tell anyone because I didn't want anyone trying to talk me out of it. When they pulled the piercing out, I felt it briefly but I was in an altered state. It is hard to explain. All I know is the Great Spirit took care of me out there. I could not have completed the dance without the year of preparation, my supporters' prayers and Spirit's help."

She went into her tent and brought out a shawl. It was black with long black fringe.

"Here girl, I want you to have this. This is one of my shawls that I have made and worn in the dance. I want you to have it in gratitude for your support. Love you," she smiled.

"Thank you. I love you too. I am deeply honored."

With that I gave her a long heartfelt hug. I needed to remember her strength and endurance in future times when I doubted my own power of faith and commitment.

My flight home to Massachusetts on the next day was restful. I was out like a light before the plane left the runway. My body was tired and exhausted but the memories would be forever in my heart. I remembered before I left, Granny Molly reminded me of the emotions that came up in the kitchen.

"You might want to take time to look deeper into the issue, it's come up for a reason," she assured.

I would pray on it, to help me understand the deeper issue and where in my life this began. It surely didn't begin in my marriage. Right now on the plane ride home, sleep was all I could muster. Sleep, yes wonderful sleep. As I drifted off my mind began to dream.

I was in the woods walking and an elderly woman with long white braids was motioning to me, calling me closer to her.

When I reached her she yelled, "Where have you been? I've been waiting for you. It's time to enter the pit. I don't have much time. You have to heal and help the women. Hurry up and find me. Wake up and get on with it."

I was jolted awake by the flight attendant.

"Excuse me, Miss. We have landed and you need to disembark from the plane."

"Okay. Thank you," I said.

I gathered my belongings, while still caught up in the dream. It was so real and lucid. As if the woman was truly out there calling for me to find her. It was a haunting feeling, one that would not leave me.

CHAPTER SIXTEEN

While I was at the Sundance ceremony, I had received a call for an interview from one of the job applications I had placed online. I returned the call, but the position had been filled. I had been away for nine days and the call may have come in earlier in the week.

Although a slight disappointment crossed my mind, I trusted that it could have not been the right job. Once again I started the grind of combing the papers and internet for job possibilities.

The next day I received a call from an elementary school in an adjacent town.

"Hello Laurel, this is John Everett. I received your name from Olivia Bartel. She raved about your children's program. I wondered if you would be available to present to three of our classes in September. Of course we will pay you. We would need a session for each class. Each class has about forty students. If you agree, please email me the class syllabus and your fee for approval."

"Yes. Thank you. I would love to." I replied.

"Great. I look forward to your program," he concluded.

Well isn't this interesting? Even more interesting was that by the end of August several schools from towns up to sixty miles away had called. They wanted to book programs for the fall semester. It seemed I was going to be busy well into the month of December.

I dutifully searched the job market and applied to several positions but my heart was not truly invested in the process. By September, I was presenting my programs three days a week and making enough to cover my expenses. I had also received a six month extension of my eligibility for unemployment benefits.

The children were full of excitement. Some of the classes were with kindergarten and preschool, while most were with middle school age. I altered the program to be appropriate for each age group, but the entire message was the same. Respect for all living things, including the earth and that we (all living things) are connected to each other. I also hoped to instill the understanding of diversity through compassion and respect.

Only years later when I met with some of these children as young adults, did I discover the impression that I had made upon them with the program.

It was wonderful to be around such young, vibrant and energetic children. It was as if, I was reliving and reminiscing my childhood.

It had seemed the Child's Sacred Pipe bundle was teaching and healing me all at the same time. Something was definitely happening. My life had become about prayer and teaching. My heart was happy. I was content and at peace. I lived in the moment and stayed present.

For the next four months, life was a whirlwind of fun and play. I was excited and inspired as my childhood dream of teaching was manifesting.

CHAPTER SEVENTEEN

By Christmas the school presentations had all been completed with the hope of rehire again the following year. As a new year began, my search for a full-time job increased, but there was still not much available.

My landlord finally found a buyer for the condo and I needed to find a new place to live by March 1st. I was grateful that she had not found a buyer the past year. But now I really needed to find a new place. Talk about the pressure I was feeling, but again I focused on prayer and trust.

I had, for many years, worked part-time in holistic work with flower essence, energy readings and different modes of hands on energy treatments. Some of the clients asked if I would teach classes on these subjects. So after praying on which classes to teach, I agreed.

The classes started as small groups in people's homes and then spread by word of mouth. Soon I was teaching enough classes and getting new clients by phone and in person to pay for my all living expenses. I was following my heart and the flow of what was placed before me. Now, if I could only find the right place to live all would fall into place.

As the month went on, life was good. No, I was not rich or living the high life, but I was making enough to live by doing what I loved.

In the middle of February, my landlord informed me that she and her husband were getting a divorce. She asked that if I had not found a place yet, if I would consider staying longer. It seemed the sale on the condo fell through and she could not afford to leave the condo vacant until she found another buyer. This was good news which gave me another couple of months to find a place. *Just trust,* I reminded myself.

I was inspired to create new classes to teach. By spring, my name had been given to several retreats and workshop facilities. These venues would be more lucrative because they could handle dozens of students in one workshop.

I needed to travel over an hour each way for some of the classes, but the joy it gave me knowing I was doing my bliss, overrode any ill effects that my body felt from the long drive.

I had noticed that the classes contained mostly women. There were a few men from time to time, but predominately they were women. The women were hoping to understand how to heal themselves and their family.

My workshops began to take form as an experiential event. People were gaining insights into themselves and their feelings. I was helping them to process their wounds in class exercises and the workshops became very fulfilling to me.

Those that came for the workshop had no idea what they were coming to learn and understand about themselves. I found that each person in the group had the same issue, a loss of self-esteem and worthiness to heal. It was very profound. I was in awe each time the Great Spirit led the right people to the class.

The spring went by quickly. It was now approaching June. I had kept in touch with the grannies over the year and was getting ready once again to support Granny Janice at Sundance.

"Are you ready to do it all again?" she asked me by phone.

"Not sure, but I'll be there for you," I reassured her.

"Then I'll see you next week, when I pick you up at the airport. Molly will be with me. She's looking forward to it. Plan for the heat, 'cause it's been hotter than a three dollar pistol," she joked.

I laughed. She was so endearing. She had a way with words that I had never heard before. On one occasion, she said her "dogs were barking." I looked around but I didn't see any dogs. I was dumbfounded. Then she laughed and said, "No, not a real dog, these dogs," and she pointed to her feet. Oh, how I loved those feisty grannies and their southern mannerisms.

CHAPTER EIGHTEEN

A week later, I was on the plane to Texas. The grannies greeted me and we were off on the four-and-a-half hour trip to the Sundance.

When we arrived, I remembered the familiar faces from the previous year. Once again my service would be kitchen and dish duty. However there would be a different kitchen mom this year.

Carla Madison worked with me in the kitchen last year, and this year *she* was the kitchen mom. Carla was a petite woman with long graying hair. She was warm and compassionate. She also was very patient and kind, truly encompassing the meaning of a "mom."

She made sure that we took regular breaks, ate snacks and drank fluids. She was nurturing and caring to all who came to the camp and kitchen. It was if she was made to be the heart of the camp. Though it was still hot and I got very tired, the eight days would go by quickly.

This year I was different. I focused on service while balancing my needs. If I started to get depleted, I asked for a break and took care of what I needed to recharge myself.

Granny Janice danced, but she did not pierce. Granny Molly and I spent time every day in the arbor to pray and support her and the other eighty or so dancers.

I felt the surge of the energy and could see spirals within the Mystery Circle, but this time as the men pierced I was able to pray without feeling their physical pain. I was able to be present and pray without connecting to the energy of their physical body. Last year unintentionally, I had a different experience because I was too open. This year, I was able to be clearer with my prayer and not attach my energy to the dancers and this provided me with a better experience.

Granny Janice was fading from time to time, but all in all she stayed strong and in her prayer.

A few of the dancers fell to the ground in exhaustion. The Medicine Chief and helpers went over to them and fanned cedar over them to bring them back to consciousness.

"Look at the dancers that have fallen and have gone into a vision. They are the closest to the Great Spirit. Maybe they will be given something to tell the people in the dance or an answer to their prayer," said Granny Molly.

I watched and when the dancers became fully conscious, they were escorted to a secluded shaded part outside the circle to reveal what they had experienced to the Chief. It was all so surreal.

"Every year the dance ceremony is different. New dancers bring new energy and prayers. Nothing stays the same, birth, death, and rebirth. It is always in cycles. Some complete their commitments to the ceremony, others begin and still others renew and recommit more years," Granny Molly added.

"I understand. Every Sacred Pipe, purification lodge and vision quest I have experienced in the past is different. I am so grateful to be able to support and be part of this ceremony," I replied.

The week flew by and finally the last day of the ceremony and the feasting celebration began.

Granny Janice once again gifted me.

"Laurel, I want you to have these moccasins. They are very special to me. They were given to me by a medicine woman. She was a very warm, caring lady. She helped many people, especially the women. They have not been worn because they were too big for me to wear. I believe they were hers and she wore them a couple of times. You might want to smudge them with sage before you try them on," she suggested.

"Thank you, Gran. They look like they will fit. I am honored to receive them," I replied.

I cleared them with sage smoke and tried them on. A perfect fit like they were made for me. They were the color of buckskin and were decorated with red and blue beads in the shape of a star. I was very grateful and humbled by the gift.

The next day, I headed back home to Massachusetts. As I said my goodbyes to everyone, I wondered what was in store for me. I hoped I would be able to return the following year. Two years of support completed and three more to go.

CHAPTER NINETEEN

Once home, I began my search for full-time work again. I had previously booked a few clients for flower essence consults a couple of days after my return from Texas. I had learned from the previous year that I needed to give myself a few days to rest after my return. I had also booked a few workshops throughout the rest of the summer.

I still hoped to find a new place to live. As I prayed in gratitude, opportunities for new clients and classes developed, but I was still waiting for the new living space.

On Labor Day weekend, I was teaching a workshop to understand the energy field. The workshop took place in a beautiful and serene setting in nature. It was a new place for me to teach. The land was in northern Massachusetts. The thirty acres of lush green oaks and pine trees and clear small pond which casted the glimmer of the sun's rays was a precious gift at the end of the trail in the woods. It was the perfect place for one to expand their awareness of energy and renew.

To my surprise a former high school classmate was in attendance.

"I thought it was you! Do you remember me? It's Lee Ann Harding."

"Yes of course, I remember. You look wonderful," I replied.

"I am so looking forward to this workshop. Who could have known what we would become twenty-five years later?"

Time had been kind to her or perhaps she had been kind to herself. She was still the beautiful, voluptuous, blonde bombshell. She still wore massive amounts of make-up, but her large blue eyes were warm and sincere. Still a knockout in her forties, she had not gained even one ounce of weight, while I on the other-hand had put on quite a few pounds since the divorce.

Why do we as women compare ourselves? Always looking for what is wrong with us instead of honoring what is good. We hold our breath and pull in our stomach to appear thinner. This increases our own anxiety because we are unnaturally tightening our stomach. We are ashamed of and disown our bodies because we don't fit what men and society view as desirable. Women used to be worshipped for the curved bellies and creative power of bringing life forth into the world.

Stop Laurel. I told myself. *Don't go there.* The destructive thoughts need to be stopped in their tracks. Sometimes we need to change our thoughts to change the energy. I guess I can use that teaching in my workshop today.

During a break from the workshop, I had two interesting conversations. One with Lee Ann Harding and one with a woman named Dottie Smith.

Lee Ann was worried about finances. She had a place to rent in a nearby town where I lived, but was having trouble finding the right tenant. As I listened to her, I asked for more detail on the living space.

"It is a two bedroom on a quiet street. The mortgage is paid, so I really just want someone to help with the taxes and help keep it heated, especially with the winter coming."

"So how much are you renting it for?" I asked.

"Are you looking for a place?" she asked.

"Actually I am," I answered.

"Oh you are the absolute answer to my prayer. I will give you a good deal since I know you. Here, I will write down the address and you can come by tomorrow if that is okay."

"Great," I replied as I retrieved the address.

Could this be also the answer to my prayer? Turned out it would be. The rent would be one hundred and fifty dollars less a month and the place was immaculate. She also had no problem with my pet Sunshine and taking clients at the apartment. In fact, she would become one within a short time.

The second interesting conversation was with Dottie, a young woman who was nearly thirty and a fitness instructor. She commented that she taught at an adult night education program and that I might want to consider getting into the school's program. She was willing to recommend me to the school.

Wonderful, I thought *a new place to teach and possible new clients.* My horizon was expanding.

I would later call the school that she had recommended with a list of courses I was available to teach. I figured these events were placed in my path and I would follow the flow of the opportunities to the maximum.

Chapter Twenty

Lee Ann and I met the following day. The apartment was wonderful. Many large windows brought tremendous light to the rooms and there was plenty of space in the bedrooms. We agreed on an end of September move in date.

You never realize how many things you accumulate over time until you need to move. I had sold many possessions before my former marriage. In just under five years, I once again had many things to give away and donate to charity.

As is the Native American custom, giving away precious items was a way to honor a new beginning or ending in your life. It was a way to give gratitude for the abundance in your life. It continued the circle of giving and receiving and the trust that we would always have enough. Large giveaways were done after ceremonies for weddings, deaths, births and healings. So I began my giveaway.

I gifted precious items to family members and close friends while the remainder was gifted to charities. It allowed me to start out fresh and much lighter on all levels. It is a way of opening up to receive more abundance in my life by clearing and releasing the old. It was a wonderful feeling to give away possessions that I valued and that could be used to enhance another person's life and bring them joy.

The move went easily. I was in a new place with more privacy. There was only one other tenant in the building and because it was a duplex, there was no one above or below me to make noise or disturb me. My prayer and meditation time would become even more peaceful.

My number of clients increased by word of mouth and I continued to teach adult education and children's programs. I was making more than enough to pay my expenses.

I received a call from a teaching hospital's intern program for nursing and pre-med doctors. It seemed someone had given them my name and number and thought I would be a great fit to offer a lecture on alternative therapies.

Here was another route for me to teach, one that I could never had imagined. To give some insight to young nurses and intern doctors on things that could go hand in hand with western medicine: the healing arts of Reiki, Kahi Loa, Crystal Light Balancing, Chakra and Meridian balancing as well as Flower Essences remedies and Aromatherapy. All of which I had training and expertise.

The pre-medical students' minds were open and soaked up the information. I was there to teach them about the mind and body connection and how it can be useful to their patients and themselves. As I explained the energy field, I reminded them that as a caregiver they can become out of balance by working long hours, losing sleep and not respecting their bodies. The workshop was a success and I was asked to return in the spring the following year.

Soon, new clients I had met through the lectures were calling for appointments. My life was no longer about searching for a job. It was about living and doing my work. I made sure that I did not over-book myself so I could give myself time to rest, regenerate and stay in balance.

As Christmas season approached, the teaching slowed down and arrangements and contracts were set in place for the classes to begin again after the New Year.

Client session work also slowed down, but I earned enough to get me through the winter months financially. I was grateful for the talents that the Great Spirit had entrusted me with to use in the world.

I made enough to live and I helped lighten people's minds, hearts and spirits, which for me was the ultimate prize. I knew I was living my bliss and my life had meaning.

The winter in New England can be tough. We were having snowfalls every other day in Massachusetts. Our small town schools closed at least once a week to plow the white, ice crusted mounds. Although the children were happy for the days off they would not be so enthused when they would have extra days added to the school year in June.

The surrounding small towns that I had lived in over the years were home to me. Oxford, North Oxford, Dudley, Charlton, Leicester, Auburn, Douglas, Sutton and Webster had some of the warmest and friendliest people. Small towns have given me space and breathing room. They were places to gather my thoughts without the hustle and bustle of an overly fast pace. Even the small city of Southbridge had some of the ambiance.

The lake in Webster was one of the most sacred places for me growing up and continued to be throughout my adult life. Much time and contemplation was spent under the pines and cedar trees on the small peninsula, reading and journaling my thoughts and insights. I would watch the gulls; ducks and geese ride the thermal waves and breezes. Bald eagles have nested and in recent years baby eaglets have added to the sacredness, a peaceful connection to nature and all of its wonderment.

With the many walks of life living in the city of Worcester, I learned to work with and adjust to each of the energies. It was chaotic but was exciting. There were many different people that inadvertently taught me about different energies. Especially being in close proximity to many people, I had to focus and utilize all that I felt around me.

I had my share of traveling through the years to many places and landscapes of deserts, beaches, mountains and forests. All the land has special energy and vibration. The trick is to tune into it and let it work within you.

As the month of February approached, I found myself very reflective, reviewing my life and the lessons learned. Winter will do that for you; a time of solace and rest, and a time to go inward and relax. I had learned over the years to slow down with the cycles of the seasons. Spring was a burst of energy and a time for approaching the new and creating new cycles in my life. Summer was the active time of work and play. Autumn was the time of abundance where one harvested from what they created in the spring. Winter was the time to slow down, rest, reflect and renew for another year and cycle.

Throughout the month, I felt a tug in my heart as I prayed. I was seeing myself in a cabin in the woods, alone on a lake with enormous pine trees. I could smell the pine cones and needles and the scent of wood smoke. This vision appeared every day for four weeks. My spirit was stirring and restless. I longed to be in those woods, a place of retreat. The place was calling me. The land beckoned me in all my waking moments and dreams to find it, luring me to it for an unknown reason that I could not comprehend. I needed to find that place. I would feverishly comb the internet until I did.

CHAPTER TWENTY-ONE

I searched the internet for cabin rentals in the woods on a lake. I searched in Maine, Vermont and New Hampshire. I found nothing that seemed to be the right place.

I prayed daily and asked for guidance and assistance. I heard a clear voice outside of me say, *"Massachusetts, 7 days of silence."*

Receiving guidance is nothing new to me. I have heard and seen things from other dimensions since I was a child. I have spirit helpers. It doesn't happen every day and at every moment, but when I sit in silence and in ceremony, I can receive guidance if it is needed.

I began my new search in Massachusetts. Sometimes the closest things to us and are right under our nose don't always make the most sense. Our logical mind believes it must be far way and out of reach.

I searched through several places and looked at the pictures of the land on the website, but it didn't feel right. Disappointed from the several days of unsuccessful searching, I surrendered and decided to take a nap.

The dream time is a powerful tool. It allows us to work out emotions and challenges from waking life, while also bringing guidance and insights from a higher plane. I was taught by the spirit world about dream work years ago by crossing dimensions and becoming the embodiment of the moon during a three day vision quest. It is here where I received a ceremony and understanding of the dream world and its symbolisms. From that day forward, dreaming became a powerful tool to receive information.

I relaxed and focused my intention on finding this place. If I was truly supposed to go there for seven days of silence I needed help finding it. I fell away from consciousness to the unconscious, a place more fluid and lucid as the world opened up.

I was again led to a cabin overlooking the lake; a small fire was lit and surrounded by a circular wall of stones. The lake was still and as clear as a mirror. I could see the reflection of my face clearly. Then slowly over my left shoulder another face appeared in the image. It was an older woman's face. Her eyes gazed intensely at me and expressed a serious intent. She was haunting in a way, not that I was fearful, but I knew that this was important. Her familiar image with long white braids offered a message. I could hear her voice distinctly.

"I'm here waiting for you among the acres of pines. Hurry up and get on with it!" she snapped.

I awoke abruptly from the nap and I assembled my thoughts.

I went to the computer and typed a*cres of pines in Massachusetts.* The internet search asked, "Do you mean, Acres of Pines campground in Massachusetts?"

Could this be the right place? I quickly went to the website and from the pictures it confirmed that this was the place. The campground was on a lake. I called the phone number and of course like most campgrounds in winter, it was closed. They would reopen May 1st.

I called once a week until at the beginning of April, there was actually someone who answered.

I asked if I could come and see the place. I told Dana Marks, the co-owner that I was looking for a retreat place before the season began. I was not looking for anything extra maybe just some firewood. She explained that they would be open Saturday May 1st.

I asked if she would allow me to arrive a couple days earlier so that no one would be around. I expected her to say no.

But surprisingly she agreed to it just this one time. I made an appointment with her to visit the grounds and find the right cabin. She was a sweet woman. As I spoke with her, I wondered if she was the woman I had seen in my dream. Only time would tell.

Two days later, I found the campground. The grounds people were in the clean-up stage and reorganizing from the winter.

Dana buzzed me in at the gate. When I met her at the office building I was disappointed to find that she was not the old woman in my dream. I explained to her that I was looking for a cabin on the water overlooking the lake. She pointed to the direction outside the office and I carefully walked up the small hill.

There were two in particular that she recommended. As I walked I felt a familiarity with the land, a homecoming if you will. When I got to the first cabin, I immediately knew it was the right one. I needed to look no further.

I ran back to the office and booked the rental. The cabin was more expensive because it was on the water but Dana gave me a great off-season price.

In three weeks, I would be in the depths of seven days of silence and whatever that meant for me. I was following the stirring within me and listening to it closely.

Chapter Twenty-Two

Knowing that this retreat would take a bite out of my finances, I wondered if I would have enough to pay my airfare to Texas in June for Sundance. I had not bought my airline ticket yet. I wanted to continue to support Granny Janice until she completed her commitment. It was also an opportunity to visit with both grannies who I talked with on a regular basis by phone. There was something about hugging their neck and hearing their life stories in person that I loved the most.

For the next three weeks my flower essence consults picked up tremendously. It was as if everyone woke up to spring a month late. I booked as many as I could while still leaving balance for myself.

Many people do not have a thorough understanding about what flower essences can do. People think they are oils that you put on your skin and smell which they are not.

They are made by using fresh blossoms and placing them in spring water and leaving them out in direct sunlight. The flower's essence is imprinted by the sun's rays and vitality. The water is bottled and used in a remedy mixture for each individual to increase the life force in the user. The process was discovered nearly eighty years ago.

It took me years of training and working with the essences individually to fully understand their healing properties. The process can seem strange to some people but once they have a consult and see how much better they feel emotionally, mentally and physically any doubt is gone. Since it is all natural there are no side effects or interactions with any medications.

A woman named Lynn, a referral from another client, was my first client of the morning. I never have any history of the person or what they are going through prior to the appointment.

The phone rang.

"Hello. Is this Laurel?" she asked.

"Yes. Is this Lynn?"

"Yes, it is," she replied.

"Okay Lynn, as I look through your energy field, I see your third eye, heart and solar plexus areas are off. This means that in your case, you have had a relationship loss in your life and you are very angry about it. You are thinking excessively and wearing down your physical body."

"How do you know this?" she gasped.

"Since I was a child, I could see inside and around a person when I focus. As I become in tune with their energy, I can see what may be causing the problem and from that I can make a flower remedy to release, energize and balance the life force. When our mind or emotions are used negatively too long we drain ourselves and feel fatigued and worn out. A remedy that has three to seven flower essences will help release as well as energize the areas of need in your body. In your case the mind, heart and solar plexus."

"I was told that you were good, but there was a part of me that thought consulting over the phone would not work. How can one possibly read another person, especially if you're not in the same room with them?" she asked.

"Ah, but I can. I can't explain it to you but it is one of my gifts that I have learned to refine. Understand, I will only enter someone's energy field if they have asked for a consult and have given permission," I replied.

"Well you are absolutely correct. My husband of eighteen years has found a younger woman and wants a divorce. He has moved out to be with her and I am pissed. I gave my life for that man. My only child has just entered college. I am alone," she trailed off in tears.

"I understand this can't be easy. However, being alone is the best thing for you right now. You can focus on "you". What do you want to do with your life? What makes you happy and excited? What things did you enjoy doing before you got married that you still have passion for? You are at an ending of your marriage but a beginning of a new life. It is okay to grieve the past and appreciate all that you have learned from the relationship. Your son was a blessing from the relationship."

"Yes, your right. Wait. How did you know I had a son? I said a child," she remarked.

"I see and pull information from the energy around you. I am being shown pictures and I have seen a young man."

"Are you always right?"

"The information is always correct. I trust the information I receive. Interpreting the information is the hardest part, but I have had a lot of experience over the years to fine tune it," I explained.

Lynn was quiet for a moment before I began again.

"I will make you a remedy tincture that contains white chestnut for obsessive thinking, holly and willow for anger and resentment, and cherry plum for the fear of being alone. We need to move some of the anger and fear to help you feel better. I will ship this out today. Take four drops under the tongue, four times a day. Let's make another appointment in a month," I said.

I continued, "Flower essences work better when you are consistent with consults. Each time the remedy will be changed and new flowers will be introduced while other are dropped from the remedy. For short term issues three to six sessions might be needed. For longer standing issues six to twelve consults. Every person is different but what I find in most cases is that people feel better within the first month. Rebalancing usually requires a minimum of at least three appointments however each person has to decide what is best for them," I explained.

"Thank you, Laurel."

"You're very welcome and blessings to you," I replied.

The next three weeks flew by as the temperature began to warm up to the high 40's. The last week of April was now upon me. In two days, I would be surrounded by nature in the woods. No appointments, no phone, just myself and the Child's Sacred Pipe Bundle. I could almost smell the cedar, pine and the burning of wood smoke. My body was feeling very relaxed in anticipation.

CHAPTER TWENTY-THREE

My four-wheel SUV was packed and ready to go. Linens, blankets, pillows, food, water, rain gear, warm clothes and toiletries. Everything needed for camping. The drive was less than an hour long through back roads and lovely small farm pastures. Most of the snow had melted and the buds on the trees were beginning to grow. After all May was just around the corner.

I pulled up to the front gate and I rang the buzzer. Dana's voice came over the intercom.

"Can I help you?" she asked.

"Yes, it is Laurel. I am here for the cabin by the lake for the week."

"Oh yes, let me buzz you in. Follow the road and turn left and meet me at the office," she instructed.

The gate rose so I could pass through. I followed the road for an eighth of a mile. The campground was deadly still. Aged pine needles were everywhere. The cedar and pine trees were dense and full. I felt as if I was in my own forest waiting for Robin Hood and his merry men to appear.

This place was magical. I felt like a child again. I remembered my Uncle Marty's camp in the woods in Connecticut. We would visit during the summertime. I remembered there were many pine trees and lady slippers. The small acre of land was like a mystical forest. One time, I had decided to climb a tree to sit in its crooked arm and watch the chipmunks and squirrels at play in the pine needles. A large red-tail hawk perched close to me on a limb and was waiting to catch its meal for the day. Its banded striped feathers were shades of brown and white.

The smaller songbirds cooed their relaxing lullabies to further captivate my attention and bring me joy.

His camp was also on a lake of beautiful blue water that sparkled with the sun's rays. Uncle Marty had a motor boat and would take my cousins and I out for a spin. He accelerated to make waves which made for an exciting bumpy ride and thrilling us to scream in delight. It was the perfect balance for me, tranquil forest and excitement of the lake.

Dana greeted me at the office.

"Hello, Laurel. It's nice to see you again. You will be pretty much by yourself. None of the seasonal campers will be back until the weekend. I've turned the gas on in the cabin for cooking and heating and I cleaned the fire pit. You planned on using it correct?" she asked.

"Yes, thank you. Is there firewood for the week?"

"Yes, I had my husband bring enough for several fires, as you requested," she replied.

"Since we are not open for a couple of days, I will give you my cell phone number in case you need to reach me. Please do not make a fire if it is too windy. I would appreciate your caution. There is a small variety store several miles down the road. It has canned goods, snacks and drinks. I will give you directions. Here is the map of the campgrounds. Feel free to explore. Your cabin is number twenty-two. Here is the key. Let me walk you outside, if you remember you can see it from the the office."

As we walked outside the smell of pine encompassed my being.

"There it is on the hill. You can park your car right in front of the porch or on the side of the building. Do you need help unloading?" she asked.

"No, thank you. I really appreciate you letting me in the campground before your official opening. I really need seclusion," I said in appreciation.

"Well Laurel, that's what you'll get. Only the clean-up crew will be here. I'll make sure they stay away from your cabin until you leave."

"Thank you again, Dana."

I drove up the short incline to the cabin. Squirrels and chipmunks were scurrying about, rustling through the matted leaves and pine needles. I drove slowly to make sure they did not meet their untimely death.

I always had a love of nature and animals but in my late teenage years as I began to learn my distant Native American Indian ancestry teachings, I had become even more keenly observant and respectful to all nature around me.

I pulled up as close as I could to the porch to be able to easily unload. It took me several trips. I guess I should have taken Dana's offer to help unload but I couldn't wait to be alone and start the retreat of silence.

Once settled in, I made a cup of tea and sat in one of my camp chairs to observe the lake from the deck. Two ducks and a flock of geese flew over. The water was calm and still. The musky smell of the woods filled my being with joy. Slowly a smile emerged and a giggle escaped me. It's adventure time. I took a short walk down to the end of the cove.

When I got to the cove there was a lovely bench overlooking the lake. It looked like a perfect place to pray and smoke the Sacred Pipe in the morning or at sunset. As I sat on the bench a large crow landed on a nearby branch. He cawed on his way over to let me know of his arrival.

"Hello, brother. I am honored to be here with you. Where is your mate?" I asked.

He cawed and called out for her. She called back and in a couple of minutes she too arrived on a lower branch of the tree.

"Well hello, Mrs. It is great to make your acquaintance. I will be here for a few days. Don't worry. I am no threat to you or the other critters. I come in peace." I confirmed.

They started to converse to each other and then finally flew off.

Well, I thought, *at least I made my intentions known.*

I still followed the teachings that I received from the first native elder woman I met. She was a Passamaquoddy woman from Maine named Agnes Hart. I met her at a powwow and was friends with her for several years before she died.

She was brought up in the woods and she said whenever we approach a new place we need to state our intention. We need to tell the first animal or creepy crawler that greets us why we are there, how long we will be there and that we mean no harm. Then they will let the others know that you have good intentions. It is a teaching I have followed every day.

The sun was setting and the sky morphed into a beautiful array of violet and pink hues. I could feel the dew settling in for the evening as the temperature started to drop. I offered a little tobacco to the four directions, above and below to the earth in gratitude. I knew this was a special place.

Once back at the cabin I heated a bowl of canned chicken soup and ate it gingerly.

An hour later, I went outside again. I realized if the weather remained fair I would probably be spending more time outside than in the cabin.

I began to gather the kindling and neatly placed the split logs to get the campfire started. It took a little more effort because the dew had already dampened the kindling. Eventually, the blaze was crackling. I wrapped myself in a blanket while holding my cup of tea and flashlight and awaited the darkness of the first evening.

When the first star appeared, I knew more were to follow. I awaited their arrival in the darkened canvas above me with anticipation.

CHAPTER TWENTY-FOUR

As the daylight was fully extinguished from the sky, a bright flash darted over the lake. Was it lightning? No, there was no thunder. A few minutes later, I heard the leaves rustling. It sounded like footsteps coming up from the cove. *Must be the critters nestling in,* I thought.

I was not one of those easily frightened women that you see in horror flicks. I actually enjoyed the darkness. When I had been through my four traditional vision quest ceremonies with Black Deer, I looked forward to the darkness of night and the starlit sky.

The sound of the footsteps seemed to be coming closer up the path.

"Hello," I called out.

Nothing but silence returned.

"Hello. Is there anybody there?" I asked.

Then she appeared, leaning heavily on a large cane. She wore a long dark skirt, a dark turtleneck and a heavy, woven colorful sweater. Her hair was long, thin, pure white and in two braids. Her hair hung over the shawl she had draped around her neck and shoulders. She looked to be in her late seventies, give or take. Her familiar lined face revealed a life of many travels.

"Get me a chair will you. I need to sit down," she demanded.

I didn't expect company, so I had to go onto the porch to get one of the plastic patio chairs.

"How about a cup of hot water for both of us," she shouted.

"Would you like a cup of tea?" I asked.

"Did I ask for tea? No, I said hot water. As for tea, I have my own," she replied.

"Okay." I replied.

So much for the silence tonight, I thought, *I have an ornery, I mean an honorary guest and I'm not sure when she is leaving.* I wasn't sure what I was in for tonight.

I brought the blanket, chair and the small table and returned with the two cups of hot water and placed them on the table. She had already made herself comfortable in *my* camp chair.

"It's about time you got here. I've been calling you for many moons," she quipped.

"Sorry." I replied.

I guess the look on my face implied that I did not understand her meaning.

"I called to you in the dream world. You have much ability to work in the spirit world and with the stars and moon. You have been grooming your powers well. You have had strong men teachers and loving women teachers. You have respected them and honored them by remaining true to the teachings," she said.

I listened to her words.

"I guess you don't remember me. I called to you when you slept on the plane from Sundance and I was over your shoulder in the lake two moons ago. I like to project a younger less wrinkled face," she chuckled as she moved her face side to side to show me her profile.

She did look familiar but I was trained not to ask many questions only to listen when an elder was speaking. Too many people cut them off and dismiss them. Or worse, they try to show off by trying to impress the elders with what knowledge they *think* they have. I, on the other hand, have gained a wealth of understanding and wisdom by observation and listening to their stories. They teach you about life. Elders are not just native people but older people from all backgrounds. They all have stories to tell and things to teach us.

"I guess we need introductions first. My name is Tula. I've been a part of this land and lake for a long time."

"I'm Laurel. So it was you, who called me in my dream?" I asked.

"The stirrings and restlessness within you are your own but I came in your dream many months ago. You see you are approaching a slowdown time, when a woman will stay in her power all the time instead of only once a month," she spoke.

"You mean my moon time, my menses? But I'm only forty-three." I added.

"Yes, you have had your moon for many years and now your cycle has become irregular, only a few times a year instead of monthly. It's the start of the change. Women have a hard time with this cycle. They fight it. You are called to work with women in the future after you teach the children. You have already started to work with the children have you not?" she asked.

"Yes. It has been almost five years that my menses have slowed. I thought it was just stress. How did you know about the children and women?" I asked.

"The spirits told me. You know you aren't the only one who can hear and see them," she smiled.

I wondered how she crossed the lake to get to my cabin. She must have come by row boat or canoe. She seemed too fragile to paddle from the other side of the lake. How did she know which cabin I would be in? She must have seen the campfire.

"Don't you worry 'bout how I got here. Your eyes can deceive you. I am not as fragile as you think. Yes. I saw your fire. Now let's get on with it," she barked.

"Here put this in your cup," she motioned.

She took a small cotton bag and filled it with a handful of dried leaves of some kind but it was too dark to see clearly.

"Let this steep in your cup. Then drink it slowly in four sips," she added.

She took the same amount and placed the bag in her cup as well. We let the tea steep for a few minutes as she spoke.

"There is much to talk about. You have been working and teaching the children. The next part of your journey will be to heal the circle within yourself, for women need much healing. In time you will teach other women to heal by what you have learned. The tea is ready. Drink it as I tell the story," she commanded.

She looked off into the flames of the fire and she began her story.

Loralee Dubeau

"There once was a time of balance between the triangle and the circle. The triangles protected the circles and honored and cherished them. They heeded the circles caution and their dreams of warning. All life was precious. The triangle needed the balance of the circle to know itself."

She continued, "The triangle was straight and assertive, full of action and strength allowing itself permission to move ahead and grow. The circle was whole already and connected to the cycles of life, birth, death and rebirth. The whole universe was inside the circle, with all the wisdom and knowledge for guidance. The circle's heart remained open to feelings, experiences and working with the natural flow of the earth, fire, water and air. Everything needed was already there."

She explained further, "The triangle knew it needed to be within the circle and connected to it. It honored the circle and realized the power it held in creating new life. It stayed close to the center of the circle and together they created a life of balance, living in harmony with the earth and all of its creatures and with each other."

She slowly took a sip from her cup. As I drank my tea there was no unusual taste but I experienced a warm flutter in my belly, a nurturing and relaxed wave of peace. My eyes became heavy as she spoke.

"Eventually, the triangle started to walk further away from the center of the circle as the years passed. It was reaching for more and striving for more power. It began to desire power to possess and own. It wanted to control the natural flow of things. It began to dishonor the circle and all things within it. Taking more than what it needed from the land, listening less to its heart and center. The circle tried to warn the triangle, trying to draw it back into the center of the circle."

She continued on, "But the need to progress and possess overwhelmed the triangle. The more it gained the further from its heart and feelings it became. Intellect became powerful but it was losing the center of its heart. No longer did it care for the circle, only for what was beyond and outside of it. No longer did it protect and love the circle."

"Later as they created new life together, it was only to satisfy the triangle's physical need, not out of love of creation. The circle was now only something to use, abuse and discard. No longer was the circle valued, trusted or given worth. New triangles were being created but

98

now separate from the circle, growing outside of it with less emotion and connection. New circles were also being created. Only now the circles were becoming wavy lines and misshapen, no longer round and full like the moon. As time went on the circles lost their own worth and value. Soon there will be no more true circles; no more heart and no wholeness in creation. Since the circle has been devalued, abused and discarded who wants to be a circle?" she welled up with tears and her voice became weepy.

"Everyone wants to be a triangle. It has three sides and it stands tall. They strive for it and are praised for it, but a circle can never truly be a triangle. For within its shape there are still round edges and still a central power that beats with the heart of the circular universe. We need circles Laurel; they hold the inner power of life and wisdom. The triangles today hold the power of greed and detachment. The world cannot survive forever this way. The circles need to reform and be made whole again and help the triangles back to the center. Until the circles reform themselves they cannot help the triangles back to the center of their circle and recreate the harmony."

She came to the end of teaching as she spoke softly, "There comes a time of calling, when what is within the misshapen circle will need to reform. It will take work to get the circle back but it can be done. You will get your circle back Laurel, I will show you the way. It is called the..."

As her voice drifted away from me, I became aware of a gathering of older women in a pit around a fire in the woods. I approached it slowly as they beckoned me. The women's faces were too far away to be seen but each one of them motioned for me to come closer. I felt my body tremble and a wave of anxiety overcame me. Where was I going and how did I get here? I could go no further, the questions I held in my mind prevented me from entering.

The next thing I remembered, I was slouched in the chair at sunrise. The cooled ashes were dampened by the dew. Tula was nowhere to be seen. I checked inside the cabin. There was no trace of her entering the cabin. I took the Child's Sacred Pipe bundle and made my way back to the bench by the cove.

There were no traces of a boat, canoe or footprints for that matter. It seems she had vanished as easily as she came. As I filled the Child's Sacred Pipe and offered my prayers, I felt a connection to the whole of the universe. I prayed in gratitude for what had transpired last night. I also was grateful for the present moment, the one that allowed me to breathe and pray in the sacred way that many people died for.

I prayed for the children in the world, those coming and leaving. I began to see them as triangles and circles. As the circles grew they became more misshapen, a deformity that happened over time. I began to understand Tula's story. The circles were the feminine and the triangles were the masculine. Each needed the other but the feminine had yielded her central power of knowing and creating. Eventually, she began to lose her power.

Had I lost mine? Is this what Tula meant when she said I would get my circle back?

I questioned in my mind, *what was the name of the tea that relaxed me so?* I would wait for her to return. I was sure it was not going to be the last time I would see her.

I packed up the bundle and went back to the cabin to eat a hearty bowl of oatmeal and dried cherries to start the day.

CHAPTER TWENTY-FIVE

I spent the rest of the day reading an inspiring book of quotes from native elders. I pondered on each and wrote down my insights. I wondered if these were their actual words or just what was the author had interpreted. A wrong interpretation can change the entire thought that was being communicated.

The sun was shining and the temp was close to 50 degrees. A brisk wind over the water made it feel cooler.

The walk through the campground was invigorating. I used the map as a guide but there were clearly marked signs throughout the grounds. There were also other cabins that were more rustic than the one I had rented. As I walked I remembered my childhood and how I loved to explore nature.

Every so often I would journey over the embankment in our backyard into the small amount of brush to explore the rocks, plants, bugs, frogs and other critters. Once, I came face to face with a skunk. I stopped dead in my tracks. I didn't move. I just informed it I was not there to cause trouble. Eventually I slowly backed away and the skunk continued on its way.

The thrill of adventure followed me into my teenage years. I would take long walks through my home town of Webster. I walked into the back of the woods that has now become the grounds of the local high school. The lake seemed to have shrunk. There used to be more trees on the little peninsula that was connected to the sandy beach and swimming area. Two walking or running tracks were created by taking down the lushness of the woodlands.

The land may have changed but I have found there is always some magical adventure around every corner wherever you are in nature. This place was no different. As late afternoon approached the birds began their chatter to close yet another day of beauty.

I gathered some pine cones on my walk and offered tobacco to the trees for their gifts. I wasn't sure how I would use them but thought they held a creative force, perhaps a pinecone wreath for Christmas. I was drawn especially to the small baby ones whose tips had broken off. I placed them carefully in my large knapsack that hung across my shoulder and chest.

Once at the cabin I heated a can of soup. I feasted on a vegetable bean soup with some oyster crackers as the sun began to set. Tonight the sky held hues of peach and light blue as the clouds started to fade.

Again I created a campfire, wondering if Tula would return. I wanted to go to the cove and wait for her but something told me to just let things happen as they should. Not trying to rush or control would probably work in my favor and, besides, I wasn't sure if she would return tonight.

I was prepared though. Two chairs were set by the fire with blankets. The hot water was on. The fire was burning and the sage and cedar that I added to the fire created an aroma of sacredness in the woods. As the stars began their nightly appearance, another flash in the sky over the lake came fast and fleeting. Once again I heard the rustling of footsteps up the path and out of the darkness she appeared.

"I see you're all ready for me. Go ahead and get the water," she said as she pointed to the cabin.

I returned with both cups and place them on the wooden table. Again she filled the cotton tea bag with an herb but this time it was with a dried root.

"Here, let this steep before you drink it."

"What are these herbs you are giving me with tea?" I asked.

"You know plants individually and you have studied and taken them for years. I want you to experience them differently by working with their spirit. Last night you relaxed with leaves. Tonight these roots will purge the body."

I settled in to listen. I had so many questions that I wanted answered. She must have read it on my face.

"Okay, go ahead and ask just this once and then you're going to listen," she nodded.

"I am wondering who you are and why you chose me," I answered.

"I didn't choose you, Spirit did. I was told someone would be coming and that I was to test you to see if you were the one," she answered.

"Test me?" I questioned.

"Yes. Could you hear and see me? Did you listen to the internal call? Well, you're here aren't you?" she winked.

She continued to answer my question.

"I was born in southeastern New York in the mountains. My mother was Iroquois and my father was a mixture of Choctaw, Blackfoot and French. My mother "Sleeps with Bear," they called her, was an herbalist and what they considered a country doctor in those days. We lived simply. There was a small community of us in the woods for a while. I met my half-side, or husband, in my early twenties and we married. We moved around a lot. His job was building and constructing houses. He went where he got contracts and I followed him. We settled in this area in Massachusetts in our late fifties. It was the longest time that we lived in one place," she smiled remembering.

"So do you have any children?" I asked.

"Nosy aren't you. No, I have no children. When you are called to the work with the sacred sometimes that is the sacrifice you give to be available to be of service to others. It can be lonely for those who never learn to become one with the silence which connects them with the whole. When you really learn to walk with the sacred you never feel that emptiness, for it truly fulfills you. As for my age, I am older than I want to remember and since age is of no importance let us drink the tea. Four sips," she commanded.

I sipped the tea. It was pungent on my tongue. This one would be harder to get down. Not as enjoyable as the previous night.

She began her teachings once more.

"So you probably understand that the circle is the feminine and the triangle is the masculine. Both are needed but women have lost their balance. By the time women get to the stage of their children not depending on them anymore, their bodies change from fertile to barren and they can't find themselves anymore. They become angry and resentful and yet they long for something that they don't quite understand. They have given too much of themselves away to others and denied their voice inside, the creative, passion and joy."

"Women are taught to be patient, kind, and nurturing but by denying their own desires and needs and not caring for their self, it leaves them empty, sad, angry and depleted because they feel no one cares and loves them. No one will care for them the way that they can love and care for themselves. Women were not made to be martyrs. They don't have to do everything by themselves."

"Where are the fathers and the men who help and support the women? The women have chased them off by being too independent and not allowing them to help. Suffering and not asking for what they need and putting themselves last, if ever at all, will make their union crumble."

"Women have lost their voice and rhythm inside. When she comes to mid-life she grieves for what could have been. She feels lost and confused. When is it her time? When can she get what she desires? Can she even ask? Does she believe she deserves it? Her self-esteem has become damaged and she has lost her way and her own inner teacher. She has lost the connection to her body and her heart. She no longer cares for either of them. She just presses on like the detached independent triangles in the world. She has lost her inner power."

"She is expected to be what masculine society expects: sexy, sub-servient, obedient and tending to the needs of all *except* for herself. If she does not comply she is mentally unstable, overly emotional and in years past, put away in asylums."

"In today's world women are given medications to dull and deaden the voice even further. It is not just lost, it is silenced forever. The inner voice needs to be heard, our wounds need to be nurtured and cleansed and the circle needs to be reformed. With a stronger circle we can create passion and give meaning to our life and be happy. Then we can open our circles to merge again with the triangles and the balance of nature will return."

I took in her words as I sipped the tea. A gurgle in my stomach made its way up my throat. I was struggling to hold down the contents of my stomach. I felt the turmoil inside me. She watched me carefully as I covered my mouth.

"What are you waiting for? Purge it; release the poisons that you have inside you. Reach down and release it," she demanded.

I didn't quite understand. *What kind of tea had she given me to make me feel so sick?*

"I didn't make you sick. You were sick already. Let it come up to release," she demanded again.

I couldn't hold it down any longer. I opened my mouth and regurgitated. Interestingly enough only a small amount of liquid passed my lips as I wretched. A wave of despair engulfed me as my mind became enraged at this old woman. I trusted her and now I was feeling all types of emotions and sick to my stomach.

"What did you give me? What kind of tea was it?" I fumed.

"It's not the tea. It is all the emotions that you need to purge. You have carried and buried the sickness for a long time," she responded.

I didn't quite understand what the woman was saying but I was angry, betrayed and sad all at once. The emotions were drowning me like a tidal wave pulling me under and I couldn't escape to breathe.

I dropped to my knees and let out a primal scream. I didn't know where it came from yet I couldn't hold it back. Once I released it, uncontrollable sobs escaped me. I wept and wept. I didn't know why I was crying but I couldn't stop. The dam had been broken and the waters were gushing and overflowing.

"Just stay with it, let the tears wash you clean," she comforted.

She placed her hand on my shoulder and gently rubbed my back. I continued to weep. It was as if I was weeping for the whole world, every child, woman, man, animal, bird, all of creation. As I wept I felt the energy from the earth surge into me and experienced a rocking sensation. I moved my body to its rhythm as I rocked back and forth on the ground. I cried wiping the tears again and again from my face. I must have been exhausted because somehow I had fallen asleep on the pine needles. The sleep led me deep into a dream.

I was in a tribal camp. I could see everyone moving about in their daily chores but somehow I was invisible to them. I came upon a small tipi and I noticed the paintings on the covering. There were the phases of the moon painted in black and white around the bottom edging. Above the moons were small stars painted like the night sky.

I remembered the teachings of Black Deer that holy people in the tribe would paint their tipis depending on their visions. I wondered if this was the sacred place for a sacred person.

As I stood admiring the paintings, a woman opened the flap and emerged. She looked directly into my eyes.

"You can see me?" I asked.

"Yes," she replied.

"Where am I?" I asked.

"In a place of healing, you are remembering the balance."

"I don't understand." I replied.

"You will."

She turned and walked away. I followed her. She walked through the camp then entered the woods. We began to walk downhill.

"Come," she beckoned me as I followed her into the woods.

In the distance was a gathering of women, older than I. They sat in a circle and motioned for me to come into the center and sit down. I felt all eyes upon me but I kept my eyes lowered to the ground out of respect. They spoke in a tribal language that I did not know but somehow could understand. They were deciding whether or not it was time for my teaching. The woman I had followed pleaded my case for me.

"She is ready. She has found us. She has the ability to work with us now."

"Will she listen? Will she face the darkness of the pit?" they asked.

All I could do was keep my eyes lowered. One by one, each elder stood and touched my womb and head with a sacred feather. I began to feel lightheaded. My body was spinning faster and faster until by reflex I closed my eyes.

I awoke face down on the ground. The fire was nothing but ashes and the sun was rising above the lake. I remained still to remember the dream and what transpired last night.

The two empty chairs were by the fire pit but Tula was long gone.

I arose from the ground to take a shower, journal my dream of the gathering of women and make my breakfast. The rest of the day would be for silent reflection.

CHAPTER TWENTY-SIX

I reflected on how sick I felt after the tea and the uncontrollable sobbing. I don't believe I had ever wept that much before, not even as a child.

I gathered the sacred bundle, walked to the cove and began the Sacred Pipe ceremony. I carefully cleaned the bowl and stem with the sage smoke and connected them together in a sacred manner.

I filled the bowl with the sacred tobacco and prayed to each of the Grandfathers of the directions. The bowl began to vibrate. It was beating in rhythm with my own heartbeat. The pulsing in my left hand had become the whole universe. I looked into the darkness of the hole being filled with tobacco prayers, deep within the red clay. I prayed to be open to insights and gentle teachings and to offer my gratitude for all things in my life, those seen and unseen.

As I drew in the first smoke and offered it to honor the directions, a peaceful feeling enveloped me, as if someone had wrapped a warm blanket around me.

I smoked further and I remembered myself as a child at five-years-old, being the center of attention and the apple of my daddy's eye. Then the memory moved further until I was ten and a big sister to a brother who was three-years-old. *He* was now the center of attention to both of my parents.

My daddy no longer played games with me. Little Tommy was being tossed the ball and taught how to catch. My daddy used to do that with me. I saw myself as a child on the outside of the family. Mommy was tending to her little boy and daddy was teaching him how to play ball. I was now the chore girl, helping mommy with the dishes, folding laundry and picking up the toys that Tommy played with; the big girl chores. I was only a helper and no longer important, at least that is the way it felt.

I loved Tommy and I wanted to play with him and daddy, only I wasn't allowed to play anymore. I was a big girl. As the years passed and I got into my teenage years, Tommy went fishing with daddy, spending more time with him.

As I smoked, I began to cry for the little girl that felt abandoned and pushed to the side, wondering why she lost her father's love and attention. The years rolled ahead to the time I was fourteen. I was a good girl, respectful, didn't cry, did what was asked and was responsible, strong and independent. This seemed to please both of my parents, especially my father. I got good grades in school and was a thoughtful caring person, putting other's needs before my own just like my mother.

Sadness engulfed me as I remembered my younger years. I believed I had a wonderful childhood, which I had but I had not realized that I stuffed away the sadness, anger and abandoned feelings. I tried to get attention by pleasing and becoming all the qualities that were expected. I realize now, there was a deep seated rebellion going on. In search for my father's love and approval I began to resent my mother and her chores and duties as a woman in the household. I decided deep within me that I was not going to be a mere housewife. I wanted to travel, have a career and have fun and that began the disconnection from what I was not yet sure of. The memory offered nothing more. The Child's Sacred Pipe was smoked completely. I was stuck at fourteen.

I couldn't believe what I had felt as a child. *How could I feel this way?* Of course I was loved and cared for. Both parents loved me. *What was this heavy emotion coming up?* I was raw and feeling guilty for what I had seen and felt. *How could I resent my mother? How could I feel abandoned by my father?* They were wonderful parents. I cried on and off throughout the day.

I wrote down my emotions onto the pages of my journal, emotions that I never knew I had. It was a tough day. I was a good person I told myself. I should not feel this way. All hell was breaking lose inside of me. *Why did the memory stop at fourteen? Was there more to come?*

CHAPTER TWENTY-SEVEN

I reflected on my emotions all day. Eventually dusk approached and I built the fire. Once it was dark I ignited it and heard the crackling of the kindling as the smoke began to rise and the fire took hold. I sat there in the darkness as the moon was waning.

As she had come the past few nights, I had a feeling that the old woman would return again.

Some time passed and the flash in the sky brought me back to the present. Once again I heard a stir in the woods and up the path. I had the water heating and had placed the two chairs with blankets around the fire. I was ready or at least prepared.

She came out of the darkness again with the cane in hand, walking with a slight limp. Tonight she had a black fringed shawl around her shoulders and a long denim skirt.

"Hello." I said.

"Ah, I see you are ready for me? That's good. Seems you had a rough day today. Your energy is all watery," she acknowledged.

"What do you mean?" I asked.

"You know what I mean. Don't act dumb all of a sudden. You read energy and you understand it. The heart and solar plexus have been releasing. Don't you feel it?" she asked.

"Yes, lots of emotions today. Stuff I didn't realize I had felt. I'm not feeling real good about myself at the moment." I replied.

"You think because you're human you have to be perfect? Who says so? What is perfect and by whose standards? Girl, you've got a lot to let go of," she shook her head.

It seemed so inappropriate to me to call her Tula. Maybe I could call her Ms. Tula or perhaps Granny Tula.

"Stop fussing with my name. I see the wheels turning in your head. *Tula* means "leaping water" in Choctaw. You can call me Grandma Tula if it makes you feel better."

I had teachings from the Cherokee, Seneca, Cree, Blackfoot, Hopi, Navaho and Sioux traditions and I spent time learning each tradition faithfully.

I had received training and been given permission to lead Sacred Pipe and purification lodge ceremonies. I had met my spirit and star teachers through each of the years of training and ceremonies. I had learned of my native heritage years ago from my great-grandmother as a young girl.

"I see you are thinking again. You're a good listener and you've had much training I'm sure, but what I came to help you with is something within you. Go get the hot water will you? I think it's time for tea," she pushed.

I rose and quickly poured the steaming water into the mugs and placed them on the small wooden table before her. She pulled out another root and yet again, it was different than the one from last night. This one was chopped into small pieces. She placed the pieces in the cotton bags and steeped them in the water. I hoped that I would not wretch the way I had the night before.

"This will have to steep a bit. The roots take longer to pass their energy to the water. Don't worry. This one is a bit easier on the body," she comforted.

"Can you tell me what kind of tea we drank last night?" I asked.

"All in due time, but not now. You need the experience to learn first. Pay attention to what you feel and sense inside," she prompted.

Again she began her story.

"The misshapen circles reach a point in their life when they recognize they are missing something. They don't feel their wholeness as a circle. They start to remember how they became misshapen and out of balance. They decide to work on reforming their circle but they need to find and understand how they became that way. As I said, some were born from mothers that had lost their circle and they will have to work harder to re-create their shape but they can do it. They can rebirth the circle but first they need to die."

Die? I thought. *What does she mean die?*

"It's time to drink the tea," she motioned by taking her cup in hand. "Drink it down with four large sips. Just breathe in and relax."

In a moment I had a flash. *Was I drinking to my death? Was this poison? I was following this woman whom I didn't really know. What on earth was I doing? I always had better sense than this.*

I drank the tea and observed the fire while a warm sensation filled my body. A deep relaxed state, yet one of heightened awareness. I felt my body sinking down into the earth. I was entering a deep dark hole. It was one that had been closed and sealed for a long time. Only now was it open to me. My mind and body surrendered. I was called to the silence of these woods following Spirit's guidance for a reason. I relaxed further into the silence. I was at the edge of discovering why I was called. I faintly heard the wise woman's words as I closed my eyes.

"Let the darkness swallow you deep. Surrender yourself. Slowly enter the pit. Soon you will be within its center."

The darkness entombed me. I fell into the deep hole and felt the motion of being gently rocked back and forth. I heard an ocean and its waves crashing in and out. I could see nothing but blackness as if I was blind to any sense of form. I breathed slowly accepting the darkness and the gentle rocking. I landed softly and was somewhere at the bottom.

Alone, yet I felt no sadness. Suspended in time, I relaxed further. The sound of waves ceased and just the silence remained. Time was non-existent. Maybe hours were passing or perhaps days and it was of no importance. Soon I became accustomed to the silence and the darkness.

A small glimmer of light above me began to expand. Silvery and bright, its rays emerged and touched my being. It was the moon herself. I was with her; or perhaps was it she who was within me as I had been told many times through various women elders? I heard her presence speak.

"I will bring awareness to the shadow inside you. The darkness is hidden to protect your ego and sense of self but it is what keeps you

separate and limited. I am the sacred grandmother within you. It is time to remember, release and rebirth."

Once again my consciousness returned to the image of myself at fourteen. I was fully developed and both parents were telling me what clothing was appropriate; nothing too tight, nothing low cut or revealing and certainly nothing sexual. That was fine with me. However, as I reached high school I felt like a freak. Girls were feminine and boys were noticing. I was not even allowed to shave my legs or wear make-up. I obeyed to please my parents and be a good girl.

After physical education class one day, one of the girls noticed my legs were awfully hairy. She started to make fun of my legs calling me a wild bear. I was distraught. That evening, with my father's razor in hand, I proceeded to shave my legs and arm pits. I carved a nice little chunk out of my lower calf that would not stop bleeding. It eventually landed me at the doctor's office for a tetanus shot and a week's grounding to my bedroom.

As the teenage acne began, I tried to camouflage my face with a base powder that I secretly took from my mother's night stand. Eventually she caught me and decided to allow me to have my own make-up but cautioned me to use it sparingly. I was told not to draw attention to myself or my female body. I realize now that I took it one step further. I began to disconnect from my body and being a girl.

I began my menstrual cycle at eight-years-old. I understood it was dirty because I was told it was to be kept secret. Wrap it, discard it and place it in the trash. When I was young, there were a couple of times I left the wrapped package on the back of the toilet and received punishment for forgetting to "get rid of the thing," in my father's words. So I learned quickly that being a girl was not as pleasant or acceptable as being a boy. Each day, I became more disconnected from myself and the feminine.

My mind wandered back to a Sunday afternoon. I was wearing a pretty knee-length paisley skirt and one of my father's friends from work stopped by to visit. He had just purchased a new sports car and he wanted to show my father and take him for a ride.

Rick had visited several times. He was a divorced man who was interested in music, dance clubs and fast cars. He loved the Beatles and that was also my favorite band since I was a young girl. I liked to listen to him talk to my parents about music and other wild stories in his life.

After my father went for a ride with him, I begged my father to let me go for a ride in the sports car with Rick. Since it was only a two-seater, only one person could ride with him at a time. My father agreed to let me go for a short ride. He told Rick, "Just around the corner and back and no speeding."

I was excited beyond belief. I was going for a ride in a cool car. Rick put the Beatles "Let it Be" song on the eight track and we were off down the street. At that moment, I felt like a true grown-up. We went further than around the block. We were each singing to the music that was cranked up all the way, drawing the attention to onlookers we passed. Rick had the sun roof open and the wind was blowing my dark locks freely into chaos. I was happy and feeling wild and untethered.

He bought ice cream at the local stand and then we drove to the nearby Webster Lake to watch the boats and enjoy the treat. After we ate our ice cream, I told him we should get back because my father would be getting upset that we were gone too long.

"You have become a real beauty, Laurel. You look more and more like your mother every day. Do you have a boyfriend at school yet?" he joked.

"No. I'm not allowed to date and I am not really interested anyways," I dismissed.

"You know there are so many things I could teach you," he spoke as he started to force his body against mine.

He began to pull up my skirt and make his way to my underwear. I was fighting, moving my legs and trying to push him off but he had my arms pinned with his upper body and he was strong. I started to scream and yell but there was no one around to hear me. I began to cry as he forced his tongue in my mouth, touched the skin beneath my underwear and forced his fingers inside me with manipulation.

In an act of defiance, I bit down hard on his tongue and clamped my teeth. It forced him to withdraw from me and I opened the car door and escaped. He called after to me as I ran wildly.

"Laurel, please get back into the car. I will take you home," he beckoned in a panic.

"No," I screamed as I started the trek home.

He followed me in the car as I ran. I was in shock and I barely remembered turning the corner on to the street where I lived. I stopped running from being out of breath and walked at a much slower pace. Again Rick pleaded to me from the car.

"Laurel, please get into the car. This doesn't look good. He'll blame you. Your father will never believe you if you tell him. I will say you came on to me. You'll disappoint him," he manipulated.

I was humiliated, feeling guilty and I didn't want to think about it much less talk about it. He betrayed me. I was ashamed.

I was about four hundred feet from my house and I got in the car but I didn't put the seatbelt on just in case I needed to escape.

He dropped me off in front of the house. As the car door slammed my father came out to wave goodbye to Rick.

"Let's forget this, okay Laurel?" he asked.

And forget it I did. I buried it deep, losing all memory of it up until now in this moment. Why now, as the small light embraced me in this darkened abyss did my memory return?

I felt a quaking around and within me; crashing sounds and loud roars were frightening me. The walls were breaking and shattering. The light I had experienced was swallowed by the darkness. All was black and desolate. The loud roar I realized was that of my own voice screaming from the memory that was brought to the surface. The sound went on and on for what seemed liked ages in this darkened pit until I exhausted myself and closed my eyes to rest.

I laid in the darkness for a long time without stirring. Eventually the glimmering light above returned once again. This time the light felt much further away from me. I could not feel its presence as before the memory had replayed itself, though I could still hear her voice.

"In this pit is the womb of who you are and your connection to nature and life. Within you is where you find the shadows of what limits you have, and the power to rebalance your true self that was created from the one light of all being. A woman must return to the silence within to heal the wounds and release the illusions from society, family and what you have been told and accepted as truth. In the silence and the darkness of the pit is where you will find what ails you and the truth in

which to heal it. You have all you need inside the pit - life, death and rebirth," she explained.

Saddened, angry and ashamed were the emotions I was experiencing. My being felt pain, I could barely breathe. This memory was repressed. I barely had remembered nor had wanted to remember. The shock and betrayal had stayed with me all my life. I had kept my all my male relationships at arms-length to stay in control and feel safe. I had never fully given all of myself, my heart or trust for fear of betrayal. The event had changed me, as I reviewed my life. I realized I had never achieved full intimacy with anyone. Not just sexual intimacy but happiness and joy. I took detours and became focused on career and traveling to escape and get away.

I acknowledged the memory and I reviewed all of my past boyfriends, dates and even my marriage. I unconsciously had relationships with men who could not fully connect to me, nor could I to them. We were all wounded.

The small light spoke again, "Yes, now you see. You did not trust, so you drew to you those people who would betray you and who could not be trusted. It was easy to blame and walk away from someone who delivered your expectations. What if you had trusted? What if you had chosen to forgive the man who was your father's friend? What if you had spoken the truth of what had happened and not felt guilt, shame or fear? What if you realized that you were a precious young woman that deserved to be respected and cherished? Just because you were a girl, you were no less valuable to society, but even more valuable. Girls are not taught this by their mothers and grandmothers. Society has changed its ways from the nurturing, love, connection and compassion of the feminine to a world of aggression, greed and excess of the masculine pleasuring their needs. Women have lost their way for hundreds and hundreds of years. They have forgotten their inner voice within their pit. They have accepted through oppression the roles that they are now expected to fulfill. It does not feel right inside them. They search for what is missing in their life. Some start searching in their late thirties but most start in their forties or fifties. They become unhappy with their life, their husbands, and their children. Their life has no meaning or purpose. As their bodies change and their hormones flux all these emotions get played out with temper and rage or uncontrollable tears. Bodies and hearts are being reminded of what the feminine spirit needs and desires. A transformation is ready to take place with a death of the old and a rebirth of the new called the Grandmother's Way," she concluded.

Grandmother's Way? It sounds indigenous. Is that what I am approaching? My menstrual cycle had become irregular in the last few years. I started getting mood swings that I countered with flower essences, essential oils and herbs.

The light above me drifted further away.

I heard the call of a crow and I opened my eyes.

Once again, I was near the ashen coals and nestled crookedly in the blanket of the chair. Grandma Tula was nowhere to be found. The morning sun was rising and burning up the mist over the lake.

I began my day with a light breakfast and a short trek on the campground's trail. Walking helped me think and process. I was raw and tears escaped me. Repressed memories and wounds limited me in my thinking and actions. I wondered again what was in the tea. It seemed to be another root. Grandma Tula did not allow me to look closely enough to recognize it. I had herbal training in my younger years but one can never know everything.

When I returned from my walk, I brought out the Child's Sacred Pipe to smoke. As I prayed in each direction, I felt the wind pick up. Each of the spirit grandfathers from the directions came forward in spirit form. Then for the first time, the spirit grandmothers placed themselves beside each grandfather. Both were present in each direction. As I smoked the Child's Sacred Pipe, I could feel the hearts of many children. Those that were hungry and in physical pain, those that were molested, mentally and physically abused, those that were lost and abandoned, those that were dying and even those that were getting ready to be birthed and enter the earth's realm. A lot of emotion passed through me as I was filled with the oneness of all children and how precious the human life was. How would they learn? What would they experience in their lifetime? I prayed hard for them all, for their journeys to be happy, for their lessons to be gentle, that their hearts would feel love and that their spirits would be fulfilled. My heart was full as I connected to the whole of it all.

I sat in the silence after the sacred smoking was completed with silent tears that trickled down my cheeks. My inner child was weeping as I connected to my pain. I allowed the memories to rise without judgment of myself and I released the repression. I was weeping for every disappointment, for every fear that I had felt, for every time I had felt unloved, forgotten or ashamed of being a girl.

The tears were silent but no less powerful than as if I had been sobbing out loud. I held the Sacred Pipe to my chest and the warm bowl comforted my heart. It represented the whole universe and it represented the whole of me. It gave me great peace.

A voice outside of me said, "You are loved all the time. There is not one minute since your birth that the light within you did not shine. The light of spirit is proof within you of that love. There is nothing outside of you that is needed to fill it. Feel it within. Shine it for others to see. You are not separate. Fear and anger causes separation. Love, compassion and forgiveness create wholeness."

A warmth and tranquility filled me. My tears dried and I could breathe fully again. There was no tension in my body, just a relaxed state of being. The Sacred Pipe ceremony would always be a way to experience the wholeness of being.

Chapter Twenty-Eight

I spent the rest of the day reading and processing my feelings in my journal. Although I was peaceful, I was also fatigued. The emotions being released exhausted my body. I walked daily to move the energy through the soles of my feet to the earth below. I was taught long ago by a native teacher to release what ails me and give it to her (the earth) to transform.

Granny Sadie was a Cree elder from Oklahoma. She told me to offer tobacco to the earth first and to ask permission to dig a small hole. As I carefully moved the moist soil with my hands I prayed for help to not displace any of the creepy crawlers from their homes. I asked the earth to help me take my sadness, grief and anger and transform it deep within her womb and to rebirth it into positive energy for the new growth of grass or plants.

At first, because it was so new then, it was not easy to speak to the small hole in the earth. I felt a little foolish with the exercise. Eventually I connected to the soil with my hands and my heart began to fill and the emotions poured out. I was grieving a pet dog that I had loved for ten years. I also was grieving a relationship with a young man who had cheated on me with another woman. This brought up emotions of anger and betrayal. Lots of words filled the hole in the earth; more than I had thought were in me. A stream of tears ran down my cheeks and into the hole.

Finally when no more could be expressed or felt, the elder instructed me to fill the hole with kind words of gratitude and love for the transformation and healing that it was giving me. I offered the four sacred plants to the earth; sage, cedar, tobacco and small pieces of sweet grass.

She handed me several seeds to plant in the hole. She said it was the gift that I offered and that new life would spring out of the pain. I covered the hole with the same soil that I had removed ever so gently and watered it lightly. The pain had been transformed and when I visited her a year later, a mound of grass had grown over the spot. I could no longer tell where I had released.

The second teaching she gave me was to walk and disperse the energy through my feet, or sit upon the earth and release it through my tail bone. Both were effective ways that I still use today.

While remembering her teachings, I also realized the power of the death and rebirth cycle in nature that happened every day. Staying present and living in the moment was really the only way one could live in harmony.

My memories floated in and out throughout the rest of the day. As an eight-year-old, I began my cycle and was taught to keep it hidden and discreet. At ten-years-old, the boys from school lifted my skirt from behind me to see my underwear. So I and the other girls in class began to wear shorts under our skirts for protection. At twelve-years-old, the boys in school began to grab at my breasts and I had to slap them away. The boys made nasty sexual comments about the girls and stole kisses from them forcibly. When I complained to the women teachers their reply was, "Get used to it, boys will be boys. Just wear baggy sweaters to not attract them."

I never wore tight clothing and I shouldn't have had to wear a tent to repress the boy's curiosity, which didn't work anyway.

So I, as well as many other girls learned quickly that if we attracted attention, it was our fault and that we could not do anything to stop the unwanted attention.

High school boys also tried to rub up against me or pinch my behind, thinking it was funny. As much as I yelled, slapped or reported the incident nothing ever changed. I was not singled out intentionally; most girls suffered the same whistles, cat calls, pawing or sexual innuendos.

As I reviewed my life, I had become less feminine so I could be equal and seen for my intelligence and abilities not my body. I valued my intellect and mechanical abilities. I was a leader and supervisor in my career for many years in my life, drawing attention away from my femininity.

If I disagreed with consensus I was an irrational female, probably "on the rag" as one of the managers had said behind my back.

The rage inside was moving up within me as the memories resurfaced. I had lost myself and given way to all the aggression of success to feel worthwhile. I wondered how many other women suppressed their emotions like I did.

I wanted my father to still notice me after my brother entered the family. So I tried hard to be good, not showing anger or tears, and helping my mother with the household. Having emotions were not acceptable. I had to be strong so I became independent enough to take care of myself.

That is exactly what I did. I educated myself, worked hard to support myself and became more masculine to be acknowledged. I thought I was balanced but I lost my circle because I didn't trust men. I kept my feminine at bay, I did not want to be too attractive for fear of being raped or attacked. I wanted to be loved for my mind, not my body. I realized now that I had rejected my feminine body and developed more masculine qualities. I became the triangle.

Again I cried. Tears flowed and I sobbed. How wounded I was. From the outside it may have seemed to other women that I had it together - self-sufficient, independent and answering to no one.

When I allowed myself to feel, I saw how I betrayed myself. I was feeling the sadness of abandonment and betrayal, the rage of being disrespected while wanting to be seen and heard. I was trying to figure out how to survive in the world while still being me.

While I knew the emotions were my own, I felt as if I was processing the repressed emotions of all women. It felt very heavy but I allowed myself to feel, cry and scream. I wanted it all to come up and release from my body. I allowed myself to experience it without guilt.

After a few hours, fatigued, I laid down for a late afternoon nap. I wrapped myself up in a warm fleece blanket and took my dream remedy flower essence drops to relax and opened up to the dream time. During my childhood illness the dream world was open to me. I learned if I stated my intention, and asked for any guidance a symbolic answer would come to me. I learned how to interpret the symbols from the dream time with the guidance of the spirits who helped me heal. As I breathed slowly like I had many times before and closed my eyes, a tranquil slumber began.

I was walking in the forest and I came to a clearing in the woods. I walked slowly towards a village of tipis and no one seemed to notice me approaching. I entered the community and watched as the children played and life went on happily. The familiar elder woman with silver colored hair and a well-worn tanned hide dress approached me. It was only she who could see me.

"Come. Follow me. I am White Swan," she demanded.

I followed her past the tipis and out of the village into the woods. The women were gathered around a fire in a circle. They had either a black, red or white shawl around their shoulders. All were seated in a circle, shaking rattles in time with their chants. The melody was beautiful as their voices crooned high and low in tune. They were building a wave of sound energy. Emotions stirred within me. There was a primal sound to their song. The voices blended tearfully together. I noticed the flames would build and then lower in concert with their voices.

"This is an ancient ceremony." White Swan spoke.

She allowed me to observe and learn the song by singing it quietly to myself. Four of the women rose from the circle when the chant was completed. They had ancient faces, maybe hundreds of years old. They were familiar. The circle again had thirteen women.

As they approached me, they had gourds containing the colors of red, black and white earth paint. As they painted my face, arms and legs, they sang a powerful chant. It sent shivers through my body. I felt faint and was afraid I would fall. The women laid me down and began to rattle over me slowly. Then they increased the rattling until it became a fast frenzy of energy. I felt myself lift out of my body, rise above the trees and begin to travel.

I traveled and reviewed my life backwards, from forty-three to birth. Not a moment was left out. Everything was seen and understood with great awareness. As I witnessed my birth I experienced my soul essence.

What completeness it held, full of inspiration and wonderment. It was a chance to experience unlimited possibilities.

Quickly, I began to move the cycle forward from birth to present. I found myself back in my body, lying on the ground with the grandmothers around me. Their song and rattles had stopped. White Swan spoke softly and tenderly.

"We have met several times now. You are entering the death cycle, a change in your body, mind and heart. We have initiated you into this cycle. Your blood will become scant and then happen only once a year for the next year. Before it does you must knowingly enter the death cycle to transform and make a smooth transition. On your cycle feed your blood in a sacred designated place to the earth and moon. Sing the death song we have taught you. It will empower and transform you. It will help you to work with us fully. It is the old way of crossing over into the cycle. Let your offering the next year embrace this phase of initiation into the Grandmother's Way."

I drifted away from the group knowing full well I could return again.

I opened my eyes and awoke from the dream state. Fully present and aware I wrote the experience in my journal. This was a big dream, an initiation into the sacred and a formal beginning to an ending phase of life.

CHAPTER TWENTY-NINE

I made a fire as dusk approached again. I was never sure if Grandma Tula would visit but I made the appropriate accommodations just in case.

As the woodlands began to slow down with the darkness, I relaxed into the silence while breathing slowly. The dampness in the air and slight chill made me wrap myself tighter in the fleece blanket. The first star appeared in the sky and as I remembered my maternal grandfather's example, I made my first prayer for the evening.

My maternal grandfather Gus Laroux, was an avid fisherman and would wait until the first evening star had appeared after a hard rain. We would make a prayer in gratitude for the worms to appear above the ground and use them to catch and feed the fish.

He used to say, "We are giving the fish one last meal before we catch them and eat them. It is the cycle of life and we must be respectful."

He had several large boxes of loam in the cellar of the house and he placed the worms we found carefully in the loam. We needed to be careful not to pull them out of the soil and break them apart for then we would be wasting their lives. Once we gathered them, we placed them in the boxes to live comfortably until we needed them for catching fish. When all of the worms were gone, he used the loam in his vegetable garden. Then when spring came, Grandpa Gus got new loam to start the process all over again.

When I looked up at the amazing stars, this tender memory surfaced. I said a prayer of gratitude to my grandfather and his teachings of respect for the natural world.

I was distracted from my thoughts by a flash in the sky. It was an blue orb that fell quickly and touched the banks of the lake and disappeared. I heard a shuffling of leaves and the sound of a human cough. I got up from my chair and looked down the path from the lake's edge. She coughed again as she appeared from the darkness.

"Get me some hot water, girl. My throat is dry," she commanded.

I raced to get our cups of hot water and placed the cups before her. She looked tired tonight. I wanted to share my dream and all I was processing but felt it better to hold off for right now.

"Been a whirlwind of a day for you, hasn't it? Your energy field is low. Lots of crying today?" she asked.

I nodded in return.

"Tears are a way for us to move the anger and fear that we hold inside us. Why anyone would want to stuff the emotions down is beyond me. They cleanse us and our being. To feel is a good thing. It is a way we connect as human beings. Some folks feel the world revolves around them. They take everything so personally. Then there are others who repress their feelings and stuff them down like a volcano that is ready to erupt at any time. The trick is to balance feeling and detachment at the same time," she spoke.

"How does one do that?" I asked.

"Be aware and compassionate with yourself; acknowledge that you are sad, angry or fearful. Look within yourself to see where it comes from. What wound have you not healed or forgiven? If one looks outside themselves for their pain, they will blame people and events and will not heal the wound. If they look within they can heal it by understanding where it started, forgiving oneself for carrying the wound, and then forgiving the event or person that may have triggered the wound that we carry. If you forgive yourself for carrying the wound and are compassionate and loving to yourself, it shifts the energy to healing so that you will not continue to carry it into the future by blaming something or someone else."

"What if someone has harmed you, aren't they responsible for your pain?" I asked.

"Humans make choices based on their knowledge and experience. They are all trying to do the best they can in any given moment. They are responsible for those choices and when they know better they can do better. People will carry those wounds until they heal them but if one blames another, they will not heal. It may have been wrong to begin with but one can continue to carry and limit their life by carrying the baggage every day. It is not happening in the present moment so why keep carrying it? Challenges are to make us stronger and more forgiving, compassionate and loving. When we have experienced pain we can be compassionate towards others who experience the same."

She continued, "We are relations to each other. All our experiences in life as human beings help us grow. Good experiences and not so good are both valuable. Do we want to carry the wound and limit our potential life or do we want to move beyond and heal the fear, anger and sadness and live our best life. It's our choice. Tell me Laurel, what have you learned? Why the tears today? What wounds do you carry?"

"I have realized that I was sad and angry at my father for abandoning me when my brother was born. I was no longer his number one. I felt abandoned and unloved. I had less time with him especially after Tom could walk and talk. He spent time playing with him instead of me. I never knew I felt that way. I feel ashamed that I feel that way now." I replied averting my eyes to look away.

"These memories are attached to emotions that you need to bring to your awareness to heal. Is there anything else?" she asked softly.

"Angry memories have come up. I remembered my father's friend attacking me sexually and all the memories of boys in school grabbing at my breasts and lifting my skirt. When I reported it to a teacher nothing was done. It made me very angry. In fact, I am outraged and embarrassed at the same time. I feel guilty, ashamed and betrayed. I am feeling so many emotions right now. It is confusing." I said as I started to cry.

"Yes, let the tears flow; allow yourself to be in this moment of truth and your emotions. Release them. You have held this in for a long time. Many women hold their feelings in. Women in society are violated every day. The power of the feminine, the true mother, is inside us all - not just in women but in men too. It allows us to feel unconditional love for ourselves and each other. If healed and acknowledged it could change the mindset from the power of control over to the power within us. It would help us all to relate, love and understand each other."

"Women have been repressed for hundreds of years but now they have begun to fight back for things like their rights to vote, control of their own bodies, and right to earn equal pay. These are all good things but what they have not changed is their mind and behavior. They have become greedy for success and power too. To become equal they have torn each other down and become hard, gossiping and controlling."

She continued further, "They no longer nurture themselves, other women or their children. They no longer listen to the great mother of wisdom within them. They have lost the intuitive of gentle knowing. They overwhelm themselves and don't listen to their bodies when they need rest. They no longer listen to their hearts and spirits about what they need or want, or how to be happy and balanced. They are teaching their daughters the same greed to succeed and to be tough and not express their emotions. So who is doing the nurturing? It is not just the women's role to nurture, a man can as well, but it is within the woman's knowing that teaches the men and children how to love unconditionally. If she loses this ability she cannot help herself or give to others. She has become hardened, cold, and non-sensual and cannot hear the stirrings within her that keep her balanced. She believes she has to please, service others and deplete herself or become completely unfeeling and controlling in a masculine way. In any event she has lost her way."

"The masculine is not the only thing to blame. Women need to stand up and remember their inner ancient voices to bring wholeness to the self and then to those in their life. We will only be treated the way we treat ourselves and the way we allow others to treat us," she informed.

"All these memories you carry. Where are the emotions of anger, fear and sadness in your body? What does it look like - color, shape, size, taste or smell? Get in touch with it. It is your teacher. What will you gain if you release and heal it?" she asked.

As I thought about my life honestly, I had been carrying this story a long time. Life could be different. I knew at that particular moment, standing with Tula and divulging deep into my emotional past that I had to forgive myself.

"Where in your body do you feel the emotion?" she asked again.

"I feel my anger in my stomach. It is brown and small and tastes sour. I feel as if I could throw up." I replied.

"Yes and that is why you vomited the second night with the tea," she noted.

"The sadness I feel in my heart is black and heavy like a stone weighing down on the center of my chest," I added.

"That is why you must let the tears flow to help release the tension," she added.

"The fear is in my groin. It feels stiff and closed down, a dark void of hard tar between my womb and tailbone." I completed.

"Fear can be hard to recognize. You must breathe in and out very slowly to relax and release the tension in your body that you recognize. Acknowledge it and release it through your feet to the earth. Take the light of the moon above you and fill those places of unbalanced emotions with love. Let it fill you completely. Many women are out of touch with their bodies. They cannot feel the flow of life moving through or when it gets stuck. One needs to find the painful memory, feel it in their body, acknowledge it and be present with it, and then forgive and love it so that it can be released and not carried any longer," she explained.

As I followed her directions, I felt my body relax and release. I could see and feel the areas in my body shift. When I came to the completion of this exercise I opened my eyes.

"Tonight we will drink another tea," she said.

She opened the brown bag and proceeded to chop and place pieces of another dried root into the cotton bags. She began her teaching as we waited for the tea to steep.

"There comes a time in a woman's life when she needs to heal the things that limit her. When her body begins to change, emotions that have been buried will surface. The sadness and anger that she has withheld will now erupt like a volcano. Her true voice will beckon to speak. This voice comes from within the pit of her womb. Her spirit will no longer be denied. The time has come for her to embrace all of who she is and no longer deny her wishes and desires for happiness. She begins to realign the sacred feminine within her. She will hear the call and return to the pit to remember her true self and no longer be what others expect her to be."

"She is no longer mother, daughter, sister, wife, her job and any other roles from society that she has accepted. She can now be free to express her voice and full being. It is her time to nurture herself. She has given to others and now it is time to give to her soul's purpose."

"Grandma Tula, isn't she *still* a mother? Does that mean that she no longer serves others?" I asked.

"Laurel, by this time the woman is older and her children should need her less. She must allow them to be responsible adults. Her body is telling her to take care of herself. That is why she is torn between self-care and nurturing others. It is time for her to put herself first and when she does she will not feel depleted."

"Society has taught women to become martyrs and from our matriarchal lineage we are taught that we are worthless unless we continuously give to others, and that being a woman means to be all and do all and accept nothing in return - as if we do not deserve to ask for what we want and need. So we deny and deplete ourselves for years until we can no longer deny the inner call and knowing that we are not balanced and not happy. The change of our hormones and body makes us change our ways. The inner voice calls us to return to joy and happiness, and to remember our desires and needs - giving us permission to nurture and sustain ourselves to be happy."

"Women need to relearn how to love the self, release the wounds that we have accumulated and, most importantly, forgive ourselves for denying the joy and love that is rightfully ours to give to ourselves. We must delve into the darkness of the "pit" to look at what needs to be healed, change our perspective and relearn how to love and support our sacredness," she added.

"Was it the pit that I returned to last night? The darkness and the voice I heard from the light of the moon above me?" I asked.

"Yes. You entered the pit, but the moon is within you. It arises from the void of creation. The pit is not a dark place of abandonment. It is your center. It is the goodness and sustenance that you need. There you will find the wisdom for your soul. Here, let's drink the tea now," she suggested.

I sipped the tea in four large gulps and the warmth in my womb became relaxed. My mind began to fade to black and to a state of nothingness and peace, a sensation of falling deeper and floating down into the abyss. No thoughts were held, just a wave of relaxation while trusting the weightless feeling of time slowing down to a standstill. I was no longer a body, just a conscious essence.

With time suspended, I was submerged into a deep sleep while feeling wrapped in a tight blanket and finally touching bottom. There was nothing else that was needed, just the stillness and silence.

CHAPTER THIRTY

As my essence stilled and my consciousness slept I was being regenerated. The dark reminded me of another time and place. The tightness wrapped around me like a cocoon reminded me of the womb of my birth. Inside the warmth of my mother I was nurtured and fed without having to think or ask. The love in my being was so perfect, knowing all and knowing nothing at the same time while having the absence of any fear.

The level of innocence in the womb is so precious. The time when the essence combines with matter to form the body is miraculous. The new body will be thrust into a world of new experiences and the senses will be bombarded.

I laid in the darkness, fearless with a connection to being part of a greater whole, one that has been there from the beginning and where there is truly no end.

Wait, I heard a sound, the slow beating of something over and over. Thump, thump, thump. There was a resonance in the energy. The rhythm continued to lull me into an even deeper relaxation. Within this space I heard an internal voice. It was a soft whisper at first and then it became loud enough to comprehend.

"You have returned to the whole of your spirit and your connection to the one heart. The sound is where the one love resides. It is always within you. You cannot find it outside of yourself. When you return to this place there is only truth for you. Your very essence is created in and from love. The pit is your center. In this dark and calm space you can remember all of who you are. It is your true north, the compass that

steers the real direction. It monitors your knowing of both the true self and its relation to the whole. When a woman has become unbalanced, she can regain her balance by re-entering her center - the pit, where she can remember unconditional love and replenish, regenerate and rebirth."

As I lay in the security of the cocoon blanket around me, the voice continued.

"Here is where you find the great mother, the nurturer of self. It is your innate right to give and receive love. To balance self, one must first feed the great love to the self. When you give it away to others over and over and give nothing to yourself, you will deplete that love and become abusive to yourself and allow others to abuse you as well. Do not search for others to fill and complete you. There is nothing outside of yourself that can fill that void. Only you can fill that hole. You are here in this pit to remember how to love and care for yourself. Your voice in the silence will tell you what you need, if you listen. It carries the great wisdom and serves as your teacher. It needs to be heard and not disowned, suppressed or repressed. It is nature's flow and rhythm within you. When you have a feeling or insight, go into the silence and name it, identify where it comes from, understand it, express it and act on it. When you listen, value, express and act upon what it needs, the strength of the feminine and the great mother's love will return you to balance."

It seemed like I had been in this great vastness for an eternity. A golden cascade above me began to flow in the dark. An amber liquid dripped on my wrapped essence, one drop at a time. It slowly covered me. It was hot. It was melting and erasing something from me, but what I could not see. Something was being transformed a little at a time. The drops of liquid lightly kept pace with the thump, thump, thump sound beating ever so slowly. As the liquid slowly covered me, it allowed me to receive its goodness. It was filling holes that I never knew I had. Changing and restructuring me. I was happy and content as the beating of the sound led my essence beyond that moment into a lost and ancient land.

My consciousness floated to a great fire in the distance. It roared as chants were sung in a low monotone. The voices followed the flames as the fire surged with highs and lows. It was a gathering of women who had formed a great circle. As I drew closer, I watched as they anointed a female infant with oils and a crushed herb. They used a red feather, then a black feather and then finished with a white feather. They anointed her womb, navel, heart and forehead. Cradled by four women they raised her to the four directions, to the sky above and touched her to the earth below. They anointed her by placing a small dot below her navel with red ochre paint. They spoke in a tribal language, yet somehow I could understand.

"This is your center from the breath of life that blew you into existence and connected you to this world. It is your lineage from the stars to the earth. The great voice of wisdom resides within this vessel. Return to this wisdom to feed the hole in you. Return to the whole of it all."

They turned to me and beckoned me to come closer and to reside in the circle of women. As they passed the infant and placed it in my hands I looked down upon her face. I recognized the child and the familiar dark spot upon her chest. It was the face and body of me that I held. The spot resembled the birthmark that I have had for years. The eyes I gazed into were my own eyes reflecting back to me. I held her gently. I was concerned for her wellbeing and safety as I supported her fragile neck and body.

The ancient women brought me back to the feminine child within me. I remembered the love as I held the symbolic form of myself in my hands. I coddled my infant self to my chest and tears began to flow. I embraced myself, my needs, my desires, my emotions, my experiences, my body, my life and my spirit. I give voice and recognition to it all. No shame or guilt had to be buried. I am a child, a young girl, a woman, and a mother to self and others. I can feed the hole within from the love of the greater whole.

I found myself floating away from the circle and back to the darkness and the drops of the amber liquid had stopped its flow.

The amber liquid was the nectar of life. It transformed and awakened me. It was "honey," - a substance that contained wisdom and life that could be remembered to help me rebirth. I clung to the memory of the infant, pulling it deep within me and I cried with joy.

Again I was awakened by the crow calling me to consciousness. I lay on my back on the ground with my arms folded tightly over my chest. My face was wet with tears.

What day was it? Had all this happened in one night? I was chilled to the bone as the fire was nothing but ashes.

CHAPTER THIRTY-ONE

I warmed myself with a cup of hot lemon water and apple spiced oatmeal. I jotted down the entire sequence. I wondered about Grandma Tula and her disappearing without a trace. The campground was deserted so there was no one to help me establish a time-line. I chose to let it go. I came here to return to the silence. I trust someone will come and get me if I over-stay my welcome.

I returned to the cove to pray with the Child's Sacred Pipe. As I began the sacred ritual once again, the ancient spirit grandfathers and grandmothers of each direction came to bear witness. I offered them the smoke in respect and gratitude. The Sacred Pipe smoked a long time for such a small bowl. Once ceremony was completed, I sat in silence holding the pipe bowl firmly to my heart.

I looked out over the lake and the sun emerged over the pine trees. Its rays cast a shimmering trail over the water in a direct line to the shore and I. The glow rippled through me. I felt the new day and a newness of life within me. I embraced this feeling with excitement.

An hour later, I trekked the trails with a burst of energy and anticipation. My walk was invigorating. With each step, I was gathering the energy from the trees, plants, the rocks, critters and everything that came in my path. I realized I was humming a tune that I did not recognize. It was a happy and airy tune. Quick bursts of high notes seemed to be calling me to something. I continued the tune throughout the walk, allowing it to lift me to new heights of awareness. When I arrived back at the cabin hours later, I realized I had missed eating my lunch.

I heated the can of stew and breathed in the aroma of the vegetables thanking each one for the sustenance they would give to me. I ate it slowly and savored its taste. The spices and the softness of the vegetables glided with ease down my throat. I ate slowly and sipped its broth-like gravy, allowing myself to be present as both I and the stew bonded in a nurturing balance.

Today was about taking care of my needs and learning to listen to my body in a new way. The experience from last night reminded me to care for and give love to me. It was important. It may be the reason I was called here in the first place.

I knew that a joyous feeling was filling my entire being as I took care of my needs. I was empowered and energized all at the same time. It was a feeling that I hadn't remembered in many, many years if truly ever. It was a feeling that became more comfortable throughout the day.

It felt good to take the time for me. I wanted to hold on to this presence of joy forever. I was reforming the circle within me slowly. I felt it happening even though I couldn't see it.

I spent the next hours until dusk in silence. I waited for more insights on the cocoon-like space that I experienced with the golden liquid and the initiation of the child I recognized as myself. There were so many things to understand, yet I knew it would all be understood in its own time. It was an experience that would somehow change me for the better.

At dusk, all kinds of birds began their communication. *Were they talking about their days events? Or about the morsels of food they ate? Or were they just welcoming each other home at the end of the day?*

They chatted excitedly and sang their end of day praises while I took the moment to bask in their wondrous sound. As the chatter died down, I began the ritual of building the fire. I praised and thanked each branch and log from the tree that gave its life for the fire and for its light and warmth.

The fire is like our inner flame and spirit. It can get out of control if too much is thrown at it or it can die out without attention and being fed. The trick is to feed and sustain it regularly to keep it balanced and nurtured.

Time passed and I saw that the flames were burning steadily. I realized the night had emerged and the stars above were in their full glory. Above me I had recognized the stars in the belt of Orion: Alnitak, Alnilam and Mintaka. A Hopi elder that I met in the southwest years earlier had said that his villages were built on the three mesas in alignment with the Orion's belt. Their ancient sky teachers said that it is where the Hopi people originated from. Other places such as Egypt and Mexico have such places that are said to be built in the Orion's belt alignment as well. There is so much to learn from the stars. Perhaps that is why ancient civilizations built buildings with their alignment.

I dozed off by the fire in my camp chair. I was startled when I felt the breath of a presence near my face.

"Sleeping already? You must be anxious to go into the pit tonight. You started without me?" Grandma Tula asked.

"No, I didn't go there. I was just resting."

I panicked. I didn't want her to think I did not appreciate her teachings and help.

"It's alright. Go and get the hot water," she said gently.

Her voice was softer and endearing, unlike the former evenings where she was short and to the point.

Again I retrieved the hot water. She nestled into my warm camp chair as I placed the cups on the wooden table. She placed a handful of mixed small dried flowers and leaves into the cotton bags and then placed them into each cup.

"Do you wonder why I sit in your chair every night?" she asked with an intense gaze.

"I guess it is because the seat is warmer and more comfortable." I replied.

"Wrong. It is because as I sit in the chair, I pick up the energy of your feelings and thoughts. You understand don't you? You read energy. In fact you have always been sensitive to people's thoughts and emotions. You have learned to clear yourself. Not allowing things to drain your energy."

"The problem with human beings is that they are not careful with their energy and their life force. We come into the world with only a certain amount of life force to live in our bodies. When it is up we drop our robes and live on in spirit. The body is precious because it is the vehicle to help us live and learn our lessons to evolve on the earth.

When we stress it with negative thoughts or emotions like anger, fear and hate, we deplete it and create uneasiness. When we abuse our bodies by neglect, excess or mental, emotional or spiritual negativity we slowly cut down our energy. Women especially do this by giving away all of their energy and repressing their thoughts and feelings. By their midlife they are depleted, unhappy, angry and anxious. Some women have never honored their own moon time of the feminine."

She continued, "My ancestors and tribal people have ceremonies to welcome each stage of life: birth, puberty, motherhood, menopause and becoming the elder. By honoring each stage with ritual, one recognizes and accepts the new stage and embraces it. Today women ignore it, fight it, and deny it. They lose themselves and their connection to the great mother within. They become disconnected from their bodies, true spirit and nature."

"Wonder why there is so much breast cancer? One of the reasons, but not the only one, is that women today give all their breasts away. Not in the physical feeding of the children for that is the natural way. Letting too many people feed off them while they suppress themselves. They deny their needs, care, worthiness and self-importance."

"Do not show your beauty as a woman or you are a prostitute and are asking for it. Do not show your emotions or you're a hysteric. Do not voice your opinion or you are bossy and irrational. Women do not even know what feminine means anymore. If women do not heal this within themselves, then how can we teach the men and our children to embrace their own softness, compassion and loving nature?" she asked as she shook her head with concern.

"You are in the cycle before menopause. The next years the bleeding will dry up and instead of releasing your power back to the earth you will keep it inside you, becoming wiser and in tune with yourself and with all around you. You need to reserve your energy for service to spirit. You have already given to others. Now it is time for you."

"I understand." I replied.

"Here, take your cup and drink the tea, four large sips," she coaxed.

When I drank the liquid there was no bitter or pleasant taste. In fact, there wasn't much taste at all.

"It may taste mild but its spirit is strong," she added.

As I relaxed and stared into the fire, a hole opened up in the flames and I was drawn into it. I felt myself floating downward in a counter clockwise spiral. This time I felt at ease. I accepted my fate willingly.

As I approached the bottom Grandma Tula was waiting for me by a fire and there were several other elder women standing in a half moon circle holding hands. They offered me a gourd of red liquid and showed me how to offer it to the earth. As they motioned, I looked up above into the dark abyss. A small sliver of light appeared and grew slowly. I recognized the cycles of the waxing moon as it grew. The elders sang a fluid tune over and over until it was embedded in my memory and I understood the ceremony and its eternal connection to the earth, the moon and myself. White cornmeal was offered for release and growth. The cycle would be repeated every month until I no longer bled and made the transition.

The wise women gathered in a circle that I had now become part of by holding the hands of Grandma Tula and White Swan. The song changed. It became softer, with no words and just a humming. As we held hands and swayed our bodies from side to side, the ground opened up and gave way. My body was swallowed as I slid into the earth. I closed my eyes and awaited my fate. My world was changing. Was I approaching my death?

"Trust," I heard in my mind, as I slid down to the bottom.

I was alone now. The elders had not made the trip with me. Lying there, I knew I had traveled many miles below the surface. There was no deeper I could go. This was the absolute bottom core. I shivered and started to shake - not from a physical chill but from a fracturing. Before me I could see a mirror of my own reflection. The mirror was smoky yet I could still see its image. It was the image of me, with all the flaws of my negative thoughts. Eventually the image changed to different ages and roles that I had become over the years to others: child, daughter, sister, co-worker, training coordinator, supervisor, ex-wife, teacher and consultant. Then it showed my shadow side: fearful, stubborn, impatient, resentful and inflexible. These were the qualities that I tried to hide. The mirror also reflected all of the light side of me: intuitive, supportive, empathetic, giving, loving, responsible, leader and generous.

The mirror was a powerful tool of truth. As I peered deeper and kept my gaze, the reflection showed an older woman, with long gray and white streaked hair. The body was plump and short. As her face came closer, I noticed its wrinkles and lines, like a road map of experiences. The face had spotted aged marks from the sun's potent rays.

I peered closer into the reflections over the aged eyes, there was an astonishing resemblance. The woman spoke to me softly and clearly.

"The time is coming for the years of the change. The spirit will look for peace and joy. It will search for transition and transcendence. Do not repress it. It is time to recognize that the red grandmother of birth and fertility and growth has left and the black grandmother of death, release and change has begun. It may take more years to complete. Then the cycle will transform you into me, the white grandmother, the wise sage, a woman of knowing and one of owning her power within and trusting its wisdom. No longer will you repress who you are; your needs and your internal knowledge of healing. You will rejoin the feminine spirit of oneness. You are in the breakdown cycle to transform the body, mind, heart and spirit. The body will change but you must transform and realign the mind and heart for the spirit's fulfillment."

I listened closely and I tried to recognize the woman and guess her age. She seemed ageless although there were bodily clues. Was she in her seventies or eighties?

"Who are you?" I asked. "Where am I?"

"I am you, the wise grandmother. You are in the "Honey Pit", the center of the womb of the feminine. All life has masculine and feminine within it to stay balanced. It is nature's law. A woman has a greater connection to the mother within her. That is why she bleeds and gives birth. The birth, death, rebirth cycle is in accordance with nature's laws. Only a woman can physically experience the cycle within her own body. She becomes the container for all life to be birthed. When she has completed this cycle and her body no longer releases life's sustaining blood of creation, she withholds this force of life within her body and gives it a creative force to use in other ways through the divine earthly harmonies of music, dance, writing, painting, crafting pottery or other objects, cultivating plants and studying a deeper knowledge of self through the stars. Each form of creative expression allows the

energy to flow through and into the world. You must choose the one that fulfills your spirit. This is the way to continue the cycle - by rebirthing for the next and final years of your life to fulfill your heart and soul's commitment. It is only at this stage that we can have the time to slow down and truly be free. This time does not have to be a time of sadness, fear, resentment and regret as many women feel. It should be a time of celebration and freedom in your life."

The signs were apparent in my body, as evidenced by many missed menstrual cycles that I had not paid much attention to. I was in the cycle of the end of the red grandmother and the dreamed moon ceremony from the tribal grandmothers was the way for me to transition slowly into the black grandmother.

"It has come time for you to remember and release the beliefs of your mind, the wounds of the heart and body, and the suppression of the spirit. That is why you have been called to the silence this week. It will take energy and time but it is what it will take for the heart and spirit to be transformed."

I became tired and my eyes felt heavy. The mirror fogged over and the presence had disappeared. A drop of the amber liquid fell upon my head. I lifted my eyes and opened my mouth. Its sweetness oozed down my throat, warmed and caressed my belly and slid deep into my womb. I was transforming from the inside out.

I remembered this sensation in my womb at one time in my life. It was there at my birth and slowly it dried and hardened over the years. Now it was being regenerated and ignited once again like a fire. The liquid energy continued to fill my being until I was feeling fluid and full.

Circles floated all around me - touching me and beginning to reform my essence. The old souls of the circles greeted me and shaped me back to my natural order.

Content, I fell into slumber as my body lay still. The sleep was regenerating me - repairing and changing me. I sensed the involuntary work of my body as the bubbles of air filled my lungs. The blood was pulsing and coursing through my veins as my heart beat in rhythm with the one eternal heartbeat. Aware subconsciously, I allowed the process to unfold.

CHAPTER THIRTY-TWO

I rested for what had seemed like an eternity. I could not move, caught in a spun web of crystalized shell. A fine threaded cocoon was built as I slept. Only my head could move slightly. I tried not to panic from the restriction and allowed my breath to rise and fall.

I waited a long time for the voice to return from the abyss. A small light like a firefly appeared above me blinking on and off. As it drew closer the soft voice once again spoke.

"You have reached the bottom and the place of knowledge and the gathering of the wise energy and commitment to your sacred self. The teachings of the ancient ways of death and rebirth are inside of you. It is time to listen to your body and inner knowing. You have reached the healing place within you. Clear out the sadness, guilt, shame and anger, the illusion of poor self-image and the swallowing of abuse from others and your own self. You hold the earth and sky within you and the inner rhythm to the natural flow."

"Your sacredness of the feminine knows your burning desires for fulfillment. Here, you can see through illusion to what is true. Gather your creative ability. Allow yourself to speak, express and acknowledge your needs and desires and take the steps to make it happen. Release the control and powers that you have given to others and detach from opinions and expectations of you. The time for change has come. The next stage of life is upon you. Honor the moon and your cycle in the way the grandmothers have shown you. It will bring you power and completion before the last cycle."

"If you have not been kind and loving to yourself, begin now. It is time to heal with the grandmothers as they teach you their way. Only then will you understand. For now, you are in the process of death but fear not, you will return to the pit again and again until you rebirth as the white grandmother."

It was all too much for me to understand. I was not scared but very tired. I had seen images and events of my life pass by and I recognized anger, shame, guilt and sadness. I allowed myself to remember and release. A primal scream sounded in my ears and as it got louder, I realized it was my own voice. The voice, buried deep within, was reestablishing itself. I could feel the strength and pain of my ancestors as the ongoing scream echoed around me. I remembered all I had done to repress my feminine. Hiding my changing body as a child and being fearful of calling attention to myself for fear of rape or being attacked. Fear of not being a good girl and winding up pregnant. I was afraid of not being pretty or desirable for a man, yet I didn't want to be seen as being too sexy. Not having my voice heard when a man tried to touch me. It was all so confusing. My instincts were to love and nurture myself and others, yet I was not to be selfish, but to put other's needs first and ahead of my own. You were only good if you were pleasing and giving to others. You needed to grin and bear it and not show anger or resentment. Stuff it down, swallow it, don't cry, and be strong. Don't feel or express your pain and dissatisfaction. You were to help others promote their dreams but not your own. It was tearing me apart as I screamed in confusion.

Sadness and rage engulfed me. Another scream escaped my lips shaking me to my core. I writhed and shook trying to release myself from the cocoon. Tears flowed and as I wept a tidal wave was being released from me. I was drowning as I released my emotions.

My consciousness was fading fast and it was all too much to bear. What is truth? What is illusion? It is so damn confusing. Somebody please help me. My mind was fracturing as the cocoon began to spin around me faster wrapping me tighter. I could no longer see through my eyes. As the web spun, complete darkness was approaching over my face. The small light in the distance was extinguished. Finally there was nothing but a void at the bottom of this pit. The silence was uncomfortable. Was this my last breath? Into the blackness I succumbed. Goodbye, Laurel.

CHAPTER THIRTY-THREE

In the dark my subconscious wandered as my spirit traveled backwards in time. I was seven-years-old. My body was changing. My breasts were growing and the hair was growing in places where it had not grown before. My mother sat me down to have a "grown up" talk.

"We need to get you a bra, Laurel. Your breasts are starting to show. It's time you learn about becoming a young woman."

"But Mommy, I'm only seven," I replied.

"Yes, but sometimes the body changes faster for some girls. I need to prepare you for what comes next," she added.

I was terrified. She told me about the menses and the proper use and disposal of the things that we did not speak of in public. She was thorough in her explanations, telling me that once one gets a period then they can become pregnant. So you must sit like a lady and no longer climb trees and rough house. She told me so many things my head was spinning and my stomach was sickened with the idea.

"I don't want a period," I rejected.

"You have no choice. This is what happens to a girl's body," she explained.

"Does a boy bleed?" I asked.

"No. His body changes in its own way. A girl bleeds because she has the ability to carry a baby. A boy doesn't."

"How does she get the baby," I asked.

She explained to me all the parts and where things went and then I was really sick. It was too much information for me to handle.

"Does it hurt when you bleed?" I asked.

"Yes, it hurts like a bad bellyache. Sometimes your back hurts and sometimes your breasts hurt but you get used to the pain. It is all a part of growing up."

"Well, I don't want it." I argued.

"It doesn't matter what you want, Laurel. It's going to happen whether you like it or not. You just have to bear it like every other woman. You get used to the pain. It's not that bad."

"I hate being a girl!" I screamed in disgust.

It was the first rejection of my sacred feminine self. I discarded the blessings of the sacred feminine at seven-years-old. I understood it as a great burden that had to be carried. The menses cycle made men uncomfortable and women ashamed. It was dirty and smelly and needed to be hidden. It was not celebrated or talked about. The body was not only a container for life but one that would be used and abused by men and our own selves. We learned to say no to be good and yes to please.

My spirit felt the pain that day. The little girl cried big girl tears of fear and the rejection of self. It would take years of rejecting myself to develop a deep and unconscious wound that took me until this moment to uncover.

My spirit floated forward to a time when I was eleven-years-old. My father was taking my young brother fishing, something that I used to do with him.

"Daddy, can I go?" I asked.

"Not this time, Laurel. You stay here with your mother and help her. I am taking Tommy. It's his turn to learn how to fish."

"But I used to go fishing with you." I pleaded.

"Yes, but now it's time to do girl things with your mother. You're too old now to be acting like a boy," he added.

I welled up with tears.

"Now Laurel, don't cry, you're too old for that. It's Tommy's turn to go fishing. We will be back soon," he said as they walked out the door.

"Laurel, stop crying. You're not a baby anymore. You're a young lady. Come help me with the dusting," my mother said as she handed me a rag.

I swallowed my tears, and wiped my eyes as I choked down the anger inside.

I hate being a girl.

My spirit floated forward again to a time when I was thirteen. One of the boys in my school was cornering the girls in the library against the book shelves and trying to feel their breasts. As he approached me and cornered me I was afraid. I put my hands up to resist but he was much stronger and he pinched my nipple and laughed. I pulled away and smacked him in the face and pushed him back. I ran to the principal and reported him. None of the other girls stood up with me. I was told that it was my fault and I must have had led him on. I had on a bulky turtle neck and my skirt was way below my knees. How much more did I need to cover?

Her reply was, "boys will be boys". I got detention for slapping him. I raged inside once again.

I hate being a girl.

Again I moved forward in time to nineteen-years-old.

I was visiting my maternal grandmother. My aunt and uncle also happened to stop by for a visit. As I greeted them, my uncle by marriage kissed me and slid his tongue into my mouth. I bit down hard. He yelled. My aunt asked what happened. He said nothing. I said nothing. What could I say, your husband tried to kiss me in a way that felt uncomfortable. I stuffed my fear and rage down again.

I hate being a girl.

I hated the attention and the burden of having to fight all the time for my body. I feared one day I would not be strong enough to fight back.

My spirit moved ahead even further in time to twenty-eight-years old. The first time I felt true passion in my body. The man I was dating was tender and caring. He was gentle and patient. He tended to my needs first. It was a wonderful experience. As time went on he wanted a baby and a wife. I wanted neither. I wasn't ready. I wanted to travel to places I had never seen. We both wanted different things in life. The relationship ended and it broke my heart. Why did he want so much from me?

I hate being a woman.

I reviewed many scenes throughout my life. This last one was the one that held the most pain. It was when I was thirty-seven and engaged to Blake. I knew how that ended, so I fast forwarded through it. I heard *the comments from others whispered into my ear like a painful mid-December wind. "It's about time, Laurel. You are practically an old maid. You know you are not getting any younger. This may be your last chance."*

As quickly as the relationship began, I married him; I left him and divorced him.

I hate being a woman.

*All this suffering and hate towards being a woman started at the age of seven. All the framework of a woman's life is imbedded in her from society's rules and misconception and their own maternal lineage of suffering. Where and when will it ever end? When will the love return to the women? When will their sacredness return? When can they be honored and adored for what they give and bring to the human world? Only when, **"they" love being a woman.***

With this understanding, my spirit and consciousness returned and my travels for now were complete.

CHAPTER THIRTY-FOUR

The crow cawed and I awoke slumped in the chair. I was exhausted. My chest was sore. It felt battered and bruised. The crust on my cheeks revealed the dried tears that I had shed. My body was stiff as if I had been wrapped and bound for days. I wondered again what day it was. I was weak and vulnerable. I needed to shower and eat.

Once I ate, I knew it was time to sleep. I did not want to think. I needed to escape. I was drowsy and could barely keep my eyes open. I decided to honor my body and crawled into bed. The sun was up and it felt strange to sleep in the daytime, but my eyes and body could no longer stay awake. I crawled and nestled under the soft fleece blanket. I was asleep before my head hit the pillow.

The ceremony began. They purified their bodies with sage and cedar smoke. The circle of women offered their blood to the earth with white cornmeal prayers. They burned the sweet grass and offered it to the moon. One by one they danced in a spiral, first clockwise and then counter clockwise. They sang their chant with loud voices rising and falling in time with their turtle rattles. The small center fire danced as they sang. They were gathering up power from the earth and the moon, restoring and remembering their sacredness within and loving their own sacred body. Their hearts were expanding and opening. They danced for all women and empowered the sacred feminine upon the earth, to be embraced by all those who desired to remember.

I saw the power move through their energy fields into their bodies and hearts and it was overwhelming. It was gentle but strong. It had no limits and was endless. It was creative and it was nurturing.

An elder approached me and offered me her hand. I joined them in the circle. I began to dance by moving my arms and feet with grace. The wind picked up and the fire's flames rose higher. The fire danced with us. The wind blew the memories away. The earth rose to meet our bodies and the moon gave us her light. We, as women, could receive this power and could access it at any time for it was stored within us. I laughed and I soared. My spirit, heart and body connected in union. As I twirled around and around the power rose through me from the earth to the moon and then back down from the moon to earth. I was the channel through which it flowed. I could feel it inside. My womb was full. I remembered who I was in my body and spirit.

*I shouted loudly for all to hear, "**I love being a woman!**"*

A knock on my door woke me from my deep sleep. It was dark. I had slept all day.

I wrapped the blanket around me and opened the side door. No one was there. Again the knock jolted me. It was coming from the front door. I opened the door and the fire pit was glowing.

"Come to the fire. We need to talk," Grandma Tula demanded. Her silhouette could barely be seen.

"Do we need hot water for tea?" I asked.

"No. Not tonight," she answered.

She sat there patiently as I lowered myself into the chair.

"You are beginning the death process. Do you remember last night?" she asked.

"Yes, the memories of my childhood." I replied.

"You have started the healing process. Release your old beliefs and wounds, the ones that you carry from your maternal lineage, the ones that society has imposed and the ones from your own personal experiences that limit you."

"This is a time of change during the death process. For you, it will be earlier than most, since you began your cycles very young. This process can be painful or it can be liberating as your bleeding cycles become less over the coming year. It is time to heal by continually returning to the pit within you. Reconnect to the wisdom that has always been inside you. The sacred feminine is your birthright. It is an understanding, the desire of your spirit. You were created to feed your spirit and express it to the world. Like most women, you have long forgotten the connection to the grandmother within."

She continued on, "As you laid in the darkness and stillness you were in your honey pit, the center inside you. You are more than the titles others gave to you. You are connected to the sacred balance made from the great source itself. The balance has changed over the generations. The sacred masculine has dominated because the women have given over their sacredness of the internal grandmother."

"They need to remember who they really are... the heart people. They have lost their hearts. They give no nurturing or sustenance to their own sacred selves. There is balance of the feminine all around you in nature, the sun and the moon and the earth and the sky. Every part of masculine has its counterpart of feminine. There is no life without it. When women come to mid-life they have given so much to others and they have rejected and dishonored themselves. They are teaching their children that women deserve nothing, should ask for nothing and are nothing. So they reject their own internal power of the grandmother."

"One has to be the woman and balance the masculine - not be the masculine and lose the feminine. Both are needed. One is not better than the other, yet only a woman can bring forth and be the vessel for life to continue."

"The circle of grandmothers has been coming to you in your dreams and visions. They are giving you the initiation. They will give you the way to help yourself and other women find and connect to the sacred again. You will pass through several tests. The women's ceremony vision quest was the first. This week is the second, answering the internal call to the silence. In the autumn you will come back here again for the third. You must listen to the voice within you now. It will be getting stronger and clearer. The grandmothers will teach you the way to heal yourself throughout the next years. Listen and follow. They will never lead you astray."

I listened carefully to her words. I wondered what was to come next.

"May I ask a question?" I asked still reminded of my mind's concern.

Grandma Tula nodded in reply.

"Can you tell me the names of the herbs I have taken? They were very powerful plant spirits." I said.

"There are many plants but the medicine you will work with will be only seven plants. You have taken five. They will work on your own spirit, body and mind for now. Then you will be introduced to the last two in the fall. It will become your special medicine. The herbs will reveal themselves to you all in due time," she replied.

"Why won't you tell me?" I asked.

"Once you become strong in their medicine energy they will speak to you and teach you themselves, but not now. A healer must connect and know the spirit of the plant's medicine to understand their use. You cannot understand this from a book. Yes, a plant will work to alleviate symptoms, but to do real healing, the spirit of the plant must be one with the healer so that it will transfer its sacred power. You will not only learn the Grandmother's Way but understand your spirit's calling and purpose," she replied.

I watched the fire as we sat in silence for a while. I was remembering the last six days, revisiting every moment and the experience of the power of each plant.

The first herb made me sleepy, *a relaxant*. The second herb made my stomach sick, *a purging*. The third herb brought up sadness and fear, *a cleansing*. The fourth herb brought up the darkness and wound, *a purification and ending*. The fifth herb brought me to my sacred self, *a healing*.

These five plants had energies and powers that created movement within me. The *spirit* of the plant was ingested the same way as the physical part of the plant. The power of healing was really in the spirit of the plant, its true life force. I was beginning to understand from personal experience but there was much more to learn.

"You will leave tomorrow and you will return here again in the autumn. Prepare for a four day vision quest in the next few months. You have done well. The grandmothers will work with you in vision and dreams and in the next months you will receive two more Sacred Pipe bundles. They will be in addition to the original one from many years ago and one placed in your care more recently. Each will have a different purpose. They will reveal their purpose when the time is right. Love them, honor them and keep them safe. Let us now make ceremony with the Child Sacred Pipe."

I was surprised. I had not told her of the bundle. I was uncomfortable because I had not smoked it with anyone other than myself. I hesitated, uncomfortable with myself and my abilities. I had the proper teaching and it was blessed. I had bonded with the bundle but still I was worried about running ceremony with an elder observing.

"This is not about your ego, Laurel. It is about Spirit's calling. You have been trained and given the right to perform ceremony for those that Spirit places in your path. You did not ask for this path. No one who is in their right mind would ever ask. Spirit has gifted you with the memory of the sky nations, the vision of the spirit world and the understanding and sensing of the energy in every living thing. These things are not taught. These are things you are born with and gifted from the Great Spirit itself. It is for you to choose to fulfill your purpose or not. I am here to guide you to the next level into the elder stage, the Grandmother's Way. You must clean out the old self and through this process you will know how to help other women."

I nodded understandingly. I was exactly where I needed to be. Everything in my life was in accordance with this present moment. I placed the sage in the shell and lit the smoke, fanning it to clear myself and the bundle. I offered the shell to Grandma Tula to smudge herself.

I began the ritual and Grandma Tula closed her eyes and rocked back and forth. I filled the small bowl with the tobacco and prayers honoring the directions. I offered it to her to hold and speak her prayers in the traditional way. She cradled it with her hands, left hand on the bowl and right hand on the small stem. She held it up pointing to the night sky.

"Oh Great Spirit, keeper of the stars and creator of all life, I honor you, the sky, the four great winds, the earth mother below and the spirit within me and all of life that connects us together. I pray in gratitude for allowing me to help this special woman. You have given her blessings and gifts that others do not understand. She will need tough skin to bear it all but she will do good work here. She does not fully understand the power you have bestowed to her but as she steps into it may she use it wisely, compassionately and courageously. I ask for her teachings and healings to be gentle in this next stage of life. May she be blessed with good health and a happy spirit, aho."

She ended her prayer and handed the Sacred Pipe back to me. I honored the directions with the smoke from the pipe. We both took a turn smoking the tobacco and it seemed to smoke forever. When I finally finished smoking, Grandma Tula sang a song in a low chant. She asked that I sing it with her. As I memorized the tune and sang it there was an empowerment that I felt inside of me. It was nurturing, yet a strong energy. As we sang each round, the energy was building inside of me. On the last round, I felt myself lift and connect to the stars and the moon. A flash appeared in the sky and I was consumed by it, swirling upward and being pulled higher and higher from the earth. I heard Grandma Tula's voice as the flash had consumed my sight.

"The moon is your power to bring down to the earth. You are able to reach dimensions far beyond this earth. You can travel anywhere you need. Call upon this power. See you soon."

My consciousness was back on earth with the Child's Sacred Pipe in hand. Grandma Tula was nowhere in sight. My body was not grounded. I was still light as a feather. I wrapped the bundle and stood up to connect to the earth while moving my legs and feet side to side.

The sky was cresting its first glimpse of light. I thought about her asking me to prepare for a four day vision quest. A vision quest ceremony is personal. It is done to ask for guidance, direction to a very important question, one that can only be answered by a higher power. One prepares themselves by gradually fasting from food and water increasing time slowly until you have prepared your body for a full four days without food or water. It is not a ceremony that is taken without serious preparation and consideration. Each day of preparation begins with prayer at sunrise. During the fast, tobacco and prayers fill robes the size of your fist to honor each of the seven directions and their different colors. And many smaller tobacco prayer ties are strung together to place outside around the area that one will be sitting and standing to create a protected and sacred space for the vision quest. It is a quiet, reflective spiritual ceremony. If one has prepared, committed and is lucky, the Great Spirit, animals or spirit helpers may bring some insight to your question.

But why was Grandma Tula telling me to prepare? What question did I have that needed answering? Then it came to me. I wanted to know the plants that Grandma had given to me. Was this the way they would be revealed?

By early afternoon I would be back home reviewing the week's events. Much had happened and even more had been revealed. I was exhausted from my emotions and mentally worn from trying to understand all that I had experienced. There was one thing that I did know. I would be returning to these woods in the autumn.

CHAPTER THIRTY-FIVE

When I returned home again I needed to sleep. I took a nap in the late afternoon and it lasted until two o'clock in the morning. This would become my new schedule for a while. I awoke every morning at two o'clock to pray with the grandmothers. It was as if my sleep would abruptly end and I would hear my name being called to wake up.

The programs in the schools continued. I was now traveling further away in Massachusetts and Connecticut to teach. Some were places I had never been to before.

I met a wonderful woman through my friend Lisa Parker, who wanted to use her land for a spiritual and community purpose.

Sharon Perkins was a nature loving woman who was very in tune with her land. She was a tree woman. The birches, the pines, the evergreens and the elms that surrounded her fifteen acres were her children. She felt the land was offering itself as a hidden space for a prayer circle or gathering.

Two months prior to meeting her, I had a dream about a former native teacher who had passed into spirit. Two Beavers asked me to lead a medicine wheel prayer circle. He had taught me years ago and I had been part of his seasonal gatherings for four years prior to his passing. With the blessing and permission from his tribe's newest leader, I embarked on teaching about the medicine wheel through the prayer circle at my friend Cathy White's apartment.

The apartment was becoming too small to seat the increased number of people who wanted to come and pray. So Sharon's offering to use the land for an outside prayer circle, once a month on a Sunday afternoon was perfect. Several in the group helped with the set up for the gathering. The space was perfect. From May until the end of October the group came together. It slowly increased to about thirty people. I had no idea it would last for four years. Sharon was very happy to be able to use the land to help people and build a community of support for herself and others.

In June, before my trip back to Sundance in Texas, Sharon asked me to come for tea. As we sat and chatted, she went into another room and retrieved a package wrapped in wool cloth.

"Laurel, I am not sure of the Native American customs. I was in a trading post on the Mohawk Trail and seen this Sacred Pipe displayed in a glass case. I knew instantly I needed to purchase it and gift it to you. In my mind I could see you leading ceremony for people with it. I couldn't leave the store without out it. I know it might seem crazy but I needed to follow my heart," she said.

I opened the red wool and found the stem and bowl of the Sacred Pipe. The bowl and stem were much larger than the Child's Sacred Pipe. The red clay bowl had four rings around the top to represent the four winds. The stem was made of sumac and measured about fifteen inches. I was overwhelmed with gratitude and thanked her.

"Sharon, thank you. It is beautiful and I am honored." I said as I hugged her.

We finished our tea and I placed the Sacred Pipe carefully into my vehicle to travel home.

I would ask to have it blessed by Chief Lone Elk at Sundance this year. It was a special day with Sharon - one that bonded us in a special long-time friendship.

I called Granny Janice and told her about the new Sacred Pipe. She offered to talk to the Chief about blessing it on my behalf. He agreed if I came a day early.

When I arrived at Sundance, I brought many gifts for Chief Lone Elk who would perform the sacred blessing of the new bundle before the dance began. It was a very special and touching purification ceremony. The spirits spoke to the Chief and provided information that this bundle was an Earth Sacred Pipe. He gifted me a small tuft feather to tie on the stem. I was honored and humbled by it all.

Being my third year as a supporter, I had befriended many people throughout the camps. The smells of burning cedar and sage over the coals that kept the energy sacred pleased my senses, and the supporters' purification ceremonies led me back to connect to ancient times.

Once the dance began, the energy started to move and the supporters began their duties in the camp. By the third day the dancers were struggling and having a hard time. The temperature was 118 degrees. There was not a cloud or breeze in sight. No mercy for the dancers. The sun was strong for three full days. Chief Lone Elk sent word to each camp to ask all the supporters to come to the arbor to pray for the dancers because they were having a hard time.

Within twenty minutes, over five hundred people were standing outside the circle singing along with the drummers to give energy to the dancers. Within minutes, clouds blew in overhead to mask the sun and a gentle breeze blew in to give comfort. The amazing effects of prayer and ceremony will always be a mystery to me.

Granny Janice picked up her feet and started to dance stronger with the other dancers. The energy continued until the end of the dance.

My favorite part of the dance is at the end, being able to shake the hands of every dancer as they leave the Mystery Circle. I thank them for their prayers for the people and their commitment to the ceremony. In their eyes I see the suffering, the sacrifice, the joy of completion, the gratitude for this way to pray and gratitude to the supporters. It always brings me to tears to see the sacredness inside them. I honor all of them that keep the old tradition of those who suffered and endured so much to keep the ceremony alive.

After the feast and before I left for home, Granny Janice once again gifted me for supporting her dance. She opened the cedar box that her husband made by hand, pulled out the Sundance fan she had used in the ceremony and then gifted both the fan and box to me.

"Laurel, I am gifting this to you because Spirit tells me that you will need it for ceremony. It has the sacred energy of Sundance for healing. Use it well. I love you," she said.

"I love you too, Gran." I choked in a whimper.

The trip home the next day was long. I had two, three hour lay-over connection flights. But by the end of the day, I was home safe and sound. Year three of my commitment to Sundance support was complete.

CHAPTER THIRTY-SIX

The rest of the summer was devoted to clients, prayer circles and my daily smoking of the new Earth Sacred Pipe Bundle from Sharon. Everything in, of and on the land was to be prayed for with it. It held a grounded energy, one that was clear and centered.

My devotion to the spiritual path that I had been on for many years was evolving quickly. This new bundle became the third.

I was being called upon and asked to lead one-on-one Sacred Pipe ceremonies for many different reasons. Some were for people who needed to ask for healing; others for people who had passed or for blessing newborns. People somehow found me. Ceremony for me is private and not something you speak or talk about in the open. Through the gathering at the monthly prayer circles, Spirit found a way for people to find help.

Sharon had no idea how important the Earth Sacred Pipe would become to the people. I blessed her every time I pray with it.

I met a lovely elder named Nettie Scott who owned a bison farm, through a woman who attended the prayer gatherings. She had a large parcel of farmland that her husband and son managed and a small store that sold the crafts of the local Native Americans, as well as bison meat from the farm. Her animals were treated humanely and with care. It was a small local business that offered meat especially for the native people - bison meat was better for the health conscious. It had more protein and less fat than beef.

Nettie was a small woman with a bright smile. She had beautiful blue eyes and pure white hair. Her eyes sparkled as she spoke to me like an old friend she had known all her life. She had a gentle sweet spirit. We talked in her store for two hours. In that time not one customer came in to interrupt us.

She asked about having an outside prayer circle gathering next year on her land upon the large hill. I agreed to pray on it and if it was meant to be, it would happen with Spirit's guidance. I also offered my assistance if she ever needed anything. At that point her smile changed to concern.

"Laurel, I have been having a hard time recently. I am struggling with a relationship with one of my friends. It is really bothering me. I am trying so hard to forgive and move forward, could you pray for me?" Nettie asked.

"I would be happy to pray for you but would you like to pray *with* me?" I offered. "I could bring the Sacred Pipe and we could pray together in your home." I explained.

"Oh yes, would you do that for me?" she spoke as her eyes filled with tears.

"Yes, I believe that is why my friend has led me to you." I responded.

I returned the following day to perform the ceremony with her.

As I began, I could feel the presence of a spirit helper beside me. Her presence was gentle as she guided me through the healing part of the ceremony. As Nettie smoked the Sacred Pipe I could see her body relax and her tearful emotions begin to subside. Her breath became slow and easy.

When the ceremony came to an end, Nettie thanked me and offered me some tea and food. As I had always been taught, I offered a little of the food outside to the spirits of the plant and animals that gave their life for the food we were about to eat and to the Great Spirit and guides in gratitude for their help.

We ate and chatted. She asked about my life and how I came to ceremony. I told her about many of my teachers throughout the years including Black Deer who had given me my first Sacred Pipe and how he had trained me and placed me on my first vision quest. We chatted about the many years I was with him in ceremony. He explained that the spirits told him I was to be trained in the ceremonial ways and if I accepted Spirit's call, he would teach me.

I had never told anyone before, but today I told Nettie that I was called to ceremony as a young child. I had seen myself leading ceremonies but there were things I didn't understand at the time. So after graduating high school, I traveled and met many elders, received many teachings and participated in many ceremonies. I was very grateful for all of my travels and the teachings I received.

The ceremonies were not something you talked about in public. You don't want to draw attention to yourself in an egotistic way. They were to be provided when Spirit led the people to me in one way or another and gave me the confirmation to help them. It was both a privilege and a responsibility to serve others. You needed to keep yourself in devotion and clean and clear of alcohol or drugs to be ready to serve at a moment's notice. Only now many years later, I began to serve the people with the Sacred Pipe ceremony.

Nettie rose from the kitchen table and said, "Would you excuse me for a minute, Laurel?"

I nodded, "Sure."

She returned holding a large pillow case that had something inside of it.

As she began to speak, I felt a rush of tears well up in my eyes. I had no idea why. The energy of what was in the pillow case was having a profound effect on me.

"Years ago, I was out west and I happened to walk into a Native American trading post. The Indian man was very nice. I told him about my farm and how I would like to buy a few of his lovely authentic crafts to sell in my store. We talked for a while and I chose a few items to purchase. As I was getting ready to leave he asked me to wait a minute," she continued. "He gave me what is in this pillow case. He told me a story about a medicine woman who had engaged him to make her a Sacred Pipe."

I could feel my body surge with energy as she spoke.

"He explained to me that as he was making it and praying he realized it did not belong to her. He kept seeing a woman in the east conducting many ceremonies and be the one who would take care of it and serve the people. When the medicine woman came and asked about the Sacred Pipe, he did not have the heart to tell her that he could not give it to her.

159

So he put her off until he could find the right woman to give it to. He asked me to take it back east and find the right person."

Nettie looked at me with tears in her eyes.

"Laurel, I am sure the woman he made this for is you. I have kept it all these years and almost forgot about it until just now. I have met many Indian people over the years and I know you have distant Indian lineage and have been trained and taught the right way. I know this precious sacred object is for you to take care of and use for the good of people. I gift this to you to complete the man's vision."

She handed it to me ever so gently, like a newborn. I removed it from the pillow case. It was a large ceremonial Sacred Pipe - much larger than the one Sharon had gifted me. Both bowl and stem were separated as is customary. There were two small feathers that were placed inside the red wool that the stem was wrapped in. The stem was decorated with thick buffalo fur and meticulously colored beading. It was beautifully crafted with love and sacredness.

I thanked and hugged her. My voice cracked as I spoke.

"Nettie, I was told years ago by an elder Red Horse, in a purification lodge that I would receive a Buffalo Sacred Pipe, but the first one I received from my teacher, Black Deer was not it. The second one was the Child's Sacred Pipe, and the third bundle was the Earth Sacred Pipe. I forgot all about it until this moment. I guess it wasn't time until now. Thank you, Nettie for fulfilling his prophecy."

I have learned over the years that things follow a divine plan, and if you are paying attention, you may find that life can be full of mystical surprises. This new bundle would be the fourth sacred being or child that would need caretaking. The intensity of my life was increasing, bringing me deeper and deeper into the sacred ceremonial life.

CHAPTER THIRTY-SEVEN

The school year began again in September and I received phone calls from schools to rebook my programs. I had intentionally left an open week in October for my return to the campground to see Grandma Tula.

I prepared for a vision quest as she requested. I fasted and prayed up to four days in the last months. Each fast was more difficult as the length of fasting was increased. Many times I cried tears of compassion for those people in the world who were truly starving. My sacrifice was only temporary and I knew there would be food to eat when my fast ended. Many people in the world did not have that luxury. My prayers during the fast were directed to those who were starving and I asked Spirit to find a way for that hunger to be filled. Each month I donated can goods to the local food bank. I was doing my part to help. Prayer is good but action is necessary.

During the fasts, I made the necessary tobacco prayer tie preparations that were required for a vision quest altar as I had been taught years before. Since Grandma Tula gave me no instructions other than to return in the fall and to be prepared, I followed the knowledge I knew.

The Buffalo Sacred Pipe was blessed by Red Horse. Unexpectedly, he was in the New England area for a few days before attending an intertribal conference. I had supported ceremonies for his community out west and he told me that one day I would have my own community. He was the one who foretold about the Buffalo Sacred Pipe coming years before. It was an honor to have him bless the Sacred Pipe from his vision. He said that Spirit was leading the way for me and to be open to the path that the Great Mystery was providing.

He was happy to see that Spirit's words had come to fruition from many years ago. The purification ceremony and its blessing were powerful. I gave the elder the traditional gifts plus a gift card. Although the elder was seventy-eight his mind and abilities showed no signs of wear and tear. I was humbled and in awe of the chance to be in ceremony with him again.

The next week of scheduled children's programs went well. Both the children and I had fun. The students embraced the understanding of being connected to all things and even learned to be kinder and gentler with the earth, their pets and each other. The teachers remarked that the children were becoming calmer and kinder as each new class of students learned from the program. I was happy that these young minds might make a positive difference in the world because of teachings from the Native American Indian elders.

It was fulfilling work for my heart and soul. It allowed me to pay my bills and at the same time give food donations and send small monetary donations to my former teachers, as a giveaway in gratitude for their teachings and the healings that I had received. As the children listened to the stories and the social songs, they learned about diversity and acceptance - something that was not being taught in history books.

My schedule was balanced with clients for flower essence consultants, classes and prayerful preparation for the vision quest. The time passed quickly and the month of October arrived.

I returned to the campground. It was the last week they were open for the year and again I would be basically alone for the week with enough wood for daily fires.

It was amazing to me how many people in the world would be afraid to be alone by themselves for a week in the woods. Yet I loved it. I soaked up the energy of the trees and the lake and the scent of wood smoke from the fire. For me it was like a homecoming, a safe place of tranquility and oneness. Some people flock to the mountains, some to the seashore, but for me, the lake and woods was my place of refuge.

I unpacked my car and brought the food, bedding and other supplies into the cabin. Before dusk, I had enough time for a walk on the trails.

As I walked among the white and red pines, their aromas filled me with peace. The trails were barely visible from the beds of pine needles, acorns and pine cones. It was autumn and the leaves from the mighty oaks covered the paths.

An hour later I returned to the cabin, ate a light meal and started the fire, and awaited Grandma Tula to find me.

I thought about our meeting last April and all that had transpired. This quest I was called to bring the Earth Sacred Pipe bundle that Sharon had gifted to me. There was a knowing that this was the one to be brought to pray with this week. As the sky became dark and the fire was burning bright, I began clearing myself and preparing myself to pray with the Sacred Pipe. I was deep in prayer when I heard the rustling of the leaves coming up the path. *Was it a critter or was it the elder?* I was not sure but continued in prayer. A brief flash across the sky drew me from my prayer. *Was it lightening or was it a falling star?* It was so quick that I only saw it out of the corner of my eye.

I finished the ceremony and wrapped and secured the bundle. I kneeled on the earth which was now wet with dew, and looked up at the stars in the sky in awe, believing that the earth could not be the only place with life on it.

I heard a low voice humming in the distance. It was soft and soothing. It was getting louder from the direction of the path. Out of the woods she appeared. Her previous cane was now a large staff with feathers and beading.

She wore a white cotton dress and was wrapped in a black ribbon fringed shawl. She stood there looking me over and peering right through me.

"You came back. Good for you. You are committed and devoted. That's why I am here. You will be my last one," she said with heaviness.

"I will be the *last one*?" I asked.

"The last person that I will pass the teachings to," she replied.

I looked at her blankly but she just sighed.

"You will understand in time. Don't rush. Just focus," she added.

"Please bring me a cup of hot water," she said gently.

I returned with the cup. She put the dried root in the cotton bag and placed it in the cup.

"Let this steep a few minutes. It will help with the purification. How have you been the last few months?" she asked.

"I have been busy, teaching classes and helping clients. I am being of service and supporting myself," I answered.

"Have you been growing and healing? You experienced a lot the last time we were together. You worked with the element of earth. You submerged into her womb and met the ancients in ceremony. Have you seen them again?"

"Yes, when I smoke in ceremony." I replied.

"It is time for you to begin. Drink the tea now. It is ready," she coaxed.

I drank the tea in four large gulps. A warm flutter surged within me and caused me to perspire. I doused the campfire with water to put it out.

As I wiped my brow, Grandma Tula grabbed my arm and led me down the darkened path. I looked for the cove's edge but it seemed that we were going deeper into the woods. I felt my feet shuffle and rustle the leaves. I could smell wood smoke. I tried to speak but the words just fumbled inside me and then disappeared from my brain. We came upon a small fire and a small dome lodge covered in large animal skins. This was where Grandma Tula would perform purification ceremony for me.

The small frail woman pulled one large stone, twice the size of a human head from the fire and placed it inside the pit in the lodge. She removed her shawl and crawled in.

"Take your outer clothes off. Leave your shirt and skirt on and come on in," she called.

I crawled in on my hands and knees, acknowledging all of my relations.

The large, lone stone took up the entire pit. It was giving off overwhelming heat. Grandma Tula had a large gourd bucket filled with water and another small gourd to pour the sacred water upon the stone. She closed the door flap and we were encased in complete darkness. She began her calling song and started the purification prayer. As she sang I was transported to another time.

My eyes were clearly open and present yet the inside of the lodge had transformed into a dark cave. As she poured water gently over the stone, the cave filled with a dim light. I could see ancient drawings on the walls and there appeared four elder women seated in a small circle, one of which was White Swan. They were wearing black shawls. Their eyes were piecing right through me. They sang a tune that seemed familiar yet I did not really know it. As they sang I began to rock my body back and forth on the ground beneath me. The song was soothing and yet emotional. I was being brought to tears. I allowed myself to weep.

"You are in the deepest waters. We are at the bottom of the sea. Our great connection to the element that sustains all of life," the four women spoke in unison.

I was transported out of the cave. We were swimming underwater, like the mammals of the oceans. They led me into another small cave under the sea. Inside the cave other women were seated and waiting in a larger circle. They were wrapped in shawls. Some shawls were red, some were black and others were white. I was asked to sit within the circle. My head began to pulse. I had to lie down. I felt my womb stir and become cramp - not painful but slightly uncomfortable.

White Swan came forward and placed a starfish upon my forehead and ran it down my body. It was an unusual sensation but it relieved the discomfort in my head and womb. As they sang I felt my body being cleansed inside and out. Waves and rippled sensations were moving through me as if I was floating on water. I relaxed and let the watery sensation rock me back and forth gently, comforting me.

"Water is sacred. It is a part of your life's blood. The white grandmother brings forth life and then the red grandmother transforms the woman to allow the body to birth physical life through her and to the earth. The black grandmother helps the water recede and eventually dry up. No longer does the woman give her flow to the earth or birth human life, but holds it within herself to sustain her own needs. Then the white grandmother returns to rebirth and helps a woman to know when to share her voice and wisdom with others. The water ebbs and flows. That is the cycle of the sea and all life and it is the cycle that is within your body. The water will cool you down as the changes make you overheat. The emotions need to be purged and cleansed. The water within you dries up and your body changes to the black shawl grandmother, until the white grandmother returns to rebirth you. All the shadows and wounds will be released with ease. The power of truth will allow your illusions to fade so that you can move into your purpose.

You will experience this and then help other women to understand and take their own journey."

I lay there as they rattled the shells back and forth over my body. My body was awakened with energy and at the same time being put to sleep. The white starfish was placed upon my heart and my consciousness began to float upwards above the sea to the sky.

The sun was shining and the sky was the color of a robin's egg. The clouds were moving quickly and effortlessly through the sky. I immersed myself within the cloud as the wind blew me gently across the sky. I was floating on the thermals as if I were a large bird. The wind began to pick up and I was being pushed harder. My mind was racing from the fear of falling and losing control of my being. The power of the wind was beyond my control. It was strong, and relentless. I felt myself spinning in a spiral gust, twirling with a great intake and exhale of breath.

"Allow the wind to blow through you to release what is no longer needed and allow the change and transformation to take place," the words came from somewhere inside of me.

I relaxed and breathed slowly in and out as old memories and illusions came to my mind to release. I went with the spiral of wind around me. Once again I felt myself being spun into a great cocoon lifting me higher in the sky.

The wind had died down and the air was quiet. I was suspended in a cocoon of soothing white light. I could feel things changing both in and outside of me. A warm glow turned into a fiery heat. I felt the sweat trickle from my skin and loosen the cocoon around me. I began to unravel. The heat expanded and the emotions exploded. I wanted to tear open the rest of the cocoon that held me. As I tugged and pulled off the last of the fibers, I was startled by a voice.

"The fire that burns inside of you is your eternal flame. No longer will it be held back and limited. No longer can fear, anger and sadness hold you back. The fire can burn things to ash and rebuild you by reminding you of your spirit's path. The next phase is about fulfillment, nurturing the seed within you. Its transformation is to be sprung forth into the world through your wisdom."

I was feeling much cooler now. I returned to consciousness and awakened to the reality of my body sitting outside in the woods on a blanket in the middle of a vision quest altar, surrounded by the prayer ties I had made over the last months. *How did I get here?* The last I remembered, it was night and I was in a purification lodge with Grandma Tula. At present I was in the light of day. I stood up and began praying to each of the directions for guidance and to give thanks. I asked to understand the unraveling of what was transpiring in my life. I asked that my heart, mind, body and spirit be transformed in a gentle way.

As I sat within the altar, the small birds came and sang their praises. The crows and blackbirds made their presence known as well. The day went by slow and was uneventful. By the end of the day, the geese and ducks journeyed from the lake to their evening place. I spent each day in prayer and gratitude and paid attention to everything and anything in the present moment. The days and nights were fairly quiet. I was in a heightened awareness by the fourth day. There was no question I had reached an altered state of consciousness. Everything had slowed down, my eyes were heavy and my body was completely relaxed. By nightfall, the hours of the last four days had merged into one blurry state of time.

The light in the sky shining through the trees that I thought was the moon was growing bigger and brighter. There was no sound just a wave of static electricity in the air as the white light became a bluish glow above me. A putrid sulphur smell was trickling down through the air.

I became very sleepy and could barely keep my eyes open. I experienced the sensation of floating in the air and being carried away. It overwhelmed me and I was unable to speak or move. My body felt paralyzed.

As the feeling dissipated, I became aware of three blonde-haired humans with their backs to me in a gray metallic room. The room seemed slanted as if I was standing at an angle. They turned to face me and I noticed their eyes. They were translucent blue. No dark pupils or white, just solid blue that seemed to glow and reach right into me.

I realized they were not human yet their tall form resembled mine. Their hair was long and flowing but I could not tell if they were male or female. They had softness and a gentle air about them. I did not feel threatened but I wondered where I was and why I was here. They looked directly into my eyes and I could hear their voices even though their small mouths were not moving.

"You know us. We are your family. We are from the same place, before you were human. You have incarnated on this star called earth this time. Do you remember your home in the Pleiades? Each night you look up to the sky and search for it and when you find the cluster of stars you feel comforted because you are remembering."

It was true I would look to the night sky many times and when I found the direction and the area of the seven sisters, I felt calm and relaxed as if a knowing had taken place. *How could they know this?*

"You have had encounters, have you not?"

I shrugged.

"We have come to help you make peace with your encounters."

The being's voice sounded female yet there was no physical way of knowing. All three of them appeared to be androgynous.

"We have come to bring your heart peace," they said in unison.

They led me to another room. There, standing in the corner of the room with her back to me, was a young dark-haired girl. She looked very similar to me when I was a teenager. She turned around to face me and I gasped in shock. Her face was not quite formed. It was mottled and the hair on the top and around the front of her face was wispy and stringy. Her eyes had the same blue iridescence as the blonde-haired beings. She was a strange creature. Her arms and hands were thin and frail and her fingers were curled like claws.

Aside from her appalling frontal appearance she had an innocent smile. My heart and emotions were drawn in compassion to her. Her sparse shoulder length hair had a violet sparkle to it.

The young female came forward and reached out to me with her thin arms. I wanted to run away but she needed something from me. I was unsure if it was appropriate.

"Do you recognize her? She is a part of you, a life that began with you but could not live on your earth star. Do you remember the moment?"

The blonde being telepathically transferred my mind back to a cruise I had taken in my late twenties.

I was sailing to Bermuda. I had a hard time sleeping and felt drawn to go up on the deck for some fresh air. Alone on the deck the winds tore through my hair as the rush of the waves sprayed the salt water into air. A bright star was shining in the distance. It began to sparkle and twinkle. The star grew brighter and brighter until it was right over me. I felt my body relax and fell into a deep sleep.

When I awoke, I was in a darkened room and a light was blinding my eyes. I felt a burning below my navel and an uncomfortable cramping. I could not move to touch it. There was a low buzzing in the room as if a fly was around my ears. The light dimmed and my eyes could barely focus. The last I could recall was seeing my own face reflecting in a dark mirror. As it slowly backed away from me, I recognized bug-like eyes staring at me and I quickly lost consciousness.

The next thing I remember, I awoke on one of the deck chairs to the rising sun. People were starting to gather and make their way to the deck.

I would have thought it was a dream except that I had two small scabs over holes in my pelvic area that were still tender to the touch. I went on with the rest of my life as usual except I missed my menses three months in a row. I felt it may be from stress. By the fourth month everything returned to normal, or so I thought.

Further on in the memory, I had not been intimate with anyone, but I had recently met a man that I was dating quite seriously for a few months after the cruise. I decided to go to my physician for birth control.

The physician required an internal check-up and other normal tests before prescribing the pill. I had noted that I was a virgin on the paperwork but he obviously had not read the paperwork. When I yelped with discomfort during the internal he was surprised to learn that I had not been pregnant before. He said that I had severe scar tissue on the walls of my cervix. I told him I had never been intimate with anyone let alone been pregnant. He said that my body begged to differ. I found the whole episode confusing.

Months later, I developed digestive distress and was ordered to have upper and lower gastro-intestinal tests. During the scan the technician asked if I had any lower stomach surgeries. I replied no. Then he stated, "Well you have a small metal clamp in your lower pelvic area."

"What?" I exclaimed.

"Don't worry, I'm not a doctor I'm probably wrong about it. Sorry I mentioned it."

The doctor reported that indeed I had a metal clamp in me from a past surgery. I also had acid reflux and that watching my diet would reduce the acid and problems. But all I heard were the words "metal clamp from your past surgery." I never had surgery, let alone a pelvic or lower stomach surgery.

As the memory faded, the blonde being explained to me.

"She is part of you and the DNA of another being. Your carried her for three months and then she was removed from you and incubated until it was time to be birthed from the pod. She cannot live on your earth. Her lungs are not like yours and as you can see, she is physically deformed. She is a hybrid like many others that have been seeded and removed from the wombs of other earth women."

"But how can you do this? This is wrong. Who gives you permission?" I yelled.

"You gave permission. Your spirit agreed to the evolution process long before you were a human being. You agreed to grow and evolve many ways with a cosmic and human purpose. All humans agree to evolve. The goal is to remember and follow the human purpose to contribute to humanity and the cosmic consciousness. All beings are from the stars and will return when they drop their human form. All beings are from the mystery of the cosmos. The purpose is to evolve and grow collectively. If you evolve by completing your purpose, you will enhance all that you are connected to and affect your planet and the cosmos."

My mind was expanding with this deep truth. I had a part in this creature's existence but I would not birth a physical human being in this lifetime. I did not need to mourn as my body started to go through the changes to the next stage with the black grandmother. I could celebrate my life as a part of this being that I may never see again. I ran and embraced her in my arms. I kissed her mottled forehead and stroked her matted hair and told her, "You are loved."

Embracing her tightly, I opened my eyes and found that I was on my blanket in the middle of the altar. The sun rose and I completed the fourth day of the quest. The prayer ties in the west were cut and the altar was open for me to leave. I waited for Grandma Tula for a few minutes but she did not return. I smoked the Sacred Pipe to complete this quest which was unlike any that I had experienced before. I offered food to the spirits that guided and took care of me. Before I ate and broke my fast, I felt compelled to jump in the lake for a cleansing. It was cold! It quickly grounded me to my body.

I ate light and drank lots of water to rehydrate often throughout the day. I still had a couple of days to recuperate and rest. I wrote down all that I could remember. Although I did not understand all of it, I trusted it would make sense in time. I went and rested in the cabin dozing on and off throughout the day. At dusk I was too tired to make a fire and went to bed early.

I learned years ago, from Anna Davey, a Cherokee elder, that the best medicine to help the body to get back in balance is sun, pure air, clean water, natural food, natural herbal medicines, exercise, rest and relaxation. What I needed most right now was rest and I was going to honor my body by giving it what it needed to rebalance.

CHAPTER THIRTY-EIGHT

I slept for seventeen hours without interruption. It was mid-morning on Saturday. This would be my last full day and night at the cabin. The weather was chilly and overcast with dark clouds.

After a breakfast of organic scrambled eggs, fruit and blueberry tea, I walked the trails of the campground. The chipmunks and squirrels were romping through the leaves and pine needles and scurrying about. The birds were singing and chirping and calling to each other. The woods were anything but quiet today, full of movement and chatter.

I walked in a heightened awareness. I noticed spider webs, ant mounds and even a small ring neck snake slithering across the trail. The time in the woods was magical and enchanting. The wind was beginning to pick up and a light mist of rain was coming in. I decided to head back to the cabin and watch the rain come in over the lake from the front porch.

The rain cloud hovered over the lake in the west and sprayed its drops on the water. The once still lake, now began to pool and ripple with the shower. The small fish came to the surface to feed. They left small concentric circles on the surface where they had been.

Although there was no storm, the shower was refreshing to the land. I could feel the plants and the trees quench their thirst and say, "aah."

I sat on the screened-in porch, opened the Sacred Pipe bundle and began my ceremony of gratitude. As I filled the bowl with the sacred mixture of tobacco, a peaceful connection to all things was present. Black Deer once told me, "The bowl contains the whole universe. It is where we place our prayers. The stem is the bridge that connects our breath to the prayers and sends them through the smoke to the Great Mystery."

In this moment, my entire being experienced that teaching to be true. As I smoked the woods became quiet. No leaves rustled, no birds chirped, no squirrels romped. It was as if the woods came to a standstill.

The gratitude I felt was for everything in my life, the experiences both happy and challenging that led me to these woods, the quest and Grandma Tula. I was not sure if I would see her tonight or ever again, for she was a mystery. She came and left in the darkness. She pushed me to explore my life and begin a transformation, for which I would be eternally grateful.

After the completion of ceremony, I sat there in silence, reviewing all that had transpired and what questions I still had to be answered. Every new experience expanded my understanding but also drove me to seek more. It pulls a person further away from their limiting beliefs while stretching the mind beyond what was once possible. Life certainly was a journey and for me, another level was just beginning.

The rain shower had stopped and I built the last fire at dusk. I sat facing the west and watched the sun slowly sink behind the trees. The air was crisp and chilly. I wrapped myself in a colorful fleece blanket to enjoy my last night in the woods.

A familiar song formed in my head. A chant I had heard before. It was the chant of the shawled grandmothers as they rattled and moved the energy in and around me for healing. It was the song that shifted the pain and discomfort and moved the emotions that were repressed to the surface.

The song became louder and louder in my mind until I found myself chanting it out loud as I rocked back and forth gazing into the fire. My attention was pulled away by a flash in the sky. Moments later, I heard her muffled cough and her steps rustling up the path. Tonight she stood in a white shawl. She seemed to glow as if a halo was placed around her entire body.

"Grandma Tula," I whispered.

"Yes, it's me. You have been through much these last days. Tell me Laurel, what have you experienced?" she asked.

"I visited an underwater cave with thirteen grandmothers and they had shawls of red, black or white. They explained the stages of a woman's life and they performed some type of ceremony on me. It was powerful using the elements of earth, water, air and fire. I experienced a ship with three humanoid beings and they allowed me to meet a hybrid girl and I was told that she was a part of me. It was very confusing but I did feel a connection to her in a motherly way." I responded.

"Laurel, my time here is almost complete. I put a call out to the one who could hear me, one who could take my teachings and keep them alive. She has to be a dreamer, a teacher, have the ability to cross dimensions, hear the spirit world, understand ceremonies and embrace the twelve teachings and tests of the Grandmother's Way."

She continued on, "Although all humans, male and female, aspire to these teachings, men primarily embrace four of these teachings and tests in their lives. It is the women who learn these four and embrace the other eight as they age. These twelve teachings are the way of the grandmother, the strong divine feminine that exists in all life and nature. There is no growth unless it is birthed from the darkness of the ancient grandmother of the divine feminine. The masculine plants the seed of vitality but the feminine grows, nurtures and expands life within herself before she births and gives away what she has created. This understanding has been forgotten by most. It is up to you to take these teachings to the women to find and heal themselves and come back to the Way so that they can help their men and children have a balanced way of life. Only when women search deep within and enter the pit, can they confront their wounds and embrace these teachings to remember who they are and their path for fulfillment."

I listened as she offered her teachings. The glow dimmed around her as her energy faded. She was giving away the ancient understandings and wisdom and I was receiving it humbly.

"Your own transformation must take place first. You accomplished the first two tests the first time that we met. You passed the test of *bravery,* moving beyond fear, when you followed the call to find me. Then you passed the test of *respect*, to be considerate and accepting of all livings things, as you respected your environment and gave me, the elder, your undivided attention respecting the story and teachings I shared with you."

"This week, with this quest you have completed more tests. The test of *perseverance,* never giving up, as you worked hard to prepare your body and mind for this week in the last several months no matter how difficult it was. You have accomplished the test of *sacrifice,* to offer yourself for the betterment of your healing, as you gave your time, finances and effort to be here this week. Lastly, you passed the test of *compassion,* where you gave comfort and accepted a being unlike yourself as part of your own even if it was hard to believe."

"The next tests will become more difficult. Will you return? Only you know the level of commitment to yourself and the Great Mystery. Tell me Laurel, what have you learned?" she asked.

"I am not sure if I have learned anything," I paused. "But what I have experienced is going deep within. There I was given a look at my life since childhood and there I was shown the wounds from experiences that I still carry. Ones that help me to understand myself and the challenges I continue to bring into my life because they are not healed. Releasing the fear of abandonment that keeps me stuck in the distrust of relationships, will help me to become more intimate and loving, not only to others but especially to myself. The ancient, circle of grandmothers are working with me in dream time and vision as their ceremonies alter and heal me. I understand that learning is done over time, after putting into practice what you understand to be true. All I can say is that I am grateful for the experiences, as I see the truth of my wounds and work on their release."

"Then you have done well. It is right that the grandmothers and Great Spirit have chosen you to lead the work," she smiled.

"What work?" I asked.

"You'll see…," she smirked.

I had never seen this lightness in her. She was usually serious and to the point. It seemed that her burden was lightened. *Did my return to complete this quest give her hope?*

"You have also been shown the existence of another part of yourself that lives in another dimension. Tell me your thoughts on this?" she prodded.

"I am not sure in this moment. I remembered when it took place and all the signs of truth along the way in my life. At first, to see her frightened me. Then once I recognized her as a part of me, a motherly love and compassion was all that I could express. Do I believe it? Was she real? It really doesn't matter. I understand she cannot exist in this world nor will I ever see her again, but I feel at peace knowing that her existence out there makes me feel whole in some way. Does that make any sense?" I asked.

"Ah yes. You wondered as you felt the changes in your body that started five years ago, if you had missed out on giving and creating life. This allows you the truth that you had not known and now you can learn to accept your body lovingly and the changes that are beginning to happen with an open heart. The body will change whether you accept it or not but if you learn to love and accept instead of resist, it can be a time of excitement and wonder - to rediscover yourself again and step into the next stage of life which can be a wiser, happier and fulfilling time than you have ever experienced."

"Please Grandma, can you tell me about the herbs we used the last time we met and the one you used this time before quest? Are they hallucinogenic?" I asked.

"All in due time you will learn about your sacred seven. They are *not* hallucinogenic. Each plant works with you, if you call upon them in a sacred way which I do before I give them to you. How they work with you will be different every time depending on the energy that needs to be moved."

"Are these the ones I will work with for a long time?" I asked.

Grandma Tula replied, "You will work with them first, to know them. Then you will learn the way to make them sacred and connect with their spirits. Only then, can you work with them on the behalf of others."

She added, "Laurel, you have been in training all your life: seeing other dimensions, and departed spirits, training in sacred ceremonies and been given the permission to perform them by elders. All the knowledge you acquired combined with the talents you have been born with, have led you to the path of sacred medicine. Holy men are chosen and trained for years through family lineage or by an elder who seeks to pass on teachings to someone worthy to work with the sacred."

"It is different for a holy woman. She receives the calling at a young age and is supplied with the natural gifts that enable her to follow a sacred road of prayer. Starting as a child and continuing through her entire life. She never leaves the road. The sacred road is who she is. Life teaches her and Great Spirit speaks directly to her all her life. There is no need to be chosen by a human being. She is chosen before she enters the womb. Her spirit has agreed to give to the people and live a life of prayer for all. When she comes into the last stage of life after menopause she becomes a very powerful healer because she has worked and prayed all her life on the behalf of others and has never wavered from Spirit's voice. She has listened and followed and has been guided her entire life. For this dedication, the medicine path will be opened to her fully. The sacrifices she goes through in her life, because of her dedication to prayer and commitment to humankind does not make for an easy life, but for her it is a burning desire that goes beyond anything else in the mundane world for her to accomplish. She lives and breathes her prayer and she is misunderstood and sometimes chastised for most cannot understand. The challenges of feeling alone and separated from mankind because of her gifts can sometimes overwhelm her, but still she continues for the sake of mankind and her love of the Great Spirit. Her prayer can help the entire world because it is one continuous sacred prayer that she has lived all her life. You understand don't you?" she asked.

As I nodded I became tearful. That pretty much explained my life up until this point. As a child, I was very sick due to a problem with my kidneys. I had many playmates from other worlds and dimensions. The departed spirits came to me all the time. As soon as I could speak, I was taught to pray by my mother in the traditional Christian way, but I never related to the specific prayer that I could not understand. So I talked directly with my own words and voice. I prayed a lot, all the time, every free moment. At school, riding in the car, playing outside, playing with my brother, in the bath, in the shower, at work and on vacations. I prayed in gratitude and for other people's healing and burdens. No one asked me. I just did it. It was who I was and how much I cared about human beings and the planet. I knew my mission before I really understood myself.

When I grew older and got out of high school, I traveled and learned different systems of healing from many indigenous elders of different cultures but the teachings brought me back to the spiritual road of my ancestors on the Native American Indian path. All the paths and teachings lead to the same place. One just has to find the spiritual path that they can embrace and follow wholeheartedly with their own spirit. So I have learned, trained and followed this spiritual tradition that has not been practiced in my lineage for four generations.

My focus has always been on praying for others. Seeking comfort and healing for them and asking for their lessons to be gentle. This prayer had become more intense since my fourth vision quest when Black Deer's spirit teacher said that he was to pass his ceremony teachings onto me. He trained me in performing purification lodges, vision quests and crossing people over and we worked together to release disenchanted spirits from homes and land. I also trained for seven years with another medicine man in the west, Red Horse before I met Black Deer. I had been on a total of eight vision quests between both teachers. The Women's Society initiation was number nine and now I had been through one with Grandma Tula.

Where was this all leading? All I could do was follow as I was guided, as I had always done and trusted. Would Grandma Tula be my next teacher for many years?

As I observed the old sage, I was grateful for the experiences this week. She gave me final instructions to continue to work with the circle of shawled spirit grandmothers in the dream time and in the Sacred Pipe ceremonies - for they would teach me and guide me to ways of healing.

Before she left, I gifted the four sacred herbs and a colorful Pendleton blanket as is customary for a giveaway.

"Grandmother Tula, it is with gratitude that I offer you these gifts for all you have done for me on this quest," I spoke.

"You have done well. *Generosity*, to share with others, is a most important test. It continues the flow of abundance. You have now completed the sixth test. Thank you, my dear."

She spoke only once more before she gave her final wave.

"More of your life will change in the next years and by the age of fifty you will not even recognize your former life. The initiation began with the vision quest into the Women's Society. This began a deeper walk into the sacred that led you here to me. Pay attention to all you discover. I'll meet you here again in the spring for another quest. Blessings to you," she said.

She departed down the darkened path. In minutes, I was alone. Her footsteps on the path could no longer be heard. As I sat by the fire, I caught a blue flash in the sky over the tall pines.

Was there was a connection to the flash and Tula's arrival and departure?

Then it hit me.

Did she say another quest here in the spring? That means I would have to stay in preparation for another six months. And how was I going to afford to rent this place again? I was committed to another year of expenses in support for Sundance in Texas for Granny Janice. Where were the finances going to come from to do both in May and June?

Once again the word trust became apparent.

If it is Spirit's will, I will be guided to find the way. I sat and waited until the last of the flames died and only the coals were left. I sang my gratitude song and gently doused the pit with jugs of water as I put the fire to sleep. It was the final completion to what had transpired this week and for which I was grateful.

CHAPTER THIRTY-NINE

When I arrived home the next day, I rested and relived the memory of everything that had happened during the past week. Both my body and mind were tired. So much had taken place. Though I tried not to leave the present moment my thoughts wandered to the spring when Grandma Tula asked me to do it all again.

I took two days off before I began my trek back into the reality of everyday life. Once rested, I returned phone calls and set up appointments for clients as well as scheduled in a couple of new schools inquiring about the native programs for children.

My life however would not be the same. Every night in dream time, the circle of the ancient grandmothers returned and led me to places for ceremony that worked on my physical and energetic body. Each morning when I awoke, I felt I was being transformed and awakened on a molecular level. The process was slow but affirming.

My day started with the journaling of my experience from dream time and the greeting of sunrise with the Sacred Pipe ceremony. Only then could I begin my client schedule or teaching program for the day. This was the order of my day to connect to the Great Spirit in devotion. It gave me a feeling of connectedness to the world.

On this particular morning, I had a Skype consultation for flower essences with a woman named Grace, who had been referred to me by another client of mine. Grace connected and appeared on the computer screen before me.

I had previously entered her energy field before she called. It is difficult to explain how I do it. I have been able to do it as long as I can remember. I relax my breathing and open myself up to becoming one with the person. Then I quickly assess the energy up and down the spine, the energy centers and the banded colors of light that I see running vertically and horizontally like a grid or matrix. Last, I check the auric field around the body to look for colors, tears, spikes or anything out of the ordinary. In the short period of time, I become one with them to see their challenges and strengths. Then I quickly pop out and disconnect from them and have the information that I need to make the flower essence.

It is a process that takes a few minutes, but it takes my mind and body longer to prepare to be able to see, feel, know and understand the client.

On this day, I saw the band in the abdominal region of her body had ruts and small tears. The color band in this area had spots of brown. The energy was not moving vertically or horizontally correctly. Her left arm had very little energy running through it. When I looked at her aura I saw she had holes on the left side of her head.

My quick assessment was that she had had some kind of trauma that affected the left side of her body and the energy of her will and power was leaking and not flowing to her left arm - the area of receiving. I also saw that the energy band at her heart had large pin holes where energy was leaking and the color was dull as if it had been hardened with a film of some kind.

The understanding I was given is that she had a loss of some kind a while ago and had not released it. It was still weighing her down. It was leaving her in a powerless state unable to accept love or care from others. She withdrew from everything. The pain in her heart had drifted to become the physical pain in her arm.

As Grace and I met over the computer by Skype, I explained what I had seen and gave her my interpretation. She was shocked by my assessment. She concluded that I was right on track. Then she told me her story and what she hoped to receive from the essences.

Grace had lost her boyfriend Joe, four years ago in a car accident. She could not get past it and had isolated herself and become depressed. She found no joy in life at all. She worked at the same job where she and Joe had met. Every day she was reliving the pain and memory of him at work. Now all of a sudden, her left arm was giving her trouble and she was unable to type and perform her job. She took a medical leave of absence to rest and see doctor after doctor but got no real answers. They found nothing wrong physically. MRI's, x-rays, blood work, nerve tests and CT scans all came back negative. She just wanted to feel better.

I gave her guidance and made her an essence remedy of seven different flowers which included *Star of Bethlehem* for trauma and *Walnut* for change. The essence was created to open up her heart, lighten her mind and release the fear she held in her body. She booked a follow up appointment for a month later.

The beauty of flower essences is that they are subtle. They give tremendous amounts of restoring energy that gently release old, stuck, dense energy. They bring issues up to the conscious to be understood and released, while helping one to feel happy and full of vitality. The trick however, is to work with the essences over a period of time, not just once. It can take three to six months for an acute issue or up to a year or more for a chronic issue. However, you must be willing to look at yourself and take actions for change. Essences help the soul to remember what it came here to do, which is to be happy and balanced.

As I said goodbye to Grace, her energy felt more hopeful and content. I looked forward to shipping the remedy to her and help her on her way to wellness.

It gave me great fulfillment to help others. I understood I could not help all people, because I knew some were too resistant to look deeply at their challenges, conditions and patterns. Some were not ready or would never be ready. I would have to turn some people away and let them find their own way. It was not personal, if I couldn't help. When people needed to learn their lessons their own way I could not and should not interfere.

I can detach from my ego and know that I cannot help everyone, nor do I need to - only those willing to accept and work on their own healing can be helped. My love for all people leaves me with the understanding of free will.

Since I was a small child, I understood that we are all connected to each other and to every living thing. We need to clear our dense energy because when we clean it up and release it, we can raise the vibration on the earth. If we became self-aware of adding good thoughts and actions in and for the world, we could change things for the better. All it took was to clean ourselves up of our wounds, patterns and destructive habits that affect the people we meet and live with daily.

Sooner or later we could be living in a much happier, loving and compassionate world. It only takes the first step of working on yourself to become self-aware and responsible for the energy you live, think and put out into your home, work, family, neighborhood and community.

That is my goal. I don't have to change the whole world, I only have to change myself and help others that ask for help.

The balance is to serve others while keeping true to my needs and spiritual growth. That is why I never miss my daily prayer and quiet time. Prayer and quiet time ground me and keep me calm during the times there may not be peace in the world.

Chapter Forty

The Christmas season arrived and the classes in schools died down once again. Thankfully my client schedule was steady. I had earned enough to purchase gift cards for my parents and brother, Tom.

This year Tom made the trip from Nevada to visit our parents for a few days at Christmas. Christmas had been a special time for me as a child. Relatives from both sides of the family would gather at my parent's home to celebrate and enjoy my mother's delicious cooking and baking. The family came and went like a realtor's open house on Christmas Eve.

Today many family members have passed on. Christmas has become a private evening of reminiscing with both my parents and my brother when he can make the trip home.

The year was ending and I realized much had happened. I had hoped I could reconnect with my brother on a deeper emotional level this year. It felt like the perfect time to have a heart to heart with him. Really talk about his life and mine. We had not been close ever since he left for the military years ago. A phone call every now and then did not capture a meaningful connection. Now that I understood and hopefully released some of my abandonment issues, I trusted the opportunity would present itself.

My brother was already at my parents' house when I arrived. I hugged him and wished him a Merry Christmas and did the same for my parents. I could see both of my parents were overjoyed to have both of their children home for the holiday.

My mother had made meatballs, which were my brother's favorite, potato salad, which was my favorite and a small sliced ham which was my father's favorite. The prize was homemade cream puffs which she had not baked in years.

We sat around the table and remembered our favorite Christmas moments from the past. I felt the love my parents, my father in particular had for both of us. His smile told it all.

After eating, gifting presents, reminiscing and clean-up, my parents were tired and went to bed. My brother and I made our way to the living room to catch up on each other's lives.

"So Laurel, what's new and exciting? Have you found a full-time job yet?" Tom asked.

"No. I am still consulting and teaching. I really enjoy it." I answered.

"You can't make a living consulting," he added.

"You sound just like Dad. Actually, I *have* been making a living at it. For the last year, I am no longer collecting unemployment benefits." I said defensively.

"Are you making enough? It can't be reliable income," he said.

"I am paying my expenses. So it's reliable enough," I defended again.

"All I'm saying is that you had a great job supervising and training people in a large company. You were somebody with a title," he said.

"Tom, I still *am* somebody," I said with tension. "I love what I do now and I am happy on my own terms and nobody else's. I am pleasing myself."

My tone of voice made my point.

Tom smiled and finally conceded, "Good for you, Laurel. At last, I don't have to compete with you."

"What are you talking about?" I asked.

"Oh come on, Laurel. I could never live up to your example. Laurel this, Laurel that," he snickered.

Still I was confused.

"You were the perfect child. Always a good girl, intelligent, self-sufficient and did what was expected. I could never measure up to you in Dad and Mom's eyes," he explained.

"I don't understand. You were the baby boy, the treasured one. Mom and Dad praised your every move." I said.

"That's not the way I remember it. I was told how smart you were and how you did everything right and how your grades were so good. I had pressure on me to measure up. I struggled in school to get B's. You were Miss straight A's and honor roll. There was a time I resented you and wished just once that your grades would slip to a B average. Your example was hard for me to live up to," he said honestly.

"Is that why you left home at eighteen and joined the Air Force?" I asked.

"Partly, I guess. I wanted to make my own life and be my own person and not have my life compared to yours. I love you Sis, but you were so pain-in-the-ass perfect. All I heard was how much better I could do to be like you," he answered.

"Are you happy now?" I asked with concern.

"Yes. I am happy. I still hope to find the right woman to share my life with. I haven't done too well in that department. I guess I am looking for Miss perfect like my older sister," he joked.

I was astonished at our conversation. I had hardly considered myself an example for him. Sure I loved him and took care of him but I also realized this year that I resented him for being the boy and taking my father's attention away from me. How strange that we had such different experiences in the same household - how both our child's ego had become wounded by our different perceptions. This was the first time I had really talked honestly to my brother in years or perhaps ever.

"Tom, I also have a confession to make. This year, I went through some time alone and realized I have some issues that I did not realize. When you were born, I felt displaced. Dad and I were really close. He was my world and I was his special little girl. When you started to walk and talk, he was so proud of his little boy. He spent time playing with you and teaching you. I felt pushed aside. I had to do things with Mom, things that I resented and resisted, like housework. I love Mom but I missed Dad's attention. I spent my life in one way or another trying to please and get that attention back. I realized I carried a wound of being afraid that I would be abandoned at some point again. Isn't that strange?" I asked.

"Laurel, you are and will always be Dad's little girl. The sun rises and sets around you. He is proud of you, so is Mom. I am surprised that you can't see that," he said.

"I see it the other way around. They adore you, their boy, and the one who will carry on the family name. You are the golden child," I said.

"What a pair we are, still carrying stuff from when we were kids. Are we both wrong?" he asked.

"I think we are both right and wrong. Mom and Dad love us both the same. We are both special to them. When one of us was getting praised, as children we interpreted it as we were no longer loved or special and that was where we were wrong. We need to believe that we are enough and worth something within ourselves to be happy. Then maybe we can each find a healthy relationship. I am happy that we were able to talk to each other so openly," I smiled.

"Yes, this has been good. It sure has opened my eyes. I feel closer to you, Laurel. We have shared a common issue and maybe now we can see things differently and change our lives for the better."

"Seeing the illusion of the story we have told ourselves for years and recognizing the truth can be the start of that change. I love you, Tommy," I said with misty eyes.

"I love you too, Sis," he said as he hugged me tightly.

I left my parent's home on Christmas Eve knowing that a healing was taking place between us. My heart that had once been held at bay, had also felt my brother's heartache, each of us thinking we were less than the other. *Why do we as children deceive ourselves? Why do we feel we don't measure up to our parents love when we already have been given everything already inside of us?* This year has shown me the truth of my illusions as I continued on the path towards my healing.

January and February were tough months. The snowstorms brought periodic power outages and cancelled phone appointments. Consults had slowed down. Money was tight this winter. I lowered the heat, used less electric, cut down on groceries and even stopped the cable.

By March, although I had enough money for the quest cabin in early May, I still needed money for the plane ticket to Texas to get to Sundance. As my fourth year of supporting Granny Janice, it would be her completion year as a dancer. Next year would be her final year of giveaway and gratitude.

It was clear during my prayer with the Sacred Pipe that I was guided to give up something. I heard the words, "detach from possessions." I wondered what possessions I had that I could release and possibly sell. I prayed in gratitude for the understanding and looked for a way to raise the extra money from selling something.

I thought about the word *detachment*, I realized it had to be something of meaning, something that had value to me at one time or that still did. *What are the possessions that I love the most*, I thought. My treasures were my books. However, there was nothing that I owned of monetary value.

Then it hit me, jewelry. Every time I traveled to different places in the past, I bought a small piece of jewelry. Nothing too expensive, never more than two hundred dollars apiece but maybe selling them all would give me enough.

When I lifted the box out of the drawer, a single piece jumped out and fell on the floor. I stood in shock. I retrieved it from the floor, looked at it carefully and then began to cry. Yes, this is the piece that I needed to detach from. It was the half-carat engagement ring from my former marriage - the possession that I kept hidden away in the box, must surely be worth something. *Why had I not gotten rid of it before?*

Because as I realized, I believed that I would never get another one - that no one would ever ask me again or love me enough to think I was worthy of one. *How sad*, I thought as my eyes welled with tears.

Another relationship could not happen as long as I was not willing to release the past, detach from this symbolic form of love and make way for a new life. I smudged it with sage smoke and offered a prayer of release that it would bring joy and happiness to whom ever bought it. The next day, I brought it to a jeweler for an appraisal and to sell the diamond. The diamond sold two weeks later and I was able to pay for the plane ticket easily. My heart was at peace and I could now go back to the Sundance and continue my commitment to Granny Janice.

Several weeks later came the first of May and I was excited to spend my week at the campground. I arrived and unloaded the overly packed vehicle. I found the firewood that was left by the work crew for the fires. I was happy that the campground allowed me the time of respite and left me completely to myself. They honored my request of not being disturbed. The cabin overlooking the lake quickly became my home away from home.

I learned in my early twenties that a home can be made anywhere as long as a connection is made to the land and environment. Whenever I traveled, I searched for the perfect place to live. That is until I met Black Deer.

Black Deer helped me to realize as I traveled with him in ceremony, that wherever I am can be home if I allowed my heart to fully connect to the land.

"If you live in your heart you are truly home, for it is there where your spirit can connect to the land and be part of the whole."

That was the lesson of travel for me - to experience and become one with every place, person and living thing. It was the greatest teaching and continues to give me comfort, no matter where my travels take me.

As I settled in, I decided to gather up some dry kindling around the cabin. There were lots of dried branches and sticks that could be gathered and stored under the covered porch.

The squirrels seemed to follow me as I gathered the small branches and stored them in the garbage bag. I assured them I was doing my best not to disturb their lovely stomping grounds.

Further down the path, two crows cackled with each other as they descended upon one of the trees close to where I was standing. I looked up into the tree and I noticed a large nest. Although I didn't think there were any young ones in the nest, they were just making sure that I kept to the path and stayed away from their nest. I acknowledged both of them, stated my good intentions and moved along. This seemed to quiet and calm them down.

I dragged the bag of kindling back to the cabin and expressed gratitude to the trees whose loss of limbs through the winter would be utilized in a good way. They would be used and honored in the fires I built this week.

At dusk, both the ducks and geese made their farewell calls as they left the calm water for the evening. The evening doves too, sang their soothing melodies. It was then I built and lit the fire, awaiting Grandma Tula's arrival.

I wondered, *how many people she had visited over the years in these woods. Did she startle them the same way she had startled me? Did she also bring them tea and pass along her teachings?*

I stared into the flames and I began to sing. The song was one that was taught to me by a Lakota woman nearly twenty years ago when I was traveling. It was a woman's song. The melody was tender in places and invoked a feeling of well-being. As I sang, I watched the flames dance and the sky darken. The song permeated my being as I felt lighter and in a heightened awareness. In my mind's eye, I could see a circle of women with shawls dancing in a circle around the fire. Each of them had a sacred rattle and was chanting along with me. As the song completed I continued to observe the vision, and eventually, one by one their ghostly forms ascended to the sky. As I watched them travel they became small balls of light that disappeared into the dark. I heard a rustling of leaves. I turned my attention to the path and once again a flash from the sky in the corner of my eye diverted my attention.

"Are you ready?" the voice asked.

I turned my attention back to the path and there she stood once again leaning on her beaded, feathered staff. She had a sparkle in her eye and a grin of pleasure on her face.

"So you're back for more are you?" she grinned.

"Yes. You asked me to return and I prepared myself for quest as you instructed," I replied.

"Good. I have brought another herb for tea. Please get us some hot water," she asked.

Already prepared, the water on the stove was on low and ready to be savored. I noticed a mint smell as she poured the leaves into the cotton bags. As it steeped in the cup, the aroma quickly confirmed that it was of the mint family.

"This one will be pleasurable to drink," she said.

I proceeded to drink it with four large sips and she seemed pleased that my memory of her teachings was still intact.

"How has your life been these past months?" she asked.

"It has been a struggle," I answered.

"What is your struggle?" she asked again.

"I have been helping clients with flower essences and teaching children's programs in schools. Money has been tight. Less consults and classes this past winter. I had to sell some jewelry and cut down on food, electric and stop cable television to survive. I still have not found another job and to be truthful I don't think I want to do anything else," I replied.

"So what do you do for fun?" she questioned as she narrowed her gaze.

"Consulting and teaching is my fun," I replied.

"No, that is your service," she replied sternly.

I was not sure where she was going with this but surely my service was my bliss, my *fun*.

"When you are not in service or working, what else do you do?" she continued.

"I pray with the Sacred Pipes and keep myself centered. I pray for others who need help and ask for guidance and direction."

"Good work, but where is your pleasure, your joy?" she questioned.

"That *is* my joy." I answered with annoyance.

Grandma Tula was agitated. She shook her head at me in disbelief. I didn't understand the point she was trying to make. I was happy. I was fulfilled. *Why all the questions? Where was this conversation leading?*

"Laurel, we create *joy* when we *play*. We become light-hearted. We laugh and release the seriousness that holds us back. Service and work can be blissful if it is meaningful to you and others but it can be heavy and dense even if it is what we want to be doing. You need the balance of play, passion and perhaps love," she winked.

"There is nothing like passion to open the heart to play and laugh. Through opening our hearts in relationships we grow and expand," she explained.

"No thanks. I have had enough relationships in my life. I enjoy being alone, being free to come and go as I please and do what I want. I can take care of myself. I don't need anyone to rescue me. I am quite competent, independent, intelligent and strong," I resisted.

"So you think you got it all together do you? Suit yourself, Miss know it all," she said.

After dowsing the campfire, I followed her into the woods once again until we came upon the lodge made of skins and the small fire with a large, lone stone. She called in the spirits with her words and sacred rattle. She crawled into the lodge acknowledging all of her relations.

"Laurel, use the pitchfork and bring in the sacred grandfather stone," she demanded.

I approached the fire with reverence and lifted the large stone. I struggled to keep it on the pitchfork. It was very heavy. I was grateful that there was only one stone for me to carry. The short path from the fire to the entrance of the lodge was feeling miles away at this moment. My arms felt as if they were going to break. The stone was ridiculously heavy. It was twice the size of a human head and felt much heavier than it should have been. I was a fairly strong person but this task was testing me. I inched my way until at last I greeted the door and helped pass the stone into the pit inside the lodge.

"Okay get in and close the flap," she directed.

Once inside the darkness was upon us. Grandma Tula opened up the ceremony with a prayer and poured the sacred water onto the stone. Hot steam rose quickly and in no time the lodge was intensely hot.

The stone was sizzling so loudly that it drowned out her song and prayer. I felt disconnected from her. All I could hear was the water simmering over the hot stone. The sound deafened my ears and took my sense of balance away.

I was hot and annoyed as I wiped my face with the bottom of my cotton shirt. I wanted to cry for some reason. I had been in many purification ceremonies over the years but this one was a completely different experience. I felt disconnected from the ceremony with the sound of steam sizzling. I could not hear her prayers.

How much longer could this continue? Eventually it should die down but it didn't. It kept getting louder and louder. I still couldn't hear Grandma's words or prayers. I took a breath and tried to relax with the steam and sound instead of getting angry. The sizzling became a rattling sound in tune with my heartbeat. My chest was uncomfortable - not in physical pain but restless. My pulse was running faster and faster with the sound and heat.

I began to cry. I lay down and rested my face on the coolness of the earth. My tears and sobs were uncontrollable. The earth just took them into her belly. I was not sure why I was crying.

"I am so tired." I screamed out loud.

I rested both my body and mind. I could no longer think or process. I wanted to escape somewhere. In the midst of all that was happening I fell asleep.

I found myself below the earth in a tunnel. The air was cool yet musty. Where was I exactly? I began to walk the tunnel following a dim light somewhere in the distance up ahead. I walked for miles and yet it seemed I was getting no closer. I decided to give up and sit down to rest my feet. The light in the distance seemed to glimmer on and off beckoning me to continue on.

I arose again and traveled further and eventually I came to the end. The light blinded me and I could see no further. I went to the edge yet I was unsure if I should completely enter it to see what was on the other side.

Do I want stay stuck here in this tunnel or should I choose to pass through. As I teetered back and forth with my decision, I felt a splash of water on my face that jolted me from my dilemma.

"Laurel, get up. The purification is completed. Let's make your altar and start you on your quest," she prodded.

I crawled out of the lodge on all fours and slowly rose to my feet.

We walked further down the path to a small opening under a pine tree. I recognized it from last autumn. Time was moving very slowly and eventually I found myself secluded inside the altar of colorful prayer ties around me. With the tobacco filled Buffalo Sacred Pipe in hand, I began my prayers with the invitation song. Grandma Tula quietly turned and disappeared into the night.

Alone in prayer with my thoughts and intentions, I was not sure why I was here. Grandma Tula asked and I answered the call. Maybe I would learn, grow and heal.

I thought about her question. Where is my joy? I really could not come up with an answer. I searched my memory of recent years and could not see joy. I saw heartache, pain, fear and responsibility but nothing more.

I searched further back into my thirties. I found myself striving for success in career, working long hours, traveling for ceremony and receiving teachings from elders - again all serious intentions.

I traveled further back in my memories to my twenties and teenage years in high school. Still I found little joy or play. *Where was my joy?* All of my life was so serious. *Where was the play?*

I traveled further still, back to seven-years-old. There I found myself dancing, singing, drawing and writing short stories – wherever my imagination would take me. I was smiling remembering it now. Why did I stop dancing, singing, drawing and writing? The memory was tough to retrieve. When I remembered the day, sadness engulfed me.

I was singing and dancing and pretending to be a singer on a big stage. I saw myself in the bathroom mirror holding my hairbrush as a microphone when my father opened the door and shouted.

"Laurel, what the heck are you doing in here? Other people need to use the bathroom. Stop the silly dancing and get out of the bathroom," *he demanded.*

I was so embarrassed. I wanted to crawl under a rock and die. My daddy thought I was being silly. That was the last time I sang and danced around for fun. I didn't want to disappoint my daddy or be irresponsible by spending too much time playing in the bathroom or anywhere for that matter.

Another memory surfaced once the door was opened. I was writing a story about a dog that was lost and I drew a picture of the dog with a sad face. I was barely eight at the time. My mother called me to help with my brother's diaper change. I was so intrigued with my story that I didn't hear her calling. She began to yell for me just as my father arrived home from work.

"Laurel, your mother is calling you. Get down here," he said sternly.

"Sorry Daddy, I guess I didn't hear her." I replied.

"What were you doing that was so important?" he asked.

"I was writing a story about a dog. Someday, I'm going to be a famous writer," I said with pride.

"Maybe you should think about doing something where you can earn a living. A writer doesn't make much money. You can't pay your

bills if you can't earn a living," he said. *"You must make enough money to take care of yourself."*

He was right. My father knew everything about the world and what was best. I needed to do something that I could make money and take of myself. So my writing and drawing were no longer pleasures that I would create and enjoy. I would find something more suitable that would make him proud.

I stayed frozen in this memory. *Are you kidding?* My need to please as a child erased all my joy and play. My father's opinion and love mattered so much to me that I gave up on my own joy and pleasure. *What have I done to myself? Where have I lost me?* I so freely gave up my pleasure to please him.

I was not angry at my father. I was angry at the little girl that was so desperate for acceptance that she gave up on joy. The tears fell down my cheeks. This was an "aha" moment. The odd thing about memories, they will only resurface when you are ready to face them.

Grandma Tula was surely leading me to this quest to open myself for change. No matter where it led me, I had unconsciously signed up and committed to see it to its completion.

CHAPTER FORTY-ONE

I spent the next twenty-four hours in solitude and prayer. I stood and prayed to each of the directions, offering my gratitude and asking for guidance and gentle healing.

"Great Spirit, Grandfathers of the four directions, the sky above and the Grandmother Earth below, I want to understand why this woman Tula has called me here. What is it I am supposed to see, learn and heal? Grandfather, I ask for the understanding and for the wisdom to see the truth of what I need to change to become a better human being."

As the second nightfall came, I was strong physically and in a heightened sense of awareness. I sang the vision quest songs as I was taught years ago. I had prepared myself in the previous months for four days and four nights of fasting. I knew from experience that every quest was different and I truly never knew what challenge the quest would bring.

As the moon rose in the east I felt gratitude, for she would light the night sky and keep me company. The nights can be long and cold. Looking at her face against the blackened night sky had always given me comfort and a sense of belonging.

I alternated standing and praying and then resting and observing. Awaiting whatever would transpire. The nights of a vision quest were usually an active time in the spirit world, for the unseen makes itself known to those who have prepared and are open. Tonight, the moon's light cast upon the trees and my altar would be the only event of significance.

I struggled to stay awake. I repeated song after song and prayer after prayer to keep my focus. The birds started to make their first calls of the day. I welcomed their song as it signaled the morning. However, on this night, they rested uneasily and called to each other several hours before the sun actually rose. It can be disappointing for a quester to be anticipating the sun to rise and having to wait much longer.

I observed my surroundings and became one with them. I felt so alive. The blood pulsing through my veins was in rhythm with the slow heartbeat of the earth. The dew on the blanket that gathered through the night was enticing to a parched throat but I refrained for I knew the Great Mystery would continue to support me through my prayers and intentions.

When the sun finally began its awakening journey, I stood and sang the sunrise song. The rough translation of the native language is, *"When the daylight rises, pray to him, pray to him. If you do that, whatever you want will be so."*

The tune was so uplifting, as if I was calling the sun to rise upon my request. The sun provides so much for us. That is why it is important to greet the sun and give thanks for another day - to witness the grandeur of our precious life that we have been given to live.

The animals awoke and started to stir. The geese and ducks found their morning places on the lake and managed to coexist. The squirrels and chipmunks scurried about in their morning play, chasing each other on the ground and in the trees, showing off their acrobatic feats. Life in the woods went on as usual. I was the only unnatural one, taking up space and hindering the natural state of being.

As the morning wore on, the ants decided to explore my blanket. I must have been placed near their earthly mounds. One by one they began marching in line to explore for food. They climbed upon the blanket and split into four lines. Each had their duties and communal responsibilities. The first group explored the prayers ties. They followed the tobacco scent and balanced like walking a tight-rope on the long string. The second group inspected the seated Sacred Pipe and traveled up the stem to the end of their road. The unimpressed third group made their way across and off the blanket into the patched grass and pine needles.

The last group decided to explore me. They crawled over my legs, up my arms and stopped to use their front legs to tap and explore. They tickled me as they crawled over my body and as uncomfortable as it was, I know they meant no harm. After all, I was the stranger in their encampment. As they explored I sang an honoring song to let them know I was not a threat. Eventually they were satisfied and retreated. That is all except for *one*. It was a very large black ant, a carpenter ant I surmised. The other ants were smaller in stature. *Could this be the leader?*

The ant made its way to a raised ripple in the blanket as the other ants paraded away. It climbed up and then rested on its throne. I was intrigued and as I prayed throughout the day I kept watch out of the corner of my eye. It never moved. It seemed happy and at peace to spend the day on the blanket with me.

Dusk arrived, for my third night of quest.

The chill in the air came from a breeze blowing across the lake. Soon the dew would be upon me. I wrapped my wool blanket around me and checked on my ant friend I named, "Annie". I touched the area near her with the tip of my fingernail and she gently touched her front legs to my skin. I was content that she was alive. Why I felt she was female I am not sure. It felt as if she was a queen on her throne watching over her loyal community and monitoring their safety. Not one single ant came to visit my blanket once she had arrived.

I sang the evening song to welcome the moon and stars and made another round of prayers while holding the Sacred Pipe, waiting for the arrival of the blanket of darkness.

The moon rose again appearing a tad brighter than the night before. In the stillness, I paid attention to every sound and shadow that appeared. Waiting in stillness to whatever may appear.

As the night wore on, I found myself barely able to keep my eyes open. I stared at the moon and a halo appeared around her. She was getting brighter and larger.

It expanded so large that its light swallowed me whole. I was immersed in the light. I had no form or body. I had levitated and was weightless and free. As I looked further into my own light, I had become round and circular, the complete embodiment of the full moon. I looked further around me and I could see the night sky and the constellations and I was among them. I cast my light into the night sky with my round presence. My circle was full and whole. I felt the powerful surge and magnetism. I could feel my light aid the flow of the waters and oceans on earth. My power was immense and balanced. I could hear her voice within me. I merged my being with it.

"You have touched the divine feminine. Feel her strength and power. Feel her warmth and compassion. It is fluid and magnetic. It surges and withdraws. You have touched your circle again. Its form is once again whole and complete. Embrace your circle and remember this night. Your circle will shine when you share the true light of its wisdom. The triangle is waiting again to merge with your balance. Open your circle fully and it will expand in power and love. It is for you to share the teachings."

I was happy and full. I felt as if I would burst. The heightened joy and contentment was beyond anything I could remember.

Slowly I began to drift. I made my way across the sky, getting lower and closer to the earth. Finally, I was back in my humanness. The lightness was still within me. I could still feel the surge of power. A change had taken place - an initiation and a remembrance. Something *was* different. Though complete transformation takes time, this was a big step. Where would it lead? I hoped beyond a doubt that it would leave me forever changed for the better.

CHAPTER FORTY-TWO

The fourth day began the same as the last three, greeting the sunrise with song and a prayer to the directions with the Sacred Pipe.

I checked on my companion Annie. There was subtle movement. She had survived the evening as I had. The dew had formed small droplets around her and kept her safe. I knew once the sun rose completely the droplets would evaporate and give her more space.

By mid-day, I was extremely fatigued. I barely had the ambition to stand so I prayed sitting down in a relaxed position on the blanket.

I turned my head to my companion and I noticed the sun's direct rays had dried both the blanket and my friend. Her body was shriveled and tiny. The once large ant was now pruned and lifeless. I gently touched the blanket near her and her body broke apart into three sections. Tears welled up in my eyes. Her presence had been significant to me. I had learned over the years about the knowledge of different life forms and the medicine gifts they have to teach us. The ant is about strength, duty and community. This was the essence of her gift and teachings.

The clouds blew in overhead and the sun dimmed in reverence to honor her passing. The birds began to chime in unison in perfect rhythm. I paid attention to their symbiotic melody. I hummed along and as I did they seemed to sing louder. Vocal sounds, not words came out of me as I honored her with tears.

Then the most amazing thing happened right before me. One by one, a trail of small ants came to retrieve their queen. The first three ants in line carried each of her pieces on their backs, and the rest fell in the long procession line behind. I sang until they were completely off the blanket and out of sight. It was amazing that even the smallest creatures have their own natural ceremony, one that I would have surely missed if I had not paid attention or made the connection. I was sure that there was more than I could understand happening in the moment but I was grateful to have been present and witness the experience.

On my final night, the wind picked up and a light rain began to fall. I hovered under the blanket protecting the Sacred Pipe. I must have dozed off for many hours, kneeling upright cradling the pipe. The bowl was warm from the grip of my hand. I heard the rustling of leaves as the birds sang their early pre-dawn tune.

Grandma Tula appeared and cut the altar ties to end the quest. We walked back to the lodge to once again purify with a giant stone. She called the spirits, placed the large stone inside the lodge, settled herself and motioned for me to crawl in.

She sang and prayed and finally asked about what had happened. As I recalled becoming the moon she commented, "Ah ha, good, good."

I recalled the ant and the song that the birds sang and that I joined in with their melody. When all was revealed, I awaited her interpretation.

"You found your circle. The moon has healed you and given it back to you. Continue to honor her with the ceremony as the grandmothers have taught you. In time you will teach other women. The triangle will appear soon. He will help you to complete your healing. There will be ebb and flow, a push and pull. Remember not to push him too far," she cautioned.

"The ant has taught you and has given you its power with its crossing - to lead by having strength, honoring your duty and creating community. It has also given you the medicine to cross over those who leave the earth. The song was created to honor and lead the passage into the spirit world. This is a great honor. Another child will come to you to teach you the way. It will be very different from the others and the responsibility will take even more effort. Remember the Great Spirit will never give you more than you can handle. You have passed three more tests and completed their teachings. The test of *fortitude,* a strong heart and mind to endure disappointments, even with the loss of the ant ally, you continued on and kept to your quest. The test of *truth,* to know which is real, that all living things must die and accepting that change is always around the corner. The last test of *humility*, the path without recognition which provides clarity and keeps you moving ahead as you listened and followed my instructions to return to another quest and another year to serve the Sundance elder and ceremony. You have done well my dear, aho," she concluded.

The ceremony ended and I looked forward to eating my first meal in days. I walked up the path to the cabin and as I turned around Grandma Tula was nowhere to be seen. She must have decided to leave me alone to rest and refuel.

After some oatmeal, a banana and a cup of tea, I took a shower and went to bed. Sleep came easily and regenerated both my mind and body. I would journal later. For now, a golden slumber awaited.

CHAPTER FORTY-THREE

My body must have been exhausted because I did not stir once. Nor did I recall any dreams. My body rested and regenerated as the time passed. I had slept a full twelve hours before my body resumed its normal functions.

It can take a couple of days to re-enter everyday life after a ceremonial vision quest. Time slows down when in solitude, especially during longer quests. Rule of thumb, I have found that the length of time of the quest is usually the time it takes to reorient yourself. This quest was for four days so it will take me at least four days to ease myself back into my daily life. With that rule in mind, I gave myself four days before I took phone clients, taught classes or had any other interactions.

I wrote in my journal all of what I experienced. I knew it was important to write while it was still fresh in my mind. This was the last evening before I headed home.

I hoped Grandma Tula would return this evening. I had a few gifts for her: the traditional gifts of the four sacred herbs, tobacco, sage, cedar and sweet grass, a new Pendleton blanket, and a handmade shawl that took many hours to fringe. The shawl was sky blue and I embroidered stars and moons along the border. Every stitch was sewn with prayer and gratitude. I hoped she would enjoy it.

At the end of the day I made my final fire in the pit. As the fire began its trail of sweet smoke, I softly sang a prayer song called, "Walking the Red Road."

I must have dozed off because I did not hear her approach. Her shadow appeared close to me as she poked me with her staff.

"Wake up, Laurel. Didn't you get enough rest today?" she chuckled.

"Sorry. I am still recovering a bit. I was hoping you would return tonight though. I have some gifts for you. Please sit down. Would like some tea or hot water?" I remembered I had the water on low on the kitchen stove.

"No. Not tonight," she answered.

"Then please excuse me for a minute while I get my giveaway from the cabin." I said.

I turned the stove off, gathered the gifts and brought them outside.

"Thank you, Grandmother for your teachings and for helping me through this quest."

As I gifted the blanket and the four sacred herbs, she nodded her head in approval. I unfolded the shawl and her eyes grew wide.

"Ah, what is this?" she crooned.

She reached and pressed it closely to her eyes. She smiled and winked at me.

"Did you make this? This is beautiful, such delicate work. I can feel the love and prayers that went into its creation. This is a masterpiece," she exclaimed.

"I am glad you like it." I smiled.

She wrapped it around her and stood from her chair. She began to sway back and forth as if she was dancing. She opened her arms wide as if she was going to take flight. The metallic white fringe shimmered in the firelight. It really was beautiful on her.

"I wonder what the spirit grandmothers will help you create for me the next time," she pondered out loud.

Next time, what did she mean? Was I going to quest again with her? I hadn't yet recuperated from this one. How can this be?

"Come back in the autumn. Stay in preparation to quest again. I know fasting is hard and the time and commitment it takes. I know it takes you away from your work and supporting yourself financially but this *is* important. I know you understand this. You are healing and understanding the Grandmother's Way. It will be the gift to help other women."

She waved goodbye and danced down the path in her new shawl.

"Wait." I called to her.

She stopped and turned to face me once more.

"You said you would reveal the herbs that I have used?" I asked.

"You are not ready yet. Definitely next time," she nodded.

Quickly she turned and disappeared down the path.

Frustration arose in my body. *What the hell? How many times do I have to go through this?* I had now completed a total of eleven vision quests.

I was barely making ends meet now. It was a burden financially to return to Sundance and the cabin twice this year. I had nothing else to sell of financial worth to make it back here in five months. I was barely making it back to Sundance next month, and that was after selling my engagement ring.

I calmed myself and knew that the Great Spirit would always support me. If I needed to return again in October, I would find a way. A door or window would open for me. This was not what I really wanted to think about, especially after just completing a quest.

I remembered a teaching that Granny Janice gave me after the first year that she had danced and pierced. I had asked her if it was hard and how she kept herself standing and dancing in the hot sun with no food or water. Her face and body were sunburned, her lips were cracked and her body was worn and tired. She closed her eyes and her smile broadened as she spoke.

"Laurel, the Great Mystery does not ask us to suffer just to sacrifice. I sacrificed my time and prepared my body by fasting and watching my diet for the year. I walked further and further every day to make my legs stronger. I sacrificed and committed to prepare myself every day and for the next four years until my prayer is complete. It is my giveaway for the healing of my granddaughter."

She continued her teaching, *"Once I began the dance, the people in the camps supported me, other dancers supported me, the Chief supported me, you supported me, Molly supported me and Great Mystery took care of me. I didn't nor could I have done this without the help and prayers of others and my commitment to preparation. Sacrifice is needed but suffering is optional,"* she concluded.

In this moment, I knew her words were correct. I would commit and sacrifice to my healing and to where Spirit was leading me. I did not need to look at it as hard and suffering. I needed to see it as my giveaway of time, expense and energy for the gifts that I would and had already received.

CHAPTER FORTY-FOUR

I drove home the next morning, unloaded the car and began my four days of recuperation. My consulting was scheduled to resume on Friday. I only booked four clients to ease myself back into reality.

When Friday arrived, my first client Jessica called promptly at ten o'clock. I had developed a routine years before to visit the client while they were sleeping on the night before their appointment. This allowed me to see the matrix of energy clearly. I always receive permission from each client prior to the appointment. Otherwise I do not enter their energy field.

The process is very quick. As I open up my energy and merge with their field for a few minutes and we both become one together. I am not inside their body but I can see where the imbalance is within them. I merge with their auric field for a few moments. I see energy symbolically and I have come to understand its meaning and interpretation. Once I see the imbalances, I create a remedy of several flower essences needed to bring the energy back into alignment.

The essences serve to bring mental and emotional wellbeing but as I said before, it may take several sessions for chronic cases.

Jessica's voice sounded weak, a clear confirmation that what I saw the night before was correct.

"Hello. Is this Laurel?" she asked.

"Yes it is. Thank you for calling, Jessica." I replied.

"Jessica, I see that you are dealing with mental exhaustion and depression. It seems you have had a traumatic loss in your life."

"Yes," she confirmed.

"I am seeing it is a child. I am sorry for your loss. Your heart space is what I call blown out energetically. You carry a lot of guilt. You feel as if you cannot go on. You need to understand that there was nothing you could have done differently to have changed the outcome."

"I was not home when it happened. I was away at a conference for work. If I was home I could have stopped it. My mother-in-law was babysitting at the time," she cried.

"Do you blame her?" I asked.

"No. I blame myself. He was my child. I should have been home. I didn't want to go to the conference but my supervisor said it was important. I needed my job. Now, I am on leave from work. I just can't go back. I will probably lose my job after all."

I listened as she told the whole story of what was going on in her life. Although I didn't need the information, I already knew intuitively but she needed to give voice to her feelings. I listened compassionately and sent her energy from my navel to help her in whatever way she needed.

She composed herself after a few minutes and said she felt a little better. She thanked me for listening.

"Jessica, I will give you a remedy that contains *Pine* for guilt, *Olive* for mental exhaustion, *Gorse* for the sadness and depression and I will add a few other essences to complete the remedy. I will ship it out to you today. Please take it as directed on the bottle. Do not worry if you are on any others medications because there is nothing that will interact with it since it is just the essence of the flower's vitality not the plant itself. No drug interaction to worry about."

I sensed she was on medication for depression and I did not want to change anything that was prescribed by a doctor. Flower essences can work in tandem with other methods of support. She thanked me and the call ended.

I eased back to my work schedule the rest of the day.

The calls had slowed down to book the fall school programs. A few of the schools had not booked their usual sessions. Since it was in May and only a few weeks of school were left in the year, I called several schools to remind them.

As I made the calls, I realized what had happened. School budgets were going to be cut in August and they did not know if there would be funding for my programs. They assured me they would call once they knew if the funding was appropriated.

This could put a dent in my finances for the last four months of the year. I continued to pray and trust but it was not easy. A few new clients kept me afloat.

When June rolled around, Sundance energy rolled in as well. With lots of physical energy and stamina in my step, I made final arrangements with the grannies for my pick-up at the airport. Excitement was in the air.

By mid-June, I arrived again in Texas. The dry air and suffering heat was there to welcome me once again. This would be the fourth year and the year of completion for Granny Janice. Next year would be the end of both our commitments to the Sundance.

"Come here and let me hug your neck," she commanded as she made her way to me in baggage claim.

Granny Molly was right behind her and I reached down to hug her as well.

These women had no idea how special they had become to me. I did not have any living grandmothers on either side of my family. They had all passed by the time I was a teenager. It was good to have both the grannies as teachers and loving support. Even though I only saw them once a year, I called them every month to keep in touch. I had only known them for five years and yet it felt as if they had been part my life forever.

Granny Janice was the mothering type. She gave me her heart and generosity. I stayed at her home when I was in Texas after each dance. She cooked for me and washed my dirty clothes before I went home, even though I protested. I never won these battles. I was her guest and friend and it made her feel good to take care of someone and feel needed.

I thanked her many times. Later as years passed, I was able to send her money and gift cards to help her financially when she fell ill and I had more income.

Granny Molly was a spiritual adviser. I was so grateful to have someone to share my deepest secrets, knowing that she understood. I shared my visions and Sacred Pipe experiences and she gave me profound insights on energy and healing modalities. She was a very wise, strong woman and I learned a lot from her. She too was generous, kind and loving.

The sisters were similar and yet they were different. Both had their own unique gifts that I treasured and was grateful to have in my life.

We started our long drive to the land. A quick downpour that morning flooded the dirt road and made it impassable. Granny Janice pulled out her cell phone to let the camp director know.

"Yes we are aware of it. We will come and get you with Chief Lone Elk's old truck. It has a higher suspension and can make it through the foot of water. Then have Granny Molly drive the car back into town and we will call her when the water recedes," Dan said.

"Alright," she replied.

"They're coming to get me and bring me to the land since I am a dancer and need to start purification. Take the car into town and once the water goes down they'll call you. Here, take my cell phone," she said.

Once Granny Janice was safely in the truck and headed to the land, Granny Molly and I drove the dirt road back to town. We headed towards a Tex-Mex restaurant where we could rest and have a bite to eat.

I shared with Granny Molly, Grandma Tula's tests and teachings of the Grandmother's Way and of my quest experience. One does not normally share all the pieces of their quest for it is personal and is meant for only themselves. I shared most of it with her because I looked to her for her wisdom.

"Sounds like the women's teaching will lead you into your next phase of being an elder. Age and having grandchildren can make one a grandmother but honoring the self and gaining wisdom is the only way to truly become the *Grandmother*. One needs to earn it. I think that is where she is leading you," she surmised.

"Granny, Grandma Tula said the triangle will appear soon. He will help me to complete my healing. There will be ebb and flow, a push and pull and remember not to push him too far. Do you think she was forewarning me that a man is coming? After my quest, I saw a gray-haired man in the shadows in my dreams several times. I can't really see his face, just his gray wavy hair. He doesn't step forward enough for me to see him. It is frustrating but also scary. I don't think I want to see him. What do you think?" I asked.

"It could be that you're processing what Grandma Tula prophesized but it could also be that there is such a man that you will meet in the future, and your fear holds the dream at bay," she added. "Sounds like a prayer you need to take to the Sundance tree."

I knew what that meant. During the breaks in between dancing and when the drummers rest, the Chief allowed the supporters to come into the Mystery Circle to pray and offer a small piece or pieces of flesh to the tree. Small pieces are cut from their arms by the Chief and the offering is placed into a red cloth and tied to the tree. It is a serious prayer and offering, for the only thing someone can truly give from oneself is to give their own flesh. Most people that are not on the red road do not understand this tradition. It is not self-destructive or an addictive process. It is done with reverence and in an honoring prayerful way.

Each of the last three years, I offered one piece of flesh for the prayer to be able to continue on my spiritual road and for the financial help to continue to live. Every year I have had enough to live on.

Maybe this year my prayer needed to change. Maybe it was time to open up to a partner who could help me to continue my spiritual path and support my purpose and whatever Spirit had in store for me. If I went to the tree, I had to be sure this is what I was asking for and willing to accept. The prayer needed to be considered carefully.

We sat in the parking lot of the restaurant for another four hours until finally the camp called and said the water had receded enough to get through. We arrived on the land and reunited with Granny Janice in our camp.

It was around sunset and my tasks in the kitchen were to begin in the morning. I had the evening to reunite with the friends I had made in prior years. As we sat around the small fire in our camp, we could see the small fires in the many other camps on the land. We drank boiled drip coffee and connected our hearts together in support of the upcoming ceremony.

Morning came early and the stirrings in the camps came before the sun was up. The dancers were called for predawn purifications and the sounds of the drums in the lodges stirred everyone awake.

After the four days of purification the tree was ceremonially brought in and the dancers had their last meal before the dancing began.

I wished Granny Janice a good dance and gave her a hug and a kiss. Then she was on her way to be sequestered for the next morning's grand entrance to the dance.

Kitchen duty was hot but there were enough breaks and time in between to get to the arbor to support the dancers. The new kitchen mom this year was a young woman named Georgia, whom I had never met. She was pleasant and easy to work with. She made sure everyone had breaks and time to go to the arbor to support the dancers.

By the third day of dancing, I knew I was ready to offer my flesh in prayer. When the late morning break in the dance began, I hurried with my wrapped offering of tobacco and my two swatches of red cloth. As I stood in the short line, I opened my heart to speak my prayer to the Great Spirit.

As Chief Lone Elk passed the Sacred Pipe for me to hold and pray with, he took my tobacco offering and the swatches of red cloth on which to place the small pieces of flesh.

"Four," he stated.

I had thought I gave him two swatches but I guess I handed him four instead. Two must have been stuck together. I did not correct him. I endured only the swiftness of his hand's expertise.

My prayer was simple.

"Great Spirit, if this man I see in dreams in meant for me and my path, please put him right in front of me so I will see and know him."

That was all I could pray because the flesh was taken quickly, placed in the swatches and tied to the tree by the Chief's helper.

I was given a ball of sage to wipe the blood dripping down my arm. The Chief had neatly cut the circular pattern in the form of the four directions.

When I returned to camp Granny Molly was waiting for me.

"So you did it? You made the prayer for him?" she questioned with excitement.

I nodded solemnly.

"Bless your heart girl, this is exciting. I know there's been a healing for you to open yourself to this. Then an even bigger one once he comes in," she suggested.

"What do you mean?" I asked confused.

"I mean, that relationships show you all the things that you still need to heal. Look out. There's more fun to come," she grinned.

"Ugh," I sighed.

More healing, just what I want, I sarcastically thought.

The dance finished and the feast was completed. Another year had ended and a new one had begun.

We drove back to Granny Janice's home where I stayed for two more days before returning home. We laughed and shared stories and stayed up into the wee hours of the morning.

"Laurel, I prayed for you in the Mystery Circle. I saw that you will work with medicine power. Once your moon stops, the power will flow even stronger. Your life will be hard at times for the work never stops. Don't worry. You will have a half-side who will support your work but remember you have to *allow* him to support," she emphasized.

"Did Granny Molly tell you about the prayer and flesh I offered to the tree?" I asked.

"No. That is between you and Great Spirit. I am telling you what I saw when I prayed for you in the Mystery Circle," she replied.

Granny went into her sacred room where she kept her special things for ceremony and returned with something wrapped in a red cloth.

"I am giving this to you. This bird's leg bone can be made into a whistle for you to use to call upon and communicate with the spirits. When the time is right you will be shown how to make the whistle correctly. Do you know which bird it comes from?"

I opened the red cloth, inspected the bone and I nodded.

"Please keep it safe until you are called to make the sacred object. It has already been blessed by the Sundance medicine man," she added.

"Where did you get this? This is very sacred." I stated.

"That is not important. We each need to follow our vision and getting this for you was mine. The rest is up to you. Listen to Spirit as you always have. In time you will know how to create and use it."

I was speechless. I knew it was of importance and yet I did not know how to create the sacredness which this piece would become. I would bring it home and place it in a safe place until the time was right. With a teary hug I thanked her and quietly thanked Great Spirit.

CHAPTER FORTY-FIVE

When I arrived home it was back to life as usual. The fourth of July was around the corner and I was asked to teach at an adult evening summer education program. I had done similar classes during the spring and fall semesters last year.

The woman who was in charge of the program, asked if I could give a two-hour class on my experiences with herbs and their application. I readily agreed but wondered if there would be enough of a turn out because after all, it was summer.

At the end of July, the lecture unexpectedly yielded fifteen new students and possible clients. One by one the women took their seats as I greeted them. Although I did have a few men once in a while, my classes were primarily filled with women.

As I closed the door to the classroom and began my speech, a handsome, medium height, average build, gray-haired man entered the room. He was in a three piece navy blue suit. Clearly he was in the wrong classroom. There was something about his eyes that captured my attention. They were grayish-blue, or green with gold flecks. It was hard to as say they seemed to change back and forth.

"Oh, you must be in the wrong class. Which class are you looking for?" I asked.

"No, I am in the right class. Healing with Plants, right? I am Peter Walters," he grinned.

I was taken aback for a moment. The wave of gray curls in the back of his hair was distracting me.

"Yes, that's right," I paused. "Okay. Please take a seat."

Next, I was off and teaching for two hours.

I had each student choose a plant. I brought different leaves, roots, and flowers that I had much experience with. I did not bring any herb that was narcotic or would have interactions with medication.

The herbs were passed around the room and each person carefully held each one. One by one they each found the one that resonated with them. I sang a song to open their hearts and I had them drink the tea with the herb they chose. I had them pay attention to their mind and body and their experience. One by one I connected to their individual energy fields to see what needed healing and why they chose the one that they did.

When I entered the energy field of Peter, I recognized a lot of heartache, failed relationships and a lack of love and belief in his self. I empathized with him on a deep level for a moment and could see he was a good person. Then I quickly moved on to the next person.

As the class came to a close, I felt myself wanting to talk to Peter. I didn't know exactly why. I asked him if I could speak with him before he left. I said goodbye to the other students and gave them each a business card with my phone number and email address in case they wanted a consult in the future.

Peter waited patiently and as the last person left we began our conversation.

"I just wanted to say if you ever wanted to talk about the class or had any questions and wanted to chat over a cup of coffee, you have my card." I stammered.

What the hell was going on? These words were coming out of my mouth before I could register them in my mind. I had lost control of my mouth. There was such intensity. I was not supposed to let this man leave without talking to him, about what I had no clue.

"Here, take my business card with my work number in case you want to get in touch with me," he winked.

Oh no, what the hell just happened. He thinks I am trying to pick him up. That is not what I was trying to do.

I began to feel flush as I spoke, "Oh no, I am sorry. I am not trying to pick you up. I don't do that. I was merely trying to ask if … if…,"

He cut me off quickly.

"Well, I wouldn't mind if you *were* trying to pick me up. I would be flattered," he smiled.

Oh no. What can I say now? How do I get out of this uncomfortable situation?

"Ah... funny," I joked. "Well... nice meeting you." I gave him a hug, walked out the door and ran to my car.

Once safely in my car, I wanted to throw up. Tears and a rush of anxiety overcame me.

Why did I hug him? What was going on? I just lost control of my words, thoughts and to top it off, I just gave an unknown man a giant heartfelt hug. I did it unconsciously - like I was being pulled toward him and I was not in control of my actions. What would he think of me? Who cares, I told myself. *Just forget about him.*

I wanted to put it out of my mind. When I returned home, I quickly went to bed to forget the whole thing.

CHAPTER FORTY-SIX

I awoke to a new day and began my morning with the Sacred Pipe ceremony. I prayed with the bundle that Sharon gifted to me. This was the one that I felt called to smoke on a daily basis. It was the way I began my day after I aligned my energy and offered a tobacco prayer to the rising sun.

I offered the tobacco prayers to each direction. I felt a centered calmness around me. The prayers were of gratitude for my life and the prior night's class.

As I began to smoke my mind trailed off to the memory of Sundance a month ago. I was again standing at the sacred tree and offering my flesh and my prayer. As I stood in the sun, with sweat dripping down my forehead and blood dripping down my right arm, I could see a man in the distance crossing the Mystery Circle coming towards me. His bushy, gray hair was blowing in the wind and appeared to be glowing with the sun's rays. I felt my heart skip a beat as he came closer to me while I held the Sacred Pipe in my hands. As he came closer his face became clearer and in focus. I recognized his face. I could hear my prayer repeat from the memory of that day.

"Great Spirit, if this man I see in my dreams is meant for me and my path, please put him right in front of me so I will see and know him."

No, I said to myself as I pulled myself from the memory. *It can't be,* I repeated in disbelief. *I must be wrong. This can't be right. It can't be him.*

I finished the ceremony and placed everything back into the bundle but my mind was whirling. I did ask for the man to be put right in front of me so I could see and know him. My vision clearly had shown me Peter from last night's class.

216

His hair was shorter and he wore glasses but it *was* him. I was not sure if this would come together or not but I clearly was not going to call or initiate any further contact.

I thought, *Spirit you take care of this because I am not sure I understand correctly.* It was a good cop-out of course. How easy it was to dismiss the vision, even as clear as it was. I put it out of my mind and went on with the rest of the day.

Four afternoon clients made the day easily breeze by. As I sat down to a dinner of fresh cod and sautéed vegetables the phone rang.

"Hello." I answered.

"Hello. Is this Laurel?" he asked.

"Yes, how can I help you?" I replied.

"Hi. This is Peter Walters, from your class last night," he explained.

My heart started to race. I felt my throat tighten.

Oh no, I thought. *What do I say? Why am I so nervous? I have never had this sense of anxiety. What the hell was wrong with me?*

"Laurel, are you there?" he asked.

I hadn't realized that my thoughts were racing and a few minutes went by before I responded.

"Yes, Peter. It's good to hear from you. How are you?"

It was all I could come up with in response.

"I'm good. I thought I would call to tell you how much I enjoyed the class last night. I found it very interesting the way you sang for the plant to come forth to meet us and how you helped us choose the right one that would be useful for last night's exercise. You have a beautiful voice. It was amazing. I felt as if you were standing over me, real close when you entered my energy field. I couldn't believe it when you said you never left the front of the room during the meditation," he said.

"Thank you. I am surprised that you were aware of my presence. Many people never notice. I am usually in and out very quickly."

"I must say I am amazed at your knowledge and abilities. You must have had a lot of training," he said.

"I have had many teachings from different indigenous elders, not only Native American. I have been taught and participated in many different ceremonies over the years in my travels, but my gifts were not part of the

217

teachings. Those were given to me by the Creator itself. I had to be taught and guided by Spirit to understand how to use them." I replied.

"You surely are one interesting lady. Are you married or in a relationship?" he pressed.

"No. Are you?" I asked.

"I am going through a divorce right now. It should be finalized in a few months," he replied.

I could hear voices in the background as he was speaking.

"Do you have the television on in the background, I can hear voices?" I asked.

"No. It's my kids. I have them every other weekend," he answered.

"Kids, how many?" I asked with trepidation.

"A boy and a girl, they are both teenagers in high school. They are good kids. My other four are in college," he said.

Oh my, he has six children. Are you kidding me? I thought.

"It must keep you busy. It must be hard on them going through the separation of their mother and yourself in the divorce?"

"Actually, they have adjusted. This divorce is from my third marriage. Their mother and I divorced eight years ago," he honestly replied.

What the hell. Who is this guy? I thought. *Married three times and six kids. What is wrong with him?*

Red flags were flying left and right saying, "Danger, keep away." *I definitely got the vision from the Sacred Pipe wrong,* I thought.

I tried to remain calm and asked one final question.

"Married three times? How long did they last, Peter?"

"My first marriage lasted five years and we had our first two children. My second marriage was for fifteen years and we had four more children. My last marriage lasted a little over seven years, now I'm awaiting the divorce. Have *you* ever been married?" he asked.

"Actually several years ago, I was married for a few months but it didn't work out. Not married long enough for kids, and besides, he didn't want any. Peter, I know this might be too personal but can I ask how old you are? Twenty-seven years of marriage puts you near fifty, right?" I asked.

"I am fifty-seven. I know it is probably unacceptable to ask your age," he added.

"Not a problem. I am closing in on forty-five." I laughed.

He is twelve years older than me. Way too old for me. I wondered if I should even continue our conversation.

We did continue our conversation for two hours non-stop. We talked about our travels and our experiences in life. I was comfortable talking with him and several times we made each other laugh in delight.

He told me he was born in Vermont and had his MBA in business. He worked in a large accounting firm in Boston. He loved his work and volunteered once a month at a food kitchen for the homeless.

The conversation was coming to a close when he asked if I would like to meet him for dinner the following evening. I hesitated, not knowing how to turn him down.

"I am sorry Peter, I already have plans."

He was persistent.

"What about next Friday night? I could meet you after work. Say seven?" he asked again.

I was confused. I really wasn't interested. He had too much baggage, was too old, lived an hour away from me and couldn't stay in a relationship, but… it was just a meeting right? Not *really* a date, maybe just interesting conversation.

"Okay." I answered. "I will meet you next Friday."

"Great. I will call you next Wednesday to firm up the location and specifics. I look forward to seeing you again. Goodbye, Laurel."

"Goodbye, Peter."

I hung up the phone and my stomach began to churn and flutter.

What had I gotten myself into? Why did I agree? Maybe I will cancel when he calls next week. Just breathe and relax. Forget about it for now.

The daily clients were enough to keep me occupied for the few days. On Monday morning Nettie, the owner of the farm who gifted me the Buffalo Sacred Pipe Bundle, called me to ask for help.

"Laurel, many people who have recently come to visit the farm seem to be struggling. Some have been sick or their family members are sick and need help. I know I asked you last year, do you think you could bring a prayer gathering here like you have on your friend Sharon's land? It would be a wonderful community service for the area," she said.

"I am sorry I did not get back to you last year. I have been busy. I will pray and ask for guidance and call you back in a couple days." I replied.

On Wednesday I called Nettie back and agreed to a once a month, outside prayer gathering during the good weather. She was excited and said she would spread the word.

Peter called promptly, at seven o'clock that evening to firm up plans.

I agreed to meet him for dinner after work at his address near Boston. He offered to cook broiled seafood and vegetables. I was impressed that he wanted to cook for me but I was hesitant about meeting him at his place that was more than an hour away.

The next two days were very stressful as I tried to figure out what I was truly resisting.

On Friday, I traveled the hour and played the scene over and over in my mind. I would stay for a quick dinner, be polite and exit as soon as possible.

As soon as I entered his condo it was obvious he had little furniture or possessions, obviously a man going through a divorce. He greeted me with a smile and warm embrace and told me that I looked beautiful. He put me at ease the moment he greeted me.

He was sautéing the vegetables while the scallops and shrimp were broiling in the oven. He put out a variety of cheese and crackers on a small plate as an appetizer until dinner was ready.

He carefully poured a glass of wine and offered me the glass.

"No thanks," I said. "I don't drink."

My reaction must have caught him off guard because he replied, "Oh, I'm sorry. Would you mind if I have one?"

"Are you a regular drinker?" I questioned. "My ex-husband had a drinking problem and I don't want to go through that again."

"I rarely drink. I thought it might be nice to unwind with wine at dinner, but if it bothers you I will refrain," he said.

Here I was in his home, on his terms and I could feel I was making him uncomfortable. I decided to let go of my control a bit.

"It's okay. Go ahead. It's your home after all," I said.

Dinner was delicious. While he was not a chef, he was definitely a man who could take care of himself by cooking, cleaning and doing his own laundry.

His place was immaculate, no clutter to speak of. We sat on his leather couch after dinner, the only piece of furniture in the living room. We talked about music, his past and my past. Not much was off limits. I explained what I was doing at present for work - readings, flower essence consults, children's programs and adult wellness classes. He explained he worked in the financial industry and gave me a thorough background of his accounting experiences.

He asked if I would like to give him a reading. He had a deck of animal cards that he had bought and been playing around with.

I agreed but only if he read me first. As we sat on the floor I pulled five cards and he interpreted them as best as he could. In my assessment, he really did not have the understanding but I was impressed at how he was willing to try to read me with no experience.

I began his short reading. I didn't really pay attention to the cards because they weren't necessary. I could see right through him, his patterns and his life. When he asked his questions I answered them. He was impressed with my reading and how I came up with things that he hadn't told me.

As the night came to a close, I bade him goodbye and he kissed me with a pleasant and passionate kiss. It set the juices flowing and ignited a fire in me that I had not experienced in a while. I knew I had better leave before it got out of control. He agreed to call me in a few days.

I drove home and was surprised that it had gone so well. The kiss stirred something in me. Maybe that's why he had been married three times. He was probably a player who had a line of women to date but I knew I was only lying to myself. I had seen this man's heart. He was a good man that believed and wanted to be in a relationship. The problem was he needed to work on learning to love and value himself first.

A week went by and I heard nothing from Peter. Maybe it didn't go as well as I thought. Maybe he was disappointed that I didn't stay the night. It didn't matter. I, for once, was not going to play games or pretend to be someone other than myself. I consoled myself into believing that it was better for me to show the real authentic me and not be accepted than to pretend to be something else to please him and be heartbroken later.

CHAPTER FORTY-SEVEN

Two weeks went by and I was looking forward to the prayer circle on Sunday afternoon on Nettie's farm. The weather was expected to be beautiful.

The phone rang and I answered.

"Hello Laurel. It's Peter," he said.

"Hello," I said disinterested.

"How are you?" he asked.

"I'm fine." I said curtly.

"It's been a couple of crazy weeks. I thought I would touch base with you," he said trying to encourage the conversation.

"Uh huh," I replied.

"You're not going to make this easy on me are you?" he chuckled.

I had nothing to say or add.

"Look, I am sorry I haven't called but I truly have been busy working late and I had the kids last weekend. I ran them around to their friends and to their summer sports program. I would like to see you again. Maybe I could come out your way this time. I know it was a lot to ask you to come out to my place. I don't mind coming out to meet you," he pleaded.

"Look Peter, I'm sure you're a nice guy but you have a lot of baggage - three marriages, six kids *and* twelve years older is a big age gap. I don't think we have a lot in common," I snipped.

"Sounds like *you're* the one with the baggage. Full of preconceived ideas what will work and what won't. Sounds to me like you're making any excuse because you're afraid of dating again and getting hurt. Hey, I get it. I may have baggage but at least I am trying to take a swing at it again," he quipped.

Ooh, I cringed. *Just who the hell does he think he is?* He pressed my buttons and pissed me off. I knew darn well that he touched the truth within me and he called me on my fear. I started to laugh slowly and then became tearful. He got to me. He really got to me.

"You're right. I was disappointed when you didn't call. I *would* like to meet with you again. I will be having a prayer circle at a friend's farm tomorrow afternoon and I would like you to join us if you are free." I invited.

"Great, then can I take you to dinner?" he asked.

"Sure," I replied.

I gave him directions to my place and looked forward to his visit.

The next afternoon, Peter arrived promptly and we headed to Nettie's. As we approached the three hundred acres of land, Peter was mesmerized by the beauty of it.

"It is so beautiful here," he commented.

"Wait until you see the spot where we will have the prayer gathering. It is on a small incline in an open field. You can see the hills and the open sky."

Nettie was waiting for us, as well as close to forty people. I was in total disbelief. I had not imagined that so many people would come. I greeted each person, introduced Peter to Nettie and then began the opening song. Each person prayed with emotion and sincerity.

When it came time for Peter to pray, I listened to his prayers closely. He prayed from his heart and not his head. It was a true prayer, not a speech from his ego for other people to hear.

I was touched and moved by his gentle emotion and caring words. It was real and in the moment. I smiled because I was glad that I had invited him and could share this experience with him.

When the gathering came to a close, I sang a final song and said goodbye to each person to make a connection. We set the date and time for the next prayer circle.

Peter and I drove away together on a spiritual high from the connection to nature and people.

"That was wonderful and moving. Thank you for inviting me, Laurel. Where shall we go to dinner?" he asked.

"I am not very hungry, but there is a sub shop ten minutes up the road. Is that okay?" I asked.

"That's fine. I was hoping to take you out for something a bit more elaborate but if it is okay with you it is fine with me," he smiled.

We sat and ate our sandwiches. We were engrossed in deep conversation about nature and our presence in the universe. It was nice to talk so effortlessly and from soul to soul rather than meaningless conversation.

I noticed as time went on, I was just listening to his voice and not paying attention to his words - only the energy they emitted. It was as if small bubbles of light went from his heart and floated to mine. All I could do was smile and stay present.

When we arrived at my place I thanked him politely and hugged him and said that I looked forward to seeing him again. He looked a bit disappointed.

"Laurel, it's still early. I could in come in for a while and visit if you like," he suggested.

"Peter, I am really tired ... maybe next time," I stammered.

"Are you playing an old tape in your head?" he coaxed.

"What?" I asked.

"Do you think there is some moral code of ethics that says it is not right to invite me into your home? You know that is silly right? You can see that you can trust me. Have I not been a gentleman both times we have met? If you can read energy, you can see my intention. Maybe it is *yourself* you can't trust?" he said with a raised eyebrow.

I raged inside.

Who the hell does he think he is? He doesn't know me. He doesn't know anything. He is just trying to manipulate me. That is what men do. They manipulate you to get what they want. They are all the same. My thoughts were rambling as he was pushing me to the edge of being uncomfortable and angry.

He must have seen by my expression that he had crossed the line and pushed the button of no return and was afraid of the consequences.

"I am sorry. I don't want to push the issue or make you uncomfortable. I was hoping to have more time with you. I really enjoy being with you but I understand. I am not trying to make you feel angry or upset. Please forgive me," he said sincerely.

I calmed myself with a deep breath and my mood lightened.

What is it about this man that makes my emotions bubble to the surface so easily? He seemed to touch the very core of me, the place of my shadow, what I mask and don't want others to see; my fears and insecurities. I could just push him away, make an excuse, or cause an argument to make him leave and never see him again. However the vision in my mind of him coming towards me at the tree, while I was in my prayer was too haunting to ignore.

"You are right. I am playing an old tape. I am trying to be in control and not manipulated. I am out of my comfort zone. I am listening to old ideas and beliefs and you're asking me to look at them. How about a compromise? You can come in for a quick coffee and then leave so I can get some rest."

"That sounds great. I promise I won't overstay my welcome," he assured.

He stayed for coffee and the longer we talked, the more at ease I felt. We talked about my support at Sundance and about the grannies. I also shared about Grandma Tula and returning to the woods to quest early October. I was pouring so much of myself out to him, probably more than he even wanted to know. I opened myself up like water flowing from a deep well that could never run dry.

As we talked he held my hand lovingly, caressing it from time to time. Then ever so gently he lifted it to his lips and kissed my hand.

"What was that for?" I asked. No one had ever kissed my hand before. It felt odd and yet special.

"It is so nice to be with such an amazing woman. I am so enchanted by you. Your talents, thoughts and the spiritual commitment you have. I have never met anyone like you. You are very special," he smiled.

My eyes welled up. I could feel he really meant it. This was not an attempt at superficial chatter. As he looked in my eyes, I could feel the truth of his words.

He tenderly took my chin with his other hand and leaned forward and kissed me passionately. He smiled as he removed his lips from mine in contentment. A moment passed and then another as time stood still. We spoke no words, yet I could feel what he was feeling and I could hear what he was thinking. I was not intentionally entering his energy field as I do with clients. It just automatically happened as if we were in one bubble together.

"This woman is amazing. She is the real deal. Why have I not found her until now? I don't want to get married again but I feel this pull to her that I can't explain. I believed she was out there. I can't believe I am with her. What could she ever see in me?" he thought.

I withdrew myself from his thoughts as they overwhelmed me. Then without thinking I felt myself out of control of my body as I reached and touched his face and began to kiss him, gently at first and then with uncontrollable passion.

My mind was saying, *"Slow down, you don't want this to go too fast. You don't want to sleep with him. What will he think of you? Don't do this. You're not a loose woman. You can't act like this. Be a good girl. Get to know him. Follow the rules. It's too soon. He'll love you and leave you. All men just want a piece of tail."*

My mind was racing back and forth. Guilt and fear were somewhere in the recessed halls of my mind and trying to control me. I was enjoying the passion, losing control and falling deeply.

"Shut up. I am a woman. I can do as I please. I can trust my inner knowing. You can't control me. I will unleash myself from your hold. No more rules." I argued in my mind.

Then with my inner power, I surrendered my heart, body and soul.

The lovemaking began slowly and tenderly. He was thoughtful as he carefully caressed places I never knew existed on my body. I was burning with a fire that I had never, I mean really never felt with anyone. It was as if I was a wild jaguar let out of my cage for the first time to explore and ravage the terrain.

He began to breathe faster as I quickened my touch all over his body. I found my way to his engorged hardness and he moaned in delight. I loved the way I could make him feel. It was not a duty or expectation as it had been with my previous partners. The idea of just getting it over with was nowhere to be seen tonight. I desired him and the connection and wanted to bring him pleasure. We climaxed simultaneously and I let out a primal scream. I could not believe that it came from deep within me. As I released, I began to sob uncontrollably. Softly at first and then it became loud body shaking wails. I could not stop. I could not control the tears. I just allowed them to release for what seemed forever.

Peter just held me in his arms and showered my forehead with kisses. No words were spoken. After a while we both fell into a deep content slumber.

Peter was staring at me in the morning when I opened my eyes. His face was angelic and his grin expressed overwhelming satisfaction.

I averted his eyes and rolled away.

"Oh no, you don't," he said mischievously as he rolled on top of me, wrestling gently and making me giggle.

"You are incredible," he stated. "I think I made love with a female Bengal tiger last night."

"No, it was actually a black jaguar." I teased.

"Are you ready for more?" he asked.

"Not in the early daylight," I shuddered.

I never made love during the day. In fact, I was hoping that I could escape from the bed without him noticing my naked body. Another hang-up I guess I had.

He proceeded to kiss me and the process began once again. I found the fire within me and unleashed its power. There was something about this man that drove me wild - the way he touched me, the way he kissed me. It sent me from zero to sixty in a few seconds. The dark curly hair on his chest drove me wild. His body was so masculine, it made me shudder.

Once again we climaxed in delight. However, this time I did not cry. I was relaxed and satisfied.

"I am sorry about the crying last night, Peter. I don't know what came over me or what happened. Thank you for helping me through it and not judging me. It was like something broke in me. I could not stop or control it," I explained.

"I think that you released something. I don't think it broke. I think *we* fixed it," he winked.

I looked at him and was stunned. He had a profound way of saying the right thing at the right time. I think I had finally met my match. I giggled in delight.

CHAPTER FORTY-EIGHT

So my relationship began with Peter Walters. For the next two months, he called me mid-week and we dated every weekend. He became enmeshed in my life and I slowly approached his.

I had met his two teenagers who were absolutely wonderful but had yet to meet the older four.

I continued with consulting and classes but several of the children's programs were not being rebooked. The loss of income would become a problem soon as winter approached and I needed to heat the apartment. I trusted I would figure a way to make ends meet with Spirit's help.

The second week of October approached and Peter missed me for the week while I was on quest. He agreed to take care of my furry companion while I was away. Usually my parents kept him when I was away.

Approaching the campground again, I was feeling gloomy. I was not sure why but I felt sadness. *Could it be I would miss Peter? Or was there something deeper going on.*

Once again, I was left to myself and the cabin. It was a rainy, damp day. I was not sure if I could get a fire going. I brought several old newspapers, fat wood and plenty of lighters. Hopefully, the rain would stop and I would be back in full swing before dusk.

The rain eventually stopped before dark and I began to build the fire. The dampness in the air snuffed out the lit newspaper. I tried several times and decided to sing the "Thunder Being" song. The song calls upon the power of the Thunder Beings from the west to come and light the fire.

As I sang, I offered the four sacred herbs and centered myself with gratitude. After I finished, I lit the fire again. With patience and trust the flame eventually took hold.

I sat in the cold, chilled air. With the water heating on the stove, I waited in anticipation for Grandma's return.

I brought the turtle rattle that I made four months ago while fasting. I was shown exactly how to make it and how I was going to use it. It would be a calling rattle, one that would be used in ceremony.

As the first night wore on, Grandma Tula did not arrive. There was no rustling of leaves or noise of any kind. In fact the woods did not stir at all. It was unusual for there to be not even a peep.

The wood burned slowly through the long dark hours until only a few glowing embers remained. I knew the sun would be rising soon. I retired to the cabin with the hint of disappointment.

Maybe she forgot. Or maybe something happened to her over the last months. Could she be ill? What if I returned and she didn't? Where would that leave me?

The questions would have to wait as I needed sleep.

I rose at noon and walked down the path to the cove. My altar ties were set up neatly facing the west overlooking the lake. *How did they get there?* I placed them on the screen porch of the cabin when I arrived yesterday. Grandma Tula must have come in the early morning when I was asleep. I needed to purify before stepping into the altar. However, I did not remember where the lodge was since she took me in the dark of night. I wandered down a couple of paths in the area until I finally found it.

A small pile of wood and one large stone were left near the lodge.

Under the stone was a note and a paper bag, "Purify yourself and begin your quest. Here are the seven herbs. Pray to them and ask them to reveal themselves to you. Ask for the spirit of their medicine to work with you. They must be placed all together in the bucket of medicine water and then placed over the heated stones. See you in four days."

The instructions were clear. I was to build the sacred fire, purify and go straight to the designated altar of prayer ties. I was to take the group of seven leaves, roots and flowers and place them in the water bucket.

There was a large amount of each herb in the paper bag but I used only a small amount of each in the water and saved the rest.

I prayed to the spirits of the lake and asked permission to retrieve the water to use with the herbs in the lodge. Within three hours, I began the purification ceremony with the giant grandfather stone.

As I began a song and prayer the lodge heated quickly and I started to perspire. I invited the spirits to be with me and help me. I felt a whoosh of cold air pass by me. Seven spirit lights were dancing above the stone pit, swirling in a circle. The lights began to morph into a body of a large brown bear. It sat across from the door flap. Its gaze stared intensely and then quickly blinked.

I poured more water on the stone to greet the bear's presence. It had shape-shifted into an older woman with long white hair. She had a long sacred feather on the left side of her head. Her hair was loose and dry like straw. It was a massive amount of hair for such a small woman.

Telepathically she spoke to me and began her story.

"I am Standing Bear Dreaming Woman. It is time for your past to be healed. I have waited for you for many years. You will heal the past generations and clear the future of the women in your family and then in many other families."

"I don't understand," I replied.

"You will. During this quest you will clear yourself and the wounds of your maternal ancestors. Thank you for being here. Listen to the stone as it sings its song. It will call the seven healing spirits into the lodge. Remember each of their songs and names for they will work with you if you humble yourself. Then take the used herbs and bury them. Give them back to the earth. Honor them and pay attention. They will do the rest, blessings to you."

As she ended her communication she first changed back into the brown furry four-legged bear for a brief moment and then into one large spirit light. A great wind was swirling in the lodge; it felt like a hurricane. I was afraid the lodge would be dismantled. Then the light disappeared through the roof and the wind was released.

I poured the sacred herbal water on the large grandfather stone and it hissed and squealed in a high pitch. A rattling noise and a specific beat were clearly audible. I memorized it and hummed along. The invisible doorway below the stone pit opened and four different roots emerged from the hole and greeted me. I fanned them with the sacred fan that Grandma Janice had gifted me.

"Welcome," I said in respect.

One by one, the roots explained their purpose and the prayer song used to call upon their spirit medicine. They each explained the power of their spirit energy.

"You have been given a great responsibility. We have given you a great gift. You have taken us into your body and mind and have made the first introduction. Now you will take us into your heart and spirit. We will teach you. Once we reveal ourselves to you, you must fast once a week for eight hours while taking us, alternating a different plant each week. We will heal you and you will take our power within you for the next thirteen moons. Then we will gift our spirits and medicine completely. People use us and discard us and do not have the proper teachings and ritual. They will never know or have the full power of the medicine. We must always be returned to the earth properly after each use. Herbalists take many years to study and know the physical science of a plant but they don't understand the spirit power. Our spirit power makes the medicine but only if the correct ceremony and songs are used. Will you commit to our medicine?" they asked.

I took a moment to really think about this. *Was I willing to receive them completely?* I was not sure of all that I was committing to. I did know that this was an honor being presented to me. I knew I had come far in the last two years and was committed to changes by healing myself and following my "calling" to wherever I was being guided. Where it was all leading I could not completely know but I trusted, as challenging as it might be. I needed to do this path whatever the physical, emotional, mental and financial cost. Yes, I was open.

"Yes. I will commit to your generous offer. I humbly offer my life for your medicine," I replied.

What did I just say? My life for your medicine, it just came out of my mouth. I knew this was a heart prayer, a real prayer.

The first plant shone brightly as it spoke to my consciousness.

"I am Cramp Bark. I am the Guardian. My bark is peeled away from my root. I help to release energetic and physical toxins. I help

231

with the feminine hormones and energy. Take me sparingly and mix with others."

The spirit of the plant showed me how and when to harvest it and how many pieces were to be used in the remedy. It also reminded me of the prayer and song needed to call upon the root's spirit before its preparation and use. It also revealed how to offer it back to the earth after its use.

The next root glowed as it began its teaching.

"I am Black Cohosh. I am the Director. I lead the healing energy to the imbalance. I balance and calm the nerves in the brain and body. I too need to be used carefully."

Once again the root sang its song and offered its teaching about how and when to harvest it and how many pieces to use in the remedy.

I listened closely as the third root began its teaching.

"I am Squaw Root. I am the Purger. I release the waste that is no longer needed and I purify the body and emotions."

It then addressed the prayer, the song, its harvest and use.

As the last root emitted its glow, I waited in anticipation. This surely was not the way I had been previously trained in herbs years ago. I was paying attention to every detail and hoped I would remember. I was learning the spirit energy, a more advanced wisdom to use in healing.

"I am Valerian. I am the Filler. I keep all the spirit energy together and allow them to merge with ease. Mind, body and heart flow in a steady relaxed pace."

The root completed its song and teaching. I thanked them all for their wisdom and knowledge that each of them communicated. I could feel my body accept their presence from the steam that sizzled and entered my pores. One by one they were entering me, not through ingesting them in a tea but rather through the inhalation of steam. I felt their power and presence more intensely and directly. I was amazed with this new way of connection.

I opened up the door flap for a moment and then closed it again to finish the final round of the purification. As I prayed and sang, three small lights appeared on the ceiling of the lodge. They merged and the great bear appeared once more. This time it stood and towered above me. I lowered my head in reverence and my averted eyes.

"Aho, Grandmother Standing Bear, welcome," I said.

The large bear morphed once again into the small woman and sat across from the closed door flap.

"There are three more above ground plant spirits that wish to work with you. You have also taken them internally but now you will meet their spirits. Their prayers and songs are different as their useable part is above the earth. The root has a song, the leaves have a song and the flower has one too. They will show you all you need. Will you commit to them for thirteen moons as well?" she asked.

"Yes Grandmother, I will," I replied.

"Blessings to you," she replied and shifted into the beautiful chocolate brown bear.

As I watched her magical display, I became aware of my own body shifting. My face was being pulled and stretched and my body was being pulled forward until I found myself on all fours. I began to scratch the earth to push my body up and realized I had claws and paws. *What was happening? Was this real?* I could only see fur. My nose was much longer and I could clearly smell the sweetness of the soil and the water. The smells were overwhelming me. I was much smaller than Standing Bear, as I was just a cub. I rolled on the floor of the lodge onto my back and I noticed an object on the ceiling shining brightly.

And then it hit me, I remember this. This was a part of the dream I had before I went to the woman's ceremony. The object began to drip a golden liquid. I recalled how sweet it was in the dream. Drop by drop, I allowed myself to receive its elixir into my oddly shaped snout. As I partook of the nectar, three plants grew instantly from the earth.

I could clearly smell the fragrance of the leaves and flower petals with my snout which lightened my spirit. One by one their leaves and flowers danced as if a gentle breeze was guiding them. The first song was whispery and quick; it was the song of the leaves. The second song was airy, a celestial high octave - the song of the flower. I touched them gently as the vibration imprinted the songs in my memory.

Once again I would be taught. The leaves and flower petals had given me their first teaching of taste with Grandma Tula and now I learned scent and sound.

The first of the three danced forward and communicated to me.

"I am the Straightener. I am Spearmint. I bring energy into a balanced order. I make it soothing and pleasing to the senses."

I quickly understood its calling song, its use and how to harvest it.

The second spirit waved its leaves to impart its wisdom.

"I am the Builder. I am Raspberry Leaf. I strengthen the energy to repair what has been lost while balancing inner and outer pain."

Quickly it expressed its method of harvest, use and energetic spirit - all that would be needed.

Finally, the last one offered its flowers, several leaves and song. They blew to the ground and I carefully collected the flowers in my small paws.

"I am the Healer. I am Sage. I increase the life force. I can do all things. I purge, guard, direct, straighten, build and fill. I am the main energy to all healings. That is why I am the healer. A healer spirit works in many ways to increase and restore the natural balance. The healer spirit has the focus, flexibility, power, presence, confidence and the ability to bless with goodness. The use of all seven of us will bring power for you to use in the right way. We loan our spirit and power to you to use and protect. This will make your medicine complete."

The sage plant's spirit communication brought a clarity and awareness. Its song was reaching far deeper within me. It was a knowing life force that already existed within me since the day I came into this world. It touched the very core of me and had meaning.

I awoke on the ground of the lodge once more as my human self. *Was it all a vision?* It really felt as if I had shape-shifted into the bear cub for it was so lucid. As I completed the song and prayers, I felt a sticky substance around my mouth and the side of my face. I rubbed my face and smelled the sweet sticky substance. I sent my tongue to the corner of my mouth and tasted. It was honey.

Had I become the bear? Had Grandmother Standing Bear crossed dimensions and brought forth real honey inside the lodge? I have seen many mysterious things on my spiritual journey. I had learned not to question but to accept that what is unseen can become seen at times. In this moment, all I could express was gratitude for the magic of it all.

I completed the purification, changed into dry clothes and made my way to the colorful altar of assembled tobacco prayer ties and robes. It was nearing dusk when I entered the altar in a sacred way and sang the invocation.

I felt alert and stimulated from the seven plants that were infused into the steam during the purification. After the initial prayers to each of the directions were complete, I sat down to rest and observe.

What I came to realize many times after hours and days in a vision quest and in seclusion, reality slows down. Breath becomes slow and my body became relaxed and at peace. It can be a struggle at times to stay awake and alert. Only by following the sun in the sky could I get a small sense of the time of day.

The evening doves began their cooing while the sparrows and robins sang their end of day praises. The dew was settling in over the water as the mist made its way into the woods.

Squirrels scattered about to their evening trees but not before hiding one or two final acorns in their stash. The lake was still and calm as the usual breeze seemed to have disappeared.

As soon as my eyes became tired, I stood and once again made my prayerful request and thanks to each direction. Every time I felt sleepy I began the process over again. Stand, pray, sing, sit and observe - that would be my routine for the next four days.

The first evening and next day were fairly uneventful. The air was cool even though it was sunny. The temperature was predicted to be in the high 40's for the daytime. I was glad I had brought the heavier wool blankets and the buffalo robe that I had used in previous quests. Wearing the fur next to my skin kept me warm. If it rained the water rolled off the skin side and kept me dry. It was perfect for all terrain and weather.

The second night was a struggle. My legs and back were stiff and aching and my mouth was dry and thirsty. It was unusual for me to be this thirsty on the second night. I sang the songs of gratitude to shift my focus. I rocked back and forth as I sang and sat upright. As hard as I struggled, I eventually dozed off for a short while.

I traveled to a familiar place, my childhood home. I entered my bedroom and I was waiting for my father to arrive home. I was looking out the window, just waiting. I paced back and forth for a long time. Realizing he was not coming, I sat and cried. I was afraid and disappointed. I couldn't count on him. I was abandoned, all by myself.

I was afraid and sad and I became angry. I began to throw my dolls around the room, pulling off their arms and legs. Realizing what I had done, I stopped and with tears in my eyes began to put the dolls back together one by one. I tried to fix the mess I made. It was not easy. I struggled, trying to figure which arm and leg belonged on which doll. I was overwhelmed and buried in a pile of doll parts. I tried to piece them together but they were not fitting together as easily as before. I feared that I may never fix them and everyone would see what I had done. I felt so ashamed. I was a bad girl. I promised myself I would never show anger again.

An owl hooted and immediately pulled me from the dream.

The dream was vivid yet I knew it was not a real memory. It was symbolic. I wondered why I chose my dolls and not my other toys to break. It revealed the anger and disappointment that I held inside. After much thought, I understood the dolls represented the feminine. Waiting for the love and attention from the masculine and in not receiving my expectation, I attacked the symbolic feminine - the dolls.

The anger and disappointment was destroying me. I needed to piece myself back together and make myself whole. The dream mirrored what I most needed to look at. I knew exactly what was coming up - what I didn't want to see, what I wanted to leave in the shadows of pain... *the failure of my marriage.*

I was ashamed and still angry at him for his lies and deception and my stupidity for not seeing it all clearly before I married him. I was bitter and resentful, not just at him but at me (the broken doll).

I continued to carry these emotions after my divorce. I didn't want to think about it. The anger arose in me as if it was happening again in the present moment. It still held an emotional charge.

I stood and began to pray, "Oh Great Spirit, help me move this pain and anger. Help me heal this guilt and shame. Please, let this healing be gentle. Thank you for all of my blessings including my lessons and challenges, aho."

I dropped to my knees and began to sob. I tried to block my shame and anger. I withheld these emotions even as a child. I just swallowed everything and put on a brave face. Every disappointment, small or large

236

went unspoken. Every injustice or criticism went undefended. The hole in me was deep.

I was breaking apart and shattering. While I held my head a scream ripped from my lips.

"No."

I wanted to escape from this reality. I was awake and very conscious. That is why the pain was so great. I had nothing to distract myself. I could not run away. I was stuck in this seven by seven foot altar. I had to face it, feel it and deal with it. *How could I move forward if this was still haunting me?*

In the darkness I could hear a rustling of leaves. Was it an animal? Was it Grandma Tula? I wasn't afraid for I knew the Sacred Pipe and tobacco prayer ties would protect me. I welcomed and hoped for anything that could distract me from the uncomfortable emotional and mental pain I was in. But nothing and no one came from the sound in the woods.

I made it through the night. The fog over the lake could be seen during the first glimmer of light as the third day began.

Shadowy figures seemed to dance in the distance on the lake. Slowly they became clearer. There were four figures on horses. As they began their race, I noticed the horses were four different colors - black, buckskin, white and chestnut. I could see that the men had white and black paint on their arms, legs and faces. They looked eerie as the mist rolled under the horses' legs. It made me shudder. *Was this a vision?* They raced in slow motion toward me as I paid careful attention to every detail. I could hear their war cries as they rode. *Were they coming for me?* They seemed to be looking down below into the mist as they rode. The white fog rolled in quickly as they raced toward the land. The dense fog disintegrated and revealed a large massive white buffalo heading straight for me. The men on horseback were mere skeletons chasing the stampeding four-legged beast. It was too close for me to escape. I clutched the Sacred Pipe in prayer and closed my eyes. I felt a sharp pain in my chest as the animal collided with me. I could feel the horns and massive head tear through me. I could not breathe. I was stabbed in the heart. It was the most horrific physical sensation I had ever experienced. I heard the sound of my flesh tearing and then all went black.

There was no more pain. *Was I unconscious? I was not sure. Was I alive? Again, I was not sure.*

I could not see anything but I was aware of something around me. I had no body but somehow my mind was thinking. *Was this the unconscious?* I was somewhere in the dark. It was not an out-of-body experience because I could not see my body lying down below me. I must have died. My body will eventually be found and the maggots and other life forms will feed off me. My flesh will decompose and return to Grandmother Earth. I was not sad, I was not happy. I was in the void of emptiness.

CHAPTER FORTY-NINE

Time passed slowly, if there was such a thing as time. *If I am dead where is the light or the tunnel? Where are my relatives to greet me?*

The crow cawed loudly several times to lure me back to consciousness. I found myself back on the blanket inside my small altar. Grandma Tula was standing and getting ready to cut the west string to release me before sunrise. I had been lost in the abyss for two days. She said nothing. I felt myself floating and followed her to the lodge in the woods.

She poured the water for the last two rounds of purification. I recalled my experience with the spirits of the plants and the information that explained how I was to use them in the morning while fasting from food, once a week for the next thirteen months. I told her of my dream of breaking my dolls and how I understood it to be about my anger and disappointment of my marriage. She allowed me to process without interruption.

Lastly, I recalled the four skeletal horsemen and the white buffalo goring me and entering my heart, becoming one with me. I could not believe the pain I had felt. It was so heavy it made me pass out. I continued to explain my understanding. The four horsemen were the grandfathers of the four directions chasing the sacred white buffalo, the hope for the people. I had received my initiation to the sacred road by merging with the white buffalo. I had prayed to the Great Spirit for a healing to move the anger, guilt and shame and this might have been a shamanic death of releasing the old. *Would merging with this sacred*

239

being heal me and help me work with medicine? Only time would tell. As always, I ended with a prayer of gratitude.

When she began the final round I could barely hear her songs. They seemed so far away. She offered no other information but closed with a prayer.

"Great Mystery, see this woman whom you have chosen, see that her healing be complete, aho."

And then it was over. We both crawled out of the lodge. She turned away and began walking down the path to return to her home.

"Wait Grandma," I called. "I have gifts for you."

I had placed the gifts under a tarp near the lodge for safe keeping. The four sacred herbs of tobacco, sweet grass, sage and cedar and the Pendleton blanket. I also gave her a pair of porcupine earrings I had made. Her time and knowledge needed to be honored, a reciprocity that continues the circle of giving and receiving.

She turned to face me but looked toward the sky as she spoke.

"Dearest Laurel, you are so kind. You have passed the test of *"honor."* You have been honest with yourself and realized truth on this quest. You have honored me by emulating the grandmother teachings. Honor gives us a code of integrity to live by. You have passed the test of *"love."* For it is your love for Great Spirit and the People that you completed your quest and teachings even when threatened with death by the four spirit horsemen and buffalo spirit. You never left the blanket. The last teaching, *"wisdom"* will take more time. Your life experiences will give you the completion of the last test if you live in awareness. In time your life's knowledge will be passed on to others. My time with you is over. I have done my part and now it is up to you. Will you choose to live and walk these teachings? If so, the next child you will add to your four will be much different. A dense energy will always surround it. You will be shown how to work with it by the spirit world. It is time for you to follow your destiny. I will pray for you wherever that may take you."

I nodded and realized this was it. I would not see her again. This was as far as she could take me. I turned for a moment to pick up my wet towel from the ground outside the lodge and when I turned back she was gone. A brief sadness engulfed me. No long goodbyes. It was completed.

I retrieved the rest of the dried herbs near the lodge and walked back to the cabin to shower, eat and journal my experiences. It had been quite an unbelievable time.

The remainder of the day I kept quiet, trying to process and reintegrate myself. Still I felt far away and disconnected.

I turned in the key to Dana at the front desk. She asked if I had enjoyed my time. I told her I had. I decided to question her about Tula.

"Dana, do you know an elderly lady named Tula around these parts? She may live somewhere across the lake," I said as I described her in detail.

Dana looked surprised.

"Yes. I believe I know who you are talking about, Mrs. Logan. Both she and her husband used to canoe on the lake. The folks we bought the campground from twelve years ago told us about the couple. They must have been in their seventies at the time. They kept to themselves mostly. They made fires in the woods but they never caused any harm. The story is they both drowned years ago in the lake during the winter. They fell through the ice crossing the lake on foot. He fell first and she fell afterwards trying to help him. Their bodies were found in the spring, such a sad story."

These could not have been the same people. She was very much present with me. I would need to check the story through library and town records. Maybe they had an obituary picture.

"Why do you ask, Laurel?" Dana asked.

"I heard about her from one of my Native American friends who knew her. I wondered if she was still around. I hadn't heard about their deaths." I replied quickly not wanting to reveal the truth.

"Oh was she a Native American Indian? Well, that makes sense doesn't it, the canoe and nightly campfires," she added.

I thanked her and began my trip home. I would return to the area at another time to unravel Tula's mystery and find the truth.

CHAPTER FIFTY

When I arrived home, I listened to the answering machine and had received only one call. It was from Peter.

"Laurel, I hope everything went well. I would like to see you once you have rested. Call me soon. I missed you."

I smiled as I listened to his voice, but I was not ready to chat or see him. After a vision quest, it can take time for a person to re-enter everyday life, because in a way, they are not the same person. They have been given insight that needs to be processed and understood to move forward and make life changes.

I had nothing booked for this week and was surprised that no one had called to book a consult. I trusted it was what I needed to recover.

I also began my fasting with the first of the seven herbs. In the early morning, I made the tea, measuring the herb and singing its song and prayers. I fasted from all food for eight hours and remained quiet and focused. I broke the fast early in the afternoon and I tried to resume my schedule.

I noticed that I was still feeling detached. I was in my apartment but I did not feel home. I felt no desire to call Peter or connect to anything or anyone. It was a strange feeling that lasted the entire week. The following Saturday, Peter came unannounced and knocked at my door.

"Laurel, I have been calling you. I was worried. I am sorry to visit unexpectedly but you didn't return my calls."

I assured him that I was fine. It was just taking a little longer for me to get back to things.

I remembered the excitement of being with Peter before. Now I was in a void. Not happy, not sad, just drifting. It was not a bad feeling. Something was definitely different. My body was not tired and I moved about with ease but I felt far away.

Peter and I went to dinner and he asked many questions about my experience. I really did not want to talk about it.

"Peter, the experience is very personal and sacred. I was given many insights and information to use in my healing. It was powerful but I am sad. I know it was possibly the last time I will encounter Grandma Tula. In fact, when I asked about her at the campground the owner Dana informed me that she had died many years ago. I don't think it is the same woman though. I have dealt with dead spirits all my life and I would know the difference," I said with confidence.

"I am here if and when you want to share or talk. I want to be included in your life," he added.

"Thanks." I replied.

I could feel distance between us. Maybe it was one that I was placing.

We spent less time together during the winter. I applied and got a part-time job on the weekends to make ends meet. I worked at a candy store on Friday and Saturday evenings and Sunday afternoons while continuing my weekly morning fast. The schedule did not leave me too much time to see Peter.

He called once a week and then twice a month. He tried his best to stay connected and I was busy making ends meet.

The candy store allowed me to interact with many children. The excitement of candy was surely a child's favorite pleasure. Seeing the smiles as the children carefully chose each piece brought me pleasure and the fifteen extra hours a week of pay made my life survivable.

As Christmas day approached, Peter suggested that we meet and I had agreed. He took me to the Christmas brunch in Sturbridge. The feast was highly praised in the local area with so many delectable pastries. Everything was delicious and satisfying.

Since we had not seen each other in two months other than phone calls, I was feeling that our relationship was at a standstill and he was probably ready to call it quits and see other women. I could feel his level of frustration when we spoke on the phone. When we finally met our conversation was strained even further.

"Laurel, I have really missed you. We rarely see each other anymore. What has changed between us? I feel as if you are pulling away from me," he said.

"I am trying to pay my bills and get by until the spring. Some of the schools have lost their funding for my programs and my consulting slows down in the winter. I plan to teach classes at night in the spring for the adult education programs. You know I need to have the funds to get to Sundance for my fifth year of support and final commitment to Granny Janice. I'm really stressed right now," I added.

"I am sure your granny will understand if you can't make it. You are wearing yourself thin working all the time. Let me help you. I don't have a lot of money since I still pay child support to my ex-wife but I can help you with groceries and that will save you some money."

"I don't want your help. I can take care of myself. I have been doing it for years and I don't need *you* to take care of me." I snapped.

"What are you afraid of? Why can't you let me help you? I care about you. You're being called to support and help people. Let me be part of helping you to make that happen," he pleaded.

I should not have shared all of the intimate details of my life with him. I had let my guard down with him. He knew too much. He was trying to control me. He wanted things his own way.

He grabbed my hand to kiss it and I pulled away. I resisted. When I looked into his eyes, I was reminded of my prayer at the sacred Sundance tree.

"Great Spirit, if this man I see in dreams is meant for me and my path, please put him right in front of me so I will see and know him."

I knew it was Peter but I didn't want to accept him. *What was I afraid of? Why was I being so stubborn?*

I heard a voice in my left ear. It was one I remembered. It was strong and commanded my attention.

"In time, a partner "the triangle" will appear. He will help you to complete your healing. There will be ebb and flow, a push and pull, remember not to push him too far."

It was Grandma Tula's reminder. *Was I pushing him too far away from me?* I sighed heavily. I became tearful as I spoke.

"Peter, I need to figure this out. I am struggling and I don't know why. Please be patient with me. I do care for you, please understand that. I know at times it feels as if I am pushing you away. Maybe I am. I just need more time. I feel as if I am being pulled in many directions." I pleaded.

"I can't say I understand but I can let you know that I am not going anywhere. You have touched my heart, Laurel. I don't want to let you go. Just know I am here for you when you figure it out," he said.

I could feel the sadness in his heart as well as the love he had for me. I just could not feel that completely for him yet. I needed more time.

He brought me home and I gave him a small kiss, hardly anything that was memorable. He hugged me and said he would call me in a few days.

Once inside, I made the brew of all of the seven herbs. I knew it was not the routine but I needed their assistance. I felt called to use them all together. I placed the steaming cup on the floor and I smudged myself with cedar and sage and opened the Buffalo Sacred Pipe Bundle.

I prayed, sang the songs to each of the plant spirits, drank the tea in four gulps and then began the Sacred Pipe ceremony with reverence.

As I prayed my tears could not be held back. I felt lost and confused and I needed help. I sat in silence as the final pinch of tobacco was placed in the bowl. This ceremony had always brought me comfort and peace in the past.

The circle of elders surrounded me. The women began to sing the grandmother's song. I listened and rocked myself back and forth. Although they had taught me the song before, I did not sing with them. I just listened.

When they were finished, they circled around me and played their turtle shell rattles. They were piecing me back together. I could feel my energetic body changing and transforming the dense energy. I tried to get in touch with my feelings and body.

My groin was pulling and I remembered the polyp that was removed from my cervix during my marriage to Blake. The doctor had found the growth on my routine yearly visit. It was huge and was causing discomfort during intercourse but I never told Blake about it. I went through the office surgery by myself. He wouldn't have been supportive anyways. I couldn't count on him.

"The polyp was created from your fear of intimacy, dating back to your experience with your father's friend when you were fourteen. You lost your sense of trust," the grandmothers explained.

I was feeling tightness in my chest now and an unbearable sharp pain. It was my heart.

"You are afraid to give your heart away to a man because you believe he will abandon you. Your childhood grief and fear of losing your father's love the day your brother was born was your illusion. You have been isolating and driving yourself away until you gain your father's love and acceptance back. You believe you need to feel independent and secure enough to take care of yourself for your father's approval. He loves you no matter what attention he gave to your brother. You never lost his favor. You lost yourself."

Grandmother White Swan spoke, "Every man in your life is paying the price for the wound you carry with your father. You are disappointed in not feeling loved and feeling that you were pushed aside because you were a girl. You lost trust because of your fearful experience with your father's friend Rick. You have chosen relationships in the past who have not loved you or who could not make a commitment to you. You chose men that you could keep at a distance or who would meet your expectations of abandonment, to feel safe and in control. This is not your destiny. To complete Spirit's work and your purpose you need to share the load. You know you can't do it all by yourself. Spirit has brought you the partner, the stable triangle to merge with your circle but you need to open that circle to let him in."

Yes, I was afraid. I had envisioned him, prayed for him and for Spirit's help to be able to fulfill my purpose and calling. Peter was the man I envisioned yet I was pushing him further away. My feminine was trying to be in balance, I did not have to fear or despise the masculine. I could join with it, for us to become one. He would help me and I would help him. Understanding it is one thing; doing it is much harder.

Was this the completion of the story that Grandma Tula spoke of?

"The inner voice needs to be heard, our wounds need to be nurtured and cleansed and the circle needs to be reformed. With a stronger circle we can create new whole circles no longer deformed. Then we can open our circles to merge again with the triangles and the balance of nature's energy will return."

I was beginning to understand. I delved into the honey pit to see my wounds. I must now reshape my circle by releasing all the illusions and stories I have built my life upon. I must release the anger and sadness and forgive myself for the illusion and belief of my father's rejection because I was a girl. I was just a child and could only understand with a young child's mind. The men I chose in my life, including my ex-husband, who have caused me pain because of the wounds I carry were all doing the best that they could do in that moment. As I cried, the pain in my heart began to release. I forgave myself for the stress I created in my body and for the false beliefs that kept me from loving myself and others. This would not be easy. To release the stories that limited me and kept me wounded for years would take conscious awareness and action. I believe the seven herbs, fasting and praying was moving and stirring this up in me just as Grandma Tula had planned.

When I completed the ceremony, a conscious decision was made. I had to stop wanting love and acceptance from my father. I had lived as a son and not as a daughter by stuffing my emotions and tears and expressed only my strength, leadership and accomplishments in hopes to receive his love and praise.

My life had changed in the last several years. I had divorced, lost my secure job, was struggling financially and my life was becoming more of the spiritual road that I had followed many years. I was working with clients, teaching and now with the four sacred bundles, I was being called upon to perform ceremonies for people who somehow found me when needed.

The work was fulfilling and was slowly transforming my life but this work would not pay the bills. Teaching workshops and flower essences consults was not a steady paycheck every week. Some weeks were good and others were slow.

The calls continued to come in to ask for help. Could I pray for an aunt or grandparent, a sick child or a troubled teen? My life was becoming more about prayer than ever before. Many people needed Sacred Pipe ceremonies and I was guided to fulfill that need.

Peter and I continued our relationship through the winter but because of the many snowstorms in New England, it was mostly by telephone.

As spring finally made its way to New England, I met a medicine man called Blue Coyote through an acquaintance. He invited me to his community's purification ceremony. He knew that I had been on the red road a while and had been given permission to run purification and Sacred Pipe ceremonies from our first initial meeting and conversation.

Blue Coyote was an incredible healer. His spirit helper would take over his voice and body and perform the ceremonies for him. It was a privilege to witness. He worked with all four levels of healing; physical, emotional, mental and spiritual. I became part of his community during the next three months.

Peter understood my commitment to the new community and accepted every other weekend dates. He put more focus into his career and spent more time with his children. For me, spending less time with him really did make my heart grow fonder of him. I began to miss him and looked forward to our next time together.

In mid-June I returned to Sundance. I flew in on a Monday morning to Austin instead of Dallas because it was closer to the land and the flight was much cheaper. Arrangements were made by the grannies for someone to pick me up at the airport which was only an hour away.

I was worried that whoever was picking me up would not know me or that I would not recognize them. My concern was eased when I noticed Katie waiting at baggage claim for me.

Katie was a fellow camper that I had worked with in the kitchen for the last two years. It was great to see her. We hugged and got reacquainted and I got caught up with what I missed in camp.

When we got to the land the grannies were waiting to hug my neck and asked about my travels. By lunchtime, I was in the kitchen preparing sandwiches and cooking potatoes for potato salad. We used mustard instead of mayonnaise to keep it fresher because of the Texas heat. It was great to be back on the sacred land and in service to the camp.

On Wednesday I received a surprise. The grannies had asked that I be allowed to be a part of retrieving the Sundance tree. It was an entire ceremony within it itself that I had not been able to witness before. As we drove out to the place where the tree had been tagged and prayed to during the year in advanced, people in a caravan of vehicles were singing prayer songs through their rolled down windows. A few of the men as warriors let out their war cries to let the tree know it was time that its life would be taken for the ceremony.

As the grannies and I stepped into the high tall grass on our journey to the tree, I had a sense to walk fast. Not understanding why, I did what I thought was right. Halfway there I stepped into a large hole. I felt my foot sink into the mound and I felt small stings. I pulled my foot out and lifted it. I had a mound of fire ants attached to my ankle and leg. I quickly prayed and asked for forgiveness for my stupidity and corrupting their home and stamped my foot on the ground several times to loosen them from my skin without killing any of them. It seemed to have worked for I only received a few initial small bites. I was lucky. If I had been bitten by all the ants on my leg, I would have probably been down for a few days.

I ran to the tree and watched the ceremony of feeding it water and tobacco prayers before watching the first ceremonial chop with an axe. Each dancer in turn was allowed to make their chop and coup to the trunk. Then the few selected men quickly chopped the rest of it as the women cried with their tremolo screams to grieve for its life. When the tree began to fall many people were there to catch it. It never touches the ground for it is sacred. It was placed on a flatbed truck and was hauled back to the gate. Once at the gate it was taken off the truck by all of us and we carried it in to the land and into the Mystery Circle to be planted in the middle of the circle. As the hundred or so people carried it in we stopped four times to rest and pray until we finally raised it up with all the beautiful robes and prayer ties from the dancers and the special items that are placed in the nest of the tree.

The top branches waved with the light wind and the drummers began their songs of praise as the tree was secured, fed water and then fed with sacred foods and a prayer.

We all danced in place and the tree gave us its power and life force. I could feel the electric waves of energy radiating from the ground up through my body to my heart. It was emotional as it surged from my heart and expanded to encompass the circle of people and back into the tree. I was grateful to feel this power and have this experience. It felt healing and energizing at the same time. Once again time slowed down. It felt like we were in the Mystery Circle for days, yet I know it was only a couple of hours.

The drummers completed their songs and we left the sacred circle and began our trek back to our camps.

"How was that?" Granny Molly asked.

"It was a wonderful, very powerful healing energy. I could feel the tree and its life force even though it has been chopped down and it should've been dead," I said.

"That tree is supernatural. It becomes the connection to the Creator and spirit world. It is the bridge from the sun to the earth. It will fill the circle with healing and will renew the energy for the coming year," Granny Janice replied. "Here Laurel, I have a piece of the tree for you that I chopped. I have a piece for each of us."

She handed me the piece and I took it back to my tent, smudged it with sage and cedar and placed it in my medicine bag around my neck. I would keep it close to my heart for the remainder of the dance and hopefully for years to come.

During my time in camp many new people from other camps came to visit before the dancing began. As customary the kitchen is expected to offer them food or drink as hospitality. I offered many of them coffee or cold sweet tea.

One man named Stanley Baxter came into the camp and was sunburned and parched. He was from a camp in Arkansas. He was going to be completing his fourth year of dance. He said he had a severe headache and hoped that it would be better before he had to begin his dance the next morning. I offered energy work for him to relieve his pain.

He smiled and said, "Sister, I would be much obliged if you could help me."

I laid my hands upon his temples at first and then slid them down to the back of his neck and then to his forehead as I prayed. I felt him relax. Pictures were coming to my mind. I could see his life and his dance. He was a special man. He would be a chief in this circle someday. He was very dehydrated and he needed to drink a lot of water today.

My body sweated profusely whenever I did energy work on someone because my body heated up. It was not intentional it just happened.

I could see he would have a good dance and that he was dancing to save his marriage. After a few moments I felt it was time to stop so I removed my hands from his head.

"How are you feeling now, Stanley?" I asked.

"Much better, my headache is gone, Sister," he replied.

"That's good. I think you are dehydrated. You need to drink a lot of water the rest of today. I know you will be fasting as of tomorrow. I will be sure when I drink during the dance to remember to drink for you and say a prayer."

"Thank you. I appreciate your kindness," he smiled.

"Will you be working in the medical tent this year?" he asked.

"No, I don't think so. I think my task will be in the camp's kitchen as in the past years."

"Too bad, your healing hands could give comfort to the dancers. If I need your assistance would it be okay to send for you during the dance?" he asked again.

"I am not sure if it is customary since they will have trained medical staff on hand. If you need assistance I would be happy to help if my camp director releases me to help you. I believe you will do just fine." I assured him.

The last day of dance was very hot and the sun was strong. It was late morning and many dancers were *falling out*, which means they were passing out and hopefully having a vision. Once they regained consciousness some of them were brought to the medical tent.

When I finished cooking the final pieces of chicken to be added to the feast mid-afternoon, a runner from the medical tent came asking for a woman named Laurel.

"Do you know where I can find Laurel?" he asked.

"I am Laurel." I answered.

"Can you come with me to the medical tent?" he again asked.

"Wait a minute, I need permission to leave."

I found the camp director Dan filling the water supply tanks.

"Dan, I have been asked to go to the medical tent, can I leave the kitchen? The chicken is cooked and ready to be brought to the feast."

"Why did they ask for you?" he asked.

I looked to the man for an answer. I had not asked him why, for in ceremony you don't ask a lot of questions.

"Chief Lone Elk asked for her," he replied.

I was puzzled. *Why would he ask for me?*

"Go. If Chief wants you, you better hurry." Dan said.

I felt called to take my sacred bundle with me but I didn't know why. When I got to the tent there was a woman lifeless but breathing.

I reported to the Chief Lone Elk directly. He was the lead intercessor of the dance. The dancers were on a short break and in between rounds.

"Your name has come up a couple of times today. Stanley and Janice have both said that I should call for you. This woman Donna is from my camp. We have doctored her but she is still struggling. Help her if you can. Do not engage in talking for she is still in Sundance vision."

He walked out of the tent and back into the Mystery Circle.

I knelt down beside her and started with a prayer. I filled the Sacred Pipe from the Earth Bundle that Sharon had gifted to me. It was the one I was called to take with me on this trip. I prayed for the woman to come back to the dance and be healed to complete her prayer. As I prayed out loud she closed her eyes. After offering the smoke to the directions, I blew the smoke over her four times in her power centers.

I could see her spirit had touched the land of the dead for she had connected with her mother. I traveled to find her. Her mother's spirit was asking me to help her to return to the living. She said that her daughter was in a dark place since she died a year ago. Her prayer was to see her mother again in this dance.

I remembered the song that was gifted to me from the ant as I honored her. I was not sure if it was the right one to sing but I was being called to sing it. I sang it four times and my spirit traveled back carefully with her spirit. By the time I was done the ceremony and closed the bundle she was fully back in her body and moving slowly. I told the medic that the woman seemed to be better but she might want to keep an eye on her. Within thirty minutes she resumed her dancing to finish the final hours to the dance's completion.

I returned to camp and Granny Molly asked what had happened. I was uncomfortable with the details so I told her that I just prayed with the Sacred Pipe over her and it seemed to bring her back from the spirit world.

"Wonderful, but I believe you did more than just prayed," she commented.

"I went to find her. She was in between worlds visiting her dead mother. Her mother asked for me to help bring her back. So I sang a song to lead her," I explained.

"Laurel, things are changing for you. In this fifth year of supporting Sundance much has changed. Spirit is pushing you and calling you to the healing and ceremonial path. Spirit is helping people to find you and bring you out from hiding your gifts. I knew you were a healer the first day I met you. It is the humbleness in which you pray and the devotion to Spirit in which you carry yourself, along with your gifts of seeing the dead, reading energy fields and your compassion to serve others. It is time for you to step forward and be ready to serve the people fully," she said.

"I am not a healer, Granny. I am a singer. I sing and pray to the spirits on behalf of others and the prayers are answered. I don't do any of the healing. I just ask for one. The Great Spirit does the work," I clarified.

"That is just what a true healer would say," she laughed.

I shook my head and began to laugh too. I was always taught never to argue with an elder and in the big picture, a title is not important but the help and love you give is.

Once the dance completed, people gathered to feast.

Granny Molly went to her tent to gather her things to pack up before the feast. She returned with a piece of red cotton fabric.

"I have something I would like to gift you," she stated.

She handed me the red cloth and I opened it carefully. It was a beautiful sacred tail feather. It was large and sturdy, in perfect condition and lovingly cared for. My eyes misted over.

"A sacred feather is earned. One is honored with its presence. The feather does not make you special. The gifting of one is the honor. I honor you Laurel for the way you have supported my sister these past five years, for the assistance to our camp and the dance. I also honor you for the way you helped the dancers Stanley and Donna so humbly and yet powerfully. I see you, Laurel and I honor you," she said.

"Thank you, Grandma," I choked.

"Now let's go find Janice and feast," she commanded.

We headed to the area where the feast was placed on a line of long tables and found Granny Janice.

Granny Janice looked tired and depleted but she smiled and asked me to help her lay her blanket of giveaway items. As supporters passed the blanket each was encouraged to take something. Granny had set aside certain blankets and gifts for the supporters in her camp and for the Chief Lone Elk and his wife.

As she handed them out to her community it gave her great pleasure. She was grateful that she had completed her prayer and commitment for the past five years which now included her giveaway.

When all the gifts were distributed, she pulled one final gift from her bag that was to be for me.

"Laurel, I know this has been hard for you financially, to come each year to support me and the dance. I know it is also has been physically demanding on your body. You northeastern people aren't used to this heat," she laughed.

"Yes, but it is a dry heat." I chuckled back.

Most Texans had told me it was hot but it was a dry heat. I never knew the difference of dry or humid, for me it was always a scorcher.

"You have been good to me over these last five years, honoring my birthday, wedding anniversary and gifting me to help my husband and I. You are a generous, kind woman. Though you are much younger than me, I consider you a wise woman elder. You hold powers beyond your years. I knew you could help Donna today. When I cross one day into the spirit world I will leave you my Sacred Pipe bundle and the eagle fan that I was gifted when I was honored as an elder grandmother by one of the dancers. It means a lot to me and I will be sure that it makes its way to you. Sacred things should be used in a sacred way. Many people collect things and do not use them and they do not have the knowledge, power or right to use them, but *you* do. You have had training by elders and by the Great Spirit. When I am gone I want my sacred things to be used by a person who will help the people, one who will make medicine and that is you. You are a sacred being that serves the Great Spirit. I believe as time goes on you will gain more medicine power, much more than you have today but with it comes the responsibility to use it wisely. Thank you, Laurel. Bless your heart for all you have done for me and many others," she said.

She handed me a large sacred tail feather. It was magnificent.

"I honor you with this feather that was gifted to me by the Medicine Chief Walking Bear. He honored me in a ceremony that made me an elder Grandmother at Sundance last year. This feather was gifted to honor me as a respected elder woman. I gift this to you now to honor you also as an elder, even though your age is only forty-six. How you live and pray in ceremony, your service to others and your wisdom is what makes you an elder. This is the highest honor and gift I can give to you. Thank you for all your support. I love you, girl," she said.

I hugged her and I cried. I would treasure, honor and use it respectfully when Spirit guided me to do so.

As camp was breaking up and we were loading up the vehicle to leave for the airport, Donna halted us to wait.

"Laurel," she called.

"Yes," I replied.

"I barely remember you, for I was in and out of consciousness. I was told you helped me and prayed over me when I fell out of dance," she stated.

"Yes. I was asked to help. I did a ceremony for you. I believe you were in between worlds." I replied.

"Yes. I saw my mother and I did not want to return because I missed her so much. She was telling me to go back and I could not return on my own. I was stuck. Then I heard someone singing and I followed the voice and it brought me back to my body."

"Yes. I sang a song that I was given on a quest. I was told it was used to honor the dead and cross them over. I was called to use it but I did not know why." I said.

"I have been so distraught this past year since my mother's death. The song you sang helped me to release her spirit to cross over and bring me back to land of the living. I was called to bring her things with me to the dance. I was going to give them to Chief Lone Elk but I am sure that these things belong to you. My mother Maria would be honored for you to have them. Please take care of them and thank you for helping me. I am sure a woman with your experience will know what to do with them," she smiled.

She hugged me, then turned and left. I held a large beautiful blue, wool blanket that held some of her mother's precious items. I would open them later in private.

As we began the drive to the airport, I had an urge to open the blanket. It got stronger and stronger. Finally, I asked the grannies to pull over at a rest stop. I told them of the strong pull to open the blanket. We began burning sage in the shell to smudge ourselves and the items inside.

I thought the personal items inside were earrings or bracelets, to my surprise it was a pipe stem and bowl separated in red wool wrappings. You could tell that both had been used for many years. They would need to be cleaned and blessed before they could be used or gifted away. I would ask Blue Coyote to bless it in his lodge at the end of summer.

"My goodness," Granny Molly exclaimed. "How many Sacred Pipe bundles do you care for now?" she asked.

"I am not sure if this one is for me or it will be gifted away." I replied.

"In light of how and why it was gifted, I believe it is for *you* to use," she assured.

My mind shifted to Grandma Tula's final words to me.

"The next child will be much different. A heavy energy will always surround it. You will be shown how to work with it from the spirit world."

"Five," I said aloud.

"What did you say, Laurel?" Granny Janice asked.

"I said this makes five bundles, five children to care for. Grandma Tula said that there would be another one to add to the four and it would be much different, a heavy energy would always surround it and that I will be shown from the spirit world how to work with it," I added.

"In the future I want you to inherit my bundle too." Granny Janice said.

Granny Molly nodded and smiled.

I could not even think of losing Granny Janice. She was still so vibrant and full of life. Hopefully she would pray with her bundle for many years. I would be honored to receive it, pray with it respectfully and most of all treasure it because it was a part of her life. She was an elder and Grandmother Sundancer and it would be a privilege to take care of the bundle but for now she had too much living to do.

"It is highly unusual to have so many bundles and for so many different purposes. Chief Lone Elk said that people caring for several bundles are people who work with medicine and are healers," Granny Janice offered.

"I believe I told her that already," confirmed Granny Molly with a grin.

I just shook my head in disbelief. Not me. I am just a servant to Spirit and helper to people. That's all. I will do what I am asked and go where I am led.

CHAPTER FIFTY-ONE

I arrived in Massachusetts late Sunday evening and drove myself home from the airport. Although I packed light, I had extra unexpected gift items to carry home.

Once home, I unpacked and retrieved my phone messages. Of course among several client bookings that needed to be taken care of, was a call from Peter.

"Hello Laurel, I hope you had a great time with the grannies and in ceremony. I know you must be tired. Please call me when you can. I would love to hear all about it. Miss you."

Poor Peter. How I struggled with this relationship. I should be excited to call him and see him but I was not. I had accumulated more experiences this week that I felt odd about sharing. He could never understand me or the life I was being called to lead. It would not be a normal life. I could not be in a normal relationship. My life would consist of much ceremony, prayer and service. *When would we have time to be a couple?*

I followed up with consult bookings the next day but did not return Peter's call. By Wednesday, I was back to consulting and on the weekend I conducted a purification lodge for Grandfather Blue Coyote's community. He had given me permission and had asked me to perform the ceremony while he was away. It was also good to be back into my regular routine of fasting once a week with the tea.

Sunday afternoon I was back to work at my second job at the candy store. At the end of my shift on Sunday when I returned home, Peter was waiting outside my apartment to meet me.

"Hi, Laurel. Glad to see you're back to your schedule," he said with sarcasm.

I could feel his anger and hurt.

"I am sorry I did not return your call," I replied.

"Are you? Are you so afraid of a relationship? You said that Spirit has shown you I am the one for you. Why are you being so stubborn? How many more hoops do you want me to jump through?" he asked.

"You don't understand. Why do you care anyways? You said you don't want to get married again, remember?"

"Yes, but things have changed. I have changed. It has been almost a year since I have met you. I want to be with you. Don't you get that?" he asked.

"You have never been in ceremony, in Sacred Pipe, in a lodge or at Sundance. You don't know the level of commitment it takes for me. You don't really get it," I argued.

"Then help me to understand. Let me learn. Let me be in ceremony with you. I am willing. Share it with me. If it is who you are let me be a part of it with you," he pleaded.

"I am afraid that once I share everything you will leave." I screamed.

"I can't promise I won't but if you trust that Spirit guided us together why do you think it won't work? It's just your fear coming up to heal, right?"

Ooh, I hated when he used my words against me. He really pushed my buttons and that is why he *was* good for me.

"Okay. I will call Grandfather Blue Coyote and ask his permission for you to sweat with the community. If he says yes, you can meet them the end of July."

Peter followed me inside and we sat on the couch. I shared my experiences at Sundance. Even though I completed my commitment of support, maybe we could return next year to support together.

"Laurel, I would like to stay tonight if it's okay," he smiled.

"Don't you have work tomorrow?" I asked.

"Yes. I brought extra clothes just in case," he winked.

"It will be a long commute for you," I advised.

"It will be well worth it just to be with you. Laurel, I have fallen in love with you," he confessed.

"Peter, I can't say I love you until I truly mean it. I do care for you but let's give it time okay."

"I will wait, Laurel. I know this will work out," he grinned.

Our passion was strong as ever. Though our time apart would have seemed to given way to awkwardness it did not. Our foreplay touching was gentle and yet made me crazed and excited. He knew exactly where to touch and kiss me. He knew my body better than I did. Judging from his excitement, bringing me pleasure also brought him more excitement. He was a very giving man. It was not all about him and that made me want to pleasure him even more. We were two people who enjoyed giving more than receiving.

I had never met a man like him. I knew he was special. He was strong yet soft. He was willful yet emotional. He was not afraid to show his heart to me. He shared his feelings, thoughts and ideas. He held nothing back.

I on the other hand withheld much in the last months. My fear still had not completely released to open my heart.

He kissed my forehead after our climax and whispered, "I love you."

He cuddled me and fell asleep. I began to cry. I felt his love. He really did mean everything he said. I could trust him. I could count on him to be there for me. I would not know how much until weeks later.

We resumed our Wednesday phone calls and dates Sunday evenings. I didn't have much time to go out with him but we made it work the best we could.

I called Grandfather Blue Coyote and asked permission for Peter to meet the community at the next purification ceremony that I conducted. I also asked if he would bless the new Sacred Pipe. His response surprised me.

"Laurel, it is important that Peter begins to take part in ceremony. If he is going to be in your life he must follow the road to support you. He will find his way. Spirit put him in your life for a reason. At the next lodge you pour, have Peter run stones for the ceremony. It will give him a way to be part of the ceremony as well as an observer. As for the Sacred Pipe blessing, we will have a private lodge ceremony just the two of us next month," he replied.

Two weeks later, Peter joined the community and observed the purification ceremony. As Grandfather Blue Coyote suggested, instead of purifying in the lodge he helped with the fire and brought each stone to the entrance of the lodge for me to place inside the pit for ceremony. He stayed outside and opened the door flap at the appropriate time when I asked. He helped with the fire and observed respectfully. As a first timer he did not participate in purification but observed the ceremony. He did however partake of the Sacred Pipe at the end of purification.

He conducted himself properly and respectfully and after discussing his experience with me I found that the Sacred Pipe had a profound effect on him. It was as if he had found his home and the way to pray that suited him. I was so happy to hear this.

He did an impeccable job of supporting the community and me. He was a natural. His presence in the community gelled as well. Everyone loved him.

In the next ceremony, two weeks later, Peter would sweat for the first time. It would be the real purification ceremony experience. I prepared him with as much teachings about the purification lodge and reminded him of the proper way to handle the Sacred Pipe. We talked about everything in detail. I held nothing back.

I explained and shared all the teachings and protocols with him while sharing my personal experiences from past years. He was fully prepared for the ceremony, or so I thought.

During the first round the door flap was closed and the ceremony began. Blue Coyote began his prayers. Peter began to hyperventilate. It seems he was claustrophobic and had never mentioned it to me. His body did well with the heat and steam but the darkness of the lodge is where his fear brought forth a memory. It took him back to his mother's womb where he struggled to come into the world. His body became stuck in the birth canal and he struggled for air. Alone in the dark tunnel his first fear for survival was deeply embedded into his psyche. Four times throughout the ceremony he almost called out to be released from the darkness but each time the door flap was opened before he spoke. He grappled with his fear and shed tears of relief when the ceremony was concluded.

He barely made it through each of the four rounds but his will moved him beyond his fear. Later he had shared that the prayer songs that I had sung during the ceremony helped him to move beyond his mental fear. It would only be at the next ceremony the following month, for Peter to realize that he had received a healing for he was never afraid of the darkness of the lodge again.

The rest of the summer consisted of clients, a couple of summer workshops and ceremony. Peter and I continued in Sacred Pipe ceremony together which helped to move our relationship forward.

At the end of August, Grandfather Blue Coyote and I prepared for purification and the blessing of the newly gifted Sacred Pipe.

During the third round the heat and steam were intense. I was forced to lay my body on the earth and feel her coolness upon my face. As usual Blue Coyote's spirit helper came in to perform the ceremony and had some unexpected words.

"This Sacred Pipe is to be used to cross-over people into the spirit world. It shall be used to help the death of the body and guide the spirit back to the place of the ancestors. This woman is being called to the holy way of medicine. She now has become the woman she was meant to be. Blue Coyote's lineage of medicine men and teachings are offering this way to her. Blue Coyote is to help her and support her if she will accept the call. She is free to accept or not."

Once again this call to the path of medicine and ceremony was calling me, at the Women's Society Initiation, years ago with Black Deer, with Grandmother Tula, and now with Grandfather Blue Coyote, this was the fourth time.

"Yes," the spirit teacher spoke again. "This will be your last and final calling."

Upon completion of the ceremony Blue Coyote was just as surprised as I.

"I will teach, help and support you in any way I can," he added.

I asked him to give me a few days to pray on my answer. After four days with a heart full of concern, I accepted the call. We talked about the way he was taught to cross people over years ago.

"I am sure the spirits will work with you directly. I will share my teachings but I believe the Crossing Sacred Pipe will lead you," he confirmed.

It didn't take long for the Crossing Sacred Pipe to be used. Lisa Parker called me in tears and had asked for me to come to the city hospital. Her father had been stricken at home and they did not believe he would make it. He was in a coma and brain dead. She asked if there was a ceremony I could perform to help him. I told her I was on my way.

I sat for a moment in silence and offered a prayer of tobacco to ask Spirit's guidance. *What, if anything, could I do to help and I did I have permission to help?*

I was led in vision to Lisa's father. He was in between worlds. He asked for a release to see his wife. He was ready to cross. I got my answer clearly. I filled the Crossing Sacred Pipe with reverence and headed to the hospital.

Knowing in the hospital that I could not smoke the pipe or use sage smoke to smudge, I brought sage water that I made to spray and clear the room and her father.

When I arrived at the hospital I spoke to Lisa.

"Lisa, I have talked to your father's spirit and he is ready to cross and be with your mother. I know this is hard to hear."

She nodded and replied, "They say there is no hope. He is on life support and the doctor said I need to make a decision."

"Let me sing to him and see if he will find his way on his own."

I sang softly to him, the four direction song, an honoring song, a prayer song and then the crossing song. I wished him peace on his journey and called upon his ancestors especially his wife to come and lead him home.

I blessed his energy centers and opened them with the sacred feather to allow his spirit to lift and leave his body.

"I think you should tell him that you love him and give him your permission to move on to have a good completion," I said.

"Give him my permission?" Lisa questioned.

"Yes. Many ill people hold on because loved ones will not let them go. They feel the pull of emotions. He is ready and you need to be ready to release him. Tell him you will be alright and that he can go on in spirit and be free from the pain and the limits of his body. I am going to find a place in the back of the hospital to smoke and pray for his release and for your loss."

I found the place to smoke and pray. In a vision, I had seen that her father needed something else to let go. I understood it was a church song that he needed.

After completing the ceremony I returned to his room. Lisa was holding his hand and in tears. Her head was lying on her father's lap.

"I did what you said. Will he cross on his own?" Lisa asked.

"I am not sure. Do you know the song, 'Amazing Grace'?" I asked.

"Yes. That was his favorite church song," she replied.

"Well that is what he needs. We need to sing the song for him," I explained.

We both began the hymn. I only knew the first verse. So we sang the verse four times. When we were through I saw his spirit lift and move up and out of the crown of his head. As it released a woman was there to meet him. I expected it was his wife. The monitor for his heart went flat. There was no resuscitation per his wishes on the health proxy.

I hugged Lisa and left her and her father's body to their privacy.

Days later, I attended the memorial service for her father. He was cremated and did not want a wake. Lisa handed me an envelope.

"What is this?" I asked.

"Just a thank you note, I really appreciate your help. I know words cannot express the gratitude for what you have done for my father but I tried," she smiled sheepishly.

"Not necessary, you are my close friend. I love you and love your father," I choked.

Later that evening, when I opened the card to read Lisa's words I was dumbstruck. Not knowing exactly how to feel in that moment. Inside the card was a generous gift card to the local grocery store. She explained she knew that in ceremony there is never a charge but felt an exchange of gratitude needed to take place.

"It is what closes the circle of giving and receiving to seal it, as you once explained to me," she wrote.

Yes, I had learned that teaching years ago. I had appreciated many elders over the years for their time and teachings with gifts and donations from my heart. I felt good that I could reciprocate my gratitude in some way back to them. So I understood Lisa's generosity and thanks but it felt awkward to be on the receiving end. It was a feeling that I would need to change in order to do the work effectively.

I would continue to lead purification ceremonies for Blue Coyote's community twice a month and taught them new songs that I had learned over the years.

Years later, I would assist the elder in ceremonial vision quests and healing ceremonies as he taught me his lineage of medicine. He became a strong ally for me. He honored me with a sacred feather and respected my visions and experience even though he was twenty-five years older than I and had much more sacred life experience.

During the late spring and summer months he traveled and asked if I would become the leader of ceremonies for his community in his lodge. He was helping me to step completely into the ceremonial role that I had been called to honor. I agreed and began to give more teachings to the community from my many experiences over the years and in time his small community became my close relatives.

In a way, we are all related because we are connected and made up of the same stuff that makes us *relations*. However when we pray together, cry together and build a sacred relationship of trust and commitment to each other over time, we become *relatives*.

I received this teaching from the wife of the Sundance Chief Lone Elk. She had explained the difference of *relation* and *relative* in a group teaching by the campfire one evening. I remembered the words of Marla Songbird.

"Relations are given love, prayers and help to understand the commitment and trust it takes to become a relative. Relatives work, pray, cry and develop a deep trust over years of service together. They can count on each other for help at any time. To move from relations to relatives one must earn that trust through their actions. We honor our relatives and pray for our relations."

The teaching came about when one woman in camp shared too much of her personal life with someone she just met. Marla wanted to make this point to help the woman realize her life and personal business is sacred and you do not share intimate information with people who are not clearly your relatives. It is still a powerful teaching for me to remember every day as I meet new people.

Everything was going well in my life and relationship with Peter until the end of September. I began to have physical discomfort in our lovemaking. I decided to get a check-up earlier than my annual exam in November. The doctor found another large polyp on my cervix. It was as big as a quarter. Once again it would need to be removed and again be tested for cancer.

We argued about whether Peter should be there for its removal. I said no. He said yes. I told him I had been alone through this before when I was married to Blake and that I had not told him about the previous office surgery.

"Laurel, you are not going through this alone. I won't let you. I will take the day off from work to be with you. You do not need to be so tough. Let me shoulder this with you," he said.

"It's nothing. You don't need to miss work because of me. It's not your problem," I said.

"It is our problem. We are a team. You don't have to do this alone," he repeated.

"I'm used to doing everything alone and by myself," I replied tearfully.

"Well no more. I want to be your half-side, Laurel. Did I say that right?" he asked.

Half-side is the term for partner or spouse in Native American teachings.

"Yes, you said it right. You mean to get married someday?" I asked.

"Yes, Laurel. I want to get a place together and get married. We have been together over a year and I am ready. Are you?" he asked.

"I would like to try living together first. It will be different living together than just dating. I suppose we could try it," I answered.

"No. Not try. We need to commit to making it work. No running away, agree?" he asked again.

It was so hard. I was struggling. *Could I trust him? Would he really be there for me?* He had a job and children, ex-wife to pay, and commitments more important. *Why did this polyp show up again?*

What was it telling me energetically that I still needed to heal? I needed insight and guidance.

"It certainly would be nice to have the support and not be alone in the office. Please let me think about it. I don't understand why another polyp has come back. There is something more to this that I need to understand. If I let you come with me and you let me down, that's it," I shouted as I further explained.

"When I was eighteen, I had chest pain and I wanted my mother to go to the hospital with me and she would not go. I guess she was tired from housework and taking care of my younger brother or maybe she thought it was not serious. I didn't ask my father because he had just come home from work and he was tired. So I drove myself to the hospital and I was terrified. I felt so alone. I waited in the waiting room all by myself feeling that no one cared. It feels so silly now but I realized then that I had to get tough and take care of myself, that I was an adult now and I was alone. It turned out that the doctor thought it might have been a gall stone attack or stress. They were not really sure. At that time, I was working seven days a week, at two jobs to pay for my car and insurance. Also at the time, I had a break-up with a boyfriend of six months. So it could have been stress who knows. I just remember not wanting to count on anyone or ask for anyone's help ever again," I explained.

"Peter, this is interesting. I am working two jobs, just like I was years ago. I am stressed about our relationship. I think this polyp and memory are significant and symbolic. When this is removed I want this to be healed so it does not return again. When Blake and I starting having stress in the relationship and I discovered his drinking and lies about his finances that he kept from me, not too soon after they found the polyp on my cervix. There is something to this. I really need to pray for clarity."

"It does sound more than coincidence," he added. "Just know I will stand by you. Whatever you need I am here for you. Please don't push me away and distance yourself. It hurts me when you do that. My relationships with women have been tough. Three marriages, all of them got tired of me. They didn't want me. I tried everything to please them but in the end I wasn't enough," he said softly.

"Sounds like you have a wound too. Were you always trying to please your mother?" I asked.

"Yes sometimes, my mother would make me feel guilty. I believe she was lonely. My parent's relationship was not the most loving. I was taught that you make do no matter how bad it is. I tried to make her happy and do little things to please her and spend time with her. I don't think it really worked. I think she was always sad and lonely with her life. She was happy to have children and grandchildren. Before she died I was in my third marriage and she told me she wanted me to be happy. Within a year of her death, my third wife asked for a divorce. My third divorce was finalized when you were at Sundance this year. Laurel, I am happy being with you. I love you," he said.

"Peter, I think you are moving too fast. You are just out of a divorce. Let's take some time and live together. I want to spend time with you, but for you to jump into another marriage before healing is not right. You need to learn that you are worthy of having someone love you for you. Not for what you can do for them or how you can please them. Do what pleases you and be happy. Don't try to find love outside of yourself. Seems like we are both trying to heal similar pieces, you are trying to please the feminine, your mother, your wives, to feel worthy to have them love you and I am trying to please the masculine, my father, and my marriage and male relationships to feel worthy and loved. We both have lost our true selves in the process of looking outside of ourselves. Maybe we were put into each other's lives to mirror our wounds so that we can each heal them. I will heal my circle so that you can heal your triangle. Then we can merge the circle and the triangle in balanced energy," I said.

"The circle and the triangle?" he asked.

"Yes. It is the great balance of energy and life. The circle represents the feminine and the triangle the masculine," I began.

I repeated the story and Grandmother Tula's words and when I completed Peter had tears in his eyes.

"That is a powerful story, Laurel," he replied.

"That reminds me. I need to make inquiries about Grandmother Tula and her husband. Dana said they died years ago. Grandmother Tula visited me at the lake and put me on vision quests. She was there, Peter. Dana must have been talking about another couple," I insisted.

"Looks like you'll be busy checking it out. I am sure you will find your answer."

He pulled me close and kissed me. I surrendered.

The next morning after Peter said goodbye and left for work, I sat with the Earth Sacred Pipe. I prayed and offered its smoke to White Swan who appeared before me. She came alone without the other twelve spirit elders.

"Aho, Grandmother. Welcome," I spoke.

"You ask about the polyp and its purpose. You still carry the wound from when you were fourteen. The secret that you keep hidden still holds shame. You lost your trust of men. Your father's friend scared you and angered you. He took your power, trust and innocence that day. You must forgive him but mostly you must forgive yourself for being afraid to speak the truth and stand up for yourself as a young woman. Keeping your silence only continues to hold the shame and loss of power. You must release and regain your power by giving voice to your pain and letting it go once and for all. The polyp is the shame and denial of your feminine. What happened that day was not your fault. However holding your silence and not telling your father for fear of losing his love only kept the wound alive. You must release the story, your shame and the polyp. Only then you will begin to heal your relationship with self, your father and be able to embrace Peter," she confirmed.

She left as soon as she gave me her insights. She must be kidding. I can't tell my father. It happened over thirty years ago. My muscles were tightening as my breath quickened. My stomach began to churn. The acid slowly began its way up my esophagus. I wanted to escape so I would not have to face the humiliation. I began to cry and shake uncontrollably. *Is this what it will take to be free? Is this what must be done to heal?* This is asking too much. I can't tell my father or Peter. I would rather die. Then I stopped and took a deep breath. *Isn't that what I was supposed to do, die to release the old self?*

I collected myself and all the strength I could muster within. I did not want to drag this wound around anymore. I was tired of it limiting my joy and happiness.

I would gather my courage and speak with my father the next evening. It did not matter if he believed me or not. I could not let my fear of losing his love stop me. Deep within me I knew he loved me and that was the truth, not the story I told myself. More importantly, I loved myself and I needed to give voice to my experience to release my shame and limitations.

I did not sleep well. I struggled on and off rehearsing my conversation with my father. I finally dozed off around four o'clock.

The next day I scheduled my surgical appointment to remove the polyp. The gynecologist had an opening in two weeks. This hopefully would give Peter enough time to change his schedule so that he could accompany me.

I had two consults which kept my mind occupied for the afternoon before I ate my dinner and drove to visit my parents.

At sunset, I drove the hour to my parent's home. They were expecting me as I had called them the day before. I entered the home with trepidation.

"Laurel, it's so nice to see you. Such an unexpected surprise, we rarely see you during the week. Come in," my mother said as she hugged me.

My father was in the living room watching baseball, his favorite pastime.

"Hi Dad," I said as I bent down to kiss his cheek.

"Hi, Laurel. The darn Red Sox's are getting creamed. They can't buy a hit. They're swinging at flies. The Jays are killing them," he said in disgust.

It was the last inning of the game, thank God. I didn't want to disturb his concentration. We watched for another ten minutes until the game was over.

"So what's new Laurel? How is that handsome man of yours?" my mother gushed.

I introduced Peter to my parents when we visited together months ago and my mother was smitten with him. Though we can't visit together often because of my schedule, both of my parents are happy I have a good man in my life.

"He is fine, Mom," I replied.

"Anything new to report?" she fished.

"We have talked about moving in together," I said looking towards my father for a reaction.

"That's a good idea. Years ago, I didn't believe in it. Today, I think it is a good idea. It gives you a good look at what your life will be like together," he said.

"Wow, Dad. I am shocked to hear you say that." I replied.

"Don't get me wrong, I still believe in marriage but I just want my kids to be happy and with the right person."

"Laurel, would you like some ice tea?" my mother asked.

"Sure that would be great, Mom," I answered.

She left and went to the kitchen. Now was my chance to be alone with my father. I began to perspire nervously.

"Dad, can I talk to you about something?" I asked.

"This sounds serious," he joked.

"It is," I replied.

I had his full attention. I felt my eyes begin to mist over. I struggled to keep my composure.

"Dad, remember a long time ago your friend Rick, the guy with the sports car?" I asked.

"Sure, it's been a long time. I think I heard he died a few years ago in a car crash. I knew his wild life would eventually kill him," he said.

"Remember the time that you let me go for a ride with him in his car when he first bought it?" I asked.

"Yes, I remember. I said around the block and you were gone for a lot longer. He was such a rebel," he confirmed.

This was getting harder by the minute. I needed to just get it out and be done with it.

"Well Dad," I paused. "The reason we were gone so long is that he took me for an ice cream. Then we went down to the lake and when we were done eating it, I asked for him to take me home but he attacked me," I started to cry.

My father was horrified as his face expressed shock. I knew he did not want to talk about this but I needed to finish.

"He pinned my arms down with one arm and with his other hand he lifted my skirt and he stuck his fingers inside me."

271

My father winced in grief.

By now my mother had entered the room and was confused with the scene.

"He forced his tongue in my mouth and I was scared. He was so strong," I said in defense.

My father lowered his head into his hands. My mother was in shock.

"I bit down hard on his tongue and managed to get away from him. I ran all the way home. He followed me with his car and said that you would never believe me if I told you. You were his friend and he said that he would say I threw myself at him but I didn't, Daddy. I didn't do anything wrong except... I didn't tell you. I was so ashamed. I felt so dirty. I didn't want you to be disappointed in me," I cried.

I sobbed like a child, weeping with such pain.

My father stood and hugged me. He said nothing at first, he just held me in his arms and that was all I needed. My mother hugged me as well. The three of us just held each other in a circle for what seemed like a long time as I released my pain.

I wiped my eyes with tissues and the conversation continued.

"Laurel, why didn't you tell me?" he asked.

"Why didn't you tell us?" my mother repeated.

"He was Dad's friend. I didn't think Dad would believe me. Besides, I was in shock and embarrassed. It has bothered me all these years. I needed to tell you. The secret was eating at me. I need to let it go by telling you. I was afraid you wouldn't love me anymore. I know that seems silly but I was young and impressionable," I said.

"Laurel, you are my daughter. I would have believed you and I probably would have pressed charges or beat the hell out of him, probably both," he yelled. "It's a good thing he is dead."

"Dad, I didn't tell you to upset you. I told you so I can finally let it go. I don't want to be ashamed anymore. I want to take my life back. Thank you both for listening," I said.

The rest of the evening was spent in quiet conversation as I revealed my upcoming office surgery in two weeks. They were concerned but I told them Peter would be accompanying me and that seemed to put them at ease.

When I left my parent's house for the long drive home, I felt a weight had been lifted from my shoulders. I was happy and lighter. *Why had it taken me so long to tell my parents?* What was important? Moving forward in my relationship with Peter and looking for a place for us to live together. I knew it was the right decision.

As for marriage, I still wanted to take my time and not rush it. Blake had rushed me before, this time I held my power and voice and chose what felt right for me. I loved Peter but I was not ready to tell him. I need to take one step at a time.

CHAPTER FIFTY-TWO

I visited the library in the campground area that week but had little success. Several days later a librarian in a nearby town led me to an archive of newspaper obituaries that confirmed Dana's information.

Tula and her husband Onas Logan had indeed drowned fourteen years ago. There was a picture of them in the article and it was definitely the same woman. It also stated that a niece, Tali Logan claimed their bodies. It made no mention of where they were buried.

I looked for more information on Tali. I was compelled to find her and speak with her. I knew it sounded ridiculous but something was driving me to find her and it would not let me go. *Could I find her? What would I say? What questions would I ask?*

Peter arrived soon after I returned to my apartment and helped me search through the address and phone directory. I found twenty names and initials for Logan's that were similar in the state of Massachusetts. None of them, however, were in the campground area. Tali must have moved way.

With Peter's help we called all twenty names and none of them were the correct relation to Tula. Then I remembered that she told me she was from New York.

"We need to look in New York, Peter. She told me that she was from New York," I stated.

I watched Peter as he tirelessly searched with me for what had now been two weeks. He searched in the evening after work and helped me make the calls. He never rolled his eyes or made me feel silly that I was searching for information of the mysterious woman who I claimed to have had a relationship with for the last two years and who had been pronounced dead fourteen years ago. *Why was he helping me? Why did he believe me?*

He caught me staring at him.

"Are you nervous about your surgery tomorrow?" he asked.

"A little, I just want it to be over." I changed the subject. "Does looking for Tali seem crazy to you? Why are you helping me?" I asked.

"Because it is important to you and I believe you. I have not had an experience like this but I believe in your gifts and if you need to find Tali Logan for some answers, I want to help you," he replied.

I hugged him and said, "Thank you, Peter. I love you."

His eyes grew wide in astonishment and filled with tears.

The words came easily and naturally without thinking. There was no hesitation. I actually surprised myself. I had finally told him that I loved him and meant it.

"Yes, I finally said it and I really mean it," I said tearfully.

He kissed my hand and then he kissed my lips. The search for Tali would resume tomorrow for this was a moment of transcendence. When we entered the bedroom together I knew for the first time, I had crossed a barrier and my wall of fear had come down. I was healing and I was finally happy. I was ready to open my heart to love and trust.

With tomorrow's upcoming surgery, it was finally time to release the polyp and the rest of the toxic energy connected to it that I no longer needed. I loved myself and the man that the Great Spirit sent to me. It was time to set myself free and live happily.

Chapter Fifty-Three

The next morning, Peter took me to my appointment and waited for me. I was an emotional and tearful wreck. I had a hard time speaking and expressing myself through the sobs. Peter was there to hold my hand until the nurse called my name.

I had prayed for a good completion, releasing the polyp that represented the fear that I was not safe sexually and physically. In letting go of the fear and denial of being a woman, I was mending my circle and reshaping my life.

The journey on the hill in Texas would lead me to Grandma Tula and the honey pit inside myself to discover my fears, wounds, self-limitations and illusions.

The power of the plant spirits were helping me to heal and the grandmother spirits were helping me to understand the Grandmother's Way. The changes can only begin to take place when a woman listens to her inner voice and follows the way of the ancient feminine teachings - gathering the twelve teachings and living them fully.

I had passed the initial phase but knew this surgery was yet another test and experience to embrace and learn.

"I release you with love. I am safe and I am free to be me." I said under my breath.

I thought that the doctor would use a numbing cream or give me a mild muscle relaxer but the doctor did neither. He went about his business talking as if it was an everyday occurrence, and for him it probably was.

I winced in pain as he cut and removed the polyp. I worked hard to relax my breathing as he cauterized the bleeding and then it was over.

He placed the polyp in a sterile container and asked, "Do you want to see it? It is a large one."

Are you kidding me? He was impressed with his work as if it was a grand prize to be paraded around. Maybe to him it was. The last doctor who removed my polyp years ago never offered me a look at it. *Why would he?*

Right now I wanted to throw up at the thought of seeing it. Then I relaxed and realized that maybe this doctor was offering me something that I needed to face, something that my body and mind had created to help me heal this shadow piece.

"Yes. I would like to see it," I replied.

He handed the glass container to me.

"We will send it to the lab to be tested for malignancy, but usually polyps are non-threatening."

I looked closely, as he handed me the container. *This piece is no longer needed in me. It has served its purpose*, I thought. *Thank you for giving me the pain and insight to heal my life.*

The malformed tissue smeared with my blood was not the easiest thing to view. I offered it gratitude for it had once been a part of me and now was removed so that I could move forward.

My body felt stronger and my emotions felt clearer. The burden was released. In less than a couple of hours I was back at home resting. The doctor's orders were to wait two weeks before resuming sexual activity and Peter, as usual, was very understanding.

I resumed my search for Tali a few days later and I finally found a good lead. In a small town near the Catskills Mountains called Big Indian, I found a *Talise Logan*. I called the number and asked for Tula or Onas Logan.

"Sorry you have the wrong number," the female voice replied.

"Oh I am sorry. Are you related to them?" I asked hoping she would confirm.

"I am their niece. They both passed a long time ago. Goodbye," she said as she hung up the phone abruptly.

I convinced Peter to drive out the following weekend with me.

"It could a romantic weekend," I encouraged.

"Laurel, how are you going to meet her? Are you going to just knock on her door? She could have you arrested."

"I don't think I would be pestered to find her if this was not going to work out," I said.

"Who is pestering you?" he asked.

"I don't know. I am being drawn to find her at every waking moment. I don't know what I will say, but it is important. I have to do this," I replied.

"Okay. We'll go but we have to get moving on finding a place to live together. We need to get a place before winter. I hate moving in the winter," he pushed.

"Okay, I promise to look seriously when we get back from Big Indian."

I had many flower essence consults booked the week before our trip. It was a good week financially. The last appointment on Friday afternoon was very interesting. The woman was calling from New York. She had sent her payment ahead and I realized she was from New Paltz, near the area I would be visiting the next day. I wondered how she heard of my services.

"Hello, Abby. This is Laurel. How did you come across my name?" I asked.

"Believe it or not I was in Texas and I got your name from one of my business associates. She said she had met you at some ceremony this year and you gave her a remedy of flower essences that helped her with her anxiety and menopause symptoms. Her name is Joan Williams," she replied.

"Yes. I know her," I answered.

At Sundance camp this year, I brought a few of my remedies with me. Over the years I learned that the mental and emotional stress can be overwhelming. So this year, I brought a few just in case people needed support.

Joan Williams was a new woman in our camp who was struggling with anxiety. I offered her one of the remedies to use for the week and gave her the rest of the bottle to take home. I also recommended a consult down the road.

278

"I appreciate her recommendation," I said.

When I scanned Abby's energy field, I could see that the lower part of her column of energy was twisted. It involved security, sexuality and a lot of fear. As I tuned in further, I could see that she had anxiety because she was molested as a child. In cases like this the person does not always remember the molestation so I needed to tread lightly.

"I see that your energy bands and power centers are off in the lower half of your body. Please understand that I am reading energy only. I am not a doctor. Sometimes the stressed energy can cause physical, emotional and mental resistance which can lead to anxiety, fear, anger, sadness, aches, pains and stiffness," I continued.

"What I am seeing is unresolved fear of security and safety matters. Sometimes it is related to something from childhood. It is affecting the lower three power centers. Does this make sense to you?" I asked.

"I think so. Could you be more specific?" she asked.

"Sometimes we are aware of it and other times we don't remember. What I see, is that it is affecting your romantic relationships. You struggle with trust issues, fear for your safety and you worry a lot about money," I answered.

"Yes. You are right. I was six-years-old when I was sexually molested by a fifteen-year-old neighbor," she answered tearfully.

"I am so sorry. Did you tell anyone or ever seek counseling?" I asked.

"No. I kept it hidden. It happened twice. I was so scared and embarrassed. He said he would hurt my dog if I told anyone, I can't believe I am telling you this now," she replied.

"I think it might be a good idea to seek counseling and maybe find a support group. You are not alone. I believe you need to deal with the repressed emotions or you will never trust or feel safe in any relationship. What happened was not your fault. You deserve to be happy," I confirmed.

After asking her a few questions that I use on my consulting questionnaire, I made a remedy that would help her with her fear, self-esteem, trust and abuse issues. The special remedy included Larch, Star of Bethlehem, Centaury and three others supportive essences.

After the consult was over, I asked her about the area of Big Indian.

"Do you live near Big Indian?" I asked.

"I live about forty miles away. The area is really pretty. It has a spring and lots of woods. There is a small resort used for retreats that is really remote. There are a couple of nice bed and breakfast inns as well. Are you interested in the area?" she asked.

"Yes, my boyfriend and I will be visiting for a weekend getaway."

"Summer and autumn are usually busy with tourists in the surrounding areas. You might want to check for accommodations ahead of time."

"Okay thanks, Abby. I will mail the essence remedy to you today. Would you like to set up another consult? It is best to follow up in three to four weeks. By that time you may need a change in the remedy."

"I think I would like to try them for two weeks first and then make the appointment later," she replied.

"That's fine. Good luck to you. Let me know if you need another consult. Goodbye."

"Goodbye, Laurel," she replied.

I checked the internet for accommodations near or in Big Indian and found nothing available.

Peter arrived for dinner. As we ate the baked salmon and wild rice that I had prepared, I explained our predicament.

"Not to worry. I took care of it. I booked us at a quaint inn. You did say there would be romance right?" he laughed.

"You're such a man," I laughed and rolled my eyes. "Seriously, thank you for making the reservations. What would I do without you?" I smiled.

As he grabbed my hand and kissed it gently he replied, "Don't worry honey, I won't give you the chance to find that out."

Chapter Fifty-Four

We began our trip at four o'clock the next morning. We both smudged ourselves and the vehicle with burning sage smoke and offered a tobacco prayer to keep us safe on the journey to New York and on our return trip home.

Peter was not as excited to beat the traffic as I was. The early start was not agreeable to him or his lack of sleep.

If the truth be told, I was too excited to sleep. So why not start out early? We took turns driving and made a few quick stops to use the rest rooms. The trip took about three moving hours.

The landscape in the mountains of southeastern New York was beautiful. We passed into the area after sunrise. We could see the mist over the mountains. Peter, an avid photographer, stopped to take several shots of the mystical beauty.

We found a breakfast café where we could eat and stretch our legs. The place was welcoming and friendly. People were relaxed and slow paced. Folks knew each other and gathered to chat about the weather and town events. It reminded me very much of places that I had been to in the White Mountains of New Hampshire and in Vermont.

In my many travels over the years, I had come to realize New England would always be my home - the land of pastures, hills, oceans, woods and beaches - the complete package. No wonder so many tourists flocked to New England in the summer and autumn.

Peter was busy chatting with the waitress and discussing directions to our inn. From what he gathered it was only a few miles away. It was now eight o'clock in the morning. Check in time was not until three o'clock this afternoon. What can we do for seven hours?

I asked the waitress for directions to the road where Talise Logan lived. She looked surprised.

"There is only one place on that road. It is a retreat place but there aren't any retreats or workshops scheduled for this weekend," she noted.

Thinking fast I replied, "I just want to see the area. I may want to book a retreat for a group of friends in the spring next year. I want to make sure it would work."

"That's fine. The owner Talise Logan should be home. She pretty much keeps to herself. I'll get you the phone number in case you want to call first," she confirmed.

"Great. Thanks," I replied.

So the retreat place that Abby spoke of yesterday is Talise's place. I find that very interesting. I realized there are no coincidences.

We ate our breakfast leisurely and chatted with the locals. They were friendly and interesting. Peter would have stayed all morning but I was ready to find Talise.

We bade goodbye to the waitress and thanked her for her hospitality.

"Do you think we should call Talise first?" Peter asked.

"No. Let's drive up the road and see the land and I will offer tobacco that all goes well."

"Okay. If you think that is best," he replied.

The long road was secluded. Just the way I liked it. The birds were singing and a doe was on the side of the road. Peter took a photograph quickly without disturbing her.

"This is beautiful and private," Peter announced. "There must be at least forty acres."

Further up the road, I asked Peter to stop the car and I got out. I offered a pinch of tobacco to the four directions, above, below and held it to my heart as I prayed.

"Great Spirit, I felt I was led here. Please let this woman see that my arrival is good. Please help me tell this woman what I need to and help me understand why I was called here. With gratitude I offer this tobacco, aho."

I offered the tobacco and let the breeze blow it over the land. I returned to the car and we began the drive to the large renovated farm house estate.

We pulled up the driveway and parked close to the building. My stomach began to whirl with worry and excitement. As I stood on the front porch and knocked on the door, a tiger swallow-tail butterfly came from the east and flew over my shoulder. This was a good sign. A butterfly is a transformative energy and coming in from the east of new beginnings and understanding was the confirmation to my prayer.

The door opened and a woman in her late-sixties answered and stood before me with a smile. She had the same facial features as Grandma Tula. Her hair was long and streaked with white and gray strands. She wore a long cotton summer dress and had a long tooth earring on her left ear.

"Are you lost? We have no retreats scheduled this weekend. I'm sorry," she said.

"Hello. My name is Laurel Cannon. I am looking for Talise Logan."

"Yes, that is me," she replied.

"I apologize for showing up unannounced. Are you the niece of Tula Logan? I believe she has led me to you for some reason."

"My aunt has been dead for many years. How could you know her?" she doubted.

"Are you a spiritual woman, Mrs. Logan?" I asked.

She nodded.

"To understand what I am about to say, you will need to have an open mind," I reassured.

She looked at Peter and waited for his introduction.

"Oh, I am sorry. This is my boyfriend, Peter Walters. We drove out here together," I said.

"So where are you from?" she asked.

"We're from Massachusetts," I answered.

Talise eventually let her guard down and invited us in for a glass of ice tea.

We sat in the living area, which was cheery and bright. I was not sure how I should begin the conversation.

"Mrs. Logan," I started.

"Please call me Talise. It means "beautiful waters" in Iroquois. My mother was a combination of tribes and my father was French and Iroquois," she offered.

I began my story and I hoped she would listen until its completion.

"Grandmother Talise, I have been on the red road for many years. I have had both male and female teachers. I have been taught and given permission to lead ceremonies and I have been guided by Great Spirit through visions. I have fasted and prayed many times over the last twenty-eight years and have come to realize that beyond the gifts the Creator has given to me, I am still being called to something sacred but not of my choosing. Three years ago, I was supporting a Sundance in Texas and in a dream an elder woman was calling me to meet her. The urge continued until through prayer, I found the place on a lake at a campground. I was called to complete seven days of silence and it is where I met Grandma Tula."

She nodded and did not bat an eye.

I continued on.

"I did not understand why I needed to be there. The first evening, I was sitting by the fire and she came up the path and sat down with me. She gave me the teachings of the circle and the triangle and said I needed to heal and then help other women heal. This was not the first time I was told that I would help the women heal, also during a vision quest initiation into a women's society I was told the same."

"I spent the week with Grandmother Tula and in the evenings she gave me different teas to help me in my healing and vision. Then she said I needed to prepare myself for a four day quest and return to her in the autumn. I returned five months later and quested with her guidance again. Then she asked me to return again the following year in both the spring and autumn. So there have been four times of teachings and questing with her. On the last quest, she said we were completed. I received the twelve teachings of the Grandmother's Way and my specific seven medicine plant spirits and their teachings. When I asked the owner of the campground about her, I was told that she had died several years before. In disbelief I searched old newspaper obituaries and found that she did indeed cross over. I had read that a niece, Tali Logan had claimed the body of the couple but there was no mention of the burial. So I searched in Massachusetts and then I remembered that she told me she was from southeastern New York, which led me to finding your phone number and address. I called you a week ago and asked for Tula and Onas Logan. I don't know why but I needed to find you, perhaps to make sense of this," I said exhausted.

"Laurel, do you see dead spirits?" she asked.

"Yes. I have seen them since I was a child but Grandma Tula did not appear to be dead. Usually I can tell the difference," I insisted.

"Auntie Tula was a powerful lady; she could leave her body and appear somewhere else when needed. She was a holy woman, not only a healer but a highly spiritual woman. She worked with a lot of women's issues. She traveled around and brought her medicine (knowledge) to help women heal. I believe you were chosen because you have similar gifts and are being called to the same path. Tell me do you care for more than one Sacred Pipe Bundle?" she asked.

I hesitated to answer, for the information was very personal to me. I nodded slowly.

"I was given one many years ago in my late twenties but in the last four years I have been gifted others," I replied.

"It is because you are nearing the grandmother stage of becoming free from the blood that gives birth. Now a woman births her wisdom and completes herself and can commit to her new or destined path. Some women change careers or find new ones once there children have left the nest. A woman finds a new found freedom to fulfill her spirit's and heart's desire. Some women use this time to become more creative. All women need to return to the soul's calling and creative expression."

She continued, "However, you are being called to do more than that. Few women receive this calling anymore. It is never one that is ever asked for or wanted. The calling comes for one who has sacrificed, trained in ceremony for years, has the gift of a seer, journeys to other dimensions and understands energy and healing. The call comes later in life, when the blood dries up and frees her from her cycles of isolation. You are being prepared. The spirit world is giving you a new training to first go through the change and heal and then to use your experience to help others. You can only help heal in others what you have healed in yourself. All of us on earth are here to work on healing and evolve ourselves but rarely is one called to give her life to the sacred anymore, working solely with Great Spirit and the path of medicine."

She continued, "Thank you for following the inner spiritual call to come and meet me. I think I know why we needed to meet. We need to have a special ceremony with the dark moon and then I will teach you the ceremony to use in the future for other women. The dark moon is on Monday. Can you stay a few days with me?"

Peter frowned.

"Laurel, I have to get back to work," he reminded.

"Laurel can stay with me and you can come back in a few days to bring her home," she suggested.

I looked to Peter with pleading eyes.

"I can come home by bus or train to Framingham so you do not have to return. Maybe you could pick me up at the bus terminal. It won't be too much out of your way."

Peter shook his head. He knew I had made up my mind. I was staying.

"It's okay. I will come back if you want to stay. Maybe we can have our romantic weekend then," he shrugged.

"Thank you, Peter. You're the best," I beamed.

I wrapped my arms around his neck and planted a big one on his lips. We both shook our heads and laughed.

"Honey, I think I am in for a wild ride with you," he smiled.

"*Life* is a wild ride, not just *my* life. I need to follow where it leads me," I added.

"I would love for you both to stay overnight this evening. I have plenty of room," Talise offered.

"Thank you. We already have a place to stay for tonight," Peter replied.

"Then I will see you tomorrow, Laurel," she nodded.

"Yes, you will. Thank you for your hospitality. I would like to offer to rent a room for the next few days," I suggested.

"I appreciate that. I am sure we can work something out."

"Perfect. See you tomorrow, Grandmother," I said.

"Thank you for honoring me as an elder. I can see you came here with a good heart," she smiled and bade me goodbye.

Peter and I found the bed and breakfast inn for the evening. It wasn't as special as the retreat land but it was clean and quaint.

As excited as I was about the upcoming days, I could feel Peter's distance. We hadn't spoken for the last twenty minutes.

Finally as we entered the room and sat down on the bed I began the conversation.

"Peter, I am sorry. I know you are disappointed. Can't we make the most of the rest of the weekend?" I asked.

He shrugged.

"I am trying to be supportive. Is this the kind of life you are going to lead? I mean *we* are going to lead?" he asked.

"I'm not sure but probably. I am in a process of change. I must listen and follow Spirit on this path," I said.

"Does that path include me?" he asked with raised eyebrows.

"I don't think you would have been put in my life if you were not included in that change," I answered.

I could feel his dismay of uncertainty. *Could he forge ahead with me and continue to be patient?* I knew the woman he was falling in love with might not be the same woman he could end up with. I knew that I needed this change, healing and transformation. It was for my betterment and to become who I was meant to be. I understood that to my very core.

He looked at me and then turned away.

"Why don't we go for a walk and then get a nice quiet dinner," I proposed.

He nodded in agreement.

As we walked hand in hand down the street we were both separate in our thoughts.

"Honey, would you like to go to that little restaurant on the corner?" he pointed.

"Sure," I replied.

We were brought to a small table in the corner, dimly lit with a red candle. I looked at the menu and realized that it had mostly Italian cuisine. I am not very fond of pasta or dishes with red sauces. Peter on the other hand loved all cuisines, especially pasta.

Though I did not want to distance him anymore than he already was feeling, I felt an urge to speak up and voice my dissatisfaction.

"Peter, there is not much on this menu that I care to eat. Everything is covered in sauce and I don't like pasta."

He looked at me with disgust.

"There are not a lot of restaurants on this street to choose from," he argued.

I began to get irritated and spoke in a huff.

"I know what I want and don't want. I am not going to eat something that makes me feel sick afterwards. I will find what I want and need," I quipped.

"Why are you getting upset over food?" he argued.

His look was all it took to trigger me. The words spewed out of my mouth before I could harness them. This good, complacent, little girl was not going to make nice and take what she got. She was going to get what she desired.

"Don't look at me that way just because I have an opinion, need or desire. You have the right to get the food you want and so should I. I am no less worthy than you and you better get used to it, Mister." I said in a huff.

"What the hell are you talking about?" he asked.

The waiter came over and asked if we were ready to order. My stern and determined emotion must have scared him away.

"I will give you a few more minutes," he said trying to escape.

"No please come back. I am ready and I have a request," I said calmly.

"Is it possible to have a piece of baked chicken with no sauce, no pasta and just some vegetables?" I asked.

The waiter looked a little puzzled but said, "Let me check on that for you," and returned to the kitchen.

Peter looked at me puzzled.

"What are you doing?" he asked.

"Getting what I want," I said with confidence.

The waiter returned and assured me it was no problem. In thirty minutes, we both had what we desired. For Peter it was spaghetti and meatballs and for me it was baked unadorned chicken and vegetables.

We chatted about meaningless subjects over dinner and decide to return to the inn. Our walk back was silent and awkward. As we got closer to the inn Peter turned to me.

"Okay, do you mind telling me what is going on with you? Why did you feel the need to attack me?" he asked.

I thought about it for a moment. I had voiced something that was very deep and emotional. It was as if I went from zero to sixty in a flash. I felt agitated and angry and I needed to express it freely, but maybe directing it at Peter was inappropriate.

"I am sorry for directing my dissatisfaction at you. It was as if something arose very deep in me that I needed to speak and I had no control over. I don't ever remember expressing anger like that before," I explained.

"Honey, are you unhappy with me? Do you still want to be together?" he asked.

"Yes, Peter. Though I think this week apart will do me good. I think I need solitude not from you but from everything. Do you think you could go back to my apartment and go through my appointment book and call my consults for the next few days? Tell them I will call them back to rebook when I return? Just apologize and say something unexpected came up. Call my parents and ask them to keep Sunshine until I return?" I asked.

"Sure," he replied.

"Thanks," I kissed him gently.

After we watched a little bit of television, I went into the bathroom to undress and get ready for bed. The stress of the day must have worked its way through me. My body was achy, dizzy and my heart began to have small palpitations.

Thirteen months had passed since my last menstrual cycle which had become almost non-existent in the last two years. The doctor assured me everything was normal in my regular physical check-up, despite my body feeling different sensations, like skipped heart beats, dizziness, fatigue, profuse sweating and tingling sensation as if ants were crawling all over me.

My desire for sex was voracious at times and at other times I had no desire at all which could pose problems in my newfound relationship moving forward. What started out as a hopeful romantic weekend had become, *I am tired and have a headache weekend*. Truthfully, I really was tired and had a headache.

Maybe Peter would be tired too, after all that transpired. It had been a long day. When I opened the bathroom door the lights were dimmed, he was undressed under the sheets and motioned me to the bed with a wink. I knew the look too well. This was not going to be a "hold me until we fall asleep" evening.

As he started to kiss me, I pulled away.

"Peter, please understand I am not feeling well. I am achy and have a headache. I am really tired. Could we just cuddle?" I asked.

"What I'm hearing is that you are tired of me. This is how my marriages ended, headaches and tired," he said as he pulled away.

"I thought you loved me? Is this it for us? Are you pulling away from me, Laurel?"

"No. Why are you so insecure? You know I love you." I affirmed.

He caressed my face, and began to kiss me and rub my back. He reached for my breast.

"Are you kidding me? I said NO! What is it that you don't understand? I own my body. I need to take care of my body when it doesn't feel well. You need to respect me. I know you have needs so take care of them yourself. Maybe I will feel more amorous in the morning but not now. Why are you trying to force yourself on me?" I argued.

I left the bed and sat down in the antique captain's chair in the corner of the room. My memories flooded back to my teenage years. Remembering my father's friend forcing his unwanted fingers into my vagina, the boys in school trying to touch my breasts, or pinch my butt. Girls put up with so much; afraid to speak up, even if they tried to protect themselves, they were still bombarded at every turn. Well not anymore. I am an adult woman and I can use my voice and say no.

I began to sob holding my head in my hands. The tears of pent up anger were released to appease my heart.

Peter was torn. He wanted to comfort me but thought holding me might not be appropriate. The poor man had no clue.

"Honey, I'm sorry. Please don't cry," he soothed.

"Don't tell me not to cry, Peter. I was told not to cry all my life and I didn't cry to please, so I could be strong like my father. I had things to cry about and release. We all do in life. Not crying limits you and numbs you. Eventually it paralyzes you and prevents you from feeling. I realize when people ask you not to cry, it is not to help you but to allow them not to feel discomfort. Just like it is making you feel uncomfortable right now. I have a right and need to cry and release my emotions. I have held too much back, swallowed too many emotions and kept secrets locked away."

I continued to moan in pain and sorrow.

"Then can I offer to hold you while you cry?" he asked.

Smart man, it was exactly what I needed.

"Yes. I would like that," I sniffled.

I got back into bed and he held me close as we laid there together with my head upon his naked hairy chest. I cried and cried until I fell asleep.

In the morning I was exhausted, as if all hell had broken loose inside. My eyes were crusted over from tears and my sinuses were stuffy and blocked. I had to blow my nose several times before my head felt relief.

I jumped in the shower before Peter awoke. Breathing in the steam of the hot water gave me a cleansing internally as well as externally. The rush of water upon my skin made me pure and whole once again.

Peter grabbed his overnight bag and jumped in the shower as soon as I was through. As we passed each other he hugged me, kissed my forehead and said good morning.

Before we left the inn, I knew I needed to share my memories that prompted my sudden outburst of tears. He held my hand as I explained about the incident with Rick and all the issues that had surfaced from entering the pit with Grandma Tula. I unloaded years of sadness, grief, fear and anger. He listened quietly with full attention until I was through.

"Laurel, I am so sorry that happened to you. Thank you for sharing it with me. Here I was pressuring you last night. How insensitive I was. I am really sorry if I added to your pain," he said.

"It is my issue to heal. I am working on it. When I told my father recently about the event he believed me and gave me comfort. I idolized him because he was the first man in my life. All daughters go through it. Their experiences, with or without their fathers, shapes their future relationships. My father passed on qualities that I can be proud of - emotionally strong, independent, intelligence and responsible. It was I who missed my father's attention when my brother was born. I decided to keep seeking his affection. I thought I had to emulate him to please him and disregard myself as a girl and then as a woman. I chased his love. I wanted his praise but in doing so I created a dysfunction in me. I lost how to express my emotions and my voice. I had repressed the fear that I was not enough."

I continued, "I drew relationships to me that didn't measure up to my father. How could they? I took on more masculine energy and less feminine energy, not balancing pieces of my own nature. I lost my center and balance as a woman. There were relationships that I had to walk away from because I was still searching for my father's love. Peter, I have always had my father's love. When my brother was born he was happy to have another male to bond with and to teach. It was *I* that hated being a girl and feeling I was not worthy of his love anymore. I can forgive myself now, for seeing things as only a child who felt displaced understood things. I have carried it for most my life. I won't let it continue to keep me in fear, or angered as an adult woman any longer. I see through my illusions and I can change my perception and change myself. I can love myself and know my worthiness by accepting all the great qualities of being a woman, like allowing myself to feel and show emotion and that includes speaking up for what I want and don't want," I explained.

"Honey, I understand. I feel this has brought us closer, you *should* communicate what you want. You deserve the very best. Thank you for sharing this with me. I love you," he smiled.

"Thank you for your patience and... I love *me* too," I laughed.

"I realized that having the polyp removed and consciously releasing it this second time has helped me to move emotions and use my voice to speak about it and share it with you. I can forgive myself for keeping it buried and I can forgive my father's friend and move forward. I have been a silent victim by keeping the emotions buried. Now I can take my voice, cleanse the emotions and empower myself. I don't have to carry it anymore. The polyp was a symbolic release," I affirmed.

We hugged and in that moment I knew our relationship took a huge step forward. Everything I had experienced these few years, the women's society ceremony, the quests, supporting Sundance, the plant spirit medicine, the circle of spirit grandmothers, the gifted Sacred Pipe Bundles, leading ceremonies in Blue Coyote's community and meeting Peter was orchestrated by a divine plan to help me heal, transform myself and put me on my destined path.

Later that morning we returned to the retreat center and I kissed Peter goodbye. Grandmother Talise was waiting for me on the front porch and waved goodbye to Peter.

"I am glad you returned, Laurel. I think we have much to discuss."

We sat on the deck in the backyard. She asked me about my teachers, training, quests and years of ceremony. I shared my Sundance support experiences, the women's society initiation and my teachings and ceremony experience.

Although I did not share all the information I received in my ceremonial quests, I offered pieces. To tell all of one's vision is to lose the power of that vision.

She listened carefully and then she asked me an unusual question.

"When was your last moon time?"

"It was thirteen months ago," I replied.

"Yes, what I was feeling is right. It is time for the transition ceremony. You are young to come to the end of your cycle. Did you start your menses young?" she asked.

"Yes. I started when I was eight and I had been fairly regular until my divorce nearly seven years ago. Then I missed two to three months and the cycles were shorter. The last two years, I have only had two cycles. Each lasted for only one day," I replied.

"Laurel, when a woman misses her menses for over thirteen months after she has been slowly missing cycles for several years, she has come to the death cycle. Her body has given her life's blood for the last time and the new cycle of a sage woman begins. Now she keeps her blood inside herself and uses it to create and rebirth an older, refined wiser self - one who is free to use the remainder of her life for self-fulfillment and joy and offering her gifts and knowledge to others. It is a wonderful but sometimes difficult time because many women are not in touch with the divine feminine energy. They have not learned to honor the moon time flow and then struggle with the death of the cycle. That is why women's ceremonies are needed to balance and build strength by supporting each other in groups. That way the energy moves horizontally and can empower," she explained.

"So it will help them to mend their circle like Grandma Tula's story said?" I asked.

"Yes. Too often it takes until the cycle begins to pause and change for them to realize there are things that they need to heal. During pre-menopause and menopause they struggle with the symptoms because they fight the inevitable natural process. If they are not happy, stressed with worry, anger and fear and have buried and swallowed their voice and emotions that is when their symptoms are the worst. If they learn to honor their cycles and heal and embrace the divine feminine earlier in life, the process is easier to accept and flow with," she answered.

"That is exactly what I have been going through," I agreed.

"The circle and the triangle is nature's *energy*. The masculine energy is: the logical, the active, the strong mind and body, the hunter, provider and protector. The feminine energy is the nurturing, intuitive, compassionate, gathering, creative, strong heart and life-giving. These are energies of nature and of life. My aunt was teaching you about the energies. Each human being, man or woman, needs a balance of both energies but as women we have detached ourselves from our feminine circle of energy. It is easier for us to reshape and mend ourselves because it is natural and within us and easier to get in touch with. When we heal our true nature, we balance our self. Then we can give the feminine energies of self and let it flow to others including the many men who have lost their balance of feminine energy of strong heart, compassion and intuition. If the whole of life loses the balance to create, attune and give life, there will be no life, only destruction. So the balance of both is the key. First the feminine, which is being lost in women, needs to be recovered to heal the wounds that stop women from living their best life."

"I understand," I nodded.

"You have also been led here for another reason," she added.

"In a dream a year ago, my mother and Auntie Tula came to me and told me that a woman would be coming who would lead, teach and help the women and carry on the woman's ceremonies. I was given confirmation last night that you are that woman. Auntie Tula's Women's Sacred Pipe Bundle needs to be gifted to you. It is no coincidence that that bundle is meant for you, for it is you that heard her call to the sacred ways."

Grandmother Talise excused herself and returned with the bundle. The woolen blanket that held it was old and frayed.

"It gives me great honor and pleasure to pass this on to you, Laurel. You have found your way to this child," she smiled.

"Thank you," I choked. "It is I who is honored."

"We will bless it in the lodge tonight," she added.

I nodded in agreement. This would become the sixth child or bundle. I hoped that I could continue to be worthy to care for, protect and follow these sacred bundles with integrity the rest of my life.

Once the gifting of the Women's Sacred Pipe was completed she continued.

"Tonight we will have a purification lodge to bless the Women's Sacred Pipe. You are free to walk the grounds this afternoon. We have nearly fifty acres and there is a small dirt path where we have the lodge. Further down the path is the fire circle. I have a few women coming over to join us this evening. The ladies will bring a potluck to share."

She smiled and walked upstairs to her office area.

I was free to explore and think. As I traveled the dirt path, I found a lodge nestled among four oak trees. It made me think of Peter. He loved trees, especially the oaks in the autumn foliage. I thought of him a lot as I wandered. I had only known him for a year and I still barely knew his children. The two youngest were the only ones I had met. The others had their own lives and seemed to be happy. I knew when we moved in together that the city of Boston would not work for me. I was a small town, community orientated person. I needed to live in a slow paced, nature filled area with woods and lakes. Hopefully we would agree on a place that suited both of us.

I traveled further down the path and found a fire pit about thirteen inches deep with a circle of thirteen large stones surrounding it. The stones were smooth, like from a river or ocean. The pit was scorched and blackened from many ceremonies. Seven feet from the edge of the pit was another stone circle - this time with stones and rocks of many shapes and earth colors. In each of the four directions hung a brightly colored prayer robe that was tied to a tree branch and filled with tobacco. The space felt sacred so I did not enter. I imagined many sacred ceremonies had taken place on this land and many of those prayers were heard and answered.

I sat outside the outer circle and just observed. The squirrels and chipmunks were scurrying about but not one entered the circle. They ran around and avoided its center as if an imaginary fence protected it. I also saw a garter snake approach the outer stones, touch it and slither in another direction without ever entering the circle. It was if nature honored the circle and respected the reason it had been created. If only we as humans could have that same respect and boundaries that nature innately understands.

The robins and chickadees were flittering in the trees, calling to their mates and perhaps warning each other of my presence. I spoke a prayer of intention and gratitude that seemed to quiet and appease them. I sat there for what seemed to be a minute thinking about the blessing of the Woman's Sacred Pipe. Somehow the time had escaped me and four hours passed. Cars had begun to arrive when I returned to the house.

I was introduced to the circle of women, all of whom were middle age and older. Their smiles and nurturing nature welcomed me to their group.

"Ladies, this is Laurel. Thank you all for coming on short notice. We must support her as she accepts my Auntie Tula's bundle. Tonight it will be blessed as she becomes the caretaker of the bundle and its ceremonies."

The ladies all smiled and nodded in unison.

We proceeded to the woods and began the preparation for the purification lodge. The sacred fire was built and the stones were appropriately placed inside. The fire was lit ceremoniously and within a couple of hours the group of women and I entered the lodge on our hands and knees. The Sacred Pipe was strung above with deer skin lacing over the stone pit. The steam would clean and bless both stem and bowl.

Grandmother Talise sang the calling song to open the ceremony as she poured water on the grandfather stones. A small blue light appeared and rested on the Sacred Pipe's bowl. I thought I might have been the only one who saw it but judging from the gasps from the other women I was not.

"Aho," Grandmother Talise said.

The light morphed into a recognizable face. It was Grandma Tula. Smiling and content she spoke to me.

"You have found your way, it is good. Continue the work of the Grandmother's Way. You will help many women to mend their circle. Thank you for accepting the call and my bundle, blessings to you dearest, Laurel."

Her face disappeared and so did the light.

"Thank you Auntie, for your blessing to the pass on your bundle," Grandmother Talise prayed.

It seems she too, had seen and heard her aunt's message. I was happy Grandma's spirit was present at the ceremony. The ceremony lasted for two hours and the women made many heartfelt prayers for the bundle and myself. When lodge was completed, we made our way back to the house, changed into dry clothes and had our potluck feast.

I thanked each of the women and Grandmother Talise for a beautiful ceremony and then retired to bed. I slept for a short time and awoke before sunrise. I was being called to smoke the Women's Sacred Pipe.

I quietly made my way to the backyard and began the ceremony. When I filled the large L-shape bowl, I noticed a couple of small circles imprinted in the stone. They were all perfectly formed, no coincidence.

After I completed my prayers and filled the Sacred Pipe, I sat in silence and waited, for what I was not sure. The sky was still dark with just a glimmer of brightness. A small ball of light began its descent toward me. The ball crashed to the earth but made no sound. The circle of thirteen grandmothers who had first appeared during the women's initiation ceremony, now sat before me.

"It is time for you to meet the black grandmother. In time the white grandmother will rebirth you to the stage of elder. It is all coming together. Thank you for honoring us and all women. We will always help you to guide others. Call upon us with this Sacred Pipe whenever you need assistance," said White Swan.

Their mystical presence left as quickly as it came. Morphing into one ball of light they ascended into the sky and disappeared. I smoked and completed the ceremony with gratitude.

Grandmother Talise awoke hours later and I shared my experience with her.

"The group of women you met last night for the Sacred Pipe blessing will return again this evening. We will have a fire ceremony of the black grandmother initiation under the waning moon of release. This afternoon I would like you to take some time to think about this transition cycle and the death of the old you and things you wish to release, - roles, wounds, people, possessions and beliefs. Write them all down and we will talk later. The ladies will again bring a potluck to share."

I took the day and walked the property, visiting the fire circle again. I opened myself to the death cycle and releasing ideas, beliefs and wounds. I wrote several pages before I felt complete. I relaxed in the backyard during the late afternoon.

The group of women arrived again as sunset was nearing. We greeted each other like old friends.

"Laurel is ready to cross into the death cycle tonight and we will support her as she embraces the journey. This is a wonderful time for her," Grandmother Talise announced.

We had our potluck dinner of tasty fresh vegetable casseroles, soups, fruit and herbal teas before the fire ceremony. We chatted and enjoyed ourselves. After clean-up, we began our focus on the ceremony.

One by one, women in white cotton dresses with black shawls over their shoulders followed each other with flashlights down the dirt path until we came upon the circle that I had visited earlier in the day. A lone woman was tending the small fire that she must have built earlier at dusk.

We formed a circle around the fire pit and Grandmother Talise began the ceremony.

"We honor the dark moon of endings and follow the cycles of death to be rebirthed again. One among us has entered the thirteen month cycle of holding her blood and power inside her. Tonight she journeys with death as she no longer discharges her energy to the earth through her body. She no longer has the energy to bring forth life. Tonight she dies to the old and reclaims herself to begin walking the path of the Grandmother's Way. Let us each make a prayer to release the old and offer it to the fire to be transformed."

One by one the ladies approached the fire in silence and offered their tobacco. I was the last in the circle to pray to the fire.

My prayer was to release the old emotions of anger and fear from the past years of my life. I released the guilt and shame of the beliefs, actions and thoughts I had carried through my life up until this moment. I cried and released my sadness of never bearing human children in this lifetime. I gave it all away to be transformed into forgiveness and unconditional love for myself.

I returned to my place in the circle among the women. One by one we played our rattles, summoning the ancient grandmother spirits of the past from both our blood lineage and the spirit world. The women sang a song together over and over until I learned and sang the song with them.

A wind arose and began to lift the flames of the fire in an upward motion, confirming the grandmothers were now among us.

"Laurel now is the time to state your intentions," Grandmother Talise motioned.

As I was instructed earlier, I walked counter-clockwise to and around the fire four times and began my speech.

"Oh Grandmothers, I thank you for coming and being here with us. My blood has dried up and can no longer give life. I stand upon the earth to anchor myself and pull up her electro-magnetic power within me fully. I lift myself to connect and follow the power of the moon and honor all her cycles and bring down that power to connect it inside of me. I prepare myself for the death cycle in my body and the liberation of my spirit."

I offered tobacco once again and continued.

"Grandmothers of the Way, I release the roles of the past as child, daughter, teenager, woman, sister, wife, lover, ex-wife, caretaker of family and friend. I release my ego of job titles and previous work. I surrender my body, mind and heart to death and open up my spirit to be free for transformation. I enter the darkness fearless and with a willing heart. Thank you for the change that has and will take place. I am no longer the woman, Laurel Cannon. I choose now to walk among you."

I offered the paper from my handwritten speech to the fire. The flames consumed it quickly. Next, I offered a blank white piece of paper to symbolize the unwritten and unlimited energy I could now become. Once again the paper quickly burned end to end, until it could no longer be seen.

I returned to the circle. Each of the women and I sat down upon the earth with black shawls draped over our shoulders. We sang four more songs softly and then laid our bodies on the earth and watched the fire crackle and spark in silent meditation. One by one each woman covered me with her black shawl, as I laid on my back sending me into the darkness of my death. The physical pain of the body began. The pain in my feet, legs and thighs were numbing. My upper torso and heart began to pulse with a stabbing pain. My shoulder blades were being pushed back in an outward motion. The stabbing pain in my shoulders and back lingered for a few for seconds until at last my eyes closed. I took one final breath before succumbing to death and my spirit's release.

I found myself among a tribal village. The familiar white shawled elder, White Swan led me into the enchantment of the woods away from the camp where the familiar grandmothers were expecting me. They shook their rattles and sang the familiar song. One by one they offered a pinch of white cornmeal to the fire, earth and moon. The leader placed a white shawl upon my shoulders and then each grandmother touched my heart and blessed me with a golden tail feather.

"Move forth as Standing Bear Dreaming Woman. You have completed the black shawl and now emerge with the white shawl. Fly and dance forth in your new cycle," they proclaimed.

The white shawl expanded and became my wings. I floated upward to the sky. The transformation was complete. I became a butterfly dancing and floating with ease. Then I remembered the elder woman spirit in the lodge during my quest with Grandma Tula. She had the same name as what I had now been given, Standing Bear Dreaming Woman.

White Swan spoke again to my consciousness.

"It all began when you were the cub following your mother. Remember she led you to the honey? She led you to where you could find the sweet feminine self. You know where the honey is and how to get there. You will grow into your new name in the years to come. Welcome to our circle Standing Bear Dreaming Woman. You have earned your wings and crossed into the Grandmother's Way," she stated.

The grandmothers repeated another chorus of song to complete the ritual as I hovered above and observed. Their singing became fainter as I felt myself slowly gliding down from above the circle and closer to the ground.

~

I awoke abruptly and found myself in a pool of perspiration and disbelief. I could not believe my eyes. I recognized the brightly colored striped blanket wrapped around me. The crazed sound of the locust feeding on the tall grass and the morning call of the rooster made me recognize my location. I was on the hill in Texas, questing in the women's society initiation. All that had happened had been a part of my initiation vision. I had seen my future - Sundance support, gifting of Sacred Pipe bundles, Grandma Tula, Peter and Grandmother Talise's black shawl ceremony. *Was this the life I would live in years to come?*

The powerful vision proved more than I had expected. I was overwhelmed and tired. The women's society's initiation had given me a direction and healing. The vision would become my direction in life. All I could do now was accept and follow the path with a willing and open heart - not forcing or trying to bring the vision forward but allowing it to unfold in its own way.

After I was brought down from the hill, I purified inside the lodge and completed the ceremony. I showered and dressed in my newly made regalia. I felt alive, grounded in my body and alert. I awaited my naming ceremony and initiation into the society as part of the tradition. I did not speak or share any part of my vision with anyone, for the women told me ahead of time it was not to be shared until it had come to pass.

Granny Molly and Granny Janice, as elders of the society placed the shawl I made months earlier around me and announced my name to the women gathered.

"The grandmother spirits name you, 'Standing Bear Dreaming Woman'. This will become your new name and medicine," they stated together.

A chill ran up my spine and my flesh began to tingle. It was a déjà vu moment. This was really happening and was no longer a dream or vision. This was now my spirit name. My new life had started to unfold just as the dreaming vision had foretold. I left Texas the next day and returned to Massachusetts with much to remember and ponder.

What was unknown to me at the time was that the vision would unfold over the next thirteen years, a much slower pace than the short few days of the ceremonial quest initiation. It would be a long, hard journey and at times an almost forgotten vision. However, piece by piece all of the vision from that women's initiation ceremony came to pass. I dreamed the life that I had come to live.

Through the journey of the next thirteen years, I learned and embraced the teachings of humility, sacrifice, bravery, perseverance, fortitude, compassion, respect, honor, truth, love, generosity and finally wisdom. The vision became a reality and transformed my life beyond my comprehension those many years ago. I found my healing, my feminine circle for wholeness, my partner, my calling to the medicine ways and the understanding of the Grandmother's Way.

EPILOGUE

It is twenty years later since the day of the vision. My life has come full circle. The vision transpired as I had been shown during the initiation quest. Though, the events did not happen as quickly as in the vision. Waiting for the signs to appear and unfold was a difficult lesson in trust and patience.

The relationship with the grannies from Texas that I met during the woman's initiation ceremony did lead me to support Granny Janice in her Sundance ceremony for five years. The relationship that I have had with both her and Granny Molly over the years have strengthened and shaped the elder I have become. I love and appreciate them both tremendously.

Granny Janice has passed on in spirit, creating a hole in my life that can never be replaced. Her spirit has visited me three times since her crossing, asking for ceremonies for her daughter and family members who still struggle with her death. She assures me someday, another Sacred Pipe bundle will be placed in my care.

The meeting of the elder spirit Grandmother Tula, the initiations to the twelve Grandmother's Way teachings, the quests in the woods and the seven spirit plants revealing their medicine ways, took four years of commitment.

The seven years of sacrifice, courage and commitment that it took in leading the ceremonies, connecting to medicine spirit teachers and humbly accepting the transferred lineage that Blue Coyote and his spirit teachers bestowed upon me to serve the people, has completed my initiation to the medicine ways.

The meeting of Grandmother Talise and the teachings of the women's ceremonies of passing from the cycles of death and rebirth happened as well. These ceremonies are only meaningful if you have first done the work within the honey pit itself. If I had not gone within to the silence and quested, the transition would not have been so complete.

As for Peter, we did find each other as the vision proposed, after I completed healing my wounds and illusions. We became half-sides in a traditional Native American wedding ceremony with the Sacred Pipe and our love and relationship grows stronger with each day that passes. Being married with the Sacred Pipe keeps you married forever even after the death of the body - not only in this life but in every lifetime you incarnate.

We took this into serious consideration. Forever really means always. Our commitment to each other is that strong. We felt if Great Spirit finally put us together we would always remain married. Our strong commitment reminds us every day to communicate our feelings truthfully and listen to each other with an open heart when our shadow self gets triggered.

Peter's children have grown and married and have precious children of their own. It warms my heart every time they call me Grandma, for that is who I have become and embraced.

I have visited my shadow pieces deep within my honey pit and have acknowledged and allowed myself to touch the pain and illusions which continued to keep me wounded. I was able to change my perception and story to see the truth of the past and release what no longer needed to be carried forward. By committing to my wholeness and transforming my circle with loving kindness to myself, I have embraced my medicine calling and purpose, my feminine circle, and helping women to heal their own circle.

The last test of *wisdom* took years to learn and will continue to grow. I share the teachings of the Grandmother's Way to transform the circles to wholeness and allow the death and rebirth cycles to continue with unconditional love. I still am moved by the "I AM LOVED" button that hangs over the visor in my car (*yes, this too was gifted from my vision*) reminding me each day to embrace my circle and love within.

Going within to enter the silence and darkness of the honey pit to find the shattered pieces in your body, mind, heart and spirit that keep you angry, sad, fearful, ashamed and guilty is the **first initiation** step to the Grandmother's Way.

Putting the pieces together, seeing through the illusions and stories that you tell yourself, feeling the emotions, expressing and releasing that part of you as a death and replacing it with unconditional love by healing your circle of the feminine is the **second initiation**.

The **third initiation** is the rebirth to free yourself and step forward into accepting the changes in your body, mind and heart by caring for and voicing your needs, desires and inner knowing and valuing your feminine self, recreating your life.

The **final initiation** is the one I have completed several years ago. Re-entering and living life to the fullest, integrating your heart and attained wisdom to enrich the lives of every being you meet.

My rebirth has also inspired my inner creativity to become a writer, a desire I had forgotten since childhood.

My gifts came early in life but I had to develop and fine tune them. My life has passed through the cycles of the death of the old misshapen circle and the rebirth and the reshaping of my circle into wholeness. My body was going through the physical cycle whether I liked it or not but I chose to consciously accept and "change" my mind, heart and spirit.

By embracing the teachings of humility, generosity, perseverance, respect, honor, love, sacrifice, truth, compassion, bravery, fortitude and wisdom, the four levels of my initiation has been masterfully completed to where I now walk the road of the Grandmother's Way. A road all women will share at some stage in life as their body, mind, heart and spirit calls for the change.

Embrace the changes in your body, heart and mind and listen to the inner stirring of the feminine voice by courageously entering *The Honey Pit*. Discover the healing to transform your circle to wholeness. It is where you will begin your own journey of *Finding the Grandmother's Way*.

ACKNOWLEDGEMENTS

To my beloved half-side and husband Paul Samuels, whose love, respect and patience continues to support my life's work. I love you most.

To my parents Raymond and Theresa Dubeau, thank you for your endless teachings of love and generosity.

To my furry companion Sammy, you will always be my sunshine.

To my editor Samantha Plourd, whose expertise helped refine and polish the story. Thank you for your work of excellence.

To Pine Acres Campground, the lovely place of respite and inspiration for this novel.

To Balboa Press, thank you for the cover design and publishing.

ABOUT THE AUTHOR

Loralee Dubeau is a flower essence, dream and intuitive consultant, lecturer, teacher and follows the Native American ceremonial path. She is an elder teacher of the Good Medicine Society, a Universal Life minister and author of *There's a Whole in the Sky*. Loralee lives in Charlton, Massachusetts with her husband Paul Samuels.

www.dream-flowerconsultant.com

Printed in the United States
By Bookmasters